DARK MATTER

DARK MATTER

A CENTURY OF SPECULATIVE FICTION
FROM THE AFRICAN DIASPORA

EDITED BY SHEREE R. THOMAS

A Time Warner Company

Aspect® name and logo are registered trademarks of Warner Books, Inc.

Warner Books, Inc., 1271 Avenue of the Americas, New York, NY 10020

Visit our Web site at www.twbookmark.com

W A Time Warner Company

Printed in the United States of America

Library of Congress Cataloging-in-Publication Data

Dark matter : a century of speculative fiction from the African diaspora / edited by
Sheree R. Thomas.
    p. cm.
  ISBN 0-446-52583-9
    1. Science fiction, American. 2. Fantasy fiction, American. 3. American
fiction—Afro-American authors. I. Thomas, Sheree R.

PS648.S3 D37 2000
813'.087609896073—dc21   00-022288

For the Generations

Jada
and
Jacqueline^2

Contents

Essays

Introduction:
Looking for the Invisible

Early one morning, in a fictitious Southern town, the residents are frightened by what they cannot see. On a sparse stage, under a sign marked STORE, Clem and Luke exchange pleasantries. As time passes on this hot summer day, Clem becomes curious, then alarmed. Something in the landscape has changed. Then Clem speaks, the "something" slowly dawning on him.

"Where is the Nigras?"

It is a query that no one can answer. All the blacks have vanished. The only ones remaining are the sick and shut-in, the ones who cannot work. The mayor mobilizes the Citizens Emergency Distress Committee in a vain effort to calm his nameless town—now paralyzed without its black labor force.

When the first black returns twenty-four hours later, he is unaware of the chaos his absence has caused. When asked of his whereabouts, he "don't rightly know." Before the curtain falls, Rastus shuffles away with a slight smile on his lips, leaving Clem and Luke to search alone for answers.[1]

In an article that appeared in the *New York Times* shortly after the *Day of Absence* debut, Obie Award–winner Douglas Turner Ward described himself as "a Negro playwright committed to examining the contours, context, and depth of his experiences from an unfettered, imaginative Negro angle of vision."[2] With these goals in mind, it is interesting that he would choose as his first play to write a speculative work that centers on black absence. In *Day of Absence*, a highly satiric play, Ward doesn't give Clem, Luke, his audience, or his readers any explanation; however, I think one could say that for a brief moment, Rastus and the other black townspeople were "dark matter."

dark' mat''er—*n*: a nonluminous form of matter which has not been directly observed but whose existence has been deduced by its gravitational effects.[3]

One of my goals with this introduction is to explain why I have chosen to use "dark matter" as a metaphor to discuss the speculative fiction of black writers and their contributions to the science fiction genre. What is "dark matter"?

After observing the motions of galaxies and the expansion of the universe for the past five decades, most astronomers believe that as much as ninety percent of the material in the universe may be objects or particles that cannot be seen. This means, in other words, that most of the universe's matter does not radiate—it provides no glow or light that we can detect.

Research suggests that dark matter may be Jupiter-sized objects, black holes, and/or unimagined "exotic" forms of matter. Scientists believe that the amount of "visible" matter in the universe is not enough to account for the tremendous gravitational forces around us. First theorized some sixty years ago by astronomer Fritz Zwicky, this "missing" or "invisible" matter was believed to reside within clusters of spiraling galaxies. Today astronomers and astrophysicists prefer to call the missing mass "dark matter," because it is the light, not the matter, that is missing.[4]

Because no one has yet found a method for detecting the components of dark matter, the theory is debated within the scientific community. As more talent and vision is brought to the field in this new century, perhaps someone will be able to answer definitively, What is dark matter? In the meantime, I will entertain a few speculative theories of my own.

Why "Dark Matter"

In his 1953 collection of cultural criticism, *Shadow and Act*, Ralph Ellison cautioned readers not to stumble

> over that ironic obstacle which lies in the path of anyone who would fashion a theory of American Negro culture while ignoring the intricate network of connections which binds Negroes to the larger society. To do so is to attempt a delicate brain surgery with

a switch-blade. And it is possible that any viable theory of Negro American culture obligates us to fashion a more adequate theory of American culture as a whole.[5]

By the same token, an examination of African diasporic speculative fiction from the past century may shed new light on both the sf genre and the mainstream literary canon. In the past there has been little research in this area. Like dark matter, the contributions of black writers to the sf genre have not been directly observed or fully explored. For the most part, literary scholars and critics have limited their research largely to examinations of work by authors Samuel R. Delany and Octavia E. Butler, the two leading black writers in the genre. Currently there is a considerable body of scholarship dedicated to the work of these formidable authors, and there is room for yet more. However, both sf and mainstream scholarship have overlooked or ignored the contributions of less well known black writers. It is my sincere hope that *Dark Matter* will help shed light on the sf genre, that it will correct the misperception that black writers are recent to the field, and that it will encourage more talented writers to enter the genre.

Before I began the research for *Dark Matter*, I had several goals in mind. The first was simply to introduce readers who have never had the pleasure of reading science fiction to a few of my favorite authors. I am speaking of the writers whose words kept me reading in the genre, writers whose visions reflected and critiqued my own culture and inspired me to write on my own. I drew up a second list of non-sf writers—"mainstream" writers whose work, I thought, certainly incorporated speculative themes and perspectives.

After I began my research, however, I realized that there was more to this genre than met the eye. As the call for submissions was shared throughout the sf and black literary communities, and the postcards—then envelopes, then manuscripts—began flooding in, I was humbled by the response. And just as I had hoped, the critical pieces began to arrive. When I finally spoke with author Charles R. Saunders, who had virtually "disappeared" (as far as the U.S. sf community was concerned) into the far reaches of Canada, *Dark Matter* began to take on a new shape in my mind. Later, while I was attending the six-week science fiction writing workshop at Clarion West in Seattle, a manila envelope arrived from him. He had forwarded me a photocopy of "The

Comet," the W. E. B. Du Bois short story published in the 1920 collection *Darkwater: Voices from Within the Veil. Dark Matter* had acquired critical mass.

With W. E. B. Du Bois now in view, my original vision for the collection broadened. My new goal in compiling this collection was to offer readers an enjoyable entrée to the diverse range of speculative fiction from the African diaspora and to encourage more talented writers and scholars to explore the genre. By uniting the works of the early pioneers in the field with that of established and emerging new writers, perhaps the necessary groundwork for the discussion and examination of the "unobserved" literary tradition has been laid.

Dark matter as a metaphor offers us an interesting way of examining blacks and science fiction. The metaphor can be applied to a discussion of the individual writers as black artists in society and how that identity affects their work. It can also be applied to a discussion of their influence and impact on the sf genre in general. While the "black sf as dark matter" metaphor is novel, the concept behind it is not. The metaphor is neither farfetched nor uncommon if one considers popular themes within the black literary tradition. An excellent example is Ralph Ellison's *Invisible Man* (1945), a novel that introduced the idea of black invisibility. Ellison's "battle royale" scene and the ending in which the alienated, invisible narrator sits alone in the basement is classic sf.

Five years after the publication of Ellison's novel, Ray Bradbury published "Way in the Middle of the Air," a short story that appeared in *The Martian Chronicles* (1950). Like the black residents in Douglas Turner Ward's *Day of Absence*, the black citizens in Bradbury's story disappear—or, more accurately, they leave. While the blacks in Ward's play return without explanation, those in Bradbury's story escape to Mars, presumably never to be seen again. Twenty years after Ellison delivered his stylized portrait of one black man's invisibility, Douglas Turner Ward's play examined this auspicious invisibility and extended it to an entire community. These works consider the impact and influence of black life on society. In each story, the absence or presence of black life is an unknown value until the end. By applying dark matter to the discussion of the sf genre, I think it will become clear that black writers have been offering distinctive speculative visions to the world far longer than is generally thought.

Blacks as Dark Matter

As the dynamics of trade relations began to change during the African Middle Ages, the continent became the source of endless speculation.[6] The visions of monstrous men and anthropophagi that had filled St. Augustine's descriptions of sub-Saharan Africa were not expelled until other Europeans such as Scotsman Mungo Park "penetrated the interior of Africa."[7] In the European tradition "blackness," an extension of Africa, is often thought of as a resistant force, racially charged matter that must be penetrated—thus the descent into darkness.

In 1899 Joseph Conrad published *The Heart of Darkness*, a work that has inspired perhaps more sf stories (and criticism) than any other work of fiction.[8] Premier genre critic John Clute writes that this twentieth-century classic's "grueling odyssey into the unknown, and its vision of the Otherness of alien life, has captured the imagination of sf writers ever since." In this description the "unknown" element alluded to is the African continent or, more specifically, the Belgian Congo of 1890; and "the Otherness of alien life" is the Africans themselves.

A century later, the phrases "heart of darkness" and "Dark Continent" continue to conjure up images of primordial blackness in our minds. (Ironically, Freud used the term "Dark Continent" to refer to the female psyche, but it is of blackness that contemporary minds think.) Blackness has exerted a power on the international racial psyche that is fantastical, perhaps more so than the dark, malformed monsters of St. Augustine's day. People have always been frightened by what they cannot see—and the specter of blackness looms large in the white imagination.

On the subject of blackness, race, and the imagination, critic and novelist Adam Lively writes:

> From the "fantastic voyage" narratives of the seventeenth and eighteenth centuries, through the exotic imperial romances of the nineteenth, and up to the science fiction of the twentieth century, imaginative literature has been a means—like any mythology—of mediating between the domestic and that which lies at and beyond the limits of knowledge.[9]

Long before *The Heart of Darkness*, the imagination had acted as an instigator of historical change. Africa became the "unknown" and blackness was equated with the "Other." Two hundred years of slavery said so. And as these thoughts became institutionalized and codified, first in the form of slavery and later in the imaginary lines of political maps that documented the scramble for Africa, the people behind the "blackness" receded into the background. They became dark matter, invisible to the naked eye; and yet their influence—their gravitational pull on the world around them—would become undeniable.

Sheree R. Thomas
January 2000

Notes

1. Douglas Turner Ward, *Happy Ending and Day of Absence* (New York: Dramatists Play Service, Inc., 1944), 35, 57.
2. Douglas Turner Ward, "American Theatre; For Whites Only?" *New York Times*, August 14, 1966.
3. NASA Jet Propulsion Lab at California Technical Institute, glossary of terms, www.nasa.jpl.gov.
4. Kim Griest, "The Nature of the Dark Matter," lecture delivered January 15, 1996, at the International School of Physics, Varenna.
5. Ralph Ellison, *Shadow and Act* (New York: Vintage Books, 1972), 253.
6. Roland Anthony Oliver and Anthony Atmore, *The African Middle Ages, 1400–1800* (New York: Cambridge University Press, 1981).
7. Mungo Park, *Travels into the Interior of Africa* (London: Eland, 1983).
8. February–April 1899 is the date of the serialized version that appeared in Blackwood's *Edinburgh Magazine*. The complete novel appeared in 1902.
9. Adam Lively, *Masks: Blackness, Race, and Imagination* (New York: Oxford University Press, 2000), 2.

DARK MATTER

SISTER LILITH

Honorée Fanonne Jeffers

(2000)

Right that moment when we climbed from the hot mud there was light. There wasn't any darkness, there was light. All light. And no rib, at least not with me. I don't even eat meat, even after all of it.

Me and that man were twins, born together, and that's why he wanted me next to his skin even after I left him, even after I didn't want him anymore, and him not letting me leave with my own child.

I felt Adam's heart start to beat at the same time as mine. The dirt was warm, we were swimming with first grace, and then we opened our eyes, let go of each other's hands. Blinked in the light. We were cold. Didn't know we were naked, but we knew we were cold. I didn't know his name, and didn't know what he had looked like all that time 'cause my eyes were closed. So I opened my eyes for him, and I thought he looked pretty good just to be getting here. Skin darker than our mud and rippling when he moved this way and that. And his eyes lit on me, smiled, and that's how I knew I was beautiful. I heard, "He is Adam. She is Lilith." And that's how I knew my name.

I heard soft rumbling. Sky streaked with red. "You are woman. He is man. You are together. Alone." And that's how I knew we were married. And the sun and the moon came up together and there were flowers under a tall tree and we lay down and we came together and we were swimming around each other again and we were finally warm and there was light light light light light light light.

Now all of a sudden, I'm bleached, I'm bone, a Jane-come-lately. All I see on those pages is God and Snake. Adam and his concubine. I just got to say that if a trophy wife was what he wanted, he sure got one. Somebody made him the most beautiful girl in the world, all right. And all that noise about her *two* sons. That is my blood on Cain's skin when he came into this world. I got the best of Adam. She got the rib out of an old man, my leavings.

How long? Time flies when you're young, married, and in love. It's always that way at first with any man. He's sweet when you're new and tight. Can't do enough for you, pick enough fruit and vegetables for you, stand on his head until his eyeballs roll, just for you. The loving five times a day, talking that sweet way all up in me. Everywhere. In the water, in front of the animals. And it was good. That one hundred (or was it two hundred?) years went by just like that.

He used to talk to me about my size all the time. He would say, "Lili, you just as little and soft and pretty as one of those doves flying 'round this tree." He would say, "I could pick you up with one of my fingers. You one sweet baby doll." Sometimes he would scare me a little when he would come in from the animals smelling a little funky and growl in my ear, "Boo, Miss Lili." Yeah, he scared me because muscles are trouble. They give the mind a sense of what can be taken. I only liked to pretend. I didn't really want to be an animal, just during season, always from behind.

After them one hundred—or was it two hundred? I can never remember—he still wasn't used to anything. Still went around grabbing all the time, picking up things for show. It was cute when we were newlyweds, but after a while—please. I could have said, "Adam, you so strong. Let me feel that big ole bump on your arm," but who has time for that? I'm a plainspoken woman. Always have been from the time my tongue moved. And I had a child to worry about by then. So I just grunt and keep on. And then when he plunk right on top of me for five minutes, I mean, what can you say to that?

They come up to me in a group one day. That bum rush of angels wearing white double-breasted suits. I knew not to trust them then. It wasn't fourth Sunday, so why all the white?

Of course, Adam was nowhere to be seen. Satan up front looking like a preacher about to pass around the collection plate twice. The man was too pretty. I guess that kind of perfection is supposed to be an asset, but it wasn't natural. You could tell there wasn't a mark anywhere on this man's body, just a smooth gold all over.

Satan took a step forward from his men. "Sister Lilith, We got us a situation here, " He said. "It seems Brother Adam is a bit discontented, and we all thought you should know." Now, this is the first I heard that my man was having problems with me. I knew how I was feeling, but didn't know it was going both ways. It hurt that somebody else was telling me my own business. Hurt more that my man was gone while I was being told. But here I was, pretending that I was walking right along with Satan. I wasn't going to give that angel the satisfaction of catching me out.

"Sister, Brother Adam says for the last century or so, things ain't been like they was." Then, from underneath one of his wings, he pulled out a white handkerchief and mopped his forehead. It wasn't a degree over seventy that day. He tucked his hankie out of sight, smoothed back his hair, and then he commenced. I should cook more fancy dishes for Brother Adam. Listen more attentively to Brother Adam's stories about the animals. Then Satan pushed his nose right into my bedroom. "You know, Sister Lilith, men really appreciate enthusiasm in the romance department. Why, a cooperative mate makes all the difference!" He didn't even have the decency to be 'shamed of himself. Thought he was being natural.

I looked Satan right in his face, asked him, "Did 'Brother Adam' tell you he don't help around the house none? That he don't pay no attention to little Cain? That he don't never ask me about *my* day or *my* stories? He tell you he don't even bother to kiss me before he come in jumping all up on me to 'cooperate' with him? I bet he don't tell you none of that, does he?"

The rest of them started looking around like they ain't never seen trees and sky before. Looking anywhere but at me. It didn't take a genius to figure out whose idea this little field trip was. Satan smiled all the wider and licked his perfect teeth so they got shiny. Kind of rolled back and forth on the balls of his feet. "Now, Sister Lilith, a lot is riding on you and Brother Adam. This concern is not only mine, this comes straight from the Top. Do you know what I'm saying here?"

"Yes, I know what you're saying, and it don't matter Who this come from. The truth is just what it is and you can take that back on up with you when you go."

Right then, the rest of Satan's crew made a noise together and stepped back and left him alone standing right next to me. He clucked his tongue at me the same way I did when Cain was having a tantrum. Like he was calm and I wasn't. "Sister, sister, I understand. I do. And I want you to know that I'm on your side. We all are. Listen, just meditate on it with me right now is all I ask." He closed his eyes and bowed his head. After a few moments, he peeped up at me and saw I was looking at him with my neck right where it always was. So he turned around, fluttered his wings all showy, then flew straight up in the air, with the rest of them following right behind.

It gets to the point where you see the path so clearly in front of you. And what and who remains is you and your child. A little piece that's always going to be yours, a little somebody all you got to do is love, and he gives you every little thing you need. Pretty soon, your womb don't move for nobody but your child.

The world was so small, I didn't worry about Adam. Back in those days, you could spit from one end of my universe to the other. I knew I was older than Adam in a lot of ways, but figured he didn't have nobody but me and Cain, and just how long could a man stay gone? A few months, a few years? Sooner or later he had to come back to me. He had to. And one day he did come back with that scar on his side.

I should have known Satan couldn't leave nobody's well enough alone. I guess that's why I ain't got a name right now. I been here forever in this place, and I know what I'm talking about. Been to hell and back and know the touch of scales on my finger. Been here longer than Adam and that woman lived. No, she ain't no wife. I don't care how long she was around, how many children she had. She ain't never going to be wife. It was me and I'm still here to prove it. Been here, longer than my child, and that's hard.

Can't go nowhere except looking at everybody and this little bit of land I got. A few flowers and a vegetable garden. Even got an apple tree—ha! All I got forever in this world is to be a watcher.

The Comet

W. E. B. Du Bois

(1920)

He stood a moment on the steps of the bank, watching the human river that swirled down Broadway. Few noticed him. Few ever noticed him save in a way that stung. He was outside the world—"nothing!" as he said bitterly. Bits of the words of the walkers came to him.

"The comet?"

"The comet—"

Everybody was talking of it. Even the president, as he entered, smiled patronizingly at him, and asked: "Well, Jim, are you scared?"

"No," said the messenger shortly.

"I thought we'd journeyed through the comet's tail once," broke in the junior clerk affably.

"Oh, that was Haley's," said the president. "This is a new comet, quite a stranger, they say—wonderful, wonderful! I saw it last night. Oh, by the way, Jim," turning again to the messenger, "I want you to go down into the lower vaults today."

The messenger followed the president silently. Of course, they wanted him to go down to the lower vaults. It was too dangerous for more valuable men. He smiled grimly and listened.

"Everything of value has been moved out since the water began to seep in," said the president, "but we miss two volumes of old records. Suppose you nose around down there—it isn't very pleasant, I suppose."

"Not very," said the messenger, as he walked out.

"Well, Jim, the tail of the new comet hits us at noon this time," said the vault clerk, as he passed over the keys; but the messenger passed silently down the stairs. Down he went beneath Broadway, where the dim light filtered through the feet of hurrying men; down to the dark basement beneath; down into the blackness and silence beneath that lowest cavern. Here with his dark lantern he groped in the bowels of the earth, under the world.

He drew a long breath as he threw back the last great iron door and stepped into the fetid slime within. Here at last was peace, and he groped moodily forward. A great rat leaped past him and cobwebs crept across his face. He felt carefully around the room, shelf by shelf, on the muddied floor, and in crevice and corner. Nothing. Then he went back to the far end, where somehow the wall felt different. He pounded and pushed and pried. Nothing. He started away. Then something brought him back. He was pounding and working again when suddenly the whole black wall swung as on mighty hinges, and blackness yawned beyond. He peered in; it was evidently a secret vault— some hiding place of the old bank unknown in newer times. He entered hesitatingly. It was a long, narrow room with shelves, and at the far end, an old iron chest. On a high shelf lay two volumes of records, and others. He put them carefully aside and stepped to the chest. It was old, strong, and rusty. He looked at the vast and old-fashioned lock and flashed his light on the hinges. They were deeply incrusted with rust. Looking about, he found a bit of iron and began to pry. The rust had eaten a hundred years, and it had gone deep. Slowly, wearily, the old lid lifted, and with a last, low groan lay bare its treasure—and he saw the dull sheen of gold!

"Boom!"

A low, grinding, reverberating crash struck upon his ear. He started up and looked about. All was black and still. He groped for his light and swung it about him. Then he knew! The great stone door had swung to. He forgot the gold and looked death squarely in the face. Then with a sigh he went methodically to work. The cold sweat stood on his forehead; but he searched, pounded, pushed, and worked until after what seemed endless hours his hand struck a cold bit of metal and the great door swung again harshly on its hinges, and then, striking against something soft and heavy, stopped. He had just room to squeeze through. There lay the body of the vault clerk, cold and stiff. He stared at it, and then felt sick and nauseated. The air seemed unaccountably foul, with a strong, peculiar odor. He stepped forward, clutched at the air, and fell fainting across the corpse.

*   *   *

He awoke with a sense of horror, leaped from the body, and groped up the stairs, calling to the guard. The watchman sat as if asleep, with the gate swinging free. With one glance at him the messenger hurried up to the sub-vault. In vain he called to the guards. His voice echoed and re-echoed weirdly. Up into the great basement he rushed. Here another guard lay prostrate on his face, cold and still. A fear arose in the messenger's heart. He dashed up to the cellar floor, up into the bank. The stillness of death lay everywhere and everywhere bowed, bent, and stretched the silent forms of men. The messenger paused and glanced about. He was not a man easily moved; but the sight was appalling! "Robbery and murder," he whispered slowly to himself as he saw the twisted, oozing mouth of the president where he lay half-buried on his desk. Then a new thought seized him: If they found him here alone— with all this money and all these dead men—what would his life be worth? He glanced about, tiptoed cautiously to a side door, and again looked behind. Quietly he turned the latch and stepped out into Wall Street.

How silent the street was! Not a soul was stirring, and yet it was high noon—Wall Street? Broadway? He glanced almost wildly up and down, then across the street, and as he looked, a sickening horror froze in his limbs. With a choking cry of utter fright he lunged, leaned giddily against the cold building, and stared helplessly at the sight.

In the great stone doorway a hundred men and women and children lay crushed and twisted and jammed, forced into that great, gaping door-way like refuse in a can—as if in one wild, frantic rush to safety, they had crushed and ground themselves to death. Slowly the messenger crept along the walls, trying to comprehend, stilling the tremor in his limbs and the rising terror in his heart. He met a business man, silk-hatted and frock-coated, who had crept, too, along that smooth wall and stood now stone dead with wonder written on his lips.

The messenger turned his eyes hastily away and sought the curb. A woman leaned wearily against the signpost, her head bowed motionless on her lace and silken bosom. Before her stood a streetcar, silent, and within—but the messenger but glanced and hurried on. A grimy news-boy sat in the gutter with the "last edition" in his uplifted hand: "Dan-ger!" screamed its black headlines. "Warnings wired around the world. The Comet's tail sweeps past us at noon. Deadly gases expected. Close doors and windows. Seek the cellar." The messenger read and staggered on. Far out from a window above, a girl lay with gasping face and sleevelets on her arms. On a store step sat a little, sweet-faced girl looking upward toward the skies, and in the carriage by her lay—but the messenger looked no longer. The cords gave way—the terror burst in his veins, and with one great, gasping cry he sprang desperately forward and ran—ran as only the frightened run, shrieking and fighting the air until with one last wail of pain he sank on the grass of Madison Square and lay prone and still.

When he arose, he gave no glance at the still and silent forms on the benches, but, going to a fountain, bathed his face; then hiding himself in a corner away from the drama of death, he quietly gripped himself and thought the thing through: The comet had swept the earth and this was the end. Was everybody dead? He must search and see.

He knew that he must steady himself and keep calm, or he would go insane. First he must go to a restaurant. He walked up Fifth Avenue to a famous hostelry and entered its gorgeous, ghost-haunted halls. He beat back the nausea, and, seizing a tray from dead hands, hurried into the street and ate ravenously, hiding to keep out the sights.

"Yesterday, they would not have served me," he whispered, as he forced the food down.

Then he started up the street—looking, peering, telephoning, ringing alarms; silent, silent all. Was nobody—nobody—he dared not think the thought and hurried on.

Suddenly he stopped still. He had forgotten. My God! How could he have forgotten? He must rush to the subway—then he almost laughed. No—a car; if he could find a Ford. He saw one. Gently he lifted off its burden, and took his place on the seat. He tested the throttle. There was gas. He glided off, shivering, and drove up the street. Everywhere stood, leaned, lounged, and lay the dead, in grim and awful silence. On he ran past an automobile, wrecked and overturned; past another, filled with a gay party whose smiles yet lingered on their death-struck lips; on, past crowds and groups of cars, pausing by dead policemen; at 42nd Street he had to detour to Park Avenue to avoid the dead congestion. He came back on Fifth Avenue at 57th and flew past the Plaza and by the park with its hushed babies and silent throng, until as he was rushing past 72nd Street he heard a sharp cry, and saw a living form leaning wildly out an upper window. He gasped. The human voice sounded in his ears like the voice of God.

"Hello—hello—help, in God's name!" wailed the woman. "There's a dead girl in here and a man and—and see yonder dead men lying in the street and dead horses—for the love of God go and bring the officers—" the words trailed off into hysterical tears.

He wheeled the car in a sudden circle, running over the still body of a child and leaping on the curb. Then he rushed up the steps and tried the door and rang violently. There was a long pause, but at last the heavy door swung back. They stared a moment in silence. She had not noticed before that he was a Negro. He had not thought of her as white. She was a woman of perhaps twenty-five—rarely beautiful and richly gowned, with darkly-golden hair, and jewels. Yesterday, he thought with bitterness, she would scarcely have looked at him twice. He would have been dirt beneath her silken feet. She stared at him. Of all the sorts of men she had pictured as coming to her rescue she had not dreamed of one like him. Not that he was not human, but he dwelt in a world so far from hers, so infinitely far, that he seldom even entered her thought. Yet as she looked at him curiously he seemed quite commonplace and usual. He was a tall, dark workingman of the better class, with a sensitive face trained to stolidity and a poor man's clothes and hands. His face was soft and slow and his manner at once cold and nervous, like fires long banked, but not out. So a moment each paused and gauged the other; then the thought of the dead world without rushed in and they started toward each other.

"What has happened?" she cried. "Tell me! Nothing stirs. All is silence! I see the dead strewn before my window as winnowed by the breath of God—and see—"

She dragged him through great, silken hangings to where, beneath the sheen of mahogany and silver, a little French maid lay stretched in quiet, everlasting sleep, and near her a butler lay prone in his livery.

The tears streamed down the woman's cheeks, and she clung to his arm until the perfume of her breath swept his face and he felt the tremors racing through her body.

"I had been shut up in my dark room developing pictures of the comet which I took last night; when I came out—I saw the dead!

"What has happened?" she cried again.

He answered slowly:

"Something—comet or devil—swept across the earth this morning and—many are dead!"

"Many? Very many?"

"I have searched and I have seen no other living soul but you."

She gasped and they stared at each other.

"My—father!" she whispered.

"Where is he?"

"He started for the office."

"Where is it?"

"In the Metropolitan Tower."

"Leave a note for him here and come." Then he stopped. "No," he said firmly, "first, we must go—to Harlem."

"Harlem!" she cried. Then she understood. She tapped her foot at first impatiently. She looked back and shuddered. Then she came resolutely down the steps.

"There's a swifter car in the garage in the court," she said.

"I don't know how to drive it," he said.

"I do," she answered.

In ten minutes they were flying to Harlem on the wind. The Stutz rose and raced like an airplane. They took the turn at 110th Street on two wheels and slipped with a shriek into 135th. He was gone but a moment. Then he returned, and his face was gray. She did not look, but said:

"You have lost—somebody?"

"I have lost—everybody," he said simply, "unless—"

He ran back and was gone several minutes—hours they seemed to her.

"Everybody," he said, and he walked slowly back with something film-like in his hand, which he stuffed into his pocket.

"I'm afraid I was selfish," he said. But already the car was moving toward the park among the dark and lined dead of Harlem—the brown, still faces, the knotted hands, the homely garments, and the silence—the wild and haunting silence. Out of the park, and down Fifth Avenue they whirled. In and out among the dead they slipped and quivered, needing no sound of bell or horn, until the great, square Metropolitan Tower hovered in sight.

Gently he laid the dead elevator boy aside; the car shot upward. The door of the office stood open. On the threshold lay the stenographer, and, staring at her, sat the dead clerk. The inner office was empty, but a note lay on the desk, folded and addressed but unsent:

Dear Daughter:

I've gone for a hundred-mile spin in Fred's new Mercedes. Shall not be back before dinner. I'll bring Fred with me.

J. B. H.

"Come," she cried nervously. "We must search the city."

Up and down, over and across, back again—on went that ghostly search. Everywhere was silence and death—death and silence! They hunted from Madison Square to Spuyten Duyvel; they rushed across the Williamsburg Bridge; they swept over Brooklyn; from the Battery and Morningside Heights they scanned the river. Silence, silence everywhere, and no human sign. Haggard and bedraggled they puffed a third time slowly down Broadway, under the broiling sun, and at last stopped. He sniffed the air. An odor—a smell—and with the shifting breeze a sickening stench filled their nostrils and brought its awful warning. The girl settled back helplessly in her seat.

"What can we do?" she cried.

It was his turn now to take the lead, and he did it quickly.

"The long distance telephone—the telegraph and the cable—night rockets and then flight!"

She looked at him now with strength and confidence. He did not look like men, as she had always pictured men; but he acted like one and she was content. In fifteen minutes they were at the central telephone exchange. As they came to the door he stepped quickly before her and pressed her gently back as he closed it. She heard him moving to and fro, and knew his burdens—the poor, little burdens he bore. When she entered, he was alone in the room. The grim switchboard flashed its metallic face in cryptic, sphinx-like immobility. She seated herself on a stool and donned the bright earpiece. She looked at the mouthpiece. She had never looked at one so closely before. It was wide and black, pimpled with usage; inert; dead; almost sarcastic in its unfeeling curves. It looked—she beat back the thought—but it looked—it persisted in looking like—she turned her head and found herself alone. One moment she was terrified; then she thanked him silently for his delicacy and turned resolutely, with a quick intaking of breath.

"Hello!" she called in low tones. She was calling to the world. The world must answer. Would the world answer? Was the world Silence!

She had spoken too low.

"Hello!" she cried, full-voiced.

She listened. Silence! Her heart beat quickly. She cried in clear, distinct, loud tones: "Hello—hello—hello!"

What was that whirring? Surely—no—was it the click of a receiver?

She bent close, moved the pegs in the holes, and called and called, until her voice rose almost to a shriek, and her heart hammered. It was as if she had heard the last flicker of creation, and the evil was silence. Her voice dropped to a sob. She sat stupidly staring into the black and sarcastic mouthpiece, and the thought came again. Hope lay dead within her. Yes, the cable and the rockets remained; but the world—she could not frame the thought or say the word. It was too mighty—too terrible! She turned toward the door with a new fear in her heart. For the first time she seemed to realize that she was alone in the world with a stranger, with something more than a stranger—with a man alien in blood and culture—unknown, perhaps unknowable. It was awful! She must escape—she must fly; he must not see her again. Who knew what awful thoughts he had?

She gathered her silken skirts deftly about her young, smooth limbs—listened, and glided into a sidehall. A moment she shrank back: the hall lay filled with dead women; then she leaped to the door and tore at it, with bleeding fingers, until it swung wide. She looked out. He was standing at the top of the alley—silhouetted, tall and black, motionless. Was he looking at her or away? She did not know—she did not care. She simply leaped and ran—ran until she found herself alone amid the dead and the tall ramparts of towering buildings.

She stopped. She was alone. Alone! Alone on the streets—alone in the city—perhaps alone in the world! There crept in upon her the sense of deception—of creeping hands behind her back—of silent, moving things she could not see—of voices hushed in fearsome conspiracy. She looked behind and sideways, started at strange sounds and heard still stranger, until every nerve within her stood sharp and quivering, stretched to scream at the barest touch. She whirled and flew back, whimpering like a child, until she found that narrow alley again and the dark, silent figure silhouetted at the top. She stopped and rested; then she walked silently toward him, looked at him timidly; but he said nothing as he handed her into the car. Her voice caught as she whispered:

"Not—that."

And he answered slowly: "No—not that!"

They climbed into the car. She bent forward on the wheel and sobbed, with great, dry, quivering sobs, as they flew toward the cable office on the east side, leaving the world of wealth and prosperity for the world of poverty and work. In the world behind them were death and silence, grave and grim, almost cynical, but always decent; here it was hideous. It clothed itself in every ghastly form of terror, struggle, hate, and suffering. It lay wreathed in crime and squalor, greed and lust. Only in its dread and awful silence was it like to death everywhere.

Yet as the two, flying and alone, looked upon the horror of the world, slowly, gradually, the sense of all-enveloping death deserted them. They seemed to move in a world silent and asleep—not dead. They moved in quiet reverence, lest somehow they wake these sleeping forms who had, at last, found peace. They moved in some solemn, world-wide *Friedho* above which some mighty arm had waved its magic wand. All nature slept until—until, and quick with the same startling thought, they looked into each other's eyes—he, ashen, and she, crimson, with unspoken thought. To both, the vision of a mighty beauty—of vast, unspoken things, swelled in their souls; but they put it away.

Great, dark coils of wire came up from the earth and down from the sun and entered this low lair of witchery. The gathered lightnings of the world centered here, binding with beams of light the ends of the earth. The doors gaped on the gloom within. He paused on the threshold.

"Do you know the code?" she asked.

"I know the call for help—we used it formerly at the bank."

She hardly heard. She heard the lapping of the waters far below—the dark and restless waters—the cold and luring waters, as they called. He stepped within. Slowly she walked to the wall, where the water called below, and stood and waited. Long she waited, and he did not come. Then with a start she saw him, too, standing beside the black waters. Slowly he removed his coat and stood there silently. She walked quickly to him and laid her hand on his arm. He did not start or look. The waters lapped on in luring, deadly rhythm. He pointed down to the waters, and said quietly:

"The world lies beneath the waters now—may I go?"

She looked into his stricken, tired face, and a great pity surged within her heart. She answered in a voice clear and calm, "No."

Upward they turned toward life again, and he seized the wheel. The world was darkening to twilight, and a great, gray pall was falling mercifully and gently on the sleeping dead. The ghastly glare of reality seemed replaced with the dream of some vast romance. The girl lay silently back, as the motor whizzed along, and looked half-consciously for the elf-queen to wave life into this dead world again. She forgot to wonder at the quickness with which he had learned to drive her car. It seemed natural. And then as they whirled and swung into Madison Square and at the door of the Metropolitan Tower she gave a low cry, and her eyes were great! Perhaps she had seen the elf-queen?

The man led her to the elevator of the tower and deftly they ascended. In her father's office they gathered rugs and chairs, and he wrote a note and laid it on the desk; then they ascended to the roof and he made her comfortable. For a while she rested and sank to dreamy somnolence, watching the worlds above and wondering. Below lay the dark shadows of the city and afar was the shining of the sea. She glanced at him timidly as he set food before her and took a shawl and wound her in it, touching her reverently, yet tenderly. She looked up at him with thankfulness in her eyes, eating what he served.

He watched the city. She watched him. He seemed very human—very near now.

"Have you had to work hard?" she asked softly.

"Always," he said.

"I have always been idle," she said. "I was rich."

"I was poor," he almost echoed.

"The rich and the poor are met together," she began, and he finished: "The Lord is the Maker of them all."

"Yes," she said slowly, "and how foolish our human distinctions seem—now," looking down to the great dead city stretched below, swimming in unlightened shadows.

"Yes—I was not—human, yesterday," he said.

She looked at him. "And your people were not my people," she said; "but today—" She paused. He was a man—no more; but he was in some larger sense a gentleman—sensitive, kindly, chivalrous, everything save his hands and—his face. Yet yesterday—

"Death, the leveler!" he muttered.

"And the revealer," she whispered gently, rising to her feet with great eyes. He turned away, and after fumbling a moment sent a rocket into the darkening air. It arose, shrieked, and flew up, a slim path of light, and, scattering its stars abroad, dropped on the city below. She scarcely noticed it. A vision of the world had risen before her. Slowly the mighty prophecy of her destiny overwhelmed her. Above the dead past hovered the Angel of Annunciation. She was no mere woman. She was neither high nor low, white nor black, rich nor poor. She was primal woman; mighty mother of all men to come and Bride of Life. She looked upon the man beside her and forgot all else but his manhood, his strong, vigorous manhood—his sorrow and sacrifice. She saw him glorified. He was no longer a thing apart, a creature below, a strange outcast of another clime and blood, but her Brother Humanity incarnate, Son of God and great All-Father of the race to be.

He did not glimpse the glory in her eyes, but stood looking outward toward the sea and sending rocket after rocket into the unanswering darkness. Dark-purple clouds lay banked and billowed in the west. Behind them and all around, the heavens glowed in dim, weird radiance that suffused the darkening world and made almost a minor music. Suddenly, as though gathered back in some vast hand, the great cloud-curtain fell away. Low on the horizon lay a long, white star—mystic, wonderful! And from it fled upward to the pole, like some wan bridal veil, a pale, wide sheet of flame that lighted all the world and dimmed the stars.

In fascinated silence the man gazed at the heavens and dropped his rockets to the floor. Memories of memories stirred to life in the dead recesses of his mind. The shackles seemed to rattle and fall from his soul. Up from the crass and crushing and cringing of his caste leaped the lone majesty of kings long dead. He arose within the shadows, tall, straight, and stern, with power in his eyes and ghostly scepters hovering to his grasp. It was as though some mighty Pharaoh lived again, or curled Assyrian lord. He turned and looked upon the lady, and found her gazing straight at him.

Silently, immovably, they saw each other face to face—eye to eye. Their souls lay naked to the night. It was not lust; it was not love—it was some vaster, mightier thing that needed neither touch of body nor thrill of soul. It was a thought divine, splendid.

Slowly, noiselessly, they moved toward each other—the heavens above, the seas around, the city grim and dead below. He loomed from out the velvet shadows vast and dark. Pearl-white and slender, she shone beneath the stars. She stretched her jeweled hands abroad. He lifted up his mighty arms, and they cried each to the other, almost with one voice, "The world is dead."

"Long live the—"

"Honk! Honk!"

Hoarse and sharp the cry of a motor drifted clearly up from the silence below. They started backward with a cry and gazed upon each other with eyes that faltered and fell, with blood that boiled.

"Honk! Honk! Honk! Honk!" came the mad cry again, and almost from their feet a rocket blazed into the air and scattered its stars upon them. She covered her eyes with her hands, and her shoulders heaved. He dropped and bowed, groped blindly on his knees about the floor. A blue flame spluttered lazily after an age, and she heard the scream of an answering rocket as it flew. Then they stood still as death, looking to opposite ends of the earth.

"Clang—crash—clang!"

The roar and ring of swift elevators shooting upward from below made the great tower tremble. A murmur and babel of voices swept in upon the night. All over the once dead city the lights blinked, flickered, and flamed; and then with a sudden clanging of doors the entrance to the platform was filled with men, and one with white and flying hair rushed to the girl and lifted her to his breast. "My daughter!" he sobbed.

Behind him hurried a younger, comelier man, carefully clad in motor costume, who bent above the girl with passionate solicitude and gazed into her staring eyes until they narrowed and dropped and her face flushed deeper and deeper crimson.

"Julia," he whispered. "My darling, I thought you were gone forever."

She looked up at him with strange, searching eyes.

"Fred," she murmured, almost vaguely, "is the world—gone?"

"Only New York," he answered; "it is terrible—awful! You know— but you, how did you escape—how have you endured this horror? Are you well? Unharmed?"

"Unharmed!" she said.

"And this man here?" he asked, encircling her drooping form with one arm and turning toward the Negro. Suddenly he stiffened and his hand flew to hip. "Why!" he snarled. "It's—a—nigger—Julia! Has he— has he dared—"

She lifted her head and looked at her late companion curiously and then dropped her eyes with a sigh.

"He has dared—all, to rescue me," she said quietly, "and I—thank him—much." But she did not look at him again. As the couple turned away, the father drew a roll of bills from his pockets.

"Here, my good fellow," he said, thrusting the money into the man's hands, "take that—what's your name?"

"Jim Davis," came the answer, hollow-voiced.

"Well, Jim, I thank you. I've always liked your people. If you ever want a job, call on me." And they were gone.

The crowd poured up and out of the elevators, talking and whispering.

"Who was it?"

"Are they alive?"

"How many?"

"Two!"

"Who was saved?"

"A white girl and a nigger—there she goes."

"A nigger? Where is he? Let's lynch the damned—"

"Shut up—he's all right—he saved her."

"Saved hell! He had no business—"

"Here he comes."

Into the glare of the electric lights the colored man moved slowly, with the eyes of those that walk and sleep.

"Well, what do you think of that?" cried a bystander. "Of all New York, just a white girl and a nigger!"

The colored man heard nothing. He stood silently beneath the glare of the light, gazing at the money in his hand and shrinking as he gazed; slowly he put his other hand into his pocket and brought out a baby's filmy cap, and gazed again. A woman mounted to the platform and looked about, shading her eyes. She was brown, small, and toil-worn, and in one hand lay the corpse of a dark baby. The crowd parted and her eyes fell on the colored man; with a cry she tottered toward him.

"Jim!"

He whirled and, with a sob of joy, caught her in his arms.

Chicago 1927

Jewelle Gomez

(2000)

High and light, the rich notes of her song lifted from the singer like a bird leaving a familiar tree. The drummer stopped and only a bass player snuck up behind her voice, laying out deep tones that matched hers. Gilda stood at the back of the dimly lit room, letting the soothing sound of music ripple through the air and fall gently around her. Her gaze was fixed on the woman singing on the tiny stage, whose body was coiled around the sound of her own voice. Gilda had come to the Evergreen each weekend for a month to hear the woman sing. LYDIA REDMOND, INDIAN LOVE CALL the window card read outside underneath her picture. On her first night walking through the streets of Chicago, Gilda had seen the sign and been drawn by the gleaming beauty of the face. The sheer simplicity of Lydia's voice rang persistently inside Gilda's head.

The smoky air and clink of glasses crowded around Gilda, filling the room almost as much as the attentive audience. Black and brown faces bobbed and nodded as they sat at the tiny tables on mismatched chairs. Others stood at the short bar watching the set along with the tall, light-skinned bartender, Morris. Some stood in the back near the entrance transfixed, as did Gilda.

She had finally created the opportunity to meet Lydia Redmond through the club's owner Benny Green. It had taken only a slight glance held a moment longer than necessary to plant the idea, and Benny treated Gilda like she was a long-missed relative. Lydia had been full of playfulness when they'd sat together at Benny's table after her show one night. The luminescence in the photograph that had drawn Gilda shimmered around Lydia when she laughed. The sorrow that cloaked so many club singers had only a small place within Lydia. When she looked into Gilda's eyes, she'd read her so intently that Gilda had to turn away. The last note of a sweet, bluesy number wavered in the air, then was enveloped in unrestrained applause and shouts. Gilda smiled as she slipped out of the door of the club's entrance into the short alley and was startled to see Benny holding a young boy by the collar.

"I ain't jivin' you, Lester. You get home to your sister right now. You want me stoppin' by to have a talk to her?"

"Naw."

"Naw what?"

"Naw sir."

"I done told you don't hang in this alley. You ain't heard they shootin' people this side of town?"

"Yes sir," the boy said blankly as if he'd been told he was standing in a loading dock.

"I'm tellin' you there's been shootin' here, boy! Don't crap out on me."

"Yes sir." Lester let himself show the surprise he felt.

"Here," Benny said as he handed the boy a folded bill. He looked about seven years old and was dressed in pants and a jacket much too large for him, like many children Gilda had seen.

"Take that to your sister." Benny's thin mustache curved up as his lips could no longer resist a smile. "Tell her come by my office tomorrow . . . no, not tomorrow. Make it the next day, tell her come at noontime. Ya hear?"

"Yes . . . yes sir." The child's face lost its stiff fear and as Benny shoved him toward the mouth of the alley, he almost smiled.

"Damn."

"A colleague?" Gilda said lightly.

"He'd like to be. How in hell can you keep 'em out the game if you can't keep 'em in the house?" Benny's voice was raw with anger.

Gilda didn't have to listen to his thoughts to sense the anxiety and concern swirling around underneath his hard tone.

"I already got two laundry women. Looks like I'ma have to hire me another one. She lost her job." Benny jerked his thumb in the direction of the darkness where the boy had disappeared. "His sister, she takes care of a passel of them."

Maybe you should open a laundry house. Gilda let the thought slip from her mind into his.

"Maybe . . . you know I got the back end of the joint, facing off North Street. . . . Maybe I'll set them girls up in there. Get us a laundry going! Damn. That's it."

"You have a good heart, Benny."

"What else I'ma do?"

"That's what I mean," Gilda said.

"Lester's okay, he just ain't got nothin' to do but hang around trying to grab some pennies. Morris had to snatch him up out some trouble last week."

"You and Morris need to be on the city council," Gilda said with a laugh as she started toward the mouth of the alley.

"Hey, you comin' by the party later? We got a fine spread." His smooth brown skin was like velvet in the light of the alley. He pulled at the cuffs of each sleeve under his jacket and smoothed his hand across his short-cut hair, readying himself to return to the bar.

"I'll be there."

"You know, cousin, you need to be careful walking these streets by yourself in the middle of the night."

"Thanks, Benny, I'm just going up to the corner. I'll be right back."

"Umph." Benny grunted his disapproval, then said with a smile, "You know I can't handle it when a good-lookin' woman stands me up."

Gilda waved as she turned and walked swiftly out to the street. She looked north, then south before she picked her direction. The air felt brisk and fresh on her smooth skin, untouched by the decades that had led her to this place. The deep brown of her eyes was still clear, sparkling with questions just as they had when she was truly a girl. Her full mouth was firm, tilted more toward a smile than a frown, and inviting, even without the faint trace of lipstick she occasionally applied.

The fragrance of fall was in the trees just as it had been every season for many years. Gilda marveled at how different each part of the country smelled; and over time, the scent of everything—grass, wood, even people—altered subtly. Nothing in her face revealed that eighty years had passed since Gilda had taken her first breath on a plantation in Mississippi. After journeying through most of the countryside and small towns west of the Rocky Mountains, this was her first stop in a major city in some years.

As she strode through the streets, Gilda was self-conscious about her clothes. Although some women had worn pants for almost fifty years, she was still frequently among a select few wherever she went. It had caused ripples of talk since her arrival in town, but she would not relent or be forced to maneuver in the skimpy skirts that were currently the rage. Her solid body was firm with muscles that were concealed beneath the full-cut slacks and jacket. The dark purple and black weave of her coat hid the preternatural strength of her arms. Her hair was pulled away from her face, in a single, thick braid woven from the crown of her head to her neck. There was nothing about Gilda that any of the men who frequented the Evergreen would call elegant, yet the way she moved through the room left most of them curious, attentive.

Gilda removed the matching beret she wore and tucked it inside a deep pocket in the lining of her jacket. Tonight, few would notice her as she passed. She turned off of the downtown street and walked toward the river. Here the noise was louder, lower. The echo of Lydia Redmond's voice receded as Gilda's body succumbed to its need. She remembered the first time she'd gone out into the night for the blood that kept her alive. Running through the hot, damp night in Louisiana with the woman, Bird, who'd first given her the gift, Gilda had been astonished at the ease of movement. They'd passed plantation fields as if they rode in carriages. She'd barely felt the ground beneath her feet as the wind seemed to lift them through the night. They'd found sleeping farmhands, sunk deeply into their dreams, and Bird, always the teacher, had allayed Gilda's fears. Whatever horror there might be in the act of taking blood was not part of this for them. Bird taught Gilda how to reach inside their thoughts, find the dream that meant the most while taking her share of the blood. In exchange for the blood Gilda learned to leave something of help behind for them and in this way remained part of the process of life.

Later, Gilda heard of those who did not believe in exchange. Murder was as much a part of their hunger as the blood. The fire of fear in the blood of others was addictive to some who became weak with need for the power of killing. Or, even worse, they snared mortals in their life of blood without seeking permission. The eyes of these killers glistened with the same malevolence she'd seen in the eyes of overseers on the plantation when she was a girl. The thud of their boot on the flesh of a slave lit an evil light inside them. Gilda avoided those with such eyes. To have escaped slavery only to take on the mantle of the slaveholders would have shamed Gilda and her mentor, Bird, more than either would have been able to bear. Instead, she thrived on the worlds of imagination that she shared with others.

We take blood, not life. Leave something in exchange. The words of that lesson pulsed through Gilda with the blood. In the exchange, it was usually easy to provide an answer to the simple needs she discovered as she took her share of the blood. In one situation a lonely woman needed to find the courage to speak aloud in order to find companionship; in another a frightened thief required only the slightest encouragement to seek another profession. Gilda enjoyed the sense of completion when she drew back and saw the understanding on their faces, even in sleep.

Gilda had lived this way for more than eighty years—traveling the country, seeking the company of mortals, leaving small seeds among those whose blood she shared. But recently, with each new town, Gilda had begun to lose her connection with mortals. She had little confidence in her ability to live in such close proximity with them and maintain her equilibrium. In the last town, she'd settled comfortably, remote enough from neighbors to avoid suspicion. Yet she'd enjoyed the life of the small black community in Missouri and been inspired by them. Their scrubbed-clean church, the farmers who distributed food from their land to people who were hungry, the women who nursed any who needed it. The burden of insults and deprivation they faced each day was only a small part of what they shared. Gilda had found herself deeply enmeshed with someone whose life was so rooted in that town, it was clear she was meant for the age in which she lived. The companionship had renewed Gilda in ways that were as important as the blood. Despite the temptation to bring someone into her life, Gilda saw that to disrupt another's would have been disaster. Again, Bird's lessons had helped her find her way through the confusion of power and desire. Gilda had moved on, leaving her cherished companion behind, finding her way onto the road alone once more. In her isolation, she'd begun to feel the weight of her years.

A sound drew her back to the moment—footsteps were approaching her quickly from behind. This was a neighborhood in which the men who worked on the railroads and in the meatpacking plants often drank hard and followed their impulses. Her caution hardened into defense when she saw two white men barreling toward her. Gilda had recently read in one of the newspapers that the Ku Klux Klan was having a large resurgence across the country and these two exuded that same kind of agitation. The larger man, dark curly hair falling in his eyes, threw his arms out to envelop her in an embrace; the other was close behind. Gilda stepped aside quickly and left him empty-handed and bewildered. She realized that both were drunk, but her evasion seemed to anger the curly-haired one. The short man, more inebriated than his companion, fell to his knees laughing at the sight of his off-balance friend.

"Come on, darlin'. A little kiss, that's what we want," he said from his kneeling position in a thick Irish brogue.

"It'll be more'n a kiss when I'm done," Curly said with a nasty edge.

Gilda glanced over her shoulder at the lights of the low building from which they'd emerged. No one else seemed to be exiting; only the distant music of a stride piano punctuated the night.

"Commere." Curly grabbed at Gilda as she easily ducked his grip. The one on his knees found it all so funny he couldn't get up. Gilda tried to back up to create enough room to turn away, planning to move so swiftly that they would never see the path she'd taken. Curly, now enraged by the failure to capture his prey, drew back his fist. His arm was broad under the heavy work jacket and his fist was massive as he struck out with the force of a wrecking ball.

Gilda stopped the man's fist in the air before it reached her face and squeezed until she heard one bone break. The man on the ground sat contentedly, still laughing as if he were listening to Fibber McGee and Molly on the radio. Rage filled Curly's face; then was replaced by fear as he saw first the anger and then the swirling orange flecks in Gilda's eyes. To come all this way and still be faced with the past made Gilda dizzy with outrage. She listened to the bones snapping in Curly's hand and in her mind saw the man who'd tracked her down when she'd escaped the plantation. A simple overseer who did not see her as human. The memory of the ease with which he'd enjoyed trapping her and his excitement as he'd anticipated raping her blazed inside Gilda's head. The hard crackle of barn hay sticking the flesh of her back as she'd prayed not to be discovered; that light in his eyes that burned everything around him; the stink of his sweat as he'd hulked above her. The feel of the knife in her hand as it had entered his body. A sound of crying. Gilda shook her head to free herself from the images of her past that crowded in.

She held the curly-haired man with her gaze, leading his mind into a foggy place where he would rest until she was done. She let his broken hand drop, sliced the thick skin on his neck with the long nail of her small finger, and watched the blood rise rapidly. A ferrous scent filled the air and she pressed her lips to the dark red line, drawing his blood inside her. A kiss had not been all he'd had in mind. Any woman alone by the stockyards was fair game to him. And no one would ever hear a colored woman's accusation of rape.

She pushed into his thoughts, to find something she might fulfill rather than let herself enjoy his terror as she drained him of life. Inside, his insecurities flooded him like a mud broth; her rape would not have been the first. Only his camaraderie with his friend, the short one on the ground, still drunk and laughing, held any importance. As she started to pull away and leave him with his life, she probed further and saw the image of a young girl, the daughter of the woman who ran the boardinghouse where he lived. A parasitic lust clouded the space around her in his thoughts. Gilda pushed them aside and inserted a new idea: *This child could be your friend*, just like the short man who sat oblivious beside them. He'd never imagined women as anything other than prey, but his investment in this girl's safety—her nurturance—might provide a renewed connection to the world around him. Gilda wiped her mouth clean and released him. He fell to the ground beside his friend, who only then looked up, puzzled. The short one who laughed almost toppled over when he tried to stand and better assess the situation.

"Hey . . . you . . . what'sa matter?" He blinked and as he swayed Gilda stepped backward away from the two, leaving them frozen in their comic tableau as she sped away.

The blood that would carry her through centuries burst inside her veins. A flush of heat rose in her body and suffused her face and neck with deepening color. Her dark skin glowed with the renewed life flowing inside her. The definition of her arms and shoulders sharpened imperceptibly with each step. Yet, even as she sighed with enjoyment of the fresh blood, she wondered why she would want all the years that lay ahead. Men of this type, of all races, filled the roads and towns wherever she went. A woman had as much chance of survival on a city street as an antelope wandering into a pride of lions. Gilda shook the image from her mind and moved away from the raw smells and animal fear.

When she was back on a main street she slowed her pace and turned to look in the shop windows, hoping to supplant the images that tried to take root. The city was growing so fast merchants barely had time to keep up with it. Elegant gowns were hung next to daytime dresses; divans reclined beside kitchen stoves. The whole city felt as if it were bursting with life.

Gilda stopped in front of a store that held tools and looked at the saws and lawn mowers, then pulled back to catch her image in the glass. According to superstition, she had no soul; therefore, she could cast no reflection. But those of her kind had lived long before Christian mythology permeated contemporary society. In the glass, Gilda recognized the face she'd always known. Almond-shaped eyes, never quite ordinary, even without the orange flecks of hunger, dark eyebrows that gave her face a grave intensity, full lips now firm with thought—the same West African features that she'd seen in many other faces as she'd traveled the country. Gilda smiled at her reflection, set her beret at an alluring angle, straightened her jacket, then hurried back toward the Evergreen.

Benny Green had bought the corner building where his club was located almost as soon as he saw the sign EVERGREEN. It was fate; the place was almost named for him. He'd been saving for years with one idea in mind—to own something, a place where colored people could be comfortable, some people would get work, and he'd be an easy part of the world because he'd created it. He didn't know how long he could keep his ownership hidden from his employees and friends, but in the months since he'd opened up he'd dodged all questions. With Prohibition it was hard enough: police looking for a handout, enforcers, who seemed to work all sides of the street, demanding their cut. Rivals were always looking for an opening so they might take over the prosperous business that the Evergreen had become. Sometimes they tried to push—causing trouble in the club, harassing patrons outside. It was simpler for Benny to let everyone think he was somebody he wasn't. He paid for protection, kept a low profile, never let his joint get in the papers, and pretended he was just a manager who reported to someone else.

The door into Benny's flat was at the top of the stairs that led up from the street behind the club. Gilda stood on the landing in a moment of anticipation. She would be in a room full of people, her people, for the first time in decades. The colored people of Chicago liked being invited to Benny's parties. She tapped on the door and a small woman in a maid's apron opened it almost immediately. Her face was suffused with a smile, which she worked very hard to maintain as she examined Gilda's austere pants and matching jacket.

"May I take your . . . wrap?" she said, barely belying her confusion.

"No, thank you. The ensemble wouldn't work without it, wouldn't you say?"

The maid laughed easily. "You can sure say that, ma'am." She swept the door open wider to usher Gilda in as she continued to chuckle.

"Kinda cute, though. Kinda cute," she repeated as she waved Gilda toward the living room and walked away.

His apartment above the bar was a rambling affair that Gilda had visited only once before. She'd heard how he'd hired an out-of-work friend to repaint. Then he'd hired another club patron, who'd just lost his job, to decorate the parlor, and when one of his waitresses needed extra money, he'd hired her to redo his dining room. Eventually one friend or another had tended the whole place. Morris always teased, "That man'll never give you a free drink. But he always got a job for ya."

The result of Benny's fragmented approach to decoration was a flash blend of opulence and primitivism, each of which seemed to be evolving. An African mask was hung amid chiffon draping in the entry hall. Through the door, Gilda saw the clean, curving lines of the period in the sideboard and divan. And everywhere were stacks of books and other things that had never found their proper places. The sound of someone plunking out Bix Beiderbecke's "In the Mist" on the piano had reached Gilda long before she entered the rooms. The pianist halted repeatedly, trying to get a grip on the snaking melody. Laughter and voices almost swallowed the sound of the effort.

In the first parlor, a long table was barely visible beneath platters of chicken, sweet potatoes, and cole slaw. Bowls overflowed with pickles and other things Gilda didn't recognize. She did recognize Hilda, the tall, slender natural redhead who waited tables at the Evergreen. Her hair and tawny skin were shown to best advantage by her crisply tailored black silk dress, cinched at the waist with a three-inch-wide belt that matched her hair perfectly. She waved at Gilda and continued on her way toward the piano where Emory, who usually played drums, was still attacking the Beiderbecke tune. His circle of wavy, mixed gray hair had receded far back on his head but he still appeared youthful as he concentrated on the tune. Gilda walked past them, wading into the scent of perfume that hung in the air. The click of high heels and deep male voices filled the room, mingling with the piano as if orchestrated by Ellington.

Through a door, in the smaller parlor she saw Benny in the dining room playing bartender behind a short, highly polished version of the mahogany bar in the Evergreen. He'd changed into a light-colored silk jacket that hung softly on him. Morris, in a reversal of his nightly routine behind the bar, relaxed on a leather and chrome barstool, his tall frame barely contained. They appeared to be intent on their conversation as Benny served him a drink, but he glanced up and noticed Gilda among the half dozen other guests mingling near the doorway.

"Come on over here, cousin," Benny shouted.

"Harlem ain't got nothin' on Chicago," Morris was saying as she approached. "Tell this man, Gilda. What Harlem got we ain't got?" Morris's light brown eyes sparkled with challenge, more playful than he'd ever appeared downstairs. His ever-present white shirt was, as usual, fresh and firm across his broad shoulders.

"I ain't sayin' nothin' against Chicago, man," Benny answered in a soft teasing voice she'd heard often when the two men were together.

"You think we ain't got no colored writers?" Morris went on. "We got colored writers here. And we got the music. Shit, you know that yourself!" Morris took a drink as if that ended the discussion. "What about Richard Wright? He got his chops here. And you ain't heard of Katherine Dunham, man?" Indignation was building like a balloon over Morris's head. "Where you think King Oliver been playing for the last five years? Same with Alberta Hunter—"

"Lemme get you something," Benny interrupted Morris, "'fore this man starts trying to run for mayor."

Gilda asked for champagne and he laughed. "Girl, you need something more'n that on a night like this."

"They may go to Harlem, but they find themselves here. In Chicago!"

"That'll do me, Benny. Honest." Gilda had no luck trying to appear demure and was relieved when she heard Lydia's voice behind her.

"Aw, Benny, stop annoying the chick. Give her what she wants. You trying to get the woman drunk?" Lydia leaned in closer to the bar. Benny, faking villainy, twirled an imaginary mustache, much larger than his own.

Gilda inhaled Lydia's scent deeply before she turned. A light blend of cinnamon and magnolia wafted from her hair, making Gilda's heart beat faster. She was startled to see that Lydia wore bronze satin pants that clung to her narrow hips. On top she wore a pale golden chiffon blouse that highlighted her copper skin, which shone through the filmy fabric.

"You like it?" Lydia asked as she watched Gilda, who seemed unable to catch her breath.

Gilda finally found her smile. "You look quite . . . chic. I believe that's the word."

Benny prepared another drink and held the short rock glass as if he didn't want to let it go.

"Come on, give," Lydia said, then took the drink.

"Lyd's kinda handy with the sewing machine," Morris said. "She even made them curtains that run 'cross the stage."

"Hey, why should you get all the gab?" Lydia teased Gilda. "Half the town's talking about your outfits. Hell, when you walk in the club I gotta turn the lights up so they stop lookin' at ya." Her laughter was totally unladylike and flew into the room, compelling others to join her. It was the same sound that filtered through her singing.

She grabbed Gilda's arm and drew her away from the bar. "Lemme show you the joint before they eject Emory and plunk me down at the piano." Gilda followed her through the kitchen to what looked like a comfortable office. Gilda stepped inside and leaned against a narrow desk, watching as Lydia crossed the room sipping from her drink. Her wavy dark hair was loose around her shoulders and the vibrant red polish on her nails gleamed in the dim light. Gilda was fascinated by the way she filled the room.

"So, uh, what do you think? About me, my singing, stuff like that." She almost sounded like a child; her enthusiasm and curiosity were unconscious and genuine.

"Your voice carries almost all the joy in the world."

"Um." She stopped and leaned against a bookcase to think for a moment.

"Benny likes you a lot," Gilda said, pausing. So many thoughts were swirling in her head, she couldn't easily choose one. Gilda felt ripples of desire expanding inside. She put her drink down and pressed her hands to the desk.

"How can you tell that?"

"He can't take his eyes off you. If you're anywhere in the room his body is turned in your direction as if you were the sun."

"Ain't you the poet?"

Gilda felt embarrassed, but there was no sign of it. Her skin remained the rich dark color it had always been.

"Ben's like my brother."

Gilda's skepticism was obvious.

"No, really. He took good care of me when I needed it and I do the same."

"Have you been friends long?"

"I was traveling with a show. 'Blue Heaven.' You ever see it?"

Gilda shook her head.

"About a year ago we're doing the gig and I got sick. Him and Morris got me to the hospital when the troupe moved on. Made sure I had everything. Then give me the job singing at the Evergreen. They are two right guys. Benny's always helping somebody with something. The colored school, this church or that one. He's got a buck for everybody."

The description fit easily with the impression that Gilda had formed since arriving in town.

"So what's your game?" Lydia made the question sound soft, not an accusation.

Gilda thought a moment. She could easily have diverted the question, but she didn't want to, at least not right away.

"I'm trying to decide what to do next," Gilda said, knowing Lydia could never understand how big a question it was.

"Stick around this burg for a while." Lydia's voice carried the same invitation to joy that Gilda had heard in her singing.

"I think I will."

"Good. Benny's gonna need someone like you."

"Someone like me?"

"Smart, figuring on the future. That's his one . . . kinda flaw, you know. Colored folks in this town need this, they need that." Lydia's eyes were unwavering as she watched Gilda listening to her. She spoke and examined Gilda at the same time. "He's always thinkin' about it, but he's got no sense of a plan. You a woman who knows somethin' about planning for the future. And he don't know how to handle those mugs that keep edging up on him." Lydia's confidence in her words and in Gilda surprised her.

Gilda looked around her at the books and ledgers. It felt like a room bursting with ideas and with life; Benny's presence was as strong here as it was downstairs in the Evergreen. Gilda wouldn't let herself listen to Lydia's thoughts. That was another lesson from Bird she'd embraced: Intruding on another's thoughts simply for personal gain was the height of rudeness. So, the reasons for Lydia's certainty remained unclear. Lydia watched Gilda watching her, as if she awaited Gilda's assent. The memory of Lydia's scent unfurled like an unexpected fog in Gilda's head and she tried to clear her mind.

"Why does the billboard say 'Indian Love Call'?" Gilda asked.

"My father was Wampanoag. Back East, you know, the Indians they named Massachusetts for. They were Wampanoag."

Gilda looked again at Lydia and recognized the bone structure. The blending of African and Indian lines was so common in this country, yet Gilda had forgotten. She'd seen many women who looked like they might be Lydia's relatives.

"Of course," she said.

"That was Benny's idea, not mine. My mother would be fit to be tied." She sipped from her glass, then set it down on a shelf and moved closer to Gilda. This time the cinnamon and flowers were real, not a memory. "She's not much for people pretending not to be colored."

"But you're not."

"Naw. Everybody likes a bit of mystery. So this year I'm it."

"What about next year?" Gilda kept her breath shallow, trying not to take in too much.

"I'll be Lebanese!"

The room was filled first with Lydia's laughter, then Gilda's. Deep inside an image blossomed for her, a tiny glimpse of her past. Inside she held a precious moment of laughter between her and one of her sisters as they'd toiled among the rows of cotton. The reason for mirth had quickly faded then. In the expansive dining room with Lydia, Gilda recaptured that forgotten joy and savored it as fully as if her sisters were still alive and in the room beside her.

This was what Gilda found so entrancing in Lydia's voice. It was rich with the happiness she'd had; very little sorrow or bitterness weighted her songs. The melodies Lydia sang each night might be mournful when delivered by someone else, but Lydia sang with the light of what was coming, not merely what had been done in the past.

They both stopped laughing, comfortable with the recognition of the feeling growing between them.

"And what's your mystery, lady?" Lydia asked as if she already knew the answer.

Gilda pressed her hand to Lydia's cheek lightly, letting herself enjoy the softness around Lydia's smile. She didn't want to pull away from the question, even though she knew she couldn't answer. Lydia stepped in closer, the full length of her body pressing its aura of heat against Gilda.

The air wavered around them, intoxicated by mist and cinnamon. Then the unnatural silence in the rest of the flat crashed around them. No piano, voices, or glasses. The ominous silence was broken by a shout and the explosion of a gun.

"Stay here!" Gilda said in a low voice, and bolted through the door. She moved quickly but without sound. When she entered the dining room, everybody was huddled on the floor, satin dresses and silk jackets askew. Through the parlor, she could see the front door forced open, almost off its hinges. The maid's face was barely visible thorough a crack in the bathroom door and Gilda waved her back.

"Shit." Gilda heard Morris.

"Everybody stay down," Gilda shouted as she listened to the entire flat—the attackers seemed to have fled. She hurried to the bar. Behind it, Benny lay on the floor. Morris held his hand to the wound in Benny's chest. His fair skin had paled as if the blood were draining from him as well.

"I told him we had to give them the joint. They been wanting in for months." Tears filled Morris's voice. "We got other stuff, we don't need this shit." Morris spoke as if his words could bind the wound.

"Quick, let me." Gilda edged Morris out of the way and knelt beside Benny. "Get them out of here." The floor around Benny was awash in his blood. The moments moved in rapid flashes for Gilda. She looked into his eyes as she tried to find his pulse. He was there and not there. Morris's apologetic voice was a low murmur as he helped people to their feet and kept the exit orderly. The woman in the maid's apron came out of the bathroom and helped Morris find people's coats.

As Benny's blood cooled around her, Gilda thought of the little boy, Lester, arriving tomorrow at noon with his sister for a job. She could feel Lydia reaching out, begging her to make everything all right as if she knew Gilda was able to hear her. All the connections Benny had with those around him in this room had created a family, and in turn he aided others holding their families together. He was able to help give life in ways different from Gilda. She fought the urge to save Benny with the power only she possessed.

Blood should not be given as an unexpected gift. Bird's admonition rang in her mind. Gilda knew of those who'd not chosen wisely, giving the gift of blood to those unable to manage the powers. She'd seen the results: deadly tyrants, intoxicated by their powers, unable to care about the havoc they created around them.

The explicit wish for the gift must be stated. How can you know who is capable of carrying such a burden? Gilda accepted all the reasons for letting Benny die. She turned to see Lydia standing at the bar looking down at them, her mouth open in horror.

"I know you can save him."

Lydia's eyes were full of that knowing. Gilda didn't understand how that could be, and at the same time knew she could not let Benny's life slip away from him, to be soaked into the hard wooden floor. But to give the blood without his direct request was against all she'd been taught. Which would be the worse transgression?

Gilda put her lips to the wound in Benny's chest, where the blood had pooled. She took his blood into her mouth and listened for his needs. His mind was full of many people he wanted to help. Pictures of people, of towns, of the Evergreen were lit inside Gilda like reflections from a mirror ball. A fascinating dizziness pulled Gilda closer to Benny's mind. Lydia was deep inside his dreams, too, and it was as she'd said: as a sister.

The most urgent image inside Benny was his love of Morris. Gilda was startled that she hadn't realized it earlier. Their bond had grown out of a mutual care for the colored people of their town. Without the guarded protection they both maintained in public, the kinship and desire between them was unmistakable. The two men were partners in business and in life. There was little time left, but Benny's thoughts kaleidoscoped through her mind like spokes on a wheel. This was a family. They had work to do. Benny's thoughts were filled with an array of faces, although his body was almost still under her hands. She could not ignore the tie that held so many together.

Gilda let herself feel rather than think about what was coming. She would give him her blood and he would survive. Benny, Morris, and Lydia would know what she was. She would have to explain the life of the blood. If he desired it, Benny could go on with his life, fully recovered, and reject that preternatural life. When the hunger came on him, he could fight as if it were a drug, until it subsided, then dissipated completely.

But Benny might also decide to live with the blood. He would have the right to ask Gilda to share with him twice again until he was strong, and she would teach him about their life as Bird had taught her. She could not guess which path he would choose. Only in the moments and years to come would Gilda know the meaning of her decision.

She could feel Lydia staring down at her. With the hard nail of her small finger, Gilda cut the skin on her wrist smoothly and held it to Benny's mouth. At first, the blood just washed down his face. She tilted his head back so his mouth would open. He began to take the blood in and Gilda felt life slowly return to his body. His eyes fluttered, then filled with confusion and relief.

Lydia's eyes showed both her gratefulness and bewilderment when Gilda looked up, Benny's warm blood staining her face and clothes. The door to the flat slammed shut and they heard Morris running.

"Benny," he bellowed as he came. Their life together had seemed about to end when he'd gone to the front of the flat to help the shocked guests leave. His anguish was carried in the tears that ran down his face onto his blood-splattered shirt. He stopped abruptly when he saw Lydia smiling. Incredulous, he looked down at Benny, whose eyes were open and had regained their focus.

A familiar vitality pulsed through Benny's body as Gilda cradled him in her arms. She sensed they would be spending much time together in the coming months.

"He's all right, Morris," Lydia said, as if she knew it was true even though she wasn't exactly sure why. Her voice was full of joy like her songs.

Black No More (excerpt from the novel)

George S. Schuyler

(1931)

NEGRO ANNOUNCES REMARKABLE

DISCOVERY

CAN CHANGE BLACK TO WHITE IN THREE DAYS.

Max went into Jimmy Johnson's restaurant and greedily read the account while awaiting his breakfast. Yes, it must be true. To think of old Crookman being able to do that. Only a few years ago he'd been just a hungry medical student around Harlem. Max put down the paper and stared vacantly out of the window. Gee, Crookman would be a millionaire in no time. He'd even be a multimillionaire. It looked as though science was to succeed where the Civil War had failed. But how could it be possible? He looked at his hands and felt at the back of his head where the straightening lotion had failed to conquer some of the knots. He toyed with his ham and eggs as he envisioned the possibilities of the discovery.

Then a sudden resolution seized him. He looked at the newspaper account again. Yes, Crookman was staying at the Phyllis Wheatley Hotel. Why not go and see what there was to this? Why not be the first Negro to try it out? Sure, it was taking a chance, but think of getting white in three days. No more jim crow. No more insults. As a white man he could go anywhere, be anything he wanted to be, do most anything he wanted to do, be a free man at last . . . and probably be able to meet the girl from Atlanta. What a vision!

He rose hurriedly, paid for his breakfast, rushed out of the door, almost ran into an aged white man carrying a sign advertising a Negro fraternity dance, and strode, almost ran, to the Phyllis Wheatley Hotel.

He tore up the steps two at a time and into the sitting room. It was crowded with white reporters from the daily newspapers and black reporters from the Negro weeklies. In their midst he recognized Dr. Junius Crookman, tall, wiry, ebony black, with a studious and polished manner. Flanking him on either side was Henry ("Hank") Johnson, the "Numbers" banker, and Charlie ("Chuck") Foster, the realtor, looking very grave, important and possessive in the midst of all the hullabaloo.

"Yes," Dr. Crookman was telling the reporters while they eagerly took down his statements, "during my first year at college I noticed a black girl on the street one day who had several irregular white patches on her face and hands. That intrigued me. I began to study up on skin diseases and found out that the girl was evidently suffering from a nervous disease known as vitiligo. It is a very rare disease. Both Negroes and Caucasians occasionally have it, but it is naturally more conspicuous on blacks than whites. It absolutely removes skin pigment and sometimes it turns a Negro completely white but only after a period of thirty or forty years. It occurred to me that if one could discover some means of artificially inducing and stimulating this nervous disease at will, one might possibly solve the American race problem. My sociology teacher had once said that there were but three ways for the Negro to solve his problem in America," he gestured with his long slender fingers, "To either get out, get white, or get along. Since he wouldn't and couldn't get out and was getting along only differently, it seemed to me that the only thing for him was to get white." For a moment his teeth gleamed beneath his smartly waxed mustache, then he sobered and went on:

"I began to give a great deal of study to the problem during my spare time. Unfortunately there was very little information on the subject in this country. I decided to go to Germany but didn't have the money. Just when I despaired of getting the funds to carry out my experiments and studies abroad, Mr. Johnson and Mr. Foster," he indicated the two men with a graceful wave of his hand, "came to my rescue. I naturally attribute a great deal of my success to them."

"But how is it done?" asked a reporter.

"Well," smiled Crookman, "I naturally cannot divulge the secret any more than to say that it is accomplished by electrical nutrition and glandular control. Certain gland secretions are greatly stimulated while others are considerably diminished. It is a powerful and dangerous treatment but harmless when properly done."

"How about the hair and features?" asked a Negro reporter.

"They are also changed in the process," answered the biologist. "In three days the Negro becomes to all appearances a Caucasian."

"But is the transformation transferred to the offspring?" persisted the Negro newspaperman.

"As yet," replied Crookman, "I have discovered no way to accomplish anything so revolutionary, but I am able to transform a black infant to a white one in twenty-four hours."

"Have you tried it on any Negroes yet?" queried a skeptical white journalist.

"Why, of course I have," said the Doctor, slightly nettled. "I would not have made my announcement if I had not done so. Come here, Sandol," he called, turning to a pale white youth standing on the outskirts of the crowd, who was the most Nordic looking person in the room. "This man is a Senegalese, a former aviator in the French Army. He is living proof that what I claim is true."

Dr. Crookman then displayed a photograph of a very black man, somewhat resembling Sandol but with bushy Negro hair, flat nose and full lips. "This," he announced proudly, "is Sandol as he looked before taking my treatment. What I have done to him I can do to any Negro. He is in good physical and mental condition as you all can see."

The assemblage was properly awed. After taking a few more notes and a number of photographs of Dr. Crookman, his associates, and of Sandol, the newspapermen retired. Only the dapper Max Disher remained.

"Hello, Doc!" he said, coming forward and extending his hand. "Don't you remember me? I'm Max Disher."

"Why certainly I remember you, Max," replied the biologist rising cordially. "Been a long time since we've seen each other, but you're looking as sharp as ever. How's things?"

The two men shook hands.

"Oh, pretty good. Say, Doc, how's chances to get you to try that thing on me? You must be looking for volunteers."

"Yes, I am, but not just yet. I've got to get my equipment set up first. I think now I'll be ready for business in a couple of weeks."

Henry Johnson, the beefy, sleek-jowled, mulatto "Numbers" banker, chuckled and nudged Dr. Crookman. "Old Max ain't losin' no time, Doc. When that niggah gits white Ah bet he'll make up fo' los' time with these ofay girls."

Charlie Foster, small, slender, grave, amber-colored, and laconic, finally spoke up:

"Seems all right, Junius, but there will be hell to pay when you whiten up a lot of these darkies and them mulatto babies start appearing here and there. Watcha gonna do then?"

"Oh, quit singin' th' blues, Chuck," boomed Johnson. "Don't cross bridges 'til yuh come tuh 'em. Doc'll fix that okeh. Besides, we'll have mo' money'n Henry Ford by that time."

"There'll be no difficulties; whatever," assured Crookman rather impatiently.

"Let's hope not."

Next day the newspapers carried a long account of the interview with Dr. Junius Crookman interspersed with photographs of him, his backers and of the Senegalese who had been turned white. It was the talk of the town and was soon the talk of the country. Long editorials were written about the discovery, learned societies besieged the Negro biologist with offers of lecture engagements, magazines begged him for articles, but he turned down all offers and refused to explain his treatment. This attitude was decried as unbecoming a scientist and it was insinuated and even openly stated that nothing more could be expected from a Negro. But Crookman ignored the clamor of the public, and with the financial help of his associates planned the great and lucrative experiment of turning Negroes into Caucasians.

The impatient Max Disher saw him as often as possible and kept track of developments. He yearned to be the first treated and didn't want to be caught napping. Two objects were uppermost in his mind: To get white and to Atlanta. The statuesque and haughty blonde was ever in his thoughts. He was head over heels in love with her and realized there was no hope for him to ever win her as long as he was brown. Each day he would walk past the tall building that was to be the Crookman Sanitarium, watching the workmen and delivery trucks; wondering how much longer he would have to wait before entering upon the great adventure.

At last the sanitarium was ready for business. Huge advertisements appeared in the local Negro weeklies. Black Harlem was on its toes. Curious throngs of Negroes and whites stood in front of the austere six-story building gazing up at its windows.

Inside, Crookman, Johnson and Foster stood nervously about while hustling attendants got everything in readiness. Outside they could hear the murmur of the crowd.

"That means money, Chuck," boomed Johnson, rubbing his beefsteak hands together.

"Yeh," replied the realtor, "but there's one more thing I wanna get straight: How about that darky dialect? You can't change that."

"It isn't necessary, my dear Foster," explained the physician, patiently. "There is no such thing as Negro dialect, except in literature and drama. It is a well-known fact among informed persons that a Negro from a given section speaks the same dialect as his white neighbors. In the South you can't tell over the telephone whether you are talking to a white man or a Negro. The same is true in New York when a Northern Negro speaks into the receiver. I have noticed the same thing in the hills of West Virginia and Tennessee. The educated Haitian speaks the purest French and the Jamaican Negro sounds exactly like an Englishman. There are no racial or color dialects; only sectional dialects."

"Guess you're right," agreed Foster, grudgingly.

"I know I'm right. Moreover, even if my treatment did not change the so-called Negro lips, even that would prove to be no obstacle."

"How come, Doc," asked Johnson.

"Well, there are plenty of Caucasians who have lips quite as thick and noses quite as broad as any of us. As a matter of fact there has been considerable exaggeration about the contrast between Caucasian and Negro features. The cartoonists and minstrel men have been responsible for it very largely. Some Negroes like the Somalis, Filanis, Egyptians, Hausas, and Abyssinians have very thin lips and nostrils. So also have the Malagasys of Madagascar. Only in certain small sections of Africa do the Negroes possess extremely pendulous lips and very broad nostrils—on the other hand, many so-called Caucasians, particularly the Latins, Jews, and South Irish, and frequently the most Nordic of peoples like the Swedes, show almost Negroid lips and noses. Black up some white folks and they could deceive a resident of Benin. Then when you consider that less than twenty per cent of our Negroes are without Caucasian ancestry and that close to thirty per cent have American Indian ancestry, it is readily seen that there cannot be the wide difference in Caucasian and Afro-American facial characteristics that most people imagine."

"Doc, you sho' knows yo' onions," said Johnson, admiringly. "Doan pay no 'tenshun to that ole Doubtin' Thomas. He'd holler starvation in a pie shop."

* * *

There was a commotion outside and an angry voice was heard above the hum of low conversation. Then Max Disher burst in the door with a guard hanging onto his coat tail.

"Let loose o' me, Boy," he quarreled. "I got an engagement here. Doc, tell this man something, will you?"

Crookman nodded to the guard to release the insurance man. "Well, I see you're right on time, Max."

"I told you I'd be Johnny-on-the-spot, didn't I?" said Disher, inspecting his clothes to see if they had been wrinkled.

"Well, if you're all ready, go into the receiving room there, sign the register and get into one of those bathrobes. You're first on the list."

The three partners looked at each other and grinned as Max disappeared into a small room at the end of the corridor. Dr. Crookman went into his office to don his white trousers, shoes, and smock; Johnson and Foster entered the business office to supervise the clerical staff, while white-coated figures darted back and forth through the corridors. Outside, the murmuring of the vast throng grew more audible.

Johnson showed all of his many gold teeth in a wide grin as he glanced out the window and saw the queue of Negroes already extending around the corner. "Man, man, man!" he chuckled to Foster, "at fifty dollars a th'ow this thing's gonna have th'numbah business beat all hollow."

"Hope so," said Foster, gravely.

Max Disher, arrayed only in a hospital bathrobe and a pair of slippers, was escorted to the elevator by two white-coated attendants. They got off on the sixth floor and walked to the end of the corridor. Max was trembling with excitement and anxiety. Suppose something should go wrong? Suppose Doc should make a mistake? He thought of the Elks' excursion every summer to Bear Mountain, the high yellow Minnie and her colorful apartment, the pleasant evenings at the Dahomey Casino doing the latest dances with the brown belles of Harlem, the prancing choruses at the Lafayette Theater, the hours he had whiled away at Boogie's and the Honky Tonk Club, and he hesitated. Then he envisioned his future as a white man, probably as the husband of the tall blonde from Atlanta, and with firm resolve, he entered the door of the mysterious chamber.

He quailed as he saw the formidable apparatus of sparkling nickel. It

resembled a cross between a dentist's chair and an electric chair. Wires
and straps, bars and levers protruded from it and a great nickel headpiece, like the helmet of a knight, hung over it. The room had only a
skylight and no sound entered it from the outside. Around the walls
were cases of instruments and shelves of bottles filled with strangely colored fluids. He gasped with fright and would have made for the door but
the two husky attendants held him firmly, stripped off his robe and
bound him in the chair. There was no retreat. It was either the beginning or the end.

Slowly, haltingly, Max Disher dragged his way down the hall to the
elevator, supported on either side by an attendant. He felt terribly weak;
emptied and nauseated; his skin twitched and was dry and feverish; his
insides felt very hot and sore. As the trio walked slowly along the corridor, a blue-green light would ever and anon blaze through one of the
doorways as a patient was taken in. There was a low hum and throb of
machinery and an acid odor filled the air. Uniformed nurses and attendants hurried back and forth at their tasks. Everything was quiet, swift,
efficient, sinister.

He felt so thankful that he had survived the ordeal of that horrible
machine so akin to the electric chair. A shudder passed over him at the
memory of the hours he had passed in its grip, fed at intervals with re-
volting concoctions. But when they reached the elevator and he saw
himself in the mirror, he was startled, overjoyed. White at last! Gone
was the smooth brown complexion. Gone were the slightly full lips and
Ethiopian nose. Gone was the nappy hair that he had straightened so
meticulously ever since the kink-no-more lotions first wrenched
Aframericans from the tyranny and torture of the comb. There would be
no more expenditures for skin whiteners; no more discrimination; no
more obstacles in his path. He was free! The world was his oyster and he
had the open sesame of a pork-colored skin! The reflection in the mirror gave him new life and strength.

He now stood erect, without support, and grinned at the two tall,
black attendants. "Well, Boys," he crowed, "I'm all set now. That machine of Doc's worked like a charm. Soon's get a feed under my belt I'll
be okeh."

Six hours later, bathed, fed, clean-shaven, spry, blonde, and jubilant,
he emerged from the outpatient ward and tripped gaily down the corri-

dor to the main entrance. He was through with coons, he resolved, from now on. He glanced in a superior manner at the long line of black and brown folk on one side of the corridor, patiently awaiting treatment. He saw many persons whom he knew but none of them recognized him. It thrilled him to feel that he was now indistinguishable from nine-tenths of the people of the United States; one of the great majority. Ah, it was good not to be a Negro any longer!

As he sought to open the front door, the strong arm of a guard restrained him. "Wait a minute," the man said, "and we'll help you get through the mob."

A moment or two later Max found himself the center of a flying wedge of five or six husky special policemen, cleaving through a milling crowd of colored folk. From the top step of the sanitarium he had noticed the crowd spread over the sidewalk into the street and around the corners. Fifty traffic policemen strained and sweated to keep prospective patients in line and out from under the wheels of taxicabs and trucks.

Finally he reached the curb, exhausted from the jostling and squeezing, only to be set upon by a mob of newspaper photographers and reporters. As the first person to take the treatment, he was naturally the center of attraction for about fifteen of these journalistic gnats. They asked a thousand questions seemingly all at once. What was his name? How did he feel? What was he going to do? Would he marry a white woman? Did he intend to continue living in Harlem?

Max would say nothing. In the first place, he thought to himself, if they're so anxious to know all this stuff, they ought to be willing to pay for it. He needed money if he was going to be able to thoroughly enjoy being white; why not get some by selling his story? The reporters, male and female, begged him almost with tears in their eyes for a statement but he was adamant.

While they were wrangling, an empty taxicab drove up. Pushing the inquisitive reporters to one side, Max leaped into it and yelled "Central Park!" It was the only place he could think of at the moment. He wanted to have time to compose his mind, to plan the future in this great world of whiteness. As the cab lurched forward, he turned and was astonished to find another occupant, a pretty girl.

"Don't be scared," she smiled. "I knew you would want to get away from that mob so I went around the corner and got a cab for you. Come along with me and I'll get everything fixed up for you. I'm a reporter from *The Scimitar*. We'll give you a lot of money for your story." She talked rapidly. Max's first impulse had been to jump out of the cab, even at the risk of having to face again the mob of reporters and photographers he had sought to escape, but he changed his mind when he heard mention of money.

"How much?" he asked, eyeing her. She was very comely and he noted that her ankles were well turned.

"Oh, probably a thousand dollars," she replied.

"Well, that sounds good." A thousand dollars! What a time he could have with that! Broadway for him as soon as he got paid off.

As they sped down Seventh Avenue, the newsboys were yelling the latest editions. "Ex-try! Ex-try! Blacks turning white! Blacks turning white! . . . Read all about the gr-r-reat discovery! Paper, Mister! Paper! . . . Read all about Dr. Crookman."

He settled back while they drove through the park and glanced frequently at the girl by his side. She looked mighty good; wonder could he talk business with her? Might go to dinner and a cabaret. That would be the best way to start.

"What did you say your name was?" he began.

"I didn't say," she stalled.

"Well, you have a name, haven't you?" he persisted.

"Suppose I have?"

"You're not scared to tell it, are you?"

"Why do you want to know my name?"

"Well, there's nothing wrong about wanting to know a pretty girl's name, is there?"

"Well, my name's Smith, Sybil Smith. Now are you satisfied?"

"Not yet. I want to know something more. How would you like to go to dinner with me tonight?"

"I don't know and I won't know until I've had the experience." She smiled coquettishly. Going out with him, she figured, would make the basis of a rattling good story for tomorrow's paper. "Negro's first night as a Caucasian!" Fine!

"Say, you're a regular fellow," he said, beaming upon her. "I'll get a great kick out of going to dinner with you because you'll be the only one in the place that'll know I'm a Negro."

Down at the office of *The Scimitar*, it didn't take Max long to come to an agreement, tell his story to a stenographer and get a sheaf of crisp, new bills. As he left the building a couple of hours later with Miss Smith on his arm, the newsboys were already crying the extra edition carrying the first installment of his strange tale. A huge photograph of him occupied the entire front page of the tabloid. Lucky for him that he'd given his name as William Small, he thought.

He was annoyed and a little angered. What did they want to put his picture all over the front of the paper for? Now everybody would know who he was. He had undergone the tortures of Doc Crookman's devilish machine in order to escape the conspicuousness of a dark skin and now he was being made conspicuous because he had once had a dark skin. Could one never escape the plagued race problem?

"Don't worry about that," comforted Miss Smith. "Nobody'll recognize you. There are thousands of white people, yes millions, that look like you do." She took his arm and snuggled up closer. She wanted to make him feel at home. It wasn't often a poor, struggling newspaper woman got a chap with a big bankroll to take her out for the evening. Moreover, the description she would write of the experience might win her a promotion.

They walked down Broadway in the blaze of white lights to a dinner-dance place. To Max it was like being in heaven. He had strolled through the Times Square district before but never with such a feeling of absolute freedom and sureness. No one now looked at him curiously because he was with a white girl, as they had when he came down there with Minnie, his former octoroon lady friend. Gee, it was great!

They dined and they danced. Then they went to a cabaret, where, amid smoke, noise, and body smells, they drank what was purported to be whiskey and watched a semi-nude chorus do its stuff. Despite his happiness Max found it pretty dull. There was something lacking in these ofay places of amusement or else there was something present that one didn't find in the black-and-tan resorts in Harlem. The joy and abandon here was obviously forced. Patrons went to extremes to show each other they were having a wonderful time. It was all so strained and quite unlike anything to which he had been accustomed. The Negroes, it seemed to him, were much gayer, enjoyed themselves more deeply, and yet they were more restrained, actually more refined. Even their dancing was different. They followed the rhythm accurately, effortlessly and with easy grace; these lumbering couples, out of step half the time and working as strenuously as stevedores emptying the bowels of a freighter, were noisy, awkward, inelegant. At their best they were gymnastic where the Negroes were sensuous. He felt a momentary pang of mingled disgust, disillusionment, and nostalgia. But it was only momentary. He looked across at the comely Sybil and then around at the other white women, many of whom were very pretty and expensively gowned, and the sight temporarily drove from his mind the thoughts that had been occupying him.

They parted at three o'clock, after she had given him her telephone number. She pecked him lightly on the cheek in payment, doubtless, for a pleasant evening's entertainment. Somewhat disappointed because she had failed to show any interest in his expressed curiosity about the interior of her apartment, he directed the chauffeur to drive him to Harlem. After all, he argued to himself in defense of his action, he had to get his things.

As the cab turned out of Central Park at 110th Street he felt, curiously enough, a feeling of peace. There were all the old familiar sights: the all-night speakeasies, the frankfurter stands, the loiterers, the late pedestrians, the chop suey joints, the careening taxicabs, the bawdy laughter.

He couldn't resist the temptation to get out at 133rd Street and go down to Boogie's place, the hangout of his gang. He tapped, an eye peered through a hole, appraised him critically then disappeared and the hole was closed. There was silence.

Max frowned. What was the matter with old Bob? Why didn't he open that door? The cold January breeze swept down into the little court where he stood and made him shiver. He knocked a little louder, more insistently. The eye appeared again.

"Who's 'at?" growled the doorkeeper.

"It's Max Disher," replied the ex-Negro.

"Go 'way f'm here, white man. Dis heah place is closed."

"Is Bunny Brown in there?" asked Max in desperation.

"Yeh, he's heah. Does yuh know him? Well, Ah'll call 'im out heah and see if he knows you."

Max waited in the cold for about two or three minutes and then the door suddenly opened and Bunny Brown, a little unsteady, came out. He peered at Max in the light from the electric bulb over the door.

"Hello Bunny," Max greeted him. "Don't know me, do you? It's me, Max Disher. You recognize my voice, don't you?"

Bunny looked again, rubbed his eyes and shook his head. Yes, the voice was Max Disher's but this man was white. Still, when he smiled his eyes revealed the same sardonic twinkle—so characteristic of his friend.

"Max," he blurted out, "is that you, sure enough? Well, for cryin' out loud! Damned if you ain't been up there to Crookman's and got fixed up. Well, hush my mouth! Bob, open that door. This is old Max Disher. Done gone up there to Crookman's and got all white on my hands. He's just too tight, with his blond hair, 'n everything."

Bob opened the door, the two friends entered, sat down at one of the small round tables in the narrow, smoke-filled cellar and were soon surrounded with cronies. They gazed raptly at his colorless skin, commented on the veins showing blue through the epidermis, stroked his ash-blond hair, and listened with mouths open to his remarkable story.

"Watcha gonna do now, Max?" asked Boogie, the rangy, black, bullet-headed proprietor.

"I know just what that joker's gonna do," said Bunny. "He's goin' back to Atlanta. Am I right, Big Boy?"

"You ain't wrong," Max agreed. "I'm goin' right on down there, brother, and make up for lost time."

"Whadayah mean?" asked Boogie.

"Boy, it would take me until tomorrow night to tell you and then you wouldn't understand."

The two friends strolled up the avenue. Both were rather mum. They had been inseparable pals since the stirring days in France. Now they were about to be parted. It wasn't as if Max was going across the ocean to some foreign country; there would be a wider gulf separating them: the great sea of color. They both thought about it.

"I'll be pretty lonesome without you, Bunny."

"It ain't you, Big Boy."

"Well, why don't you go ahead and get white and then we could stay together. I'll give you the money."

"Say not so! Where'd you get so much jack all of a sudden?" asked Bunny.

"Sold my story to *The Scimitar* for a grand."

"Paid in full?"

"Wasn't paid in part!"

"All right, then, I'll take you up, Heavy Sugar." Bunny held out his plump hand and Max handed him a hundred-dollar bill.

They were near the Crookman Sanitarium. Although it was five o'clock on a Sunday morning, the building was brightly lighted from cellar to roof and the hum of electric motors could be heard, low and powerful. A large electric sign hung from the roof to the second floor. It represented a huge arrow outlined in green with the words BLACK-NO-MORE running its full length vertically. A black face was depicted at the lower end of the arrow while at the top shone a white face to which the arrow was pointed. First would appear the outline of the arrow; then, BLACK-NO-MORE would flash on and off. Following that the black face would appear at the bottom and beginning at the lower end the long arrow with its lettering would appear progressively until its tip was reached, when the white face at the top would blazon forth. After that the sign would flash off and on and the process would be repeated.

In front of the sanitarium milled a half-frozen crowd of close to four thousand Negroes. A riot squad armed with rifles, machine guns, and tear gas bombs maintained some semblance of order. A steel cable stretched from lamp post to lamp post the entire length of the block kept the struggling mass of humanity on the sidewalk and out of the path of the traffic. It seemed as if all Harlem were there. As the two friends reached the outskirts of the mob, an ambulance from the Harlem Hospital drove up and carried away two women who had been trampled upon.

Lined up from the door to the curb was a gang of tough special guards dredged out of the slums. Grim Irish from Hell's Kitchen, rough Negroes from around 133rd Street and 5th Avenue (New York's "Beale Street"), and tough Italians from the lower West Side. They managed with difficulty to keep an aisle cleared for incoming and outgoing patients. Near the curb were stationed the reporters and photographers.

The noise rose and fell. First there would be a low hum of voices. Steadily it would rise and rise in increasing volume as the speakers became more animated and reach its climax in a great animal-like roar as the big front door would open and a whitened Negro would emerge. Then the mass would surge forward to peer at and question the ersatz Nordic. Sometimes the ex-Ethiopian would quail before the mob and jump back into the building. Then the hardboiled guards would form a flying squad and hustle him to a waiting taxicab. Other erstwhile Aframericans issuing from the building would grin broadly, shake hands with friends and relatives, and start to graphically describe their experience while the Negroes around them enviously admired their clear white skins.

In between these appearances the hot dog and peanut vendors did a brisk trade, along with the numerous pickpockets of the district. One slender, anemic, ratty-looking mulatto Negro was almost beaten to death by a gigantic black laundress whose purse he had snatched. A Negro selling hot roasted sweet potatoes did a land-office business while the neighboring saloons, that had increased so rapidly in number since the enactment of the Volstead Law that many of their Italian proprietors paid substantial income taxes, sold scores of gallons of incredibly atrocious hootch.

"Well, bye, bye, Max," said Bunny, extending his hand. "I'm goin' in an' my luck."

"So long, Bunny. See you in Atlanta. Write me general delivery."

"Why, ain't you gonna wait for me, Max?"

"Naw! I'm fed up on this town."

"Oh, you ain't kiddin' me, Big Boy. I know you want to look up that broad you saw in the Honky Tonk New Year's Eve," Bunny beamed.

Max grinned and blushed slightly. They shook hands and parted. Bunny ran up the aisle from the curb, opened the sanitarium door, and without turning around, disappeared within.

For a minute or so, Max stood irresolutely in the midst of the gibbering crowd of people. Unaccountably he felt at home here among these black folk. Their jests, scraps of conversation, and lusty laughter all seemed like heavenly music. Momentarily he felt a disposition to stay among them, to share again their troubles which they seemed always to bear with a lightness that was yet not indifference. But then, he suddenly realized with just a tiny trace of remorse that the past was forever gone. He must seek other pastures, other pursuits, other playmates, other loves. He was white now. Even if he wished to stay among his folk, they would be either jealous or suspicious of him, as they were of most octoroons and nearly all whites. There was no other alternative than to seek his future among the Caucasians with whom he now rightfully belonged.

And after all, he thought, it was a glorious new adventure. His eyes twinkled and his pulse quickened as he thought of it. Now he could go anywhere, associate with anybody, be anything he wanted to be. He suddenly thought of the comely miss he had seen in the Honky Tonk on New Year's Eve and the greatly enlarged field from which he could select his loves. Yes, indeed there were advantages in being white. He brightened and viewed the tightly-packed black folk around him with a superior air. Then, thinking again of his clothes at Mrs. Blandish's, the money in his pocket, and the prospect for the first time of riding into Atlanta in a Pullman car and not as a Pullman porter, he turned and pushed his way through the throng.

He strolled up West 139th Street to his rooming place, stepping lightly and sniffing the early morning air. How good it was to be free, white and to possess a bankroll! He fumbled in his pocket for his little mirror and looked at himself again and again from several angles. He stroked his pale blond hair and secretly congratulated himself that he would no longer need to straighten it nor be afraid to wet it. He gazed raptly at his smooth, white hands with the blue veins showing through. What a miracle Dr. Crookman had wrought!

As he entered the hallway, the mountainous form of his landlady loomed up. She jumped back as she saw his face.

"What you doing here?" she almost shouted. "Where'd you get a key to this house?"

"It's me, Max Disher," he assured her with a grin at her astonishment. "Don't know me, do you?"

She gazed incredulously into his face. "Is that you sure enough, Max? How in the devil did you get so white?"

He explained and showed her a copy of *The Scimitar* containing his story. She switched on the hall light and read it. Contrasting emotions played over her face, for Mrs. Blandish was known in the business world as Mme. Sisseretta Blandish, the beauty specialist, who owned the swellest hair-straightening parlor in Harlem. Business, she thought to herself, was bad enough, what with all of the competition, without this Dr. Crookman coming along and killing it altogether.

"Well," she sighed, "suppose you're going downtown to live, now. I always said niggers didn't really have any race pride."

Uneasy, Max made no reply. The fat, brown woman turned with a disdainful sniff and disappeared into a room at the end of the hall. He ran lightly upstairs to pack his things.

An hour later, as the taxicab bearing him and his luggage bowled through Central Park, he was in high spirits. He would go down to the Pennsylvania Station and get a Pullman straight into Atlanta. He would stop there at the best hotel. He wouldn't hunt up any of his folks. No, that would be too dangerous. He would just play around, enjoy life, and laugh at the white folks up his sleeve. God! What an adventure! What a treat it would be to mingle with white people in places where as a youth he had never dared to enter. At last he felt like an American citizen. He flecked the ash of his panatela out of the open window of the cab and sank back in the seat feeling at peace with the world.

SEPARATION ANXIETY

Evie Shockley

(2000)

W hat holds us to places is people. we make up all kinda stories about how it's the sunrise over the ocean, the way we can't sleep without sirens or wake without garbage trucks crashing down the street below our window, the kind of greens/bagels/pad thai we can only get in this neighborhood, but in the end if our lover-boy or sistah-girl is crossing the river, the country, the ocean, to lay down a new life far away, we're right behind em—if we get invited. no thought for that geographical spot we couldn't live without last week. and, just the same, if lover or mother or father is stuck to a place like white on rice, we likely to be sitting still, no matter how hard the wanderlust makes us throb between the legs. no matter how much greener the grass on the other side.

i know this from living it. if your life tells you different, you write your own story. this is mine, and here's how it was:

i never dreamed i would want to leave the ghetto. i was born and raised in the ghetto, and i figured if i ever had children, they were gonna be born and raised in the same place. with our people, you know. where we could see, hear, taste, smell, and feel our culture all around us. it was on the sidewalks in the macs' rolling stroll and the girls' whip-fast double-dutch. it was in the broad noses and black granite surfaces of the sculptures in our public buildings. it was in the aromas of collards and catfish cooking that surfed the wind down residential streets. this was the whole point of creating the ghetto—the african american cultural conservation unit, as the official name goes—to preserve our way of life. everyone on both sides of every counter, desk, and door in this place shared my blood, my relationship to this country's messed-up history. here, i knew exactly who i was. african american. and, best of all, i was a primary cultural worker, the most prestigious rank of employment in the whole unit. a dancer of black dances.

i remember when it all changed.

"peaches!"

i was stretching, on the floor of the main rehearsal studio, in my customary spot—as one of the furaha dance theater's two female leads, i always practiced in an area where the floor wasn't warped or splintering at all. *point, forehead to knees, hold-two-three-four, release.* roosevelt, my baby brother, strode in, obviously hot-n-bothered, but not too off-center to give his muscular legs an admiring glance in the front mirror as he crossed the room. he was waving a bright red flyer at me. *flex, stretch, hold-two-three-four, release—inhale deeply, point, exhale, stretch.*

"peaches, have you seen this?" as i spread my legs 180 degrees wide, for my next set of stretches, he stepped in front of me and dropped to a seat on the floor, cross-legged, yoga-style, in one effortless motion. skimming the paper quickly, i stopped short, my body wrenching back to center from the beginning of a left-side stretch. it began: *effective immediately, residents of african american cultural conservation unit #1 should further organize waste disposal by separating waste associated with sexual activity and sexual health from other categories of waste.*

"they can't be serious!"

"i knew you hadn't seen this shit."

i opened my mouth, but couldn't figure out what to do with it. i reread the flyer, more slowly. "they can't be serious."

"they gonna be counting your kotex, sistahgirl. straight up. and my condoms."

there's always a "they," i've come to see. this "they" was the national department of ethnic and cultural conservation, the "decc." contrary to my words, the decc took its governmentally mandated mission very seriously. very.

the decc was established round about 2095 or so, when the american national legislature determined that the best way to keep white racist hegemony from wiping out all the rest of us—from slowly starving our bodies or minds, or perpetrating an out-n-out massacre—was to make us some sacred space. set aside some areas of the country where african americans, latinos, asians, jews, american indians, and the rest could be minding our own business, in every sense of the phrase. you know?

talk about happy. african americans and latinos got up and headed for our respective conservation units with a quickness. in mass numbers—ninety, ninety-five percent of us. we were all about conserving our *lives*. american indians, who already had some land of their own but no economic base besides a few casinos, traded their national autonomy for the guaranteed funding that the new law would grant each unit. jews and asian americans were more divided, as groups, over whether or not they wanted to live separate from white america. but things got so hot for folks who tried to stay, it just wasn't worth it. people of color were *wishin* for the days when the klan and groups like that would just burn a damn cross and be done with it. around the turn of the twenty-second century, police were still trying to enforce the anti-hate-crime laws, but they couldn't be everywhere at once. it wasn't like all whites were into the violence thing, but there were more than enough who were. by the time things settled down, population outside the conservation units was ninety-four percent white, and folks inside the units were busy hooking things up the way we'd always dreamed of—to suit *ourselves*.

the government liked that. conservation of cultures was key, everyone agreed. so along with folks getting their own geographical spaces came the duty to contribute to the national archives of american cultures. the president instituted the decc to handle the collection of records and cultural materials. for a long time, the agency worked on organizing historical evidence. that was cool. but the time came, not twenty-five years ago, when the decc began to focus on collecting records and creating archives "as-we-go." so nothing would be lost, as they put it. started slow and mild: send in copies of all programs and bulletins. videotapes of all live performances. a copy of all books published by ghetto companies to go to the national library of congress, on top of the copy sent to the central unit library. copies of all mxds recorded went in. likewise, photographic records of gallery installations. birth, marriage, death certificates—double-filed. no big deal. african americans had seen the downside of being nearly recordless, from the days of slavery and reconstruction, so we were proud that recognizing the value of our culture was now the law. but then the law began to grow.

"why can't it be just like in the good days?" he was saying. "you separate your trash from recyclables, period. you wanna be really super-citizen, you separate your recyclables—glass from paper, aluminum from plastic. there was a purpose beyond just being nosy."

"so what you saying, roo? you ready to break up outta here?" i smiled at his instant discomfort. i knew what the answer was before i asked. his face so familiar to me, the odd green eyes from some great-grand who didn't live into our lifetimes, the wide smile just like mine, the eyebrows thick and expressive, bouncing up and down when he got excited, with the random rhythms of a basketball in play.

"i ain't saying that."

all the threatened, oppressed groups got three main conservation units each, in different areas of the country. in these spaces, whites can't enter without permission, in person or by way of any commercial or cultural intrusions. in our unit—the east coast unit, affectionately known to the residents as the ghetto—you don't have to see no white people if you don't want to. the ghetto controls its own tv stations, its own radio stations. our movies are black, our commercials are black, our schools teach black history, our theaters produce black plays. nobody's "universal" aesthetics to define us, nobody's standards to live up to but our own. the profits stay in the ghetto and benefit *us*. true, money didn't seem to go as far these days as it used to, and there were those who worried bout how we were importing more from outside the unit—basics, like toilet paper and tires—than we were exporting—which was mainly cultural products. but we had a lot more ownership and management of businesses in the ghetto than we had ever had before, according to our history books.

the ghetto's government-sponsored dance company is all-black, and roo and me, we rule. roo is the body as light, the essence of motion, beauty in function. women fall at his feet after performances like he drugged em. me, i ain't bad, if i do say so myself. the company's name, "furaha," is a swahili word that means "joy." my dancing is a prayer for joy, a blessing that my movements produce like sweat, and i'll share it with anyone who'll sit still for two seconds. we pack our auditorium here in the ghetto nearly every performance. and when we make our biannual tours of cities outside the unit, audiences eat us up. i wish sometimes i could ask them what it is in our work that moves them, out there. but that kind of contact is no longer allowed—hasn't been legal since i was in grade school.

in thoughtful silence, i returned to my warm-up. roo stretched out facing me, mirroring my movements, as he had so often before. growing up, he was always determined to be able to do any moves i could do, so he'd be competitive for a space in any dance company i got into. my tag-along brother, who followed me right into the place where he was born to be.

when i heard the footsteps of the rest of the company, i blushed. the red flyer, flat screaming by my foot, was gonna trigger another fight between me and trevette. i snatched it up, folded it, and tucked it into the waistband of my leggings, beneath the oversized t-shirt i wore. luckily for me, she chased in after mari had stepped to the front of the room. mari is the company leader and choreographer, and she don't take no stuff after her rehearsals start. trevette went straight to her place and took first position. i refused to meet her eyes in the mirror, but i could feel her gaze, hot, on my shoulders.

as soon as mari dismissed us, trevette broke for the locker room. i was thinking, *praise god,* because i was not ready to talk to her. surprised me that she didn't try to corner me in the rehearsal studio. i trailed into the locker room after much delay, stopping first to ask a question of mari, to check with roo about his dinner plans, to gossip with a couple of other dancers about a blind date one of them had the night before. i thought i was just being careless, the first two times my lock didn't open after i punched in the code, but the third time i entered the numbers more carefully. when it still flashed red, i grew concerned. not just my clothes, but my keys and my wallet were locked away. the other women slipped quickly into their street clothes and vanished. when i looked up and saw no one, i made a dash for the door to the men's changing room, intending to catch roo before he left, so he could give me a ride home. turned the corner at full speed, and ran smack into trevette.

she grabbed my wrists, one in each of her slender, strong hands. "can i help you?"

"girl, you scared me to death!"

"where you headed so fast?"

i looked at my wrists, then met her gaze fully. she peeled her fingers from around my arms. "i need to make sure roosevelt doesn't leave without me—i'm locked out of my locker and can't get to my car keys."

"i'll drive you home."

"i—" i didn't even bother. i couldn't avoid talking to her forever, even if i wanted to.

"what's wrong with your locker?" she asked.

"i don't know! i entered my password three times, but it won't open."

"let me try." she hunched over the lock's keypad for a second or two and then i heard the high-pitched beep and saw the green light.

"how did you do that?"

"truth?"

"course."

self-satisfaction rose in her eyes like biscuits in a tin. "i changed your password at the beginning of rehearsal."

"unh!" i made this inarticulate noise of indignation and reached for the door of my locker. quick like silver, she pressed the lock button. and i still didn't have the current password. "trevette!"

"sit with me a minute, peaches." she brushed cool fingers down the side of my arm from shoulder to elbow, so lightly i might have only felt their breeze passing over my skin. i sat.

"you know, i didn't give you my password for you to lock me out of my own locker."

"please come with me." direct, but uncertain, she spoke, like a soldier giving a command to a superior officer. i stared at her knees, unable to speak. "peaches, this is it. you swore that if i ever got to the breaking point, you'd pack up and go with me. now, i know you've seen the new decc order. next thing you know, they gonna be archiving our dirty drawers! this is the last straw for me. it's time to go! maybe you were counting on changing roosevelt's mind before now, but i can't help that. i ain't gonna wait to get up outta here until there's some law against it!"

"trevette, this is home," i whispered, almost a moan. "we do important work here. i love this place, this immersion in what's ours."

"i know. but we won't be giving up our work. just doing it for a different audience. we'll be free to see what black minds and black bodies can do with white music or white choreography. come on—how many times can we perform *revelations* without becoming robots on stage? our work is getting so sterile, girl. giving it some fresh sights and sounds to work with don't mean we gotta reject black dance."

i plunged my face into the pool of indecision in my cupped palms.

"eleanor johnson. how long we been tight?"

"um, how old are we?" the ritual question in answer to ritual question. born two days apart, on the same street, neither of us could remember the time before we were inseparable.

"exactly. and nothing can change the way i feel about you. i love
you. i want the best for you. i want you happy and safe." trevette sighed
heavily. "we done had this conversation so many times. the good things
about this unit are good. real good. sometimes i feel like i could lie down
in the middle of 125th street and roll around like a dog in clover, i'm so
full of satisfaction: some gospel song that moves my heart, some dance
step calling up mother africa that pops into my mind as i'm walking
around watching the rhythms of folk just doing their own day-to-day on
the street, some beautiful boy-face peeping up at me over a book and
smiling about learning. that stuff feels real good."

i waited silently for the "but."

"but i can't help remembering what granddaddy used to say. you were
there, too, you heard him. 'history is a cycle, y'all,' he kept saying. 'this
unit is separation today, but it'll be segregation tomorrow, mark my
words. it's freedom now, but there gonna come a day when it'll be a trap.
it's the right to love your own we needed so bad, but it's gonna be a
heavy duty to some generation ahead.'"

of course i remembered. roo and i spent all kinda time at trevette's
house after our mother died. i could still see the old man, rocking on the
parkers' front porch, sporting a dingy cotton undershirt and loose jeans,
speaking about the old days before the ghetto was created. he had only
been a teen when the law was passed, and he was old-old when trevette
and me was girls. in his last weeks, he used to mumble to himself as he
rocked, eyes fixed on some memory in his head, saying over-n-over,
"conservation. reservation. conservation. concentration," like a chant.
we knew what he was talking about, long-ago gatherings of american indians and a certain group of asian americans, but we couldn't figure out
why he was connecting those times of deprivation and harassment to
our peaceful retreat, our lawful homeland.

"i'm feeling it heavy, peaches. i don't think you can put a box around
a culture. and i don't like feeling like somebody's anthropology project."

"trevette, i—"

"i'm done with it, girlfriend. and, brother or no brother, i want you
with me when i go."

*   *   *

that evening, i piled into my favorite chair, this big overstuffed thing that i found in a clearance sale near the ghetto border. tucking my bare feet into a corner for warmth, i unfolded the flyer and stared at the words on the page again, trying to tell myself not to be insulted.

decc alert

effective immediately, residents of african american cultural conservation unit #1 should further organize waste disposal by separating waste associated with sexual activity and sexual health from other categories of waste. waste items covered under this category include, but are not limited to:

> *feminine hygiene products (internal and external)*
> *male and female condoms,*
> *packaging for reproductive and anti-reproductive medical technologies,*
> *discarded sexual pleasure implements, etc.*

pink containers will be provided to each household for collection purposes, and should be placed with the household's other color-coded receptacles for pick-up.

—executive order #46,877, pursuant to the ethnic and cultural conservation act.

no use. i was pissed. i remembered, vaguely, that i had heard rumors of decc interest in the so-called "reproductive patterns" of american racial and ethnic groups, but i hadn't counted on more micromanagement of our lives to get the details. hell, this was for real an invasion of privacy! they already tracked our food consumption, monitored our reading, recorded our entertainment choices. they had so many categories for separating our waste for disposal, the street looked like a rainbow on trash day, lined with row after row of different color bins. all in the name of history and cultural conservation. anytime someone complained—and trevette had done her share of complaining—the decc issued its standard response. that we owe it to our grandchildren and their grandchildren to preserve a record of what african american culture was like in the twenty-second century. remember the middle passage era! they always added. "unknowable" history. few first-person accounts of what the kidnapped africans thought about their tragedy, how they coped, what they did, day-to-day, to survive the holds of the slavers.

when roosevelt dropped by, as he always did if he was anywhere near my street, i interrupted his flow on his latest romantic conquest to see if i could get him to change his mind about leaving. "i've been thinking that trevette's right," i started. "you know? this new order is over the top. maybe it's time to get, while the getting's good."

"chick, you gotta do what you gotta do." he stood up, went to the window, turning his back to me.

"i'm talking bout you doing it, too!"

"ain't gonna happen."

"come on, man! everything we do is *data* these days! i feel like this society has regressed to the days of animal testing, and this time it's us, instead of rabbits and mice, that get studied."

"if you hadda studied, yourself, a little harder in your history classes, you'd know that black folks got studied even back then. remember that tuskegee thing?" he glanced my way, and i nodded. "that shit happened then, it's probably still going on, and it ain't gonna stop no time soon."

i thought that over. "well, at least, if it's happening now, it's probably limited to the ghetto and the other units. if we went out into the open territory, they couldn't single us out. we'd get the same treatment as the whites." my eyes narrowed. "and we deserve that, too! i know you noticed how our studio's starting to decline, repairs not getting made like they oughta, salaries not keeping up with costs like they used to. i got my eyes open when we tour out there. they may rush us from hotel to stage to hotel, trying to keep us from accidentally breathing white culture—"

"yeah, i see their dope, next-generation equipment, their fancy facilities. but are you dancing for the money or what?" roo challenged me.

"hell, no!" i swallowed and brought my voice back down. "i'm dancing to see where my body and mind can take me, wherever beauty is. and i don't like seeing 'road closed' signs in my path."

he shook his head, his short, locked hair a spiky mane, dark against the twilight filling the window. "see, how you gonna act? like i don't hear you when trevette be all on your case to leave the ghetto? you say all the things *i* feel, when you talk to her. it is *large*, what we do up in here. we dance the dances that our ancestors of the twentieth century created from pain and pork chops, you know what i'm saying? and those dances have the trace of all prior african-american dances in them. we keep it real for our young people, so that they grow up with their history living all around them."

"i'm getting a little tired of that old shit." i said this so quietly, i wasn't sure if it had left the realm of thought.

"don't say that."

"i'm serious, roo. there are times when this emphasis on the past like to drown me. all these authenticity rules! gotta have eighty percent historical content in each program. can't change not a step in performing some nineteenth or twentieth century dance. it's like we're fossils, walking around. i need to see if maybe black dance got a *future*." i got up, went to stand beside him at the window. "i do love the ghetto. but I'm not sure it's enough."

he looked into my face, his expression queer, his eyes muted. "you should go, peaches," he said, finally.

"not without you."

"without me. go with trevette. she's as much your family as i am."

"yeah, but i can't be choosing between family members. we all go, or we all stay."

"no. trevette is out the door, and you know it."

i could feel the waters rising inside me, frustration that would flood my eyes in a minute. "she won't leave without me!" trevette just couldn't do me like that. she of all people knew how much roo and me needed each other. parents and grandparents gone, our uncles way over in the west coast unit, our only aunt with her latino husband and their kids living somewhere out there, out of reach, virtually out of contact, because of the government's worries bout introducing "foreign elements" into ghetto culture. my little brother was my support, my responsibility. i could still see him, six years old and already growing like a vine, ashy ankles hanging out below the hem of his jeans, begging our parents for dance lessons "like peaches."

roo put his arm around me, pulling me against his lean frame. sighing. "when i look at the streets of this unit, when i scan the audience at the end of a performance, when i shop, when i play, the people i come in contact with look like me. the vibe they send out is on my wavelength. not like they just got one groove—they got a million—but wherever they're at, is someplace i can reach, or at least see. they all colors, but they all colored, if you know what i mean."

we laughed. i did know.

"what moves me as a person, as a dancer, is the giving and getting, getting and giving, that goes on between me and them. my art is more interactive than individual. and i can't get what i need, to dance like i mean it, if my audience is never black."

"there are black folks out there," i interrupted.

"yeah, barely. it's not the same." he took my hand, studying my fingers, the nails clipped to the pink. "but that's me. you're a different person, girl. you got to go for what you know. your art thing is about expressin—like a glass that keeps filling up from the bottom and flowing over the top like crazy. something comes from deep inside you, and gotta come out. period. now, whatever you need to keep that flow flowing, that's what i want you to have. if it's love, then stay close to love. if it's change, then you gotta follow the tracks that lead on away from here."

brother. brother. osun's favorite son, sending me off like an unwilling esu to the crossroads. not without you. i pulled the mudcloth drapes across my window. "love, then," i said, and hugged him close.

the next day was sunday. i was glad, as they say, to go into the house of the lord, get me some good old gospel music from a choir of voices as large and pretty as the sky. blue, but sunny. trevette and i sat together in our usual pew, rocking side by side to the music, amening through the sermon. i liked watching trevette out of the corner of my eye, enjoying the ways she enjoyed service, fascinated by the way her mahogany skin seemed to glow with a special fire. i kept expecting roosevelt to drag in late, like most other sundays, but he never showed.

in the parking lot, me and trevette discussed our plans for the rest of the day, in a conversation salted with "praise the lords" and peppered with handshakes exchanged with members of the congregation passing around us. "i wonder where roo is," i mentioned.

"um-hm," trevette murmured. "i was thinking, let's go out for dinner instead of cooking. we can talk without worrying about what's gonna burn."

"you think he went creeping so late last night that he couldn't even make it to church?"

"i think if he was as worried about being with you as you are about being with him, he'da been here by now, for sure." trevette grinned, and i had to laugh. "now, are you down with going to sylvia's, or what?"

"let's do it!"

we had a long wait, since we weren't the only folks who thought about eating at sylvia's after church. but it was worth it. collards and fried chicken, steaming and salty, and cornbread like sweetless cake dipped in butter. green beans and macaroni-n-cheese. when we leaned back, forty-five minutes later, we both wished we had on the loose-fitting robes we wore at home. trevette unbuttoned the skirt of her fuchsia suit, relieved that her jacket was long enough to hide her shamelessness.

"we gonna need a workout and a half in the morning, girlfriend," i moaned.

"word." trevette was concentrating on breathing. "nobody would believe that dancers could eat with so little health consciousness and still do the things we do with our bodies."

"why you talking that health consciousness shit? that's white people madness! black folks' bodies can survive anything, so long as we get a steady diet of greens—don't you know your history?" i hooted, pulling out the old joke.

"well, that may be true, but i got to get used to thinking about the kind of lifestyle i'm gonna have out there," trevette replied seriously, and brought me all the way down. i didn't speak, just frowned and stared into my empty plate. when the silence began to hurt, she continued, the words leaking out, low and slow, like they were rubbing her throat raw. "i put in my application with the decc yesterday."

i had anger in my palms, my thighs, the roots of my hair, the balls of my feet. "you just gonna go on off and leave a body?" i shouted. "well, go on, then. me and roo will just have to make it without you."

"peaches, i want you to come, too. the company that's sponsoring me will sponsor you, too, gladly. we can do more as a pair for their repertoire than i can alone."

"i don't know why you gotta split us up like this, you know?" i took out my wallet and swiped my card down the sensor in our table, so hard it didn't read. in tears, i snatched the card out of the slot and stormed away without paying, yelling over my shoulder, "you gonna be so rich, you take care of dinner!"

i shouldn't have been driving, but i tore out of the parking lot, headed for roo's apartment. i didn't see a thing all the way there, driving the familiar route out of habit and getting there on god's will. i didn't even have the decency to be grateful.

"roosevelt! roo! roosevelt!" i yelled, banging on the door. no answer, not even the "go away" i sometimes got if i interrupted him in an intimate moment. hmm. i went back out to the parking lot to see if his ride was there—hadn't even thought about it on the way in. it was gone. i decided to sit in my car and wait for him. parked where i could see the entrance, i settled back.

it was torment. i didn't have a thing to do but think.

for the first hour, i thought endlessly about how furaha would reorganize itself after trevette left. i imagined myself as the only female lead, tried to comfort myself with the idea that i would get the judith jamison solo i'd always wanted. but no, they'd likely replace her. and there was something wrong with all the potential replacements, in my mind. michelle—too short. donita—too uninspired. sapphire—not fluid enough. i finally realized that the biggest problem with all of them was that they weren't trevette.

the second hour, it got worse. i started imagining all the things that coulda gone wrong to keep roo from at least letting me know where he was. not that i was trying to be my brother's keeper, but when you grow up tight-tight like me and roo, you feel the need for connection, you get into patterns. sundays, we pretty much always saw each other at church, but if not, we'd hook up in the afternoon to chill. trevette was often with us, along with anyone else we were close to. his lovers either hated me or adored me—and they found out fast which option worked for anyone who wanted to be a part of his life for more than a night. we'd lost our mother before we were ten years old, and our father barely lived to see us graduate. we were the core of each other's family, and others could love us both or hit the road.

so where was he? in an accident, in a fight, in a drug-induced state of forgetfulness? he didn't really do drugs, feeling the way he did about his body and his dancing, but occasionally his friends seduced him into experiencing some high that was supposed to take him to new levels of creativity and heighten his awareness of his body's possibilities. if he was down this road, he'd definitely avoid me, knowing that i'd give him hell, during or after the fact.

maybe that was it. just when i needed him so bad. well, he had no way of knowing. i pulled out of the lot and headed for home. i knew he'd turn up at my door before long.

except he didn't. sunday night, i simply worried. monday morning, i woke up, on top of the bed and still wearing my clothes, in a mild panic. by tuesday's rehearsal, i was hysterical.

"mari, have you seen or heard from roosevelt?" i had asked everyone in the company, not including trevette, of course, but no one knew anything.

"honey, no, i haven't, and if he's not here on time, he's liable to get his solo reassigned. he knows i don't play that," mari responded matter-of-factly.

he never came to rehearsal. i couldn't think, couldn't concentrate on anything going on. my mind was full of worst-case scenarios: accidental o.d.? car wreck, and him comatose or unidentifiable? stabbed by some crazy ex-lover and left to bleed in a dumpster? i stumbled through my steps and almost broke my ankle on a partnered jump i tried with russell, who was standing in for roo. afterward, i broke down and went over to trevette, who i hadn't spoken to since sylvia's.

"i know what you're going to ask me," she said as i walked up. "and i don't know why you think i know anything that nobody else here knows."

"you're closer to him than the rest."

"closer than you?"

that one hit me right between the eyes. i burst into tears.

"aw, peaches, for christsake! i'm sorry. i know how you must feel. i'm worried, too," she said, hugging me. "how can i help?"

we called the police and filed a missing persons report. we phoned every hospital in the unit. we checked with his landlord. we drove around to his friends' homes and his favorite hangouts, asking for him. we put his photo and our plea for information on the web. nothing. no one had seen him since saturday evening. finally, we came back to where we'd started, in my apartment, where i sank into my armchair, exhausted, my hands shaking on my knees. "trevette, i don't know what i would be doing by now if you weren't here. thanks, girlfriend. i mean it."

"don't thank me—"

"no, really. i feel so bad about how i treated you on sunday, too. i don't wanna hold you back from following your dream. we don't have to want the same things outta life, you know?"

trevette's pretty, round face was sad, and she kept quiet for a minute. "hmm. what i think is, we all do what we have to do, and we try not to hurt the ones we love while we doing it, but sometimes that shit happens anyway."

i nodded. "so true."

"but i wonder, is it really true that we don't want the same thing? i know this probably ain't the time to say it, but isn't it more that roosevelt doesn't want what you and me both want?"

i balled my fists tightly, to keep the shaking from being so visible. "you know, you're right, in a way. i could never think of leaving him to go out of the unit and do my thing. it seems so selfish. not that my love for the ghetto ain't real or deep or strong, but i do need some things i can't find or ain't allowed to have here. and if roo would come with, i'd be gone in a heartbeat."

"well, let's believe you'll have plenty more chances to convince him that he should try the world outside the ghetto."

"amen. amen."

the weeks that followed felt more and more unreal to me. i learned to do what i'd never done on a dance floor, to go through the motions with my limbs and torso, while my head was someplace else. i walked around, always on the verge of being run over on the streets or falling down stairs, because i didn't see out through my eyes, i saw into my mind, where i was making lists: call the hospitals again, inquire at different private dance companies within the ghetto, check with the morgue. . . . despite my morbid worries, this last item didn't make my first few lists, and when i finally admitted to myself that i should do it, i almost fell out from the pain. but he wasn't there, either, so i kept on investigating as though my life depended on it.

i wandered around the ghetto randomly, and the one thing i was looking for was bout the only thing i didn't find. the only other things that really registered with me were the bright red decc flyers posted on every corner, reminding us about that hateful new executive order. i sorta cringed every time i noticed them, cause it just made it harder for me to ignore the fact that trevette was going to be leaving soon. i'd start searching again, more desperately than ever.

the police hated to see me coming.

"still no news, ms. johnson."

"have you found any new leads? are you even trying? you don't expect me to believe that y'all can't find my little brother in this unit if you want to!"

"he's a missing person, ms. johnson, not an enemy of the state. and he's a grown man. we've only got so many eyes, ears, and hands around this force, and there are other cases that get equal and greater priority than your brother's."

"but—"

"ma'am. just go home and wait. there's no telling what a man might need to do on his own. it doesn't necessarily mean trouble. i bet he shows up soon. in the meantime, try not to worry—we'll keep looking."

that answer blew my mind. maybe it was that state of mindlessness that made me listen to trevette when she dropped by that afternoon.

"i heard from the decc. my application was approved."

"i'm happy for you, girlfriend," i said, and started to cry. when i could talk again, i moaned, "i'm going to be all alone here."

"if you want out, i can have your paperwork expedited. we could leave together."

"how can i leave not knowing what's happened to my brother?"

trevette bit her lip. "i think it's what he'd want you to do."

i thought about the conversation we'd had in my apartment that saturday afternoon, the last time i saw him. *you should go, peaches,* he'd said. *without me.* i thought about rehearsal tomorrow, and mari's constant fight to inject new life into the moves and music that were getting so ingrown and dull to me. the popular music that sampled itself in cycles, so that you could never tell what century a cut was from, or whether you were listening to an oldies station or the latest release. there was something in roo that wanted to fight through this enforced boredom, to try to get to the other side by going straight through the heart of our culture. i could see inspiration in his dancing, where my own had beauty and grace, but no spark, not any longer. not for a while now.

finally, i thought about what the officer had said that morning. lost or found, maybe roo had parts of his life that i couldn't share—and vice versa. that hurt, but waiting by the phone in my apartment wouldn't change that fact, or bring him back if he was gone for good.

"let's do it," i said, trevette's hand in mine like a promise, her breaking smile like a star i could steer by.

and we did. my application passed through the decc so fast it left burns on some folks' desks. then we had to sign contracts, witnessed by pale decc agents in dark suits, acknowledging that we understood we could never return to the ghetto, and that our contact with persons inside the unit would be limited and monitored, to ensure that no "contamination" of black culture occurred. we caught each other's glance, quick-fast, the only sign we made of our pact to try to use our exile to break down the hundred-plus-year-old walls between the ghetto, the other units, and the rest of the world.

the air transport took us up and out, west and south, into geography we knew more as historical landscape than a place we could travel to in today's world. our new company was located in a city cradled between hills and river, between north and south, called cincinnati. we'd been there only once before in our lives. i stared down at the hills and highways rolling beneath us. silently, trevette reached into her bag and handed me a folded paper.

dear peaches,

i'd rather for you to be mad at me than for you to go on mourning a dead brother who's still kicking it here in your former home. so here's the truth: i'm safe and happy, and ready to get back to my life, which i left long enough to let you go. mari is going to whup my ass (on the dance floor) before she lets me get back into my lead position, but she'll get over it. i'm going to be tearing up the joint, up in here, and you better do the same out there. make something beautiful, girl, and i'll hear about it. i'll know.

love always,

roosevelt franklin johnson

p.s. trevette ain't nothing but the victim of my stubbornness and determination, and she didn't ever lie to you even if she didn't tell you everything she knew, so don't give her a hard time! she is the only person i know who loves you as much as i do.

i read it six times, sixty times, i don't know how many ways i set my eyes across that page. i felt a different feeling every time i read it, though—i know that much. when i folded it up again, and finally looked into trevette's eyes, i said the only thing that i could say after my long weeks of worry and grief.

"he's all right!" i whispered.

she sighed in relief, giving me a quick kiss of apology. hand-n-hand, we peered out the transport window, looking for signs of home in this foreign land, falling gently toward earth.

TASTING SONGS

Leone Ross

(2000)

At the time, the only problem I had sleeping with another woman in my wife's bed was the sweat.

I make no apologies for the affair. No, actually, that's not true. I apologize, even today. When I say that, I don't mean the days that screamed with silence, when all you could hear in our house was the click-click of Sasha's heels and the taunt of her zippers, her snap fastenings, I swear I could even hear her fingers against the buttons of her shirts as she walked around me, *through* me, dressing, sitting in front of the fridge spearing cold akee and saltfish into her mouth because she didn't have the energy to cook, packing Jake's little bag, all in awful silence, handing him, wordless, to her sister, whose disapproving back called out to me as she left with my son, yelling, *Adulterer, adulterer,* with every self-righteous step, as Sasha turned back to the battle, one only she could win. I don't mean the sound of my pleas that eventually became whimpers and soared into shouting and then dipped down to the indignity of whispered pleas once more, begging her to forgive me, *Please, just talk to me, say anything, I'm sorry, I'm so sorry, Sash.* I don't mean any of those things. I mean the apology inside of me. To Sasha and to Brianna. To both of them.

I'm putting this all down, sitting on the veranda of our new house. For Jake, I think. He should know, and I realize that having him read it as an addendum to our will is a damned cowardly way, but I can think of no other.

This is still the new house to me, even though we've been here twenty years; Jake departed for college two years ago. Jake, do you dream of this house? When my subconscious pulls down images of home, it always chooses the old house, the house of my own childhood, the one my mother left for me. On Hope Road, the dogs howling over the fence, cats mating at night, bunches of hibiscus laden with crazed hummingbirds, clumps of love bush, splayed in orange chaos across the hedges at the front, a difficult driveway that Sasha could never reverse into. But my son's dreams must be strident with this new house, the only one he's ever known, the place where his parents embarrass him by laying their hands on each other, even in their disgraceful forties. When he comes out from Miami on Spring Break I see him watch ghosts here: ghosts of himself, hurting his knees and knuckles, playing marbles, doing homework. But it's still the new house to me; it reveals none of my childhood. Or my sins.

It's the house Sasha insisted on, after Brianna. *Number One*, she said. *I can never live in this old house*, she said. *I don't care if you first walked here and your fucking mother breastfed you here. Buy a new one.* I remember those words because they were the first ones she said to me after she found me and Brianna grappling like lost animals in her bed, the sheets stinking with good-byes. Sasha made it clear: *Moving out of this house is the first step. And then I will think about me and you.* I could smell victory; I blew my savings on a deposit immediately, put the old house on the market, bought new furniture, decorated. Sasha would have nothing to do with it. It was penance. She swigged Red Stripe and watched me pack our clothes, wrangle on the phone with estate agents, laying one imperious, broken nail on the fabric swatches I placed before her, a yes or a no handed down from her hurt high. My patience and sorrow were tested in those weeks, with the inquiring looks from decorators who could not understand how a man with broad shoulders could walk on glass around his matchbox wife. She's small, Sasha. Small with a strength that makes her taller than me, and if you strike her, she burns.

She said that she could smell the sweat everywhere, that it was like some oil slick that had infected the old house, as if the liquid had touched each surface, had dived into her underwear drawer, insidious in the folds of frothy G-strings and off-white panties for long-gone heavy period days, as if it poured itself among the cutlery and evaporated into the air, contaminating her. I told her that Brianna only ever came to the house that one time, but she didn't believe me. There were times when I found her washing herself like a woman after rape, scrubbing at her skin until brown was red, watching Brianna disappear down the plug hole of the sunken shower, then reinfecting herself as she stepped onto the bath mat. And, of course, the photographs had to go. God help me, it hurt to destroy them. Simply, some of the most inspired work I've ever done, seasoned with desire and the eroticism of guilt. *How would you feel if I fucked someone else, Jerry?* She said it to me conversationally, our second day in the new house, Jake playing with a star-covered mobile in his cot, her moving closer to him, despite herself, smiling at his first smiles that were really gas. Yes, a casual tone, over my son: *I should. I should go to one of Lillian's sick parties and fuck the first man I meet. Can you see that in your mind's eye, Jerry? Sure you can. That's Number Two. Picture it for me.* Sasha. She knows me, and she says it like it is. I suppose that I understand why her first words came out of her sore, and why they hurt my ears. She could see the way I coveted Brianna. I still, yes, even now, feel an old stirring when I think of Brianna, her body, the way she moved, my inability to bring her peace.

I was twenty-eight, and we'd been married for a year. I left my wife for weeks at a time, to work. It was June, hot, but less than ninety degrees in the shade, when I returned to Jamaica and her from a harried, thirsty tour of Central America, rolls of film stuffed into every orifice. They were full of female pulchritude: a woman who told me she couldn't remember her age, who covered her face the first three times I spoke to her, whose wrinkles I made into journeys; her daughter, blind, who lived on her tiptoes and the money she made kissing men; a twelve-year-old with burnt sienna skin and eerie eyes, yellow and green, like a cat's, that she rolled back until there was nothing there but the whites, a habit from childhood days when she was teased as a *temba*, a goddess fallen from the sky; another girl whose face had been torn apart by jealous acid. It's my gift: to hold up women's beauty and show it to them, to revisit the faces and breasts and feet that they'd judged wanting, old, withered, not enough, too much, and have them see them anew. And they cleaved to me, eagerly, afraid, I suppose, that they'd forget that they were beautiful once I was gone.

My mother often told me that my sweet mouth would get me into trouble, that no love followed a man whose lips dripped honey. My mother died having only ever seen one photograph that I'd taken of her, despite my irritation. She said it frightened her enough. I'd made her beautiful after a lifetime of *You never gwine get a man, man goin' breed you an' lef' you fe pretty gyal, yes him ah beat you, but tek it an' pray, after all, where you gwine get one next man?*—all about my father, an empty soul, defined only by his fine Chinese origins that he wore as if he'd made them himself, and his splendid cruelty to my mother. And to me. Years of blood and invisibility. But I don't want to talk about that.

I met Brianna at one of Lillian's parties. I remember that I walked up to the door and laughed. It was covered with purple balloons and silver condoms: someone's idea of convenience and questionable humor. I pushed it open and played Name That Drug as weed and coke competed with the smell of women's thighs and the orange peel that simmered in oil-filled, antique vats. Along the brittle corridor, couples kissed and groped, twisting hands in the shadow of thighs, their laughter and moans tinkling on the air. One man, resplendent in a heart-shaped eye patch, pushed peach chiffon aside to bite his partner's neck under the dark ceiling. Somewhere, bass buzzed insidiously.

As I walked through the house, groups of beautiful people chatted and paused to nod at me; a woman masturbated in a far-off corner, her groans unheard by the rest; a man lifted a sodden mouth from his companion's vagina and waved. He was the only person I recognized; I'd taken pictures of him in the moonlight last year, his two-year-old son in his arms, his love for the child marred only by my knowledge of his promiscuity. I'd spent three months in the company of Jamaica's high-red, most debauched crowd, all happy to be captured on film by a young, up-and-coming, feted, new photographer. They'd amused me, and I'd amused Sasha, telling her the outrageous gossip I collected every night. She wasn't interested in that kind of scene. As I stood in the middle of the bacchanalia, I breathed deeply, trying to get clean air into my lungs, regretting my decision to come. It was the kind of place that made me stop feeling.

Lillian passed me by, and stopped to air-kiss my cheeks. She was so covered in gold that she clanked as she moved: Countless gold loops fell down her face; they were in her eyebrows, her cheeks, lips, and ears, drowning her delicate throat. Bracelets, like sand-colored spaghetti hoops, dangled from her arms, and twisted bunches of jewels glinted around both ankles. I wasn't surprised when she opened her mouth and gave me a glimpse of rubies, embedded in her teeth like flecks of ketchup.

"Nice to see you, Jerry," she purred.

"And you're as gorgeous as usual, Lil." I felt like squinting in her opulence.

"Not as gorgeous as you, baby!" She slipped a hand between us and squeezed me. "Want to take some pictures of me later?" I murmured an excuse; she wanted me as a lover, but I was a good boy, my wife's boy, and embarrassingly faithful. Besides, I had all the pictures I wanted of Lillian. She was a shallow woman, made even worse by her overt sexuality. Those were the days when I liked to chase the mystery of a woman, when obvious was no challenge for my art.

"Another time, eh?" She grinned, undefeated, and then clapped her hands. The busy, frenzied lovers around us paused in their play and looked up. She spread her arms. "This evening's entertainment will begin in five minutes. By the pool."

Brianna sat on the steps of the swimming pool, her hands, skirt, and bare feet soaked in water. We gathered around her, our fashionable cynicism held like a weapon before us. I wondered what she was doing there. She was too clean for us.

She was the barest woman I've ever seen. Her fragile skull was nearly bald, newly shaved. She wore no makeup, no jewelry. Her skin was enough decoration, buffed and unblemished, like squeaky, gleaming leather. It was as if she'd never played as a child, never skinned her knee, or eaten too-green mangoes and stained herself on their flesh, as if she'd never brushed a market woman's arm, taking with her the rebellion or camaraderie of daily higglering. She was very still. A man called out, "What a pretty gyal, to rass!" crinkling her brow with what looked like embarrassment. I'm sure my mouth was open. My fingers itched. I wanted to squeeze her for juice.

The night lay down on us as Brianna Riley began to sing. A slice of moon soared above the trees as the sound of her took me back to my childhood bed, the pillows soaked with sweat and tears as my father denounced my dreams. I let her stretch her gift along the length of my spine, pausing to touch each bone, sweeping around to cup her music to my face, the sound of her filling my eyes, kicking at the cotton clouds, silencing the crickets. Jamaicans, as she would have known, are a demanding audience, but in the middle of the seediness, we were suddenly, pathetically eager. She was that good. She pushed our facades aside with her gentle, crooning melody and she reminded me of drunken Christmas cake on a Sunday morning, of cricket matches in perfect whites, of children on their way home from church, of tamarind balls searing the mouth, of Chinese skipping in Kingston playgrounds. Three men shambled from the poolside and fled to the parking lot. I could hear the rumble of their car engines as her voice fell silent. I clapped until my fingertips felt scalded, and watched as the island's strangest elite surrounded her like mosquitoes.

Later that evening, Lillian and I entertained her, long after the last of the crowd slipped away. She listened to us intently, balanced in the middle of the pool, her elbows on a plastic float. Her dress drifted around her, like a huge lily. Her big, seal eyes flickered over us both.

"Lillian is the one who gave me the money to do my demo tapes," she said. Her speaking voice was pleasant, but normal. I restrained my disbelief; I didn't know Lillian to be a generous woman. I glanced at our hostess. Surely she could tell that this woman would never become part of her sordid little circle of adorers.

"And now you have a deal?" I asked.

"Yes. Well . . . almost. Warner Brothers are very interested," she said.

"Of course they are. She's so cute!" said Lillian. I wanted to swat her, like a fly.

"They like my . . . voice." She stopped. I noticed that she half answered, or ignored questions, as if she was unused to idle chitchat. "Jerry, can I ask you about your parents' background? You have a very . . . interesting . . . look."

"My father is a Chinese Jamaican and my mother is Indian and black. Hence the eyes." She tilted her head.

"Yes, my dear, Jerry is our favorite onlooker," said Lillian. "We all want him, but he won't play our little games with wifey at home." Her laughter disturbed the pool water. "I must check the locks." She rose, tinkling.

Brianna looked dismayed. "Oh—I'll go. I'm keeping you from your bed. I'm so sorry." She reached out a long, sinuous arm and paddled to the poolside, shot me a look that I didn't understand. "It's just nice to talk. . . ." I watched her take a breath before she stepped out of the water. "Could I call a taxi?"

Lillian shook her head. "No, no. Stay if you want. . . ."

"I can take you home," I said.

I watched her struggle. "All right," she said, finally.

*   *   *

In my car, after she'd dried and changed, she was silent. I made up for it, coaxing laughter from her like a pathetic court jester, driving as slowly as I could. I didn't want the night to end. I nearly crashed into a tattered goat strolling through Half Way Tree in my efforts to watch her and drive at the same time. She was so calm, even regal, and yet she'd carelessly taken Lillian's monogrammed towel with her, holding it in her lap as if it were a purse.

We reached her home too quickly. I followed her out, making sure that she was safe. Dawdled at the door, looking for the words to delay her. I can honestly say that in that moment, I became two men. One, the faithful husband, a man I pushed aside. The other, totally led by desire. I wanted to kiss Brianna until sunrise, because she looked like the kind of woman who would have liked that. I gestured at the towel. "Lillian will want that back," I joked.

"Oh, yes. I'll . . . take it to her." She twisted the damp cloth in her hands. I could tell that she wanted to stay, and yet something greater urged her away.

"I could come back and take you up there," I offered inanely.

"No. No. I'll do it."

Desperately, I reached through the bullshit.

"Brianna. I'm a photographer. Would you consider . . ."

She looked alarmed. "No, I don't like taking photographs. I'm sorry. I have to go."

I sat in the car outside her house for half an hour, imagining her under my lens.

I said at the beginning that I make no apologies. What I meant was that I make no excuses. I drove home fantasizing. I hugged my wife. My sexual interest in Brianna had nothing to do with Sasha. Women will dismiss this as cliché, but I know it's one of those clichés that is utterly true. I can understand why women feel betrayed by the deceit of infidelity, how conned they feel at a change of plan, of structure, without their being involved, how their men change the rules, lie, dip, dive, curve underneath them, avoiding discovery. I can see how foolish they feel, why the idea of their man naked with another somebody offends the ego and the heart. But I don't understand why they think that sexual arousal for another woman has anything to do with them. Wanting to possess a different woman does not reflect on the beloved. So I went home and kissed my wife.

Jake hadn't been born yet, and we spent a quiet night together, re-grouping. She wanted to hear my stories of San Jose and Costa Rica and Brazil. She said that she missed me, and I knew it was true, in between her job as senior editor at Randall Publishers. She rolled a spiff for us as she spoke, sifting the ganja between her fingers, discarding tiny seeds and debris in a silver-colored ashtray. Real weed. The first time I showed her hash in London, we both laughed. She'd turned the black clump be-tween her palms, wondering. The first time I met her, at her sister's house, she was rolling a spiff. She looked up at me as I walked into the living room, and I wondered how anyone could be so compact, so com-plete. Watching Sasha lick the edge of a piece of Rizla comforts me. Watching her lids weighed down by the buzz makes me feel safe. As moths burnt themselves on the lamplight, I looked at my wife's face, half in shadow, and let myself resent the comfort and the safety.

"Sash, how do you feel about the women I take pictures of?"

She put her head to one side. Inhaled. I could see her shoulders re-laxing.

"What do you mean?"

"I spend a lot of time with other women."

"So?" She passed the spiff to me. I took a puff, felt it glide inside me.

"Some women would be jealous. Have you ever been jealous?"

She laughed and coughed. "They're no competition."

"Seriously, Sash."

"Would you give them up?"

I shook my head.

"Do you sleep with them?"

Again, a shake of the head. Part of me wishes that she'd asked the question differently, that she'd allowed herself to stop trusting me in that moment. If she'd asked me if I was considering it, I would have said yes, laid my head on her knee, and confessed like a child, sought ways to go past Brianna. But she didn't.

"I don't worry about it, Jerry. Really. I know you love me, and I know we're friends. I know you wouldn't mess with that, so I married you. You told me that . . . the other thing . . . didn't matter. First man who ever said that to me. So, I married you, knowing that I was enough."

I didn't notice her pain. It was so familiar. Let the weed paint pictures of Brianna Riley in my head. I suppose I pretended that I had permission.

We take sweat for granted. I remember what I was told at school, that sweat was the body's way of cooling itself; I suppose everyone remembers that. Brianna used to say that if that was the case, a volcano lived inside her, constantly waiting to be cooled. I liked that image; when we became lovers, I would imagine, when I was inside her, that I touched that inferno and made her sweat all the more. She sweated and hummed when we made love. Song and sweat. To be defined by such things. To love one and hate the other so much that you can't see your own reflection in the eyes of others. But I knew what it was like to be defined in twos: pictures and need. I didn't admit it when I was a young man, but I loved the women I took pictures of, needing me. One wasn't enough. I believed in quantity over quality.

Two days later, I went back to Brianna's house and knocked on the door. She opened it and looked at me as if I had never left.

"Hello," she said. I felt absurd.

"Can I come in?" I said.

Her stance was odd, her hands behind her back, breasts pushed forward, like a kid hiding a present. Her face worked.

"Tell me you're not attracted to me, B, and I'll leave." An old approach, but sometimes they're the best.

"Please try and understand." Her voice was low. "I can't have a relationship with you or anybody. Can't you accept that?"

"Are you attracted to me?" I grinned. "What happen, babylove? I don't look *nice* to you?"

"I have to go—"

"Don't I?" I said.

"Yes, okay? That what you want to hear? Yes."

I reached for her, but she backed away, her hands still behind her. There was a kind of mute appeal in her face.

"Brianna, what are you holding—"

I stared. Water pattered around her bare feet, drenching them. Fat, unceasing drips, like the leaks we'd had in the roof at high school. Faster and faster.

"Brianna, you're spilling something—what—"

Her voice broke into pieces.

"I'm spilling *myself*. Okay?"

She raised her hands to my eyes.

"It's called hyperhydrosis."

We were sitting in her apartment. Like her, it was bare. The plastic-covered sofa was the only piece of furniture in her living room. The floorboards were naked, too. I glanced up at a light switch. It was shrouded with plastic. I wondered what her bed looked like.

"Most people with it get very clammy palms, but I'm a severe case."

"Have you always had it?" I asked.

She nodded hesitantly, then plunged forward. "When I was a little girl, no one wanted to play with me. Even grown-ups said I was nasty. I couldn't do anything about it . . . I hid my hands in my pockets. I wore gloves that got soaked in twenty minutes." She laughed softly, bitterly. "I learned to live in twenty-minute increments, which is as long as it takes before they . . . start getting bad. Then I had to sit on them. I rubbed them on my clothes. The kids laughed."

She held her slightly cupped hands in a glass bowl on her lap, as if they didn't belong to her. I watched the water bubble to the surface of her skin and roll over her fingers. The bowl was half full.

"I can't imagine how you felt," I said.

"No, you can't," she snapped. "My parents took me to a dermatologist, and she gave me something that looked like roll-on, to put on my fingers, but it didn't help. Then they sent me for a kind of electric shock treatment, but afterwards I couldn't eat or drink . . . or talk, because there wasn't any saliva in my mouth. It made me dry for about a week, and I was happy. But it gave me heart palpitations. I could've dealt with that. But my parents said it cost too much money for the treatment. My mother said it was God's way, and I had to accept it. But I hate it. *Hate* it!"

"But there must be something—"

"Yes there is, there always is. An operation, but I can't afford it. When I got the money from Lillian and Warners were interested, I was going to have it done. But the guy at Warners keeps jumping up and down—he loves my voice, but he calls the sweat a *hook*. He thinks it'll fascinate the fans."

"I can see that," I said.

"I don't care." The bowl tilted, spilling drops on her bare knees. "People think I'm nasty. They think I smell. They think it's my fault. You know how Jamaican people scornful. They point at me: 'Is time you clean up youself, mi dear.' Like I can't see what I am! I won't let anyone feel *sorry* for me!"

I sat beside her. She scrambled to get away, the bowl wavering dangerously. She grabbed for it, but it slipped out of her hands and shattered on the floor. She leapt to her feet, ignoring the glass.

"Brianna, you'll cut yourself."

"Get out of my house!"

"No." I moved toward her, trying to get her out of the way of the shards, but she shrank from me, scrubbing her hands against her T-shirt. Big wet splotches stained her chest, soaking through to her nipples.

"Please, please, Jerry, please go. It gets worse. It gets worse—"

"When you're upset?"

"Yes!" She sounded as if she wanted to cry. I watched her hands weep, instead. They were all but gushing now, their merciless flow darkening her wooden floor.

"I have to get something to hold my hands over—"

I grabbed her shoulders. "No. We can clean it up afterwards. I can. Move out of the way of the glass and stay here." She pushed at my chest with her elbows, sweat pumping from her palms, coursing down her wrists onto my shirt.

I grabbed her face and held it. I made her look at me. "This is *part* of you. You've got wet hands, B. You can't even push me away. Why not? You want to. What's the worse thing about this? Huh?"

Her face crumpled. "That . . . I can't touch anybody, not even my . . . mother. . . ."

"Touch me," I said.

Her hands circled my neck. I felt water soak my back as I gave Brianna Riley her first kiss. I felt like the hero in some cynically penned drama. It was what I needed in those days. Extremes. Drama. Don't we all?

I took pictures of Brianna and carried them home for Sasha to admire. Hundreds of them. She was as fascinated as me by the woman's strange condition. Sometimes I caught her bending over them in my darkroom and workspace, thoughtful. She came over to me for a hug.

"Oh, I understand her so much, y'know? She must feel so out of control, like her body just does things and she can't change it. I know how she feels." I held her close and tried to remember which shirt I'd left at Brianna's house.

I transformed Brianna's apartment into a studio and worked furiously, my new lover stepping around the equipment, anxious that she not damage anything. I slid my lens across her gleaming skin. I shot her bald head from the depths of a coconut tree. I cross-referenced her pores with her eyes and caught her as whizzing demigoddess; a wanton tease; a child; running across the parking lot; naked, rolled in dirt and sand like a zebra; tiptoed, capturing the sweet arch of her back; rough and ready as a ragamuffin; as dance hall queen; as prostitute; as maid. She was the most adaptable model I'd ever had. And water, yes, water everywhere. I poured food coloring into her palms and together we watched, enthralled, as she made a mauve waterfall in her back garden, the liquid pouring from her, spraying into the air in lovely droplets, in sumptuous curves, simmering in the heat of our country. I made her lift her hands above her head and clicked my shutter as she rained on herself, and it was amazing to watch her laugh. To watch my wife laugh, delighted that I had found a muse, happy in the smoky pretense of her husband's growing ability. I never thought she would find out. Truly. If she couldn't see it in the glow of Brianna's eyes, I guessed that I'd done all I could do.

"Jerry, I need some money."

"What for?" I rolled over and tweaked her nipple, then brought one of her fingers up and watched liquid mount her aureole.

"The operation," she said. I looked at her, startled. "I've decided to do it anyway. My voice is what's most important, and Warners is just going to have to take that."

"Ah . . ." I was shocked now. "You still want the operation?"

She frowned. "I always told you that."

"Yes, but . . ." I was suddenly embarrassed. I thought that my old magic had transformed her, that the pictures were enough. Hadn't I excised my mother's pain with a single photograph?

She looked at me, suddenly comprehending. She laughed, splashing my cheek. "You actually think pretty pictures make it all okay?"

"No, no, I mean, this has been a problem all your life . . ." I lied. I fixed my face into sympathy.

She laughed again. "You are so arrogant, baby. So sweet with the arrogance." She got off the bed, her body twisting into parenthesis. "There's another reason why I need money."

"Yes?"

"I'm pregnant."

A *New York Times* critic once damned me to hell, in the days before my computer was crammed with kiss-kiss E-mails from my agent: "The way that Jeremy Butler brings his models to the frame suggests coercion of the lowest kind. Underneath the smiles are screaming women, if you can only bend close enough to hear them." I crumpled the review and dismissed him. But after Brianna I've often wondered whether I cured any of the women I captured. I wonder if I truly did cure my mother, or whether I just wanted to believe that I had. I realized that I imagined all of them changed, confident, careless in the knowledge of their beauty forever, a swath behind me, all made up of whole and hearty ladies, purring in the knowledge of the wondrousness that Jerry Butler showed them. Now I wonder if I made it worse; whether the magic faded and left them emptier than before. I used them. I may not have touched any of them except Brianna, but I look at my old work and see how I masturbated with their souls.

"Sasha will just have to hold her corner and chill," said Lillian. We sat in her living room. She was a dread by then, her fake locks twisted and alien down her back, wrapped in scarlet, amber, and jade, her skirt long and wide, hiding her feet. I knew she was the wrong person to talk to as soon as I said it, but I needed someone to tell me it wasn't a big deal, and Lillian's carelessness was stunning in its consistency.

"Shit," I said, out loud.

Lillian sucked her teeth, waved the air. "How many men you know in Jamaica that have children out of doors? Nearly all of them. C'mon, Jerry. And anyway, what does Sasha expect?"

"I'm not that kind of man," I said.

"Of course you are, my dear."

I didn't tell Sasha. Denial is such a convenient thing. I just kept on going. But I watched my wife, paying our bills, giving the maid daily instructions, cutting her toenails, reading me manuscripts in bed. I listened to her whisper into my ear at night: *I can't take it, God, I can't take it.* I once read a survey of what Caribbean women said at the point of orgasm. Jamaican women say that a lot, apparently: *I can't take it.* Bajan women say, *Do me so, oh Lord.* Grenadian women say, *Ram me, Jesus Christ, ram me, boy.* I wonder if God looks down and asks what the hell He has to do with it.

I watched Brianna swell and sweat. I gave her money. As the baby grew inside her, she grew obsessed. She wanted, she said, to hold this baby in dry arms, and sing to it. It was the sum of all her thoughts: holding her child, moistened only by the blood of the birth, introducing herself with the sound of her voice. She'd told the record company that she was having the operation, and, reluctantly, they agreed that they would sign the deal without it. But after the baby, they said. When she shaped up, they'd start recording. I was proud of her determination.

We booked her in for the operation six weeks before her due date. It was a simple procedure, but it was expensive. I crept off to New York for my latest exhibition. I walked around the exhibiting hall, discussing mounting, lighting, which shots would be made available to the public as three-hundred-dollar prints, which ones would make two-dollar postcards. The curator fluttered around me, lip-glossed, his vocabulary studded with "darlings." "Brianna is just the best of your work, hon," he said. "You just get better and better. Who is she, anyway?"

I looked at the pictures and thought about my lover, my mistress. She was nervous the morning I'd left, and I'd only been able to steal a little while with her. Sasha couldn't understand where I had to go just hours before she drove me to the airport.

"You can't be here? You can't cancel?"

"B, I have to make some money. Come on, now."

She was propped up in bed, bulbous, like a big, naked moon. She had me pile her houseplants around her on the sheets, and began to water them, dipping her busy fingers into their pots and feeding them with herself, roots up. I'd seen her do it countless times, and wasn't amused anymore. Recently, each time she did something bizarre with her hands, I loved Sasha more. I had begun to think of ways of extricating myself.

She looked up. "They're going to collapse my lungs." She was near tears.

Groaning, contrite, I pushed a plant out of the way and stroked her face. I could give her comfort—it wasn't so much to ask for. The operation was keyhole surgery. The specialist would work through each armpit, cauterizing the nerve that induced sweating. To get to the nerve he would deflate her lungs, left side, right side. I thought of Sasha and her breasts. Her nipples always hardened alternately, as if they were playing hide and seek with my mouth.

"Think of holding the baby, sweetheart." Wincing, I checked my watch. Sasha would be raising her eyebrows at me by the time I got back.

"All right," Brianna said. She sighed. She let the tears dry. She never wiped her face. It was silly to do so. She was lucky that she didn't need makeup. "Yes. It's going to be a girl, y'know. That's what the doctor said."

"I know." I refused to think of my child coming into the world in a month. Perhaps if Brianna had been the kind of woman who threatened taking the kid into Sasha's face, I would have fallen out of denial. But she wasn't. So I didn't.

A week later, I unlocked the burglar bars around our veranda. Our maid, Michelle, stood waiting for me, her face impassive. She'd been picking the parasitic love bush off the hedges in the garden. Her hands were stained orange.

"Hello, Mr. Jerry," she said.

"Hello, Michelle. Where's Mrs. Butler?"

"She not here. She gone down to the office, say she comin' back late."

Something in her tone made me look up from the padlock I was twisting into place. She was pushing her lips out in that kissing gesture that Jamaicans do when they want to point at something, but don't want to use their hands.

"S'maddy here to see you, Mr. Jerry," she said.

Brianna was sitting on our bed. She wore a red T-shirt with a rip under one arm, and close-fitting jeans. I stared at her flat stomach, uncomprehending. Part of me was poised to snatch her from my marital bed the minute liquid threatened. Another part was utterly aroused by her in that marital bed, those miles of perfect skin, remembering how each time I touched her it felt new. Yet another part was outraged at her audacity. How could she come to my home? Dimly, I realized that she'd started weeping when I stepped into the room. The outrage died. Curiosity and lust and pity took over. I held her.

"Did you lose the baby?"

"No. The baby's at home. I had it early. You weren't here."

I looked down at her hands, reached to touch them, but she pulled away, was down on her knees before I could stop her, dragging arid palms across the electric sockets, across the carpet.

"So you're dry! Great! So what—"

"Look at what I can do." She began to slap herself. Big, open-handed, full-palmed slaps, cracking across her face, faster and faster. I could feel Michelle listening at the door as I stumbled to Brianna's side, nearly tearful myself. I grabbed her hands and forced them down. The skin of her fingers was cracking. It was eerie to touch them.

Her skin was bone-dry, like my throat.

She told me that she went into labor half an hour afer her surgery. In fifteen hours she held her baby boy, exhausted, wanting me, but looking down at this little person, neat and dry and safe in her arms. "Boy, we musta missed that penis," the nurse chuckled at her. Brianna watched the Jamaican dawn playing with the windows of her room, and she thought how nice it was that I'd gotten her a private room, away from the labor ward screams. She opened her mouth and waited for the taste of her song. What came out was less than a bark. The surgeons said they couldn't do anything. *An unfortunate side effect*, they said. *Never seen anything like it.*

She climbed into my arms and I forgot about Michelle as Brianna scratched and wailed and pulled me inside her, thrusting her hips at me, our wet cheeks sliding against each other as I cried, too, telling her I was sorry, so sorry that she was sad, between whining and groans and acres of curious dryness and the sound of her coming over and over, like she'd never stop, and in all of it I don't know how I heard that tiny gasp behind me, my wife standing at the bedroom door, her eyes so big that they suddenly saw all the world. I turned, I tell you, from my lover, God knows how I heard that small, hurt sound in between Brianna's orgasmic sorrow, but I did. I can hear it now.

I'm glad that I've written it all down. I'll ask Sasha whether she thinks I should keep it for Jake. I'll trust her feelings on the matter. Perhaps she won't want to change his dreams. Perhaps they would be twisted, like my own. I dream of Brianna, not smooth, or burnished, or wet, but surrounded by options: was it a knife, a rope, a razor blade, drugs, did she vomit, did she hate me, did she bleed, did it hurt? Lillian got the news on the wind and came up to the house, dragged me into the yard to tell me. It made page five of the *Daily Gleaner:* SINGER SUICIDE AFTER BOTCHED OPERATION. The *Gleaner* was never subtle, and they spread my lover's face all over their pages, frozen in a death mask. I know something. I know she wouldn't have killed herself if I had followed her that day. But I chose. I chose my wife's disbelieving eyes, and that small sound of hurt. I chose to heal the only thing I could heal.

My wife always wanted a son. When we came to the new house, Jake in my arms, she finally threw out her off-white underwear, saved for heavy periods, the ones she hadn't worn for years. I remember her words: *Number Three, Jerry: Let this be enough. Will it be enough? It has to be enough.* I said yes, that my son was enough. That I'd never touch an-other woman.

Jake is coming home tomorrow. He's grown to be a fine man. Bright, responsible, not at all interested in photography. He has Sasha's feeling for words, and he's studying linguistics and sociology. He's had the same girl since he was sixteen. They cuddle and wind love bush in each other's hair when they're here. Sometimes, when she thinks we're not looking, his girl sucks salt water off his fingers and teases him about an-other one of her shirts ruined. But she doesn't mind the sweat. Neither does Jake. He waters the plants at the front of the yard with his hands, and Sasha smiles.

CAN YOU WEAR MY EYES

Kalamu ya Salaam

(2000)

At first Reggie wearing my eyes after I expired was beautiful; a sensitive romantic gesture and an exhilarating experience. For him there was the awe of seeing the familiar world turned new when viewed through my gaze, and through observing him, I vicariously experienced the rich sweetness of visualizing and savoring the significance of the recent past.

I'm a newcomer to the spirit world, so occasionally I miss the experience of earth feelings, the sensations that came through my body when I had a body. I can't describe the all-encompassing intricate interweave of spirit reality—"reality" is such a funny word to use in talking about what many people believe is so unreal. I can't really convey to you the richness of the spirit world or what missing human feelings is like. I'm told eventually we permanently forget earth ways, sort of like when we were born and forgot all those prebirth months we spent gestating in our mother's womb; in fact, most of us even forget what it feels like to be a baby. Well, the spirit world is something like always being a baby, constant wonder and exploration.

Reggie must have had an inkling of the immensity of the fourth dimension—which is as good a name as any for the spirit world—or maybe Reggie guessed that there was a meta-reality, or intuited that there was more to eyes than simply seeing in the physical sense. But then again, he probably didn't intuit that this realm exists because, like most men, centering on his intuition was difficult for Reggie, as difficult as lighting a match in a storm or imagining being a woman. In fact, his inability to adapt to and cope with woman-sight is why he's blind now.

I was in his head, and I don't mean his memories. I mean literally checking his thoughts, each one existing with the briefness of a mayfly as Reg weighed the rationality of switching eyes. This was immediately following those four and a half anesthetized days I hung on while in the hospital after getting blindsided by a drunk driver a few blocks beyond Chinese Kitchen, where I had stopped to get some of their sweet-and-sour shrimp for our dinner. Through the whole ordeal Reggie never wavered. Two days after my death and one day before the operation, Reginald woke up that Monday morning confident as a tree planted by the water. Reggie felt that if he took on my eyes, then he would be able to have at least a part of me back in his life.

He assumed that with my eyes maybe he could stop seeing me when he brushed, combed, and plaited Aiesha's thick hair or sat for over an hour daydreaming at her bedside while she slept, looking at our daughter but thinking of me. Or maybe he thought once my chestnut-colored pupils were in his head, my demise wouldn't upset him so much that he'd have to bow his head like he was reverently praying, the way Sister Carol had done in church before she'd jump up to testify the day before.

Reginald was so eager to make good as a husband and father, to redeem whatever he thought was lost because of the way he came up. I am convinced he didn't really know me. He had this image, this ideal, and he wanted that in the worst way. Wanted a family, a home. And I was the first woman he ever loved and who ever loved him. All the rest had been girls still discovering themselves. We married. I had his child. And for him everything was just the way it was supposed to be. For me, well, let us just say, some of us want more out of life without ever really identifying what that more is and certainly without ever attaining that more. So, in a sense, I settled—that's the woman Reginald married. And in another sense, there was a part of me that remained restless. I hid that part from Reginald, but I always knew. I always, always knew me and, yes, that was what really disoriented Reginald. He loved me and I could live with his love, but until he wore my eyes he never got a glimpse of the other me.

I used to think there was something wrong with me. I should have been totally happy. Of course, I loved our daughter. I loved my husband. I could live with the life we had, but . . . But this is not about me. This is about the man whom I married. I married Reginald more because he loved me so much than because I loved him back like that—I mean, I loved him and all, but would never have put his eyes into my head if he had been killed and I had been the one still alive, on the other side.

After we went through all the organ donation legal rigamarole, we actually celebrated with a late-night seafood dinner; that was about eight and a half months before Aiesha was born. Just like getting married, the celebration was his idea, an idea I went along with because I had no good reason not to, even though I had a vague distaste, a sort of uneasiness about the seriousness that Reginald invested into his blind allegiance to me. You know the discomfort you experience when you have two or three forkfuls left on your plate and you don't feel like eating anymore, but you have always been taught not to waste food so you eat that little bit more? Eating a few more morsels is no big thing, but nonetheless forcing yourself leaves you feeling uneasy the rest of the evening. I can see how I was, how I hid some major parts of myself from Reginald, and how difficult I must have been to live with precisely because he didn't really know the whole person he was living with. He so sincerely worshiped the part of me that he envisioned as his wife, while inside I cringed, and he never knew—despite my smiles—how sad I sometimes felt, because I knew he didn't know and I knew I was concealing myself from him. Besides, what right did I have not to eat two little pieces of chicken or not to go celebrate my husband's decision to dedicate his life to me?

In hindsight, I came to realize I shouldn't have let him give me things I didn't want. Reginald would have died if he had known that having or not having a baby didn't really make that much difference to me. He wanted . . . You know, this is really not about me. When we went to celebrate our signing of the donation papers, I didn't know then that I was pregnant, but even if I had, we wouldn't have done anything differently. Stubborn Reginald had his mind made up and, at the time, I allowed myself to be mesmerized by the sincerity and dedication of Reg's declaration—my husband's pledge to wear my eyes was unmatched by anything I had previously imagined or heard of. When somebody loves you like that, you're supposed to be happy, and if you aren't, well, then, you just smile and, well, I think when he saw the world through my eyes, he saw both me and the world in ways he never imagined.

The doctors told Reginald there usually weren't any negative side effects, although in a rare case or two there were some unexplained hallucinations, but even for those patients, counseling smoothed out the transition. The first week after the operation went okay and then the intermittent double visions started. For Reggie it was like he had second sight. He saw what was there, but then he also saw something else.

Sometimes he would go places he never knew I went and get a disorienting image flash from a source about which he previously would never have given a second thought, like the svelte look of a waiter at a café, a guy whose sleek build I really admired. Reginald never envisioned me desiring some other man. I don't know why, but he just never thought of me fantasizing sex with someone else, and now suddenly Reginald looks up from a menu and finds himself staring at a man's behind. Needless to say, such sightings were disconcerting. Or like how the night I got drunk on tequila would flash back every time I saw limes. Reginald is in a supermarket buying apples and imagines himself retching, well, he thinks he's imagining dry heaves, but he's really seeing the association of being drunk with those tart green, lemon-shaped fruit. And on and on, until Reggie's afraid to go anywhere new, afraid he'll run into another man I had made love to that he never knew about, like this person he saw in a bookstore one day, a bookstore Reginald never went in but which I used to frequent. That's how I had met Rahsaan. Reggie just happened to be passing the place, looked inside the big picture window, and immediately peeped Rahsaan. When he looked into the handsome obsidian of Rahsaan's face with its angular lines that resembled an elegant African mask, Reginald got the shock of his naive life. He didn't sleep for two whole days after that one.

And when he closes our eyes to sleep, it's worse. A man should never know a woman's secret life; men cannot stand so much reality. Their fragile egos can't cope. It's like they say in Zimbabwe: men are children and women are mothers. Being a child is about innocence, about not knowing the realities that adults deal with every day. Men just don't know the world of women. So after Reginald adopted my eyes, you can just imagine how often he found himself laying awake at night, staring into the dark trying to make sense out of the complex of images he was occasionally seeing. Imagine Reginald awakened by the terror of a particularly vivid dream, one in which he saw himself, saw how he had treated me, sometimes abusing me when he actually thought he was loving me. Like when we would make mad love, and he wanted me to suck him, he would never say anything, just shove my head down to his genitals. Sex didn't feel so exquisitely good to him to see his dick up close, the curl of his pubic hair.

Although the major episodes kept him awake and eventually drove him down to the riverside, it was the unrelenting grind of daily life's thousands of tiny tortures that propelled poor Reg over the edge. Looked like every time he turned around in public he felt unsafe, felt vulnerable to assault from men he previously would never have bothered to notice. Seemed like my eyeball radar spotted potential invaders everywhere Reg looked: how to dodge that one, don't get on an elevator with this one, make sure there's always another person nearby when you're in a room with so-and-so. And even though as a man Reg was immune to much of the usual harassment, it became a real drag having to expend a ton of precautionary emotional energy in the course of taking a casual stroll down the block to buy some potato chips. The strain of always being on guard was too much for Reg; he became outraged: nobody should have to live like this is the conclusion he came to.

He never knew when the second sight would kick in, and the visioning never lasted too long, but the incidents were always so viscerally jolting that they emotionally disoriented him. In less than two weeks, it had reached the point that just looking at makeup made Reg sick. He unconsciously reacted to seeing some shades of lipstick by wetting his lips with his tongue, like there was something inappropriate about him having unpainted lips—a vague but powerful feeling that he was wrong for being like he was started to consume him. And he couldn't bear to watch cable anymore.

The morning Reginald blinded himself, he stood on the levee staring into the sun without squinting. Silent tears poured profusely down his cheeks. He kept saying he had always thought our life together was beautiful, and he never knew I had suffered so. And then he threw a twelve-ounce glass, three-quarters full of battery acid, onto his face, directly into our unblinking eyes. A jogger that morning found Reginald on his knees, shrieking. The runner ran to a house and begged the people who lived there to call an ambulance for a black guy folded over on the levee screaming about he didn't want to see anymore, couldn't stand to see anything else.

LIKE DAUGHTER

Tananarive Due

(2000)

I got the call in the middle of the week, when I came wheezing home from my uphill late-afternoon run. I didn't recognize the voice on my computer's answer-phone at first, although I thought it sounded like my best friend, Denise. There was no video feed, only the recording, and the words were so improbable they only confused me more: "Sean's gone. Come up here and get Neecy. Take her. I can't stand to look at her."

Her words rolled like scattered marbles in my head.

I had just talked to Denise a week before, when she called from Chicago to tell me her family might be coming to San Francisco to visit me that winter, when Neecy was out of school for Christmas vacation. We giggled on the phone as if we were planning a sleepover, the way we used to when we were kids. Denise's daughter, Neecy, is my godchild. I hadn't seen her since she was two, which was a raging shame and hard for me to believe when I counted back the years in my mind, but it was true. I'd always made excuses, saying I had too much traveling and too many demands as a documentary film producer, where life is always projected two and three years into the future, leaving little space for here and now.

But that wasn't the reason I hadn't seen my godchild in four years. We both knew why.

I played the message again, listening for cadences and tones that would remind me of Denise, and it was like standing on the curb watching someone I knew get hit by a car. Something had stripped Denise's voice bare. So that meant her husband, Sean, must really be gone, I realized. And Denise wanted to send her daughter away.

"I can't stand to look at her," the voice on the message was saying again.

I went to my kitchen sink, in the direct path of the biting breeze from my half-open window, and I was shaking. My mind had frozen shut, sealing my thoughts out of reach. I turned on the faucet and listened to the water pummel my aluminum basin, then I captured some of the lukewarm stream in my palms to splash my face. As the water dripped from my chin, I cupped my hands again and drank, and I could taste the traces of salty perspiration I'd rubbed from my skin, tasting myself. My anger and sadness were tugging on my stomach. I stood at that window and cursed as if what I was feeling had a shape and was standing in the room with me.

I think I'd started to believe I might have been wrong about the whole thing. That was another reason I'd kept some distance from Denise; I hadn't wanted to be there to poke holes in what she was trying to do, to cast doubts with the slightest glance. That's something only a mother or a lifelong friend can do, and I might as well have been both to Denise despite our identical ages. I'd thought maybe if I only left her alone, she could build everything she wanted inside that Victorian brownstone in Lincoln Park. The husband, the child, all of it. Her life could trot on happily ever after, just the way she'd planned.

But that's a lie, too. I'd always known I was right. I had been dreading that call all along, since the beginning. And once it finally came, I wondered what the hell had taken so long. You know how Denise's voice really sounded on my answering machine that day? As if she'd wrapped herself up in that recorder and died.

"Paige, promise me you'll look out for Neecy, hear?" Mama used to tell me. I couldn't have known then what a burden that would be, having to watch over someone. But I took my role seriously. Mama said Neecy needed me, so I was going to be her guardian. Just a tiny little bit, I couldn't completely be a kid after that.

Mama never said exactly why my new best friend at Mae Jemison Elementary School needed guarding, but she didn't have to. I had my own eyes. Even when Neecy didn't say anything, I noticed the bruises on her forearms and calves, and even on Neecy's mother's neck once, which was the real shocker. I recognized the sweet, sharp smell on Neecy's mother's breath when I walked to Neecy's house after school. Her mother smiled at me so sweetly, just like that white lady Mrs. Brady on reruns of *The Brady Bunch* my mother made me watch, because she used to watch it when she was my age and she thought it was more appropriate than the "trash" on the children's channels when I was a kid. That smile wasn't a real smile; it was a smile to hide behind.

I knew things Mama didn't know, in fact. When Neecy and I were nine, we already had secrets that made us feel much older; and not in the way that most kids *want* to feel older, but in the uninvited way that only made us want to sit by ourselves in the playground watching the other children play, since we were no longer quite in touch with our spirit of running and jumping. The biggest secret, the worst, was about Neecy's Uncle Lonnie, who was twenty-two, and what he had forced Neecy to do with him all summer during the times her parents weren't home. Neecy finally had to see a doctor because the itching got so bad. She'd been *bleeding* from itching between her legs, she'd confided to me. This secret filled me with such horror that I later developed a dread of my own period because I associated the blood with Neecy's itching. Even though the doctor asked Neecy all sorts of questions about how she could have such a condition, which had a name Neecy never uttered out loud, Neecy's mother never asked at all.

So, yes, I understood why Neecy needed looking after. No one else was doing it.

What I *didn't* understand, as a child, was how Neecy could say she hated her father for hitting her and her mother, but then she'd be so sad during the months when he left, always wondering when he would decide to come home. And how Neecy could be so much smarter than I was—the best reader, speller, and multiplier in the entire fourth grade—and still manage to get so many F's because she just wouldn't sit still and do her homework. And the thing that puzzled me most of all was why, as cute as Neecy was, she seemed to be ashamed to show her face to anyone unless she was going to bed with a boy, which was the only time she ever seemed to think she was beautiful. She had to go to the doctor to get abortion pills three times before she graduated from high school.

Maybe it was the secret-sharing, the telling, that kept our friendship so solid, so fervent. Besides, despite everything, there were times I thought Neecy was the only girl my age who had any sense, who enjoyed reciting poems and acting out scenes as much as I did. Neecy never did join the drama club like I did, claiming she was too shy, but we spent hours writing and performing plays of our own behind my closed bed-

room door, exercises we treated with so much imagination and studious-
ness that no one would ever guess we were our only audience.

"I wish I had a house like yours," Neecy used to say, trying on my
clothes while she stood admiring herself in my closet mirror, my twin.
By fall, the clothes would be hers, because in the summer Mama always
packed my clothes for Neecy in a bundle. *For my other little girl*, she'd say.
And beforehand Neecy would constantly warn me, "Don't you mess up
that dress," or "Be careful before you rip that!" because she already felt
proprietary.

"Oh, my house isn't so special," I used to tell Neecy. But that was the
biggest lie of all.

In the years afterward, as Neecy dragged a parade of crises to my
doorstep, like a cat with writhing rodents in her teeth—men, money,
jobs; *everything* was a problem for Neecy—I often asked myself what
forces had separated us so young, dictating that I had grown up in my
house and Neecy had grown up in the other. She'd lived right across the
street from my family, but our lives may as well have been separated by
the Red Sea.

Was it only an *accident* that my own father never hit me, never stayed
away from home for even a night, and almost never came from work
without hugging me and telling me I was his Smart Little Baby-Doll?
And that Mama never would have tolerated any other kind of man?
Was it pure accident that *I'd* had no Uncle Lonnie to make me itch
until I bled with a disease the doctor had said little girls shouldn't have?

"Girl, you're so lucky," Neecy told me once when I was in college and
she'd already been working for three years as a clerk at the U Save Drug-
store. She'd sworn she wasn't interested in college, but at that instant
her tone had been so rueful, so envy-soaked, that we could have been
children again, writing fantastic scripts for ourselves about encounters
with TV stars and space aliens behind my closed bedroom door, both of
us trying to forget what was waiting for Neecy at home. "In my next life,
I'm coming back *you* for sure."

If only Neecy had been my real-life sister, not just a pretend one, I always thought. If only things had been different for her from the time she
was born.

I called Denise a half hour after I got her message. She sounded a little better, but not much. Whether it was because she'd gathered some

composure or swallowed a shot or two of liquor, this time her voice was the one I've always known: hanging low, always threatening to melt into a defeated laugh. She kept her face screen black, refusing to let me see her. "It's all a mess. This place looks like it was robbed," she said. "He took everything. His suits. His music. His favorite books, you know, those Russian writers, Dostoyevsky and Nabokov, or whatever-the-fuck? Only reason I know he was ever here is because of the hairs in the bathroom sink. He *shaved* first. He stood in there looking at his sorry face in the mirror after he'd loaded it all up, and he . . ." For the first time, her voice cracked. "He left . . . me. And her. He left."

I couldn't say anything against Sean. What did she expect? The poor man had tried, but from the time they met, it had all been as arranged as a royal Chinese marriage. How could anyone live in that house and breathe under the weight of Denise's expectations? Since I couldn't invent any condolences, I didn't say anything.

"You need to take Neecy." Denise filled the silence.

Hearing her say it so coldly, my words roiled beneath my tongue, constricting my throat. I could barely sound civil. "The first time you told me about doing this . . . I said to think about what it would mean. That it couldn't be undone. Didn't I, Neecy?"

"Don't call me Neecy." Her words were icy, bitter. "Don't you know better?"

"What happens now? She's your daughter, and she's only six. Think of—"

"Just come get her. If not, I don't . . . I don't know what I'll do."

Then she hung up on me, leaving my melodramatic imagination to wonder what she'd meant by that remark, if she was just feeling desperate or if she was holding a butcher knife or a gun in her hand when she said it. Maybe that was why she'd blacked herself out, I thought.

I was crying like a six-year-old myself while my cab sped toward the airport. I saw the driver's wondering eyes gaze at me occasionally in his rearview mirror, and I couldn't tell if he was sympathetic or just annoyed. I booked myself on an eight-forty flight with a seat in first class on one of the S-grade planes that could get me there in forty minutes. Airbuses, I call them. At least in first class I'd have time for a glass or two of wine. I convinced the woman at the ticket counter to give me the coach price because, for the first time in all my years of flying, I lied and said I was going to a funeral. My sister's, I told her, tears still smarting on my face.

If you could even call that a lie.

Three more months, just ninety days, and it never would have happened. If Denise had waited only a few months, if she'd thought it through the way I begged her when she first laid out the details of her plan, the procedure would not have been legal. The Supreme Court's decision came down before little Neecy was even born, after only a couple hundred volunteers paid the astronomical fee to take part in the copycat babies program. To this day, I still have no idea where Denise got the money. She never told me, and I got tired of asking.

But she got it somehow, somewhere, along with two hundred thirty others. There were a few outright nutcases, of course, lobbying to try to use DNA samples to bring back Thomas Jefferson and Martin Luther King; I never thought that would prove anything except that those men were only human and could be as unremarkable as the rest of us. But mostly the applicants were just families with something left undone, I suppose. Even though I never agreed with Denise's reasons, at least I had some idea of what she hoped to accomplish. The others, I wasn't sure. Was it pure vanity? Novelty? Nostalgia? I still don't understand.

In the end, I'm not sure how many copycat babies were born. I read somewhere that some of the mothers honored the Supreme Court's ban and were persuaded to abort. Of course, they might have been coerced or paid off by one of the extremist groups terrified of a crop of so-called "soulless" children. But none of that would have swayed Denise, anyway. For all I know, little Neecy might have been the very last one born.

It was three months too late, but I was moved by the understated eloquence of the high court's decision when it was announced on the News & Justice satellite: *Granted, what some might call a "soul" is merely an individual's biological imprint, every bit as accidental as it is unique. In the course of accident, we are all born once, and we die but once. And no matter how ambiguous the relationship between science and chance, humankind cannot assign itself to the task of re-creating souls.*

I'm not even sure I believe in souls, not really. But I wished I'd had those words for Denise when it still mattered.

She actually had the whole thing charted out. We were having lunch at a Loop pizzeria the day Denise told me what she wanted to do. She

spread out a group of elaborate charts; one was marked HOME, one FA-
THER, one SCHOOL, all in her too-neat artist's script. The whole time she
showed me, her hands were shaking as if they were trying to fly away
from her. I'd never seen anyone shake like that until then, watching
Denise's fingers bounce like rubber with so much excitement and fervor.
The shaking scared me more than her plans and charts.

"Neecy, please wait," I told her.

"If I wait, I might change my mind," Denise said, as if this were a log-
ical argument for going forward rather than just the opposite. She still
hadn't learned that *doubt* was a signal to stop and think, not to plow
ahead with her eyes covered, bracing for a crash.

But that was just Denise. That's just the way she is. Maybe that's who
she is.

Denise's living room was so pristine when I arrived, it was hard to believe it had witnessed a trauma. I noticed the empty shelves on the
music rack and the spaces where two picture frames had been removed
from their hooks on the wall; but the wooden floors gleamed, the walls
were scrubbed white, and I could smell fresh lilac that might be artificial
or real, couldn't tell which. Denise's house reminded me of the sitting
room of the bed and breakfast I stayed in overnight during my last trip
to London, simultaneously welcoming and wholly artificial. A perfect
movie set, hurriedly dusted and freshened as soon as visitors were gone.

Denise looked like a vagrant in her own home. As soon as I got there,
I knew why she hadn't wanted me to see her on the phone; she was half
dressed in a torn T-shirt, her hair wasn't combed, and the skin beneath
her eyes looked so discolored that I had to wonder, for a moment, if Sean
might have been hitting her. It wouldn't be the first time she'd been in
an abusive relationship. But then I stared into the deep mud of my
friend's irises before she shuffled away from me, and I knew better. No,
she wasn't being beaten; she wouldn't have tolerated that with Neecy in
the house. Instead, my friend was probably having a nervous breakdown.

"Did he say why he left?" I asked gently, stalling. I didn't see little
Neecy anywhere, and I didn't want to ask about her yet. I wished I
didn't have to see her at all.

Answering with a grunt rather than spoken words, Denise flung her
arm toward the polished rosewood dining room table. There, I saw a single piece of paper laid in the center, a typewritten note. As sterile as

everything else. In the shining wood, I could also see my own reflection standing over it.

"Haven't you read it?" I asked her.

"Neecy's in the back," Denise said, as if in response.

"Shhh. Just a second. Let's at least read what the man said." My heart had just somersaulted, and then I knew how much I didn't want to be there at all. I didn't want to think about that child. I picked a random point midway through the note and began reading aloud in the tone I might have used for a eulogy: ". . . You squeeze so hard, it chokes me. You're looking for more than a father for her, more than a home. It isn't natural, between you and her—"

"*Stop it,*" Denise hissed. She sank down to the sofa, tunneling beneath a blanket and pulling it up to her chin.

I sighed. I could have written that note myself. Poor Sean. I walked to the sofa and sat beside my friend. My hand felt leaden as I rested it on the blanket where I believed Denise's shoulder must be. "So you two fought about it. You never told me that," I said.

"There's a lot I didn't tell you," Denise said, and I felt her shivering beneath the blanket. "He didn't understand. Never. I thought he'd come around. I thought—"

"You could change him?"

"Shut up," Denise said, sounding more weary than angry.

Yes, I felt weary, too. I'd had this conversation with Denise, or similar ones, countless times before. Denise had met Sean through a video personal on the Internet where all she said was, "I want a good husband and father. Let's make a home." Sean was a nice enough guy, but I had known their marriage was based more on practical considerations than commitment. They both wanted a family. They both had pieces missing and were tired of failing. Neither of them had learned, after two divorces, that people can't be applied to wounds like gauze.

And, of course, then there was little Neecy. What was the poor guy supposed to do?

"She's in her room. I already packed her things. Please take her, Paige. Take her." Denise was whimpering by now.

I brushed a dead-looking clump of hair from Denise's face. Denise's eyes, those unseeing eyes, would be impossible to reach. But I tried anyway, in hopes of saving all of us. "This is crazy. Take her where? What am I going to do with a kid?"

"You promised."

Okay, Mama. I will.

"What?"

"You promised. At the church. At the christening. You're her god-mother. If anything happened to me, you said you would."

I thought of the beautiful baby girl, a goddess dressed in white, her soft black curls crowned with lace—gurgling, happy, and agreeable despite the tedium of the long ceremony. Holding her child, Denise had been glowing in a way she had not at her wedding, as if she'd just discovered her entire reason for living.

Tears found my eyes for the first time since I'd arrived. "Denise, what's this going to mean to her?"

"I don't know. I don't . . . care," Denise said, her voice shattered until she sounded like a mute struggling to form words. "Look at me. I can't stand to be near her. I vomit every time I look at her. It's all ruined. Everything. Oh, God—" She nearly sobbed, but there was only silence from her open mouth. "I can't. Not again. No more. Take her, Paige."

I saw a movement in my peripheral vision, and I glanced toward the hallway in time to see a shadow disappear from the wall. My God, I realized, the kid must have been standing where she could hear every hurtful word. I knew I had to get Neecy out of the house, at least for now. Denise was right. She was not fit, at this moment, to be a mother. Anything was better than leaving Neecy here, even getting her to a hotel. Maybe just for a day or two.

I couldn't take care of both of them now. I had to choose the child.

"Neecy?" The bedroom door was open only a crack, and I pressed my palm against it to nudge it open. "Sweetheart, are you in here?"

What struck me first was the books. Shelves filled with the colorful spines of children's books reached the ceiling of the crowded room, so high that even an adult would need a stepladder. Every other space was occupied by so many toys—costumed dolls, clowns, stuffed animals— that I thought of the time my parents took me to F.A.O. Schwarz when I was a kid, the way every square foot was filled with a different kind of magic.

The bed was piled high with dresses. There must have been dozens of them, many of them formal, old-fashioned tea dresses. They were the kind of dresses mothers hated to wear when they were young, and yet love to adorn their little girls with; made of stiff, uncomfortable fabrics and bright, precious colors. Somewhere beneath that heaping pile of clothes, I saw a suitcase yawning open, struggling uselessly to swallow them all.

"Neecy?"

The closet. I heard a sound from the closet, a child's wet sniffle.

Neecy, why are you in the closet? Did your daddy beat you again?

She was there, inside a closet stripped of everything except a few wire hangers swinging lazily from the rack above her head. I couldn't help it; my face fell slack when I saw her. I felt as if my veins had been drained of blood, flushed with ice water instead.

Over the years, I'd talked to little Neecy on the telephone at least once a month, whenever I called Denise. I was her godmother, after all. Neecy was old enough now that she usually answered the phone, and she chatted obligingly about school and her piano, acting and computer lessons, before saying, *Want to talk to Mommy?* And the child always sounded so prim, so full of private-school self-assuredness, free of any traces of Denise's hushed, halting—the word, really, was *fearful*—way of speaking. It wasn't so strange on the phone, with the image so blurry on the face screen. Not at all.

But being here, seeing her in person, was something else.

Neecy's hair was parted into two neat, shiny pigtails that coiled around the back of her neck, her nose had a tiny bulb at the end, and her molasses-brown eyes were set apart just like I remembered them. If the girl had been grinning instead of crying right now, she would look exactly as she'd looked in the photograph someone had taken of us at my sixth birthday party, the one where Mama hired a clown to do magic tricks and pull cards out of thin air, and we'd both believed the magic was real.

Denise was in the closet. She was six years old again, reborn.

I'd known what to expect the whole time, but I couldn't have been prepared for how it would feel to see her again. I hadn't known how the years would melt from my mind like vapors, how it would fill my stomach with stones to end up staring at my childhood's biggest heartache eye-to-eye.

Somehow, I found a voice in my dry, burning throat. "Hey, sweetie. It's Aunt Paige. From California."

"What's wrong with my mommy?" A brave whisper.

"She's just very upset right now, Neecy." Saying the name, my veins thrilled again.

"Where'd Daddy go?"

I knelt so that I could literally stare her in the eye, and I was reminded of how, twenty-five years ago, Neecy's eyelids always puffed when she cried, narrowing her eyes into slits. China-girl, I used to tease her to try to make her laugh. Here was my China-girl.

I clasped the child's tiny, damp hands; the mere act of touching her caused the skin on my arms to harden into gooseflesh. "I'm not sure where your daddy is, sweetie. He'll come back."

Hey, Neecy, don't cry. He'll come back.

Staring into Neecy's anguish, for the first time, I understood everything.

I understood what a glistening opportunity had stirred Denise's soul when she'd realized her salvation had arrived courtesy of science: a legal procedure to extract a nucleus from a single cell, implant it into an egg, and enable her to give new birth to any living person who consented— even to herself. She could take an inventory of everything that had gone wrong, systematically fix it all, and see what would blossom this time. See what might have been.

And now, gazing into Neecy's eyes—the *same* eyes, except younger, not worn to sludge like the Neecy quivering under a blanket in the living room—I understood why Denise was possibly insane by now. She'd probably been insane longer than I wanted to admit.

"Listen," I said. "Your mom told me to take you to get some pizza. And then she wants us to go to my hotel for a couple of days, until she feels better."

"Will she be okay?" Neecy asked. Her teary eyes were sharp and focused.

Yes, I realized, it was *these* tears ripping Denise's psyche to shreds. This was what Denise could not bear to look at, what was making her physically ill. She was not ready to watch her child, herself, taken apart hurt by hurt. Again.

Neecy was dressed in a lemon-colored party dress as if it were her birthday, or Easter Sunday. Did Denise dress her like this every day? Did she wake Neecy up in the mornings and smile on herself while she reclaimed that piece, too? Of course. Oh, yes, she did. Suddenly, I swooned. I felt myself sway with a near-religious euphoria, my spirit filling up with something I couldn't name. I only kept my balance by cling-ing to the puffed shoulders of the child's taffeta dress, as if I'd made a clumsy attempt to hug her.

"Neecy? It's all right this time," I heard myself tell her in a breathless whisper. "I promise I'll watch out for you. Just like I said. It's all right now, Neecy. Okay? I promise."

I clasped my best friend's hand, rubbing her small knuckles back and forth beneath my chin like a salve. With my hand squeezing her thumb, I could feel the lively, pulsing throbbing of Neecy's other heart.

GREEDY CHOKE PUPPY

Nalo Hopkinson

(2000)

"I see a Lagahoo last night. In the back of the house, behind the pigeon peas."

"Yes, Granny." Sitting cross-legged on the floor, Jacky leaned back against her grandmother's knees and closed her eyes in bliss against the gentle tug of Granny's hands braiding her hair. Jacky still enjoyed this evening ritual, even though she was a big hard-back woman, thirty-two years next month.

The moon was shining in through the open jalousie windows, bringing the sweet smell of Ladies-of-the-Night flowers with it. The ceiling fan beat its soothing rhythm.

"How you mean, 'Yes, Granny'? You even know what a Lagahoo is?"

"Don't you been frightening me with jumby story from since I small? Is a donkey with gold teeth, wearing a waistcoat with a pocket watch and two pair of tennis shoes on the hooves."

"Washekong, you mean. I never teach you to say 'tennis shoes.'"

Jacky smiled. "Yes, Granny. So, what the Lagahoo was doing in the pigeon peas patch?"

"Just standing, looking at my window. Then he pull out he watch chain from out he waistcoat pocket, and he look at the time, and he put the watch back, and he bite off some pigeon peas from off one bush, and he walk away."

Jacky laughed, shaking so hard that her head pulled free of Granny's hands. "You mean to tell me that a Lagahoo come all the way to we little house in Diego Martin, just to sample we so-so pigeon peas?" Still chuckling, she settled back against Granny's knees. Granny tugged at a hank of Jacky's hair, just a little harder than necessary.

Jacky could hear the smile in the old woman's voice. "Don't get fresh with me. You turn big woman now, Ph.D. student and thing, but is still your old nen-nen who does plait up your hair every evening, oui?"

"Yes, Granny. You know I does love to make mako 'pon you, to tease you a little."

"This ain't no joke, child. My mammy used to say that a Lagahoo is God horse, and when you see one, somebody go dead. The last time I see one is just before your mother dead." The two women fell silent. The memory hung in the air between them, of the badly burned body retrieved from the wreckage of the car that had gone off the road. Jacky knew that her grandmother would soon change the subject. She blamed herself for the argument that had sent Jacky's mother raging from the house in the first place. And whatever Granny didn't want to think about, she certainly wasn't going to talk about.

Granny sighed. "Well, don't fret, doux-doux. Just be careful when you go out so late at night. I couldn't stand to lose you, too."

She finished off the last braid and gently stroked Jacky's head. "All right. I finish now. Go and wrap up your head in a scarf, so the plaits will stay nice while you sleeping."

"Thank you, Granny. What I would do without you to help me make myself pretty for the gentlemen, eh?"

Granny smiled, but with a worried look on her face. "You just mind your studies. It have plenty of time to catch man."

Jacky stood and gave the old woman a kiss on one cool, soft cheek and headed toward her bedroom in search of a scarf. Behind her, she could hear Granny settling back into the faded wicker armchair, muttering distractedly to herself, "Why this Lagahoo come to bother me again, eh?"

The first time, I ain't know what was happening to me. I was younger them times there, and sweet for so, you see? Sweet like julie mango, with two ripe tot-tot on the front of my body and two ripe maami-apple behind. I only had was to walk down the street, twitching that maami-apple behind, and all the boys-them on the street corner would watch at me like them was starving, and I was food.

But I get to find out know how it is when the boys stop making sweet eye at you so much, and start watching after a next younger thing. I get to find out that when you pass you prime, and you ain't catch no man eye, nothing ain't left for you but to get old and dry-up like cane leaf in the fire. Is just so I was feeling that night. Like something wither-up. Like something that once used to drink in the feel of the sun on it skin, but now it dead and dry, and the sun only drying it out more. And the feeling make a burning in me belly, and the burning spread out to my skin, till I couldn't take it no more. I jump up from my little bed just so in the middle of the night, and snatch off my nightie. And when I do so, my skin come with it, and drop off on the floor. Inside my skin I was just one big ball of fire, and Lord, the night air feel nice and cool on the flame! I know then I was a soucouyant, a hag-woman. I know what I had was to do. When your youth start to leave you, you have to steal more from somebody who still have plenty. I fly out the window and start to search, search for a newborn baby.

"Lagahoo? You know where that word come from, ain't, Jacky?" asked Carmen Lewis, the librarian in the humanities section of the Library of the University of the West Indies. Carmen leaned back in her chair behind the information desk, legs sprawled under the bulge of her advanced pregnancy.

Carmen was a little older than Jacky. They had known each other since they were girls together at Saint Alban's Primary School. Carmen was always very interested in Jacky's research. "Is French creole for werewolf. Only we could come up with something as jokey as a were-donkey, oui? And as far as I know, it doesn't change into a human being. Why does your Granny think she saw one in the backyard?"

"You know Granny, Carmen. She sees all kinds of things, duppy and jumby and things like that. Remember the duppy stories she used to tell us when we were small, so we would be scared and mind what she said?"

Carmen laughed. "And the soucouyant, don't forget that." She smiled a strange smile. "It didn't really frighten me, though. I always wondered what it would be like to take your skin off, leave your worries behind, and fly so free."

"Well, you sit there so and wonder. I have to keep researching this paper. The back issues come in yet?"

"Right here." Sighing with the effort of bending over, Carmen reached under the desk and pulled out a stack of slim bound volumes of *Huracan*, a Caribbean literary journal that was now out of print. A smell of wormwood and age rose from them. In the 1940s, *Huracan* had published a series of issues on folktales. Jacky hoped that these would provide her with more research material.

"Thanks, Carmen." She picked up the volumes and looked around for somewhere to sit. There was an empty private carrel, but there was also a free space at one of the large study tables. Terry was sitting there, head bent over a fat textbook. The navy blue of his shirt suited his skin, made it glow like a newly unwrapped chocolate. Jacky smiled. She went over to the desk, tapped Terry on the shoulder. "I could sit beside you, Terry?"

Startled, he looked up to see who had interrupted him. His handsome face brightened with welcome. "Uh, sure, no problem. Let me get . . ." He leapt to pull out the chair for her, overturning his own in the process. At the crash, everyone in the library looked up. "Shit." He bent over to pick up the chair. His glasses fell from his face. Pens and pencils rained from his shirt pocket.

Jacky giggled. She put her books down, retrieved Terry's glasses just before he would have stepped on them. "Here." She put the spectacles onto his face, let the warmth of her fingertips linger briefly at his temples.

Terry stepped back, sat quickly in the chair, even though it was still at an odd angle from the table. He crossed one leg over the other. "Sorry," he muttered bashfully. He bent over, reaching awkwardly for the scattered pens and pencils.

"Don't fret, Terry. You just collect yourself and come and sit back down next to me." Jacky glowed with the feeling of triumph. Half an hour of studying beside him, and she knew she'd have a date for lunch. She sat, opened a copy of *Huracan*, and read:

SOUCOUYANT/OL' HIGUE (Trinidad/Guyana)

Caribbean equivalent of the vampire myth. "Soucouyant," or "blood-sucker," derives from the French verb "sucer," to suck. "Ol' Higue" is the Guyanese creole expression for an old hag, or witch woman. The soucouyant is usually an old, evil-tempered woman who removes her skin at night, hides it, and then changes into a ball of fire. She flies through the air, searching for homes in which there are babies. She then enters the house through an open window or a keyhole, goes into the child's room, and sucks the life from its body. She may visit one child's bedside a number of times, draining a little more life each time, as the frantic parents search for a cure, and the child gets progressively weaker and finally dies. Or she may kill all at once.

The smell of the soup Granny was cooking made Jacky's mouth water. She sat at Granny's wobbly old kitchen table, tracing her fingers along a familiar burn, the one shaped like a handprint. The wooden table had been Granny's as long as Jacky could remember. Grandpa had made the table for Granny long before Jacky was born. Diabetes had finally been the death of him. Granny had brought only the kitchen table and her clothing with her when she moved in with Jacky and her mother.

Granny looked up from the cornmeal and flour dough she was kneading. "Like you idle, doux-doux," she said. She slid the bowl of dough over to Jacky. "Make the dumplings, then, nuh?"

Jacky took the bowl over to the stove, started pulling off pieces of dough and forming it into little cakes.

"Andrew make this table for me with he own two hand," Granny said.

"I know. You tell me already."

Granny ignored her. "Forty-two years we married, and every Sunday, I chop up the cabbage for the saltfish on this same table. Forty-two years we eat Sunday morning breakfast right here so. Saltfish and cabbage with a little small-leaf thyme from the back garden, and fry dumpling and cocoa-tea. I miss he too bad. You grandaddy did full up me life, make me feel young."

Jacky kept forming the dumplings for the soup. Granny came over to the stove and stirred the large pot with her wooden spoon. She blew on the spoon, cautiously tasted some of the liquid in it, and carefully floated a whole ripe Scotch Bonnet pepper on top of the bubbling mixture. "Jacky, when you put the dumpling-them in, don't break the pepper, all right? Otherwise this soup going to make we bawl tonight for pepper."

"Mm. Ain't Mummy used to help you make soup like this on a Saturday?"

"Yes, doux-doux. Just like this." Granny hobbled back to sit at the kitchen table. Tiny graying braids were escaping the confinement of her stiff black wig. Her knobby legs looked frail in their too-beige stockings. Like so many of the old women that Jacky knew, Granny always wore stockings rolled down below the hems of her worn flower print shifts. "I thought you was going out tonight," Granny said. "With Terry."

"We break up," Jacky replied bitterly. "He say he not ready to settle down." She dipped the spoon into the soup, raised it to her mouth, spat it out when it burned her mouth. "Backside!"

Granny watched, frowning. "Greedy puppy does choke. You mother did always taste straight from the hot stove, too. I was forever telling she to take time. You come in just like she, always in a hurry. Your eyes bigger than your stomach."

Jacky sucked in an irritable breath. "Granny, Carmen have a baby boy last night. Eight pounds, four ounces. Carmen make she first baby already. I past thirty years old, and I ain't find nobody yet."

"You will find, Jacky. But you can't hurry people so. Is how long you and Terry did stepping out?"

Jacky didn't respond.

"Eh, Jacky? How long?"

"Almost a month."

"Is scarcely two weeks, Jacky, don't lie to me. The boy barely learn where to find your house, and you was pestering he to settle down already. Me and your grandfather court for two years before we went to Parson to marry we."

When Granny started like this, she could go on for hours. Sullenly, Jacky began to drop the raw dumplings one by one into the fragrant, boiling soup.

"Child, you pretty, you have flirty ways, boys always coming and looking for you. You could pick and choose until you find the right one. Love will come. But take time. Love your studies, look out for your friends-them. Love your old Granny," she ended softly.

Hot tears rolled down Jacky's cheeks. She watched the dumplings bobbing back to the surface as they cooked; little warm, yellow suns.

"A new baby," Granny mused. "I must go and visit Carmen, take she some crab and callaloo to strengthen she blood. Hospital food does make you weak, oui."

I need more time, more life. I need a baby breath. Must wait till people sleeping, though. Nobody awake to see a fireball flying up from the bedroom window.

The skin only confining me. I could feel it getting old, binding me up inside it. Sometimes I does just feel to take it off and never put it back on again, oui?

Three A.M. 'Fore day morning. Only me and the duppies going to be out this late. Up from out of the narrow bed, slip off the nightie, slip off the skin.

Oh, God, I does be so free like this! Hide the skin under the bed, and fly out the jalousie window. The night air cool, and I flying so high. I know how many people it have in each house, and who sleeping. I could feel them, skin-bag people, breathing out their life, one-one breath. I know where it have a new one, too: down on Vanderpool Lane. Yes, over here. Feel it, the new one, the baby. So much life in that little body.

Fly down low now, right against the ground. Every door have a crack, no matter how small.

Right here. Slip into the house. Turn back into a woman. Is a nasty feeling, walking around with no skin, wet flesh dripping onto the floor, but I get used to it after so many years.

Here. The baby bedroom. Hear the young breath heating up in he lungs, blowing out, wasting away. He ain't know how to use it; I go take it.

Nice baby boy, so fat. Drink, soucouyant. Suck in he warm, warm life. God, it sweet. It sweet can't done. It sweet.

No more? I drink all already? But what a way this baby dead fast!

Childbirth was once a risky thing for both mother and child. Even when they both survived the birth process, there were many unknown infectious diseases to which newborns were susceptible. Oliphant theorizes that the soucouyant lore was created in an attempt to explain infant deaths that would have seemed mysterious in more primitive times. Grieving parents could blame their loss on people who wished them ill. Women tend to have longer life spans than men, but in a superstitious age where life was hard and brief, old women in a community could seem sinister. It must have been easy to believe that the women were using sorcerous means to prolong their lives, and how better to do that than to steal the lifeblood of those who were very young?

Dozing, Jacky leaned against Granny's knees. Outside, the leaves of the julie mango tree rustled and sighed in the evening breeze. Granny tapped on Jacky's shoulder, passed her a folded section of newspaper with a column circled. *Births/Deaths.* Granny took a bitter pleasure in keeping track of who she'd outlived each week. Sleepily, Jacky focused on the words on the page:

Deceased: Raymond George Lewis, 5 days old, of natural causes. Son of Michael and Carmen, Diego Martin, Port of Spain. Funeral service 5:00 p.m. November 14, Church of the Holy Redeemer.

"Jesus. Carmen's baby! But he was healthy, don't it?"

"I don't know, doux-doux. They say he just stop breathing in the night. Just so. What a sad thing. We must go to the funeral, pay we respects."

Sunlight is fatal to the soucouyant. She must be back in her skin before daylight. In fact, the best way to discover a soucouyant is to find her skin, rub the raw side with hot pepper, and replace it in its hiding place. When she tries to put it back on, the pain of the burning pepper will cause the demon to cry out and reveal herself.

Me fire belly full, oui. When a new breath fueling the fire, I does feel good, like I could never die. And then I does fly and fly, high like the moon. Time to go back home now, though.

Eh-eh! Why she leave the back door cotch open? Never mind; she does be preoccupied sometimes. Maybe she just forget. Just fly in the bedroom window. I go close the door after I put on my skin again.

Ai! What itching me so? Is what happen to me skin? Ai! Lord, Lord, it burning, it burning too bad. It scratching me all over, like it have fire ants inside there. I can't stand it!

Hissing with pain, the soucouyant threw off her burning skin and stood flayed, dripping.

Calmly, Granny entered Jacky's room. Before Jacky could react, Granny picked up the Jacky-skin. She held it close to her body, threatening the skin with the sharp, wicked kitchen knife she held in her other hand. Her look was sorrowful.

"I know it was you, doux-doux. When I see the Lagahoo, I know what I have to do."

Jacky cursed and flared to fireball form. She rushed at Granny, but backed off as Granny made a feint at the skin with her knife.

"You stay right there and listen to me, Jacky. The soucouyant blood in all of we, all the women in we family."

You, too?

"Even me. We blood hot: hot for life, hot for youth. Loving does cool we down. Making life does cool we down."

Jacky raged. The ceiling blackened, began to smoke.

"I know how it go, doux-doux. When we lives empty, the hunger does turn to blood hunger. But it have plenty other kinds of loving, Jacky. Ain't I been telling you so? Love your work. Love people close to you. Love your life."

The fireball surged toward Granny. "No. Stay right there, you hear? Or I go chop this skin for you."

Granny backed out through the living room. The hissing ball of fire followed close, drawn by the precious skin in the old woman's hands.

"You never had no patience. Doux-doux, you is my life, but you can't kill so. That little child you drink, you don't hear it spirit when night come, bawling for Carmen and Michael? I does weep to hear it. I try to tell you, like I try to tell you mother: Don't be greedy."

Granny had reached the back door. The open back door. The soucouyant made a desperate feint at Granny's knife arm, searing her right side from elbow to scalp. The smell of burnt flesh and hair filled the little kitchen, but though the old lady cried out, she wouldn't drop the knife. The pain in her voice was more than physical.

"You devil!" She backed out the door into the cobalt light of early morning. Gritting her teeth, she slashed the Jacky-skin into two ragged halves and flung it into the pigeon peas patch. Jacky shrieked and turned back into her flayed self. Numbly, she picked up her skin, tried with oozing fingers to put the torn edges back together.

"You and me is the last two," Granny said. "Your mami woulda make three, but I had to kill she, too, send my own flesh and blood into the sun. Is time, doux-doux. The Lagahoo calling you."

My skin! Granny, how you could do me so? Oh, God, morning coming already? Yes, could feel it, the sun calling to the fire in me.

Jacky threw the skin down again, leapt as a fireball into the brightening air. *I going, going, where I could burn clean, burn bright, and allyou could go to the Devil, oui!*

Fireball flying high to the sun, and oh, God, it burning, it burning, it burning!

*   *   *

Granny hobbled to the pigeon peas patch, wincing as she cradled her burnt right side. Tears trickled down her wrinkled face. She sobbed, "Why allyou must break my heart so?"

Painfully, she got down to her knees beside the ruined pieces of skin and placed one hand on them. She made her hand glow red hot, igniting her granddaughter's skin. It began to burn, crinkling and curling back on itself like bacon in a pan. Granny wrinkled her nose against the smell, but kept her hand on the smoking mass until there was nothing but ashes. Her hand faded back to its normal cocoa brown. Clambering to her feet again, she looked about her in the pigeon peas patch.

"I live to see the Lagahoo two time. Next time, God horse, you better be coming for me."

Rhythm Travel

Amiri Baraka

(1996)

Your boy always do that. You knock, somebody say come in. You open the door, look around, call out, nobody there. You think!

But then, at once, music come on. If you watching, there's a bluish shaking that flickers—maybe "Misterioso" will surround you. The music is wavering like light. The room seems to shift to step.

Then you recognize what you hear: yo' man. "Aw, brother, you at it again. You in here, ain't you?"

A laugh. This dude.

"Yeh, I'm in here, you hear me. You feel me. Here I am."

He appears, laughing. And pointing at you. "Hey, man. I'm still developing this."

"What you call this?"

"Anyscape. The first one. Molecular Anyscape. The RE soulocator—that was the improvement. T-Dis-Appear. Nick names. Perfect Nigger. American Citizen. Ellisonic. Migration. I got a name for each step."

"And now?" I rolled my eyes as he materialized before me, dissing the Dis Report on Appearance.

"This is next to last. I can dis appear, dis visibility. Be un seen. But now, I can be around anyway. Perceived, felt, heard. I can be the music! How they gon' steal it, if it's me? Yeh. But now I got something even heavier!"

This dude is out—it ain't no jive. He had done those things, and he never swore me to secrecy either. He just fixed it so I couldn't remember nothing, except when I came back.

"Further out? The cloth refiner?" He said he needed to make the cloth fade more so he could get in and out the bank without any hysteria. I figured it took a few hundred thousand to get where he was technically.

"How come they don't detect the money splitting?"

"Well, I ain't been able to stabilize the cloth thing. Sometimes people see the money floating and go off. But I still get away."

"How come they don't say nothin?"

"Well, it's hard to explain, I guess. Floating money. They studying it."

"Oh!"

"A few weeks more. I'll rob the mammyjammas clean!"

"Wow!" I thought of a stream of exclamations, but I could only analyze it while hearing it. I needed to reflect, but your boy wouldn't allow it.

"But now, B. dig this! I pushed the anyscape into rhythm spectroscopic transformation. And then I got it tuned to combine the anywhereness and the reappearance as Music!"

"What? You know, brother, this is some deep technical stuff."

"Aw, no it ain't. It's science. I can teach people how to make and use these . . ."

"What?"

"Now I added Rhythm Travel! You can Dis Appear and Re Appear wherever and whenever that music played."

"What?"

"So if you become 'Black, Brown & Beige,' you can Re Appear anywhere and anytime that plays."

"Go anywhere?"

"Yeh, like if I go into 'Take This Hammer,' I can appear wherever that is, was, will be sung."

"Yeh, but be that song, you be on a plantation . . ."

"I know." He was grinning. "I went to one." He was staring me down, winking without his eye.

"I seen some brothers and sisters digging a well. They were singing this, and I begin to echo. A big hollow echo. A sorta blue shattering echo. The Bloods got to smilin. Because it made them feel good, and that's the way they heard it anyway.

"But the overseers and plantation masters winced at that. They'd turn their heads sharply back and forth, looking behind them and at the slaves. Man, the stuff I seen!"

"You mean you been rhythm traveling already?"

"Yeh. I turned into some Sun Ra and hung out, inside gravity. You probably heard of the scatting comet. Babs was into that."

"Really? Man . . . so?"

"I know. Why? What I'm gonna do with it? Yeh, but I'm just explaining now. I got a lotta tests."

"I guess so."

"But, I want you to try it."

"Hey now . . ." I backed up a bit.

"Hey brother," he said, grinning with that wink of his. "Ain't no danger. Just don't pick no corny tune."

BUDDY BOLDEN

Kalamu ya Salaam

(2000)

a bunch of us were astral traveling, pulsating on the flow of a wicked elvinesque polyrhythmic 6/8 groove. although our physical eyes had disappeared from our faces, we still had wry eyebrows arched like quarter moons or miniature ram's horns. every molecule of our thirsty skin was a sensitive ear drinking in the vibes. at each stroke of sweat-slicked drumstick on skins, our wings moved in syncopated grace. shimmering cymbal vibrations illuminated the night so green bright we could feel the trembling emerald through the soles of our feet. deep red pulsing bass sounds throbbed from our right brain lobes, lifting us and shooting us quickly across the eons. we moved swiftly as comets, quiet as singing starlight.

as we neared the motherwomb, firefly angels came out to escort us to the inner sanctum. with eager anticipation i smelled a banquet of hip, growling, intense quarter notes when we entered the compound. a hand-carved coconut-shell bowl brimming with hot melodies radiating a tantalizing aroma sat steaming at each place setting, heralding our arrival. whenever i rode this deeply into the music, i would never want to return back to places of broken notes and no natural drums.

on my way here i heard nidia, who was in a prison in el salvador. she had been shot, captured. her tormentors were torturing her with continuous questions, sleep deprivation, psychological cruelty, and assassination attempts against her family. she sang songs to stay strong. singing in prison, i dug that.

once we made touchdown, we kissed the sweetearth (which tasted like three parts blackstrap molasses and one part chalky starch with a dash of sharply tart orange rind) and smeared red clay in our hair. then lay in the sun for a few days listening to duke ellington every morning before bathing. i was glad to see otis redding flashing his huge carefree smiles and splashing around in the blue lagoon. finally after hugging the baobab tree (the oldest existing life force) for twenty-four hours we were ready to glide inside and hang with the children again. whenever one returned from planet earth, we had to take a lot of precautions. you never know what kinds of human logic you might be infected with. since i had spent most of my last assignment checking out far-flung galaxies, on my first examination i was able to dance through the scanner with nary a miscue. my soul was cool.

i only had ten centuries to recuperate before returning to active rotation, so i was eager to eat. the house was abuzz with vibrations. a hefty-thighed cook came in and tongue-kissed each of us seated at the mahogany table, male and female, young and old, whatever. that took about six centuries. she was moving on cp time and when i tasted her kiss i understood why.

up close her skin was deeper than a sunken slave ship and glowed with the glitter of golddust pressed across her brow and on the sides of her face just above her cheekline. she wore a plum-sized chunk of orangish yellow amber as a pendant, held in place by a chain braided from the mane of a four-hundred-pound lion. her head was divided into sixteen sectors each with a ball of threaded hair tied in nubian knots, each knot exactly the same size as the spherical amber perfectly poised in the hollow of her throat. i was so stunned by the beauty force of her haunting entrance, i had to chant to calm myself.

"drink deeply the water from an ancient well," was all she said as she spun in slow circles. tiny bells dangled between the top of the curvaceous protrudence of her posterior and the bottom of the concavity of the arch in the small of her back where it met her waist and flared outward to the expanse of her sturdy hips. suspended from a cord she wore around her waist, the hand-carved, solid gold bells gave off a diminutive but distinctive jingle which rose and fell with each step.

emanating a bluegreen aura of contentment, she didn't look like she had ever, in any of her many lifetimes, done anything compromising such as vote for a capitalist (of whatever color) or succumb to the expediency of accepting any system of domination. she didn't say a word, instead she hummed without disrupting the smiling fullness of her lips. she wasn't ashamed of her big feet as she stepped flatfootedly around the table, a slender gold ring on the big toe of each foot.

her almond-shaped, kola-nut-colored eyes sauntered up to each of our individualities, sight-read our diverse memories, and swam in the sea of whatever sorrows we had experienced. she silently drank all our bitter tears and became pregnant with our hopes. she looked like she had never ever worn clothes and instead had spent her whole life moving about in the glorious garment of a nudity so natural she seemed like a miracle you had to prepare yourself to witness as she innocently and righteously strode through the sun, moon, and star light.

when she neared me she effortlessly slinked into a crouched, garden-tending posture and, with sharp thrusting arm movements, choreographed an improvised welcome dance. (how else, except by improvisation, could her movements mirror everything i was thinking?) placing my ear to her distended stomach, i guessed six months. she arched her back. a ring shout undulated from her womb. i got so excited i had to sit on my wings to keep still.

when she stood up to her full six-foot height with her lithe arms akimbo, i couldn't help responding. i got an erection when she placed her hand on the top of my head. she laughed at my arousal.

"drink your soup, silly" she teased me, and then laughed again, while gently tracing her fingers across my face, down the side of my neck, and swiftly brushing my upper torso, briefly petting the hummingbird rapidity of my chest muscle twitches. and then the program began.

a few years after monk danced in, coltrane said the blessing in his characteristic slow solemn tone. you know how coltrane talks. as usual, he didn't eat much. but we were filled with wonder anyway. then bob chrisman from the black scholar gave a short speech on one becomes two when the raindrop splits. everybody danced in a͵ppreciation of his insights.

when we resumed our places, the child next to me reflected aloud, "always remember you are a starchild. you will become any reality that you get with unless you influence that reality to become you. we have no power but osmosis and vibrations. as long as you don't forget your essence, it's all right to live inside something else." the child hugged me while extrapolating chrisman's message.

a voice on the intercom was calling for volunteers to help move the mountain even though i wasn't through with my soup and still had a couple of centuries left, i rose immediately. i had drunk enough to imagine going up against the people who couldn't clap on two and four. "earth is very dangerous," the voice intoned. "the humans have the power to induce both amnesia and psychic dislocation."

the child smiled at me and sang, "i'll wait for you where human eyes have never seen." we only had time to sing 7,685 choruses because i had to hurry to earth. our spirits there were up against some mighty powerful forces and the ngoma badly needed reinforcements. but i took a couple of months to thank the chef for sitting me next to the child.

"no thanx needed. i simply gave back to you what you gave to me." then in a divine gesture she lovingly touched each of my four sacred drums: head, heart, gut, and groin. cupping them warmly in both her hands, she slow-kissed an eternal rhythm into each. before i could say anything she was gone, humming the child's song: ". . . where human eyes have never seen, i'll wait for you. i'll wait for you."

i got to earth shortly after 1947 started. people were still making music then. back in 1999 machines manufactured music. real singing was against the law.

walking down the street one day i saw what i assumed was a soul sister. she was humming a simple song. i sensed she was possibly one of us. she looked like a chef except with chemically altered hair on her mind in-stead of black puffs of natural nubianity. i spoke anyway. she walked right through me.

i turned around to see where she had gone. but she was gone. i looked up and i was on the bandstand. i was billie holiday. every pain i ever felt was sobbing out of my throat. i looked at my blueblack face. the fist splotches from where my man had hit me.

> "I'd rather
> for my man
> to hit me,
>   than
>   for him
> to jump
>   up
> and quit me."

i sang through the pain of a broken jaw.

"have you ever loved somebody who didn't know how to love you?" i asked the audience. in what must have been some kind of american rit-ual, everyone held up small, round hand mirrors and intently peered into their looking glass. the music stopped momentarily as if i had stumbled into a bucket of moonlit blood. my left leg started trembling. every word felt like it was ripped from my throat with pieces of my flesh hanging off each note. i almost fainted from the pain, but i couldn't stop singing because whenever i paused, even if only for a moment, the thought of suicide pressed me to the canvas. and you know i couldn't lay there waiting for the eight count, knocked out like some chump. i was stronger than these earthlings. i had to get up and keep on singing, but to keep on making music took so much energy. i was almost ex-hausted. and when i stopped, the pain was deafening. exhausting to sing. painful to stop. this was a far heavier experience than i had fore-seen.

i kept singing, but i also felt myself growing weaker. drained. "i say, have you ever given your love to a rascal that didn't give a damn about you?"

this was insane. when would i be able to stop? there was so much money being exchanged that i was having a hard time breathing. i could feel my soul growing dimmer, the pain beginning to creep through even while i was singing. so this was what the angels meant by "hell is being silenced by commerce." legal tender was choking me.

for a moment i felt human, but luckily the band started playing again. some lame colored cat had crawled up on the stage and was thawing out frozen conservatory school clichés. made my bunions groan. but i guess when you're human you got to go through a lot of trial and error. especially when you're young in earth years. the whole time i was on that scene i felt sorry for the children. most of them had never seen their parents make love.

humans spend a lot of their early years playing all kinds of games to prepare themselves to play all kinds of games when they grow up. the child-rearing atmosphere was so dense the only thing little people could do was lie awake naked under the covers and play with themselves but only whenever the adults weren't watching cause if those poor kids got caught touching each other, they were beaten. can you imagine that?

damn, i thought smelly horn wasn't ever going to stop, prez had to pull his coat, "hey shorty, don't take so long to say so little."

as soon as the cat paused, i jumped in, "have you ever loved somebody . . ." yes, i had volunteered, but i had no idea making music on earth would be this taxing.

when our set ended, i stumbled from the stand totally disoriented. by now i almost needed to constantly make music in order to twirl my gyroscope and keep it spinning. after the set, i found it very difficult to act like a human and sit still while talking to the customers. i kept wanting to hover and hum. but i went through the changes, even did an interview.

"the only way out is to go through it all," i found myself saying to an english reporter who was looking at me with insane eyes.

he did his best to sing. "you've been hurt by white people in america and i want to let you know that there are white people who love and respect you." i could hear his eyes as clear as sid catlett's drum. i appreciated his attempts, but those were some stiff-assed paradiddles he was beating. the youngster was still in his teens and offered me a handkerchief to wipe the pain off my face. i waved it away, that little bandanna wouldn't even dry up so much as one teardrop of my sadness. at that moment what i really needed was a lift cause the scene was a drag.

"the only way to go through it all is to go through it all. yaknow. survive it and sing about it," i said, holding the side of my head in the cup of my hand and speaking with my eyes half closed and focused on nothing in particular.

"why sing about it?" he said, eager as a pig snouting around for truffles. (even though he wasn't french, i could see he had sex on his mind.)

"cause if you keep the pain within you'll explode." he reached for his wallet about to offer me money. for sure he was a hopeless case. once i dug he didn't understand creativity, i switched to sociology. "millions of people been molested as children." he had been there, done that. he was starting to catch my drift. "men been beating on women. you know i was a slave. that means i was violated. that means i was broke down. that means i would lay there and take it. in and out. lay there. still. i have heard reports that i was a prostitute. but i never sold myself just for money, i lay down because there was no room to stand up. in and out. in and out. till finally, they ejaculated. and finished. for the moment, for the night . . . till . . . whenever." i looked up and his mind was on the other side of the room; i had lost him again.

poor child doesn't have a clue. that's why he's looking all pitiful at me. i couldn't find a way to unfold the whole to him. i wanted to say more, but their language couldn't make the changes. he will probably write a treatise on the downtrodden negro in tomorrow's paper.

sho-nuff, next day—quote:

So-and-so is an incredibly gifted Black American animal. People were actually crying in the audience when she howled "No Body's Bizness" in the voice of a neutered dog. This reporter is a registered theorist on why White people are fascinated by listening to the sounds of their victims' pathetic crying. I had the rare opportunity to interview the jazzy chick. Although she was not very familiar with the basic principles of grammar, I managed to get a few words from her illiterateness once she took some dope which I had been advised to offer her.

I asked her what harmonic system she employed. My publisher had authorized me to offer her music lessons. I quote her answer verbatim.

"I sing because, like the Funky Butt Brass Band used to holler, you got to open up the window and let the bad air out."

That was it. When I turned off my voice-stealing machine, she said, "I got a lot of s——t in me. If I don't get it out, I'll die."

If she doesn't die first, there will be a concert tonight. Cheeri-O.

unquote.

i couldn't wait to get back to the motherwomb. . . .

But, just as I was about to fly, I woke up. I was cuddled next to Nia's nakedness, her back to me, my arm embracing her breasts, and my leg thrown up in touch with the arc of her thighs.

I stared into the deep acorn brown of her braided hair. I couldn't see anything in the unlighted room except the contours of the coiled beautiful darkness of her braids. After a few seconds the sweet familiar scent of the hair oil she used began lulling me back to sleep.

Unfortunately, I didn't have enough sleep time left to continue my flight dreams. And I spent the rest of the day trying to decide . . . no, not decide, but remember. I spent the rest of the day trying to remember whether I was a human who dreamed he was something else or was indeed something else doing a temporary duty assignment here on planet earth.

Aye, and Gomorrah . . .

Samuel R. Delany

(1967)

And came down in Paris:

Where we raced along the Rue de Medicis with Bo and Lou and Muse inside the fence, Kelly and me outside, making faces through the bars, making noise, making the Luxembourg Gardens roar at two in the morning. Then climbed out and down to the square in front of St. Sulpice where Bo tried to knock me into the fountain.

At which point Kelly noticed what was going on around us, got an ashcan cover, and ran into the pissoir, banging the walls. Five guys scooted out; even a big pissoir only holds four.

A very blond young man put his hand on my arm and smiled. "Don't you think, Spacer, that you . . . people should leave?"

I looked at his hand on my blue uniform. *"Est-ce que tu est un frelk?"*

His eyebrows rose, then he shook his head. *"Une frelk,"* he corrected. "No, I am not. Sadly for me. You look as though you may once have been a man. But now . . ." He smiled. "You have nothing for me now. The police." He nodded across the street where I noticed the gendarmerie for the first time. "They don't bother us. You are strangers, though . . ."

But Muse was already yelling. "Hey come on! Let's get out of here, huh?" And left. And went up again.

And came down in Houston:

"God damn!" Muse said. "Gemini Flight Control—you mean this is where it all started? Let's get *out* of here, *please!*"

So took a bus out through Pasadena, then the monoline to Galveston, and were going to take it down the Gulf, but Lou found a couple with a pickup truck—

"Glad to give you a ride, Spacers. You people up there on them planets and things, doing all that good work for the government."

—who were going south, them and the baby, so we rode in the back for two hundred and fifty miles of sun and wind.

"You think they're frelks?" Lou asked, elbowing me. "I bet they're frelks. They're just waiting for us to give 'em the come-on."

"Cut it out. They're a nice, stupid pair of country kids."

"That don't mean they ain't frelks!"

"You don't trust anybody, do you?"

"No."

And finally a bus again that rattled us through Brownsville and across the border into Matamoros where we staggered down the steps into the dust and the scorched evening with a lot of Mexicans and chickens and Texas Gulf shrimp fishermen—who smelled worst—and *we* shouted the loudest. Forty-three whores—I counted—had turned out for the shrimp fishermen, and by the time we had broken two of the windows in the bus station, they were all laughing. The shrimp fishermen said they wouldn't buy us no food but would get us drunk if we wanted, 'cause that was the custom with shrimp fishermen. But we yelled, broke another window; then, while I was lying on my back on the telegraph office steps, singing, a woman with dark lips bent over and put her hands on my cheeks. "You are very sweet." Her rough hair fell forward. "But the men, they are standing around watching *you*. And that is taking up *time*. Sadly, their time is our money. Spacer, do you not think you . . . people should leave?"

I grabbed her wrist. "*Usted!*" I whispered. "*Usted es una frelka?*"

"*Frelko in español.*" She smiled and patted the sunburst that hung from my belt buckle. "Sorry. But you have nothing that . . . would be useful to me. It is too bad, for you look like you were once a woman, no? And I like women, too. . . ."

I rolled off the porch.

"Is this a drag, or is this a drag!" Muse was shouting. "Come *on!* Let's go!"

We managed to get back to Houston before dawn, somehow.

And went up.

And came down in Istanbul:

That morning it rained in Istanbul.

At the commissary we drank our tea from pear-shaped glasses, looking out across the Bosphorus. The Princes Islands lay like trash heaps before the prickly city.

"Who knows their way in this town?" Kelly asked.

"Aren't we going around together?" Muse demanded. "I thought we were going around together."

"They held up my check at the purser's office," Kelly explained. "I'm flat broke. I think the purser's got it in for me," and shrugged. "Don't want to, but I'm going to have to hunt up a rich frelk and come on friendly," went back to the tea; *then* noticed how heavy the silence had become. "Aw, come *on*, now! You gape at me like that and I'll bust every bone in that carefully-conditioned-from-puberty body of yours. Hey you!" meaning me. "Don't give me that holier-than-thou gawk like you never went with no frelk!"

It was starting.

"I'm not gawking," I said and got quietly mad.

The longing, the old longing.

Bo laughed to break tensions. "Say, last time I was in Istanbul—about a year before I joined up with this platoon—I remember we were coming out of Taksim Square down Istiqlal. Just past all the cheap movies we found a little passage lined with flowers. Ahead of us were two other spacers. It's a market in there, and farther down they got fish, and then a courtyard with oranges and candy and sea urchins and cabbage. But flowers in front. Anyway, we noticed something funny about the spacers. It wasn't their uniforms: they were perfect. The haircuts: fine. It wasn't till we heard them talking—They were a man and woman dressed up like spacers, trying *to pick up frelks*! Imagine, queer for frelks!"

"Yeah," Lou said. "I seen that before. There were a lot of them in Rio."

"We beat hell out of them two," Bo concluded. "We got them in a side street and went to *town*!"

Muse's tea glass clicked on the counter. "From Taksim down Istiqlal till you get to the flowers? Now why didn't you say that's where the frelks were, huh?" A smile on Kelly's face would have made that okay. There was no smile.

"Hell," Lou said. "Nobody ever had to tell me where to look. I go out in the street and frelks smell me coming. I can spot 'em halfway along Piccadilly. Don't they have nothing but tea in this place? Where can you get a drink?"

Bo grinned. "Moslem country, remember? But down at the end of the Flower Passage there're a lot of little bars with green doors and marble counters where you can get a liter of beer for about fifteen cents in lira. And there're all these stands selling deep-fat-fried bugs and pig's gut sandwiches—"

"You ever notice how frelks can put it away? I mean liquor, not . . . pig's guts."

And launched off into a lot of appeasing stories. We ended with the one about the frelk some spacer tried to roll who announced: "There're two things I go for. One is spacers; the other is a good fight. . . ."

But they only allay. They cure nothing. Even Muse knew we would spend the day apart, now.

The rain had stopped, so we took the ferry up the Golden Horn. Kelly straight off asked for Taksim Square and Istiqlal and was directed to a dolmush, which we discovered was a taxicab, only it just goes one place and picks up lots and lots of people on the way. And it's cheap.

Lou headed off over Ataturk Bridge to see the sights of New City. Bo decided to find out what the Bolma Boche really was; and when Muse discovered you could go to Asia for fifteen cents—one lira and fifty krush—well, Muse decided to go to Asia.

I turned through the confusion of traffic at the head of the bridge and up past the gray, dripping walls of Old City, beneath the trolley wires. There are times when yelling and helling won't fill the lack. There are times when you must walk by yourself because it hurts so much to be alone.

I walked up a lot of little streets with wet donkeys and wet camels and women in veils; and down a lot of big streets with buses and trash baskets and men in business suits.

Some people stare at spacers; some people don't. Some people stare or don't stare in a way a spacer gets to recognize within a week after coming out of training school at sixteen. I was walking in the park when I caught her watching. She saw me and looked away.

I ambled down the wet asphalt. She was standing under the arch of a small, empty mosque shell. As I passed, she walked out into the court-yard among the cannons.

"Excuse me."

I stopped.

"Do you know whether or not this is the shrine of St. Irene?" Her English was charmingly accented. "I've left my guidebook home."

"Sorry. I'm a tourist too."

"Oh." She smiled. "I am Greek. I thought you might be Turkish be-cause you are so dark."

"American red Indian." I nodded. Her turn to curtsy.

"I see. I have just started at the university here in Istanbul. Your uni-form, it tells me that you are"—and the pause, all speculations re-solved—"a spacer."

I was uncomfortable. "Yeah." I put my hands in my pockets, moved my feet around on the soles of my boots, licked my third from the rear left molar—did all the things you do when you're uncomfortable. You're so exciting when you look like that, a frelk told me once. "Yeah, I am." I said it too sharply, too loudly, and she jumped a little.

So now she knew I knew she knew I knew, and I wondered how we would play out the Proust bit.

"I'm Turkish," she said. "I'm not Greek. I'm not just starting. I'm a graduate in art history here at the university. These little lies one makes up for strangers to protect one's ego . . . why? Sometimes I think my ego is very small."

That's one strategy.

"How far away do you live?" I asked. "And what's the going rate in Turkish lira?" That's another.

"I can't pay you." She pulled her raincoat around her hips. She was very pretty. "I would like to." She shrugged and smiled. "But I am . . . a poor student. Not a rich one. If you want to turn around and walk away, there will be no hard feelings. I shall be sad though."

I stayed on the path. I thought she'd suggest a price after a little while. She didn't.

And *that's* another.

I was asking myself, *What do you want the damn money for anyway?* when a breeze upset water from one of the park's great cypresses.

"I think the whole business is sad." She wiped drops from her face. There had been a break in her voice, and for a moment I looked too closely at the water streaks. "I think it's sad that they have to alter you to make you a spacer. If they hadn't, then *we*. . . . If spacers had never been, then we could not be . . . the way we are. Did you start out male or female?"

Another shower. I was looking at the ground and droplets went down my collar.

"Male," I said. "It doesn't matter."

"How old are you? Twenty-three, twenty-four?"

"Twenty-three," I lied. It's reflex. I'm twenty-five, but the younger they think you are, the more they pay you. But I didn't want her *damn* money—

"I guessed right then." She nodded. "Most of us are experts on spacers. Do you find that? I suppose we have to be." She looked at me with wide black eyes. At the end of the stare, she blinked rapidly. "You would have been a fine man. But now you are a spacer, building water-conservation units on Mars, programming mining computers on Ganymede, servicing communication relay towers on the moon. The alteration . . ." Frelks are the only people I've ever heard say "the alteration" with so much fascination and regret. "You'd think they'd have found some other solution. They could have found another way of neutering you, turning you into creatures not even androgynous; things that are—"

I put my hand on her shoulder, and she stopped like I'd hit her. She looked to see if anyone was near. Lightly, so lightly then, she raised her hand to mine.

I pulled my hand away. "That are what?"

"They could have found another way." Both hands in her pockets now.

"They could have. Yes. Up beyond the ionosphere, baby, there's too much radiation for those precious gonads to work right anywhere you might want to do something that would keep you there over twenty-four hours, like the moon, or Mars, or the satellites of Jupiter—"

"They could have made protective shields. They could have done more research into biological adjustment—"

"Population Explosion time," I said. "No, they were hunting for an excuse to cut down kids back then—especially deformed ones."

"Ah, yes." She nodded. "We're still fighting our way up from the neopuritan reaction to the sex freedom of the twentieth century."

"It was a fine solution." I grinned and absently rubbed my crotch. "I'm happy with it." I've never known why that's so much more obscene when a spacer does it.

"Stop it," she snapped, moving away.

"What's the matter?"

"Stop it," she repeated. "Don't do that! You're a child."

"But they choose us from children whose sexual responses are hopelessly retarded at puberty."

"And your childish, violent substitutes for love? I suppose that's one of the things that's attractive. You really don't regret you have no sex?"

"We've got you," I said.

"Yes." She looked down. I glanced to see the expression she was hiding. It was a smile. "You have your glorious, soaring life—*and* you have us." Her face came up. She glowed. "You spin in the sky, the world spins under you, and you step from land to land, while we . . ." She turned her head right, left, and her black hair curled and uncurled on the shoulder of her coat. "We have our dull, circled lives, bound in gravity, *worshiping* you!" She looked back at me. "Perverted, yes? In love with a bunch of corpses in free fall!" Suddenly she hunched her shoulders. "I don't like having a free-fall-sexual-displacement complex."

"That always sounded like too much to say."

She looked away. "I don't like being a frelk. Better?"

"I wouldn't like it either. Be something else."

"You don't choose your perversions. *You* have no perversions at all. *You're* free of the whole business. I love you for that, spacer. My love starts with the fear of love. Isn't that beautiful? A pervert substitutes something unattainable for 'normal' love: the homosexual, a mirror, the fetishist, a shoe or a watch or a girdle. Those with free-fall-sexual-dis—"

"Frelks."

"Frelks substitute"— she looked at me sharply again—"loose, swinging meat."

"That doesn't offend me."

"I wanted it to."

"Why?"

"You don't have desires. You wouldn't understand."

"Go on."

"I want you because you can't want me. That's the pleasure. If someone really had a sexual reaction to . . . us, we'd be scared away. I wonder how many people there were before there were you, waiting for your creation. We're necrophiles. I'm sure grave robbing has fallen off since you started going up. But you don't understand. . . ." She paused. "If you did, then I wouldn't be scuffing leaves now and trying to think from whom I could borrow sixty lira." She stepped over the knuckles of a root that had cracked the pavement. "And that, incidentally, is the going rate in Istanbul."

I calculated. "Things still get cheaper as you go east."

"You know," and she let her raincoat fall open, "you're different from the others. You at least *want* to know—"

I said, "If I spat on you for every time you'd said that to a spacer, you'd drown."

"Go back to the moon, loose meat." She closed her eyes. "Swing on up to Mars. There are satellites around Jupiter where you might do some good. Go up and come down in some other city."

"Where do you live?"

"You want to come with me?"

"Give me something," I said. "Give me something—it doesn't have to be worth sixty lira. Give me something that you like, anything of yours that means something to you."

"No!"

"Why not?"

"Because I—"

"—don't want to give up part of that ego. None of you frelks do!"

"You really don't understand I just don't want to buy you?"

"You have nothing to buy me with."

"You are a child," she said. "I love you."

We reached the gate of the park. She stopped, and we stood time enough for a breeze to rise and die in the grass. "I . . ." she offered tentatively, pointing without taking her hand from her coat pocket. "I live right down there."

"All right," I said. "Let's go."

A gas main had once exploded along this street, she explained to me, a gushing road of fire as far as the docks. Overhot and overquick, it had been put out within minutes. No building had fallen, but the charred facias glittered. "This is sort of an artist and student quarter." We crossed the cobbles. "Yuri Pasha, number fourteen. In case you're ever in Istanbul again." Her door was covered with black scales; the gutter was thick with garbage.

"A lot of artists and professional people are frelks," I said, trying to be inane.

"So are lots of other people." She walked inside and held the door. "We're just more flamboyant about it."

On the landing there was a portrait of Ataturk. Her room was on the second floor. "Just a moment while I get my key—"

Moonscapes! Marsscapes! On her easel was a six-foot canvas showing the sunrise flaring on a crater's rim! There were copies of the original Observer pictures of the moon pinned to the wall, and pictures of every smooth-faced general in the International Space Corps.

On one corner of her desk was a pile of those photo magazines about spacers that you can find in most kiosks all over the world: I've seriously heard people say they were printed for adventurous-minded high school children. They've never seen the Danish ones. She had a few of those too. There was a shelf of art books, art history texts. Above them were six feet of cheap paper-covered space operas: *Sin of Space Station #12, Rocket Rake, Savage Orbit.* . . .

"Arrack?" she asked. "Ouzo, or pernod? You've got your choice. But I may pour them all from the same bottle." She set out glasses on the desk, then opened a waist-high cabinet that turned out to be an icebox. She stood up with a tray of lovelies: fruit puddings, Turkish delight, braised meats.

"What's this?"

"Dolmades. Grape leaves filled with rice and pignolias."

"Say it again?"

"Dolmades. Comes from the same Turkish word as 'dolmush.' They both mean 'stuffed.'" She put the tray beside the glasses. "Sit down."

I sat on the studio-couch-that-becomes-bed. Under the brocade I felt the deep, fluid resilience of a glycogel mattress. They've got the idea that it approximates the feeling of free fall. "Comfortable? Would you excuse me for a moment? I have some friends down the hall. I want to see them for a moment." She winked. "They like spacers."

"Are you going to take up a collection for me?" I asked. "Or do you want them to line up outside the door and wait their turn?"

She sucked a breath. "Actually, I was going to suggest both." Suddenly she shook her head. "Oh, what do you want!"

"What will you give me? I want something," I said. "That's why I came. I'm lonely. Maybe I want to find out how far it goes. I don't know yet."

"It goes as far as you will. Me? I study, I read, paint, talk with my friends"—she came over to the bed, sat down on the floor—"go to the theater, look at spacers who pass me on the street, till one looks back; I am lonely too." She put her head on my knee. "I want something. But," and after a minute neither of us had moved, "you are not the one who will give it to me."

"You're not going to pay me for it," I countered. "You're not, are you?"

On my knee her head shook. After a while she said, all breath and no voice, "Don't you think you . . . should leave?"

"Okay," I said, and stood up.

She sat back on the hem of her coat. She hadn't taken it off yet.

I went to the door.

"Incidentally." She folded her hands in her lap. "There is a place in New City you might find what you're looking for, called the Flower Passage—"

I turned toward her, angry. "The frelk hangout? Look, I don't need money! I said anything would do! I don't want—"

She had begun to shake her head, laughing quietly. Now she lay her cheek on the wrinkled place where I had sat. "Do you persist in misunderstanding? It is a spacer hangout. When you leave, I am going to visit my friends and talk about . . . ah, yes, the beautiful one that got away. I thought you might find . . . perhaps someone you know."

With anger, it ended.

"Oh," I said. "Oh, it's a spacer hangout. Yeah. Well, thanks."

And went out. And found the Flower Passage, and Kelly and Lou and Bo and Muse. Kelly was buying beer so we all got drunk, and ate fried fish and fried clams and fried sausage, and Kelly was waving the money around, saying, "You should have seen him! The changes I put that frelk through, you should have seen him! Eighty lira is the going rate here, and he gave me a hundred and fifty!" and drank more beer. And went up.

GANGER (BALL LIGHTNING)

Nalo Hopkinson

(2000)

Issy?"

"What."

"Suppose we switch suits?" Cleve asked.

Is what now? From where she knelt over him on their bed, Issy slid her tongue from Cleve's navel, blew on the wetness she'd made there. Cleve sucked in a breath, making the cheerful pudge of his tummy shudder. She stroked its fuzzy pelt.

"What," she said, looking up at him, "you want me wear your suit and you wear mine?" This had to be the weirdest yet.

He ran a finger over her lips, the heat of his touch making her mouth tingle. "Yeah," he replied. "Something so."

Issy got up to her knees, both her plump thighs on each side of his massive left one. She looked appraisingly at him. She was still mad from the fight they'd just had. But a good mad. She and Cleve, fighting always got them hot to make up. Had to be something good about that, didn't there? If they could keep finding their way back to each other like this? Her business if she'd wanted to make candy, even if the heat of the August night made the kitchen a hell. She wondered what the rass he was up to now.

They'd been fucking in the Senstim Co-operation's "wetsuits" for about a week. The toys had been fun for the first little while—they'd had more sex this week than in the last month—but even with the increased sensitivity, she was beginning to miss the feel of his skin directly against hers. "It not going work," Issy declared. But she was curious.

"You sure?" Cleve asked teasingly. He smiled, stroked her naked nipple softly with the ball of his thumb. She loved the contrast between his shovel-wide hands and the delicate movements he performed with

them. Her nipple poked erect, sensitive as a tongue tip. She arched her
back, pushed the heavy swing of her breast into fuller contact with the
ringed ridges of thumb.

"Mmm."

"C'mon, Issy, it could be fun, you know."

"Cleve, they just going key themselves to our bodies. The innie become a outie, the outie become a innie. . . ."

"Yeah, but . . ."

"But what?"

"They take a few minutes to conform to our body shapes, right?
Maybe in that few minutes . . ."

He'd gone silent, embarrassment shutting his open countenance
closed; too shy to describe the sensation he was seeking. Issy sighed in irritation. What was the big deal? Fuck, cunt, cock, come: simple words to
say. "In that few minutes, you'd find out what it feels like to have a poo-
nani, right?"

A snatch. He looked shy and aroused at the same time. "Yeah, and
you'd, well, you know."

He liked it when she talked "dirty." But just try to get him to repay
the favor. Try to get him to buzzingly whisper hot-syrup words against
the sensitive pinna of her ear until she shivered with the sensation of his
mouth on her skin, and the things he was saying, the nerve impulses he
was firing, spilled from his warm lips at her earhole and oozed down her
spine, cupped the bowl of her belly, filled her crotch with heat. That
only ever happened in her imagination.

Cleve ran one finger down her body, tracing the faint line of hair
from navel past the smiling crease below her tummy to pussy fur. Issy
spread her knees a little, willing him to explore further. His fingertip
tunneled through her pubic hair, tapped at her clit, making nerves sing.
Ah, ah. She rocked against his thigh. What would it be like to have the
feeling of entering someone's clasping flesh? "Okay," she said. "Let's try
it."

She picked up Cleve's stim. So diaphanous you could barely see it,
but supple as skin and thrice as responsive. Cocked up onto one elbow,
Cleve watched her with a slight smile on his face. Issy loved the chubby
chocolate-brown beauty of him, his fatcat grin.

Chortling, she wriggled into the suit, careful to ease it over the ban-
dage on her heel. The company boasted that you couldn't tell the dif-

ference between the microthin layer of the wetsuits and bare skin. Bullshit. Like taking a shower with your clothes on. The suits made you feel
more, but it was a one-way sensation. They dampened the sense of
touch. It was like being trapped inside your own skin, able to sense your
response to stimuli but not to feel when you had connected with the
outside world.

Over the week of use, Cleve's suit had shaped itself to his body. The
hips were tight on Issy, the flat chest part pressed her breasts against her
rib cage. The shoulders were too broad, the middle too baggy. It sagged
at knees, elbows, and toes. She giggled again.

"Never mind the peripherals," Cleve said, lumbering to his feet. "No
time." He picked up her suit. "Just leave them hanging."

Just as well. Issy hated the way that the roll-on headpiece trapped her
hair against her neck, covered her ears, slid sensory tendrils into her ear-
holes. It amplified the sounds when her body touched Cleve's. It grossed
her out. What would Cleve want to do next to jazz the skins up?

As the suit hyped the pleasure zones on her skin surface, Issy could
feel herself getting wet, the mixture of arousal and vague distaste a wetsuit gave her. The marketing lie was that the suits were "consensual aids
to full body aura alignment," not sex toys. Yeah, right. Psychobabble.
She was being diddled by an oversized condom possessed of fuzzy logic.
She pulled it up to her neck. The stim started to writhe, conforming itself to her shape. Galvanic peristalsis, they called its ability to move.
Yuck.

"Quick," Cleve muttered. He was jamming his lubed cock at a tube
in the suit, the innie part of it that would normally have slid itself into
her vagina, the part that had been smooth the first time she'd taken it
out of its case, but was now shaped the way she was shaped inside. Cleve
pushed and pushed until the everted pocket slid over his cock. He lay
back on the bed, his erection a jutting rudeness. "Oh. Wow. That's different. Is so it feels for you?"

Oh, sweet. Issy quickly followed Cleve's lead, spreading her knees to
push the outie part of his wetsuit inside her. It was easy. She was slippery,
every inch of her skin stimmed with desire. She palmed some lube from
the bottle into the suit's pouched vagina. They had to hurry. She strad-
dled him, slid onto his cock, making the tube of one wetsuit slither
smoothly into the tunnel of the other. Cleve closed his eyes, blew a
small breath through pursed lips.

So, so hot. "God, it's good," Issy muttered. Like being fucked, only she had an organ to push back with. Cleve just panted heavily, silently. As always. But what a rush! She swore she could feel Cleve's tight hot cunt closing around her dick. She grabbed his shoulders for traction. The massy, padded flesh of them filled her hands; steel encased in velvet.

The ganger looked down at its ghostly hands. Curled them into fists. Lightning sparked between the translucent fingers as they closed. It reached a crackling hand toward Cleve's shuddering body on the bathroom floor.

"Hey!" *Issy yelled at it. She could hear the quaver in her own voice. The ganger turned its head toward the sound. The suits' sense-memory gave it some analog of hearing.*

She tried to lift her head, banged it against the underside of the toilet. "Ow." The ganger's head elongated widthways, as though someone were pulling on its ears. Her muscles were too weakened from the aftershocks. Issy put her head back down. Now what? Think fast, Iss. "Y . . . you like um, um . . . chocolate fudge?" she asked the thing. Now, why was she still going on about the fucking candy?

The ganger straightened. Took a floating step away from Cleve, closer to Issy. Cleve was safe for the moment. Colored auras crackled in the ganger with each step. Issy laid her cheek against cool porcelain; stammered, "Well, I was making some last night, some fudge, yeah, only it didn't set, sometimes that happens, y'know? Too much humidity in the air, or something." The ganger seemed to wilt a little, floppy as the unhardened fudge. Was it fading? Issy's pulse leapt in hope. But then the thing plumped up again, drew closer to where she lay helpless on the floor. Rainbow lightning did a lava-lamp dance in its incorporeal body. Issy whimpered.

Cleve writhed under her. His lips formed quiet words. His own nubbin nipples hardened. Pleasure transformed his face. Issy loved seeing him this way. She rode and rode his body, "Yes, ah, sweet, God, sweet," groaning her way to the stim-charged orgasm that would fire all her pleasure synapses, give her some sugar, make her speak in tongues.

Suddenly Cleve pushed her shoulder. "Stop! Jesus, get off! Off!"

Startled, Issy shoved herself off him. Achy suction at her crotch as they disconnected. "What's wrong?"

Cleve sat up, panting hard. He clutched at his dick. He was shaking. Shuddering, he stripped off the wetsuit, flung it to the foot of the bed. To her utter amazement, he was sobbing. She'd never seen Cleve cry.

"Jeez. Can't have been that bad. Come." She opened her thick, strong arms to him. He curled as much of his big body as he could into her embrace, hid his face from her. She rocked him, puzzled. "Cleve?"

After a while, he mumbled, "It was nice, you know, so different, then it started to feel like, I dunno, like my dick had been *peeled* and it was inside out, and you, Jesus, you were fucking my inside-out dick."

Issy said nothing, held him tighter. The hyped rasp of Cleve's body against her stimmed skin was as much a turn-on as a comfort. She rocked him, rocked him. She couldn't think what to say, so she just hummed a children's song: *We're stirring cocoa beneath a tree/ sikola o la vani/ one, two, three, vanilla/ chocolate and vanilla.*

Just before he fell asleep, Cleve said, "God, I don't want to ever feel anything like that again. I had breasts, Issy. They swung when I moved."

The wetsuit Issy was wearing soon molded itself into an innie, and the hermaphroditic feeling disappeared. She kind of missed it. And all the time she was swaying Cleve to sleep she couldn't help thinking: For a few seconds, she'd felt something of what he felt when they had sex. For a few seconds, she'd felt the things he'd never dared to tell her in words. Issy slid a hand between herself and Cleve, insinuating it into the warm space between her stomach and thigh till she could work her fingers between her legs. She could feel her own wetness sliding under the microthin fiber. She pressed her clit, gently, ah, gently, tilting her hips toward her hand. Cleve stirred, scratched his nose; flopped his hand to the bed, snoring.

And he'd felt what she was always trying to describe to him, the sensations that always defied speech. He'd felt what this was like. The thought made her cunt clench. She panted out, briefly, once. She was so slick. Willing her body still, she started the rubbing motion that she knew would bring her off.

Nowadays any words between her and Cleve seemed to fall into dead air between them, each not reaching the other. But this had reached him, gotten her inside him; this, this, this, and the image of fucking Cleve pushed her over the edge and the pulseburst of her orgasm pumped again, again, again as her moans trickled through her lips, and she fought not to thrash, not to wake the slumbering mountain that was Cleve.

Oh. "Yeah, man," Issy breathed. Cleve had missed the best part. She eased him off her, got his head onto a pillow. Sated, sex-heavy, and drowsy, she peeled off the wetsuit—smiled at the pouches it had molded from her calabash breasts and behind—and kicked it onto the floor beside the bed. She lay down, rolled toward Cleve, hugged his body to her. "Mm," she murmured. Cleve muttered sleepily and snuggled into the curves of her body. Issy wriggled to the sweet spot where the lobes of his buttocks fit against her pubes. She wrapped her arm around the bole of his chest, kissed the back of his neck where his hair curled tightest. She felt herself beginning to sink into a feather-down sleep.

"I mean the boiled sugar kind of fudge," Issy told the ganger. It hovered over her, her own personal aurora. She had to keep talking, draw out the verbiage, distract the thing. "Not that gluey shit they sell at the Ex and stuff. We were supposed to have a date, but Cleve was late coming home and I was pissed at him and horny and I wanted a taste of sweetness in my mouth. And hot, too, maybe. I saw a recipe once where you put a few flakes of red pepper into the syrup. Intensified the taste, they said. I wonder. Dunno what I was thinking, boiling fudge in this heat." Lightning-quick, the ganger tapped her mouth. The electric shock crashed her teeth together. She saw stars. "Huh, huh," she heard her body protesting as air puffed out of its contracting lungs.

Issy uncurled into one last, languorous stretch before sleep. Her foot connected in the dark with a warm, rubbery mass that writhed at her touch, then started to slither up her leg.

"Oh, God! Shit! Cleve!" Issy kicked convulsively at the thing clambering up her thigh. She clutched Cleve's shoulder.

He sprang awake, tapped the wall to activate the light. "What, Issy? What's wrong?"

It was the still-charged wetsuit that Cleve had thrown to the foot of the bed, now an outie. "Christ, Cleve!" Idiot.

The suit had only been reacting to the electricity generated by Issy's body. It was just trying to do its job. "S'all right," Cleve comforted her. "It can't hurt you."

Shuddering, Issy peeled the wetsuit from her leg and dropped it to the ground. Deprived of her warmth, it squirmed its way over to her suit. Innie and outie writhed rudely around each other; empty sacks of skin. Jesus, with the peripherals still attached, the damned things looked like they had floppy heads.

Cleve smiled sleepily. "I's like lizard tails, y'know, when they drop off and wiggle?"

Issy thought she'd gag. "Get them out of my sight, Cleve. Discharge them and put them away."

"Tomorrow," he murmured.

They were supposed to be stored in separate cases, but Cleve just scooped them up and tossed them together, wriggling, into the closet.

"Gah," Issy choked.

Cleve looked at her face and said, "Come on, Iss; have a heart; think of them lying side by side in their little boxes, separated from each other." He was trying to joke about it.

"No," Issy said. "We get to do that instead. Wrap ourselves in fake flesh that's supposed to make us feel more. Ninety-six degrees in the shade, and we're wearing rubber body bags."

His face lost its teasing smile. Just the effect she'd wanted, but it didn't feel so good now. And it wasn't true, really. The wetsuit material did some weird shit so that it didn't trap heat in. And they were sexy, once you got used to them. No sillier than strap-ons or cuffs padded with fake fur. Issy grimaced an apology at Cleve. He screwed up his face and looked away. God, if he would only speak up for himself sometimes! Issy turned her back to him and found her wadded-up panties in the bed-clothes. She wrestled them on and lay back down, facing the wall. The light went off. Cleve climbed back into bed. Their bodies didn't touch.

The sun cranked Issy's eyes open. Its August heat washed over her like slops from a bucket. Her sheet was twisted around her, warm, damp, and funky. Her mouth was sour and she could smell her own stink. "Oh, God, I want it to be winter," she groaned.

She fought her way out of the clinging cloth to sit up in bed. The effort made her pant. She twisted the heavy mass of her braids up off the nape of her neck and sat for a while, feeling the sweat trickle down her scalp. She grimaced at the memory of last night.

Cleve wasn't there. Out for a jog, likely. "Yeah, that's how you sulk," she muttered. "In silence." Issy longed to know that he cared strongly about something, to hear him speak with any kind of force, the passion of his anger, the passion of his love. But Cleve kept it all so cool, so mild. Wrap it all in fake skin, hide it inside.

The morning sun had thrown a violent, hot bar of light across her bed. Heat. Tangible, almost. Crushed against every surface of her skin, like drowning in feathers. Issy shifted into a patch of shade. It made no difference. Fuck. A drop of sweat trickled down her neck, beaded a track down her left breast to drip off her nipple and splat onto her thigh. The trail of moisture it had left behind felt cool on her skin. Issy watched her aureole crinkle and the nipple stiffen in response. She shivered.

A twinkle of light caught her eye. The closet sliding door was open. The wetsuits, thin as shed snakeskin, were still humping each other beside their storage boxes. "Nasty!" Issy exclaimed. She jumped up from the bed, pushed the closet door shut with a bang. She left the room, ignoring the rhythmic thumping noise from inside the closet. Cleve was supposed to have discharged them; it could just wait until he deigned to come home again.

Overloading, crackling violently, the ganger stepped back. Issy nearly wept with release from its jolt. Her knees felt watery. Was Cleve still breathing? She thought she could see his chest moving in little gasps. She hoped. She had to keep the ganger distracted from him, he might not survive another shock. Teeth chattering, she said to the ganger, "You melt the sugar and butter—the salty butter's the best—in milk, then you add cocoa powder and boil it all to hard crack stage. . . ." Issy wet her lips with her tongue. The day's heat was enveloping her again. "Whip in some more butter," she continued. "You always get it on your fingers, that melted, salty butter. It will slide down the side of your hand, and you lick it off—so you whip in some more butter, and real vanilla, the kind that smells like mother's breath and cookies, not the artificial shit, and you dump it onto a plate, and it sets, and you have it sweet like that; chocolate fudge."

The sensuality in her voice seemed to mesmerize the ganger. It held still, rapt. Its inner lightnings cooled to electric blue. Its mouth hole yawned, wide as two of her fists.

As she headed to the kitchen, Issy made a face at the salty dampness beneath her swaying breasts and the curve of her belly. Her thighs were sticky where they moved against each other. She stopped in the living room and stood, feet slightly apart, arms away from her sides, so no surface of her body would touch any other. No relief. The heat still clung. She shoved her panties down around her ankles. The movement briefly brought her nose to her crotch, a whiff of sweaty muskiness. She straightened up, stepped out of the sodden pretzel of cloth, kicked it away. The quick movement had made her dizzy. She swayed slightly, staggered into the kitchen.

Cleve had mopped up the broken glass and gluey candy from yesterday evening, left the pot to soak. The kitchen still smelled of chocolate. The rich scent tingled along the roof of Issy's mouth.

The fridge hummed in its own aura, heat outside making cold inside. She needed water. Cold, cold. She yanked the fridge door open, reached for the water jug, and drank straight from it. The shock of chilly liquid made her teeth ache. She sucked water in, tilting the jug high so that more spilled past her gulping mouth, ran down her jaw, her breasts, her belly. With her free hand, she spread the coolness over the pillow of her stomach, dipping down into the crinkly pubic hair, then up to heft each breast one at a time, sliding cool fingers underneath, thumb almost automatically grazing each nipple to feel them harden slightly at her touch. Better. Issy put the jug back, half full now.

At her back, hot air was a wall. Seconds after she closed the fridge door, she'd be overheated and miserable again. She stood balanced between ice and heat, considering.

She pulled open the door to the icebox. It creaked and protested, jammed with frost congealed on its hinges. The fridge was ancient. Cleve had joked with the landlady that he might sell it to a museum and use the money to pay the rent on the apartment for a year. He'd only gotten a scowl in return.

The fridge had needed defrosting for weeks now. Her job. Cleve did the laundry and bathroom and kept them spotlessly clean. The kitchen and the bedroom were hers. Last time she'd changed the sheets was about the last time she'd done the fridge. Cleve hadn't complained. She was waiting him out.

Issy peered into the freezer. Buried in the canned hoarfrost were three ice-cube trays. She had to pull at them to work them free of hard-packed freezer snow. One was empty. The other two contained a few ice cubes between them.

The ganger took a step toward her. It paddled its hand in the black hole of its mouth. Issy shuddered, kept talking: "Break off chunks of fudge, and is sweet and dark and crunchy; a little bit hot if you put the pepper flakes in, I never tried that kind, and is softer in the middle, and the butter taste rise to the roof of your mouth, and the chocolate melt all over your tongue; man, you could almost come, just from a bite."

Issy flung the empty tray into the sink at the other end of the kitchen. Jangle-crash, displacing a fork that leapt from the sink, clattered onto the floor. The thumping from inside the bedroom closet became more frenetic. "Stop that," Issy yelled in the direction of the bedroom. The sound became a rapid drubbing. Then silence.

Issy kicked the fridge door closed, took the two ice-cube trays into the bathroom. Even with that short walk, the heat was pressing in on her again. The bathroom was usually cool, but today the tiles were warm against her bare feet. The humidity of the room felt like wading through spit.

Issy plugged the bathtub drain, dumped the sorry handful of ice in. Not enough. She grabbed up the mop bucket, went back to the kitchen, fished a spatula out of the sink, rinsed it. She used the spatula to dig out the treasures buried in the freezer. Frozen cassava, some unidentifiable meat, a cardboard cylinder of grape punch. She put them on a shelf in the fridge. Those excavated, she set about shoveling the snow out of the freezer, dumping it into her bucket. In no time she had a bucketful, and she'd found another ice-cube tray, this one full of fat, rounded lumps of ice. She was a little cooler now.

Back in the bathroom, she dumped the bucket of freezer snow on top of the puddle that had been the ice cubes. Then she ran cold water, filled the bathtub calf-deep, and stepped into it.

"Sssss . . ." The shock of cold feet zapped straight through Issy's body to her brain. She bent—smell of musk again—picked up a handful of the melting snow and packed it into her hair. Blessed, blessed cold. The snow became water almost instantly and dribbled down her face. Issy licked at a trickle of it. She picked up another handful of snow, stuffed it into her mouth. Crunchy-cold freon ice, melting on her tongue. She remembered the canned taste from childhood, how her dad would scold her for eating freezer snow. Her mother would say nothing, just wipe Issy's mouth dry with a silent, long-suffering smile.

Issy squatted in the bathtub. The cold water lapped against her butt. Goose bumps pimpled the skin of her thighs. She sat down, hips pressing against either side of the tub. An ice cube lapped against the small of her back, making her first arch to escape the cold, then lean back against the tub with a happy shudder. Snow crunched between her back and the ceramic surface. Issy spread her knees. There was more snow floating in the diamond her legs made. In both hands, she picked up another handful, mashed it into the V of her crotch. She shivered at the sensation and relaxed into the cool water.

The fridge made a zapping, farting noise, then resumed its juddering hum. Damned bucket of bolts. Issy concentrated on the deliciously shivery feel of the ice melting in her pubic hair.

"Only this time," Issy murmured, "the fudge ain't set. Just sat there on the cookie tin, gluey and brown. Not hard, not quite liquid, you get me? Glossy-shiny dark brown where it pooled, and rising from it, that chocolate-butter-vanilla smell. But wasted, 'cause it wasn't going to set."

The television clicked on loudly with an inane laugh track. Issy sat up. "Cleve?" She hadn't heard him come in. With a popping noise, the TV snapped off again. "Cleve, is you?"

Issy listened. Nope, nothing but the humming of the fridge. She was alone. These humid August days made all their appliances schizo with static. She relaxed back against the tub.

"I got mad," Issy told the ganger. "It was hot in the kitchen and there was cocoa powder everywhere and lumps of melting better, and I do all that work 'cause I just wanted the taste of something sweet in my mouth and the fucker wouldn't set! I backhanded the cookie tin. Fuck, it hurt like I crack a finger bone. The tin skidded across the kitchen counter, splanged off the side of the stove, and went flying."

Issy's skin bristled with goose bumps at the sight of the thing that walked in through the open bathroom door and stood, arms hanging. It was a human-shaped glow, translucent. Its edges were fuzzy. She could see the hallway closet through it. Eyes, nose, mouth were empty circles. A low crackling noise came from it, like a crushed Cheezies bag. Issy could feel her breath coming in short, terrified pants. She made to stand up, and the apparition moved closer to her. She whimpered and sat back down in the chilly water.

The ghost-thing stood still. A pattern of colored lights flickered in it, limning where spine, heart, and brain would have been, if it had had those. It did have breasts, she saw now, and a dick.

She moved her hand. Water dripped from her fingertips into the tub. The thing turned its head toward the sound. It took a step. She froze. The apparition stopped moving, too, just stood there, humming like the fridge. It plucked at its own nipples, pulled its breasts into cones of ec-toplasm. It ran hands over its body, then over the sink; bent down to thrust its arms right through the closed cupboard doors. It dipped a hand into the toilet bowl. Sparks flew, and it jumped back. Issy's scalp prick-led. Damn, the thing was electrical, and she was sitting in water! She tried to reach the plug with her toes to let the water out. Swallowing whimpers, she stretched a leg out: Slow, God, go slow, Issy. The move-ment sent a chunk of melting ice sliding along her thigh. She shivered.

She couldn't quite reach the plug and if she moved closer to it, the movement would draw the apparition's attention. Issy breathed in short, shallow bursts. She could feel her eyes beginning to brim. Terror and the chilly water were sending tremors in waves through her.

What the fuck was it? The thing turned toward her. In its quest for sensation, it hefted its cock in its hand. Inserted a finger into what seemed to be a vagina underneath. Let its hands drop again. Faintly, Issy could make out a mark on its hip, a circular shape. It reminded her of something. . . .

Logo, it was the logo of the Senstim people who'd invented the wetsuits!

But this wasn't a wetsuit, it was like some kind of, fuck, ball lightning. She and Cleve hadn't discharged their wetsuits. She remembered some of the nonsense words that were in the warning on the wetsuit storage boxes: "Energizing electrostatic charge," and "Kirlian phenomenon." Well, they hadn't paid attention, and now some kind of weird gel of both suits was rubbing itself off in their bathroom. Damn, damn, damn Cleve and his toys. Sobbing, shivering, Issy tried to toe at the plug again. Her knee banged against the tub. The suit-ghost twitched toward the noise. It leaned over the water and dabbed at her clutching toes. Pop-crackle sound. The jolt sent her leg flailing like a dying fish. Pleasure crackled along her leg, painfully intense. Her knee throbbed and tingled, ached sweetly. Her thigh muscles shuddered as though they would tear free. The jolt slammed into her crotch and Issy's body bucked. She could hear her own grunts. She was straddling a live wire. She was coming to death. Her nipples jutted long as thumbs, stung like they'd been dipped in ice. Her head was banging against the wall with each deadly set of contractions. Issy shouted in pain, in glory, in fear. The suit-ghost leapt back. Issy's butt hit the floor of the tub, hard. Her muscles were twitching spasmodically. She'd bitten the inside of her mouth. She sucked in air like sobs; swallowed tinny blood.

The suit-ghost was swollen, bloated, jittering. Its inner lightning bolts were going mad. If it touched her again, it might overload completely. If it touched her again, her heart might stop.

Issy heard the sound of the key turning in the front door.

"Iss? You home?"

"No. Cleve." Issy hissed under her breath. He mustn't come in. But if she shouted to warn him, the suit-ghost would touch her again.

Cleve's footsteps approached the bathroom. "Iss? Listen, did you drain the wet . . ."

Like filings to a magnet, the suit-ghost inclined toward the sound of his voice.

"Don't come in, Cleve; go get help!"

Too late. He'd stuck his head in, grinning his open, friendly grin. The suit-ghost rushed him, plastered itself along his body. It got paler, its aura-lightnings mere flickers. Cleve made a choking noise and crashed to the floor, jerking. Issy levered herself out of the bath, but her jelly muscles wouldn't let her stand. She flopped to the tiles. Cleve's body was convulsing, horrible noises coming from his mouth. Riding him like a duppy, a malevolent spirit, the stim-ghost grew paler with each thrash of his flailing body. Its color patterns started to run into each other, to bleach themselves pale. Cleve's energy was draining it, but it was killing him. Sucking on her whimpers, Issy reached a hand into the stim-ghost's field. Her heart went off like a gatling gun. Her breathing wouldn't work. The orgasm was unspeakable. Wailing, Issy rolled away from Cleve, taking the ghost-thing with her. It swelled at her touch, its colors flaring neon-bright, out of control. It flailed off her, floated back toward Cleve's more cooling energy. Heart pounding, too weak to move, Issy muttered desperately to distract it the first thing that came to her mind: "Y . . . you like, um, chocolate fudge?"

The ghost turned toward her. Issy cried and kept talking, kept talking. The ghost wavered between Issy's hot description of bubbling chocolate and Cleve's cool silence, caught in the middle. Could it even understand words? Wetsuits located pleasurable sensation to augment it. Maybe it was just drawn to the sensuousness of her tone. Issy talked, urgently, carefully releasing the words from her mouth like caresses:

"So," she said to the suit-duppy, "I watching this cookie tin twist through the air like a Frisbee, and is like slow motion, 'cause I seeing gobs of chocolate goo spiraling from it as it flies, and they spreading out wider and wider. I swear I hear separate splats as chocolate hits the walls like slung shit and one line of it strafes the fridge door, and a gob somehow slimes the naked bulb hanging low from the kitchen ceiling. I hear it sizzle. The cookie tin lands on the floor, fudge side down, of course. I haven't cleaned the fucking floor in ages. There're spots everywhere on that floor that used to be gummy, but now they're layered in dust and maybe flour and desiccated bodies of cockroaches that got trapped, reaching for sweetness. I know how they feel. I take a step toward the cookie tin, then I start to smell burning chocolate. I look up. I see a curl of black smoke rising from the glob of chocolate on the light bulb."

Cleve raised his head. There were tears in his eyes and the front of his jogging pants was damp and milky. "Issy," he interrupted in a whisper.

"Shut up, Cleve!"

"That thing," he said in a low, urgent voice. "People call it a ganger; doppel . . ."

The ganger was suddenly at his side. It leaned a loving head on his chest, like Issy would do. "No!" she yelled. Cleve's body shook. The ganger frayed and tossed like a sheet in the wind. Cleve shrieked. He groaned like he was coming, but with an edge of terror and pain that Issy couldn't bear to hear. Pissed, terrified, Issy swiped an arm through its field, then rolled her bucking body on the bathroom tiles, praying that she could absorb the ganger's energy without it frying her synapses with sweet sensation.

Through spasms, she barely heard Cleve say to it, "Come to me, not her. Come. Listen, you know that song? '*I got a weakness for sweetness . . .*' That's my Issy."

The ganger dragged itself away from Issy. Released, her muscles melted. She was a gooey, warm puddle spreading on the floor. The ganger reached an ectoplasmic hand toward Cleve, fingers stretching long as arms. Cleve gasped and froze.

Issy croaked, "You think is that it is, Cleve? Weakness?"

The ganger turned its head her way, ran a long, slow arm down its body to the floor, back up to its crotch. It stroked itself.

Cleve spoke to it in a voice that cracked whispery on the notes: "Yeah, sweetness. That's what my Issy wants most of all." The ganger moved toward him, rubbing its crotch. He continued, "If I'm not there, there's always sugar, or food, or booze. I'm just one of her chosen stimulants."

Outraged tears filled Issy's mouth, salty as butter, as flesh. She'd show him, she'd rescue him. She countered:

"The glob of burned sugar on the light? From the ruined fudge? Well, it goes black and starts to bubble."

The ganger extruded a tongue the length of an arm from its mouth. The tongue wriggled toward Issy. She rolled back, saying, "The light bulb explodes. I feel some shards land in my hair. I don't try to brush them away. Is completely dark now; I only had the kitchen light on. I take another step to where I know the cookie tin is on the floor. A third step, and pain crazes my heel. Must have stepped on a piece of light bulb glass. Can't do nothing about it now. I rise onto the toes of the hurting foot. I think I feel blood running down from heel to instep."

The ganger jittered toward her.

"You were always better than me at drama, Iss," Cleve said.

The sadness in his voice tore at her heart. But she said, "What that thing is?"

Cleve replied softly, "Is kinda beautiful, ain't?"

"It going to kill us."

"Beautiful. Just a lump of static charge, coated in the Kirlian energy thrown off from the suits."

"Why it show up now?"

"Is what happens when you leave the suits together too long."

The ganger drifted back and forth, pulled by one voice, then the other. A longish silence between them freed it to move. It floated closer to Cleve. Issy wouldn't let it, she wouldn't. She quavered:

"I take another step on the good foot, carefully. I bend down, sweep my hands around."

The ganger dropped to the floor, ran its long tongue over the tiles. A drop of water made it crackle and shrink in slightly on itself.

"There," Issy continued. "The cookie tin. I brush around me, getting a few more splinters in my hands. I get down to my knees, curl down as low to the ground as I can. I pry up the cookie tin, won't have any glass splinters underneath it. A dark sweet wet chocolate smell rising from under there."

"Issy, Jesus," Cleve whispered. He started to bellow the words of the song he'd taunted her with. The ganger touched him with a fingertip. A crackling noise. He gasped, jumped, kept singing.

Issy ignored him. Hissing under his booming voice, she snarled at the ganger, "I run a finger through the fudge. I lick it off. Most of it on the ground, not on the tin. I bend over and run my tongue through it, reaching for sweetness. Butter and vanilla and oh, oh, the chocolate. And crunchy, gritty things I don't think about. Cockroach parts, maybe. I swallow."

Cleve interrupted his song to wail, "That's gross, Iss. Why you had to go and do that?"

"So Cleve come in, he see me there sitting on the floor surrounded by broken glass and limp chocolate, and you know what he say?" The ganger was reaching for her.

"Issy, stop talking, you only drawing it to you."

"Nothing." The ganger jerked. "Zip." The ganger twitched. "Dick." The ganger spasmed, once. It touched her hair. Issy breathed. That was safe. "The bastard just started cleaning up; not a word for me." The ganger hugged her. Issy felt her eyes roll back in her head. She thrashed in the energy of its embrace until Cleve yelled:

"And what you said! Ee? Tell me!"

The ganger pulled away. Issy lay still, waiting for her breathing to return to normal. Cleve said, "Started carrying on with some shit about how light bulbs are such poor quality nowadays. Sat in the filth and broken glass, pouting and watching me clean up your mess. Talking about anything but what really on your mind. I barely get all the glass out of your heel before you start pulling my pants down."

Issy ignored him. She kept talking to the ganger. "Cool, cool Cleve. No 'What's up?'; no 'What the fuck is this crap on the floor?'; no heat, no passion."

"What was the point? I did the only thing that will sweet you every time."

"Encased us both in fake skin and let it do the fucking for us."

The ganger jittered in uncertain circles between the two of them.

"Issy, what you want from me?"

The ganger's head swelled obscenely toward Cleve.

"Some heat. Some feeling. Like I show you. Like I feel. Like I feel for you." The ganger's lower lip stretched, stretched, a filament of it reaching for Issy's own mouth. The black cavity of its maw was a tunnel, longing to swallow her up. She shuddered and rolled back farther. Her back came up against the bathtub.

Softly: "What do you feel for me, Issy?"

"Fuck you."

"I do. We do. It's good. But what do you feel for me, Issy?"

"Don't ridicule me. You know."

"I don't know shit, Issy! You talk, talk, talk! And it's all about what racist slur you heard yesterday, and who tried to cheat you at the store, and how high the phone bill is. You talk around stuff, not about it!"

"Shut up!"

The ganger flailed like a hook-caught fish between them.

Quietly, Cleve said, "The only time we seem to reach each other now is through our skins. So I bought something to make our skins feel more, and it's still not enough."

An involuntary sound came from Issy's mouth, a hooked, wordless query.

"Cleve, is that why . . ." She looked at him, at the intense brown eyes in the expressive brown face. When had he started to look so sad all the time? She reached a hand out to him. The ganger grabbed it. Issy saw fireworks behind her eyes. She screamed. She felt Cleve's hand on her waist, felt the hand clutch painfully as he tried to shove her away to safety with his other hand. Blindly she reached out, tried to bat the ganger away. Her hand met Cleve's in the middle of the fog that was the ganger. All the pleasure centers in her body exploded.

A popping sound. A strong, seminal smell of bleach. The ganger was gone. Issy and Cleve sagged to the floor.

"Rass," she sighed. Her calves were knots the size of potatoes. And she'd be sitting tenderly for a while.

"I feel like I've been dragged five miles behind a runaway horse," Cleve told her. "You all right?"

"Yeah, where'd that thing go, the ganger?"

"Shit, Issy, I'm so sorry. Should have drained the suits like you said."

"Chuh. Don't dig nothing. I could have done it, too."

"I think we neutralized it. Touched each other, touched it: we canceled it out. I think."

"Touched each other. That simple." Issy gave a little rueful laugh. "Cleve, I . . . you're my honey, you know? You sweet me for days. I won't forget any more to tell you," she said, "and keep telling you."

His smile brimmed over with joy. He replied, "You, you're my live wire. You keep us both juiced up, make my heart sing in my chest." He hesitated, spoke bashfully, "And my dick leap in my pants when I see you."

A warmth flooded Issy at his sweet, hot talk. She felt her eyelashes dampen. She smiled. "See, the dirty words not so hard to say. And the anger not so hard to show."

Tailor-sat on the floor, beautiful Buddha-body, he frowned at her. "I 'fraid to use harsh words, Issy, you know that. Look at the size of me, the blackness of me. You know what it is to see people cringe for fear when you shout?"

She was dropping down with fatigue. She leaned and softly touched his face. "I don't know what that is like. But I know you. I know you would never hurt me. You must say what on your mind, Cleve. To me, at least." She closed her eyes, dragged herself exhaustedly into his embrace.

He said, "You know, I dream of the way you full up my arms."

"You're sticky," she murmured. "Like candy." And fell asleep, touching him.

Song "Weakness for Sweetness" quoted with permission of singer Natalie Burke and composer Leston Paul, ©1996.

THE BECOMING

Akua Lezli Hope

(2000)

> "Go all the way back this time
> Sometime it feel good to go back
> And start it all over again
> Here it is, three o'clock in the morning,
> Can't even close my eyes,
> Can't even find my baby,
> Can't be satisfied."

She took the cube from the holoplayer, trying to hold the flickering holo image of the blues man in her mind. He was dark as some museum's rare mahogany. What hour was it anyway? She pulled her tellya from her skinsuit's top pocket and pressed "time." It whispered back in the husky voice of that ancient singer, "hundred."

She loved the way his voice hunkered down over "hundred," guttural vowels and rich-throated. The top holoartists weren't like this. They were sinewave castrati, whose falsettos sounded like plugged-nose keening. She listened to more singers now, after her Great Becoming. She had a voice once, but it was always the horns, the muscular vibratos, the burnished mineral ululations, the flesh-beckoning brum-bra-tata-tas, and soul-awakening yayeeyaah, yeas, those wails, transcendent, that set her very liver to quiver. The horn. *WHEN THE DAY HAS TURNED TO EVENING, SOME WHO WALK THE CITY'S CANYONS.* Precious, precious metal saxophones were her first joy, metal like the City's Muse.

One long seasonless day in the past, she met the City's Muse. Oh, the tellya's "thoughts for good days" said never think about the past, but she had to remember. She had to think about when she had decided on her becoming, when she would have to leave Nuyorc if she did not become *something*.

All that lay between recognition with guaranteed income and the mind-blocked boredom of the Cottage Industries was Decision. The Great Becoming. Many avoided the decision. Others never had to make it. Then, too, there were those who were never offered the choice. *My family at least had the choice.* She patted the thermafur loungebed and felt its responsive underpurr as it rolled along her thigh—an inaccessible and undreamt-of luxury had she chosen telecommuting, the Cottage Industries, the slaveboxes. *I thought there was honor in the choosing, I was honored by the offer. Jason never had to choose. It's been ten years since my Great Becoming.*

Her one friend, her one lover, Jason of the full firm mouth, Jason of the thick thighs and languorous laughter, Jason, how his nipples would thicken under her tongue, how he could wrap around her.

It was an unnegotiable day and Cenpark was greening. She'd been listening to one of her minidiscs, the reproduction on them far surpassed the new encryption capsules. Besides, she was younger then, needed to have something in her hands, needed to be hearing and holding. He was similarly attired: zipsuit, thermapeds, sling bag, and headlamp. *Must be my age,* she thought. One couldn't tell anymore. City hick that she was, she felt unschooled in the subtlety of rank and dress. Nuyorc core was socially more egalitarian than the Manhattanae. Here in Cenpark, up- and downtown stores and eateries catered much more to tourist traffic than anywhere else in Boswash, than any other of the domed Mahattanae.

"Heyo, visitor."

"Journo, babe. Que happenin this here?"

"Umm nada much, jus listening, breezin."

"Rap, babe. It's better than tellya."

She loved this core, her home. Her mom and dad were official artisans and city bards. They spent a lot of time in the street, plying their creations or entertaining touristas. They spent their downtime teaching her and Bud, her brother.

They were most special, they were artisans and street players. They had talent and choice. She spent her young years studying violin, cello, bassoon, flute, and finally the horn. The enormous breath changer. She craved it in her hands, its mouth in her mouth, part of her passed through it, it transformed her, finger and key, breath and lip, the reed vibrating tones that colored the mind.

A good life and she got to choose. She told him all this. She opened her eyes realizing his hand was on her left breast, massaging it as she spoke. She grabbed his wrist, only half angry, held his hand.

"Your nomen, brother?"

"Jason, sistah, from Clevelands." He was ten years her senior. Neither artisan clothes nor the look of touristas, and where were the scabs or calluses that swell on finger pads, where were the contacts, the eyeshades? No, he was a technoman and from the Midwest, an oddity like a Cenpark tree, a dark-skinned technoman, like her and unlike her.

Jason, the great listener, the wish-toucher, became her friend, her first and only lover. She fashioned from him the love of her life. Not to say he was that love, but she connected the nerve endings of the flesh of her need and her creation to the spine of what he was. Her want and its partial (but oh so much closer than before) fulfillment became one.

And how, after the last shout, the last sunburst, after the heart pulse left her head and the lips and tongues unswelled and all the tides receded and the colors were no longer of the neon jungle—he would unwrap himself from her, push her from her nesting curl around his body, and turn his back. And she would be hurt, wanting to be held till, wanting the small eddies and salt of her joys, his passions, to be still shared . . . he was so tender and insistent in their beginnings. But his dark blank back would not reveal any after feelings. *Why does he hide?* she would think and he would instruct her to "Hold me, baby, please hold me, baby. Hold me tight, rock me, baby." Always she would press against his hard back, one arm curled between, one arm and one leg over him, and she would rock him past sleep. She was wrong, in part, he was not hiding so much as he was selfish—why should he hold her after he had spent so much energy awakening her to his will—this was just a continuation of her fulfilling his will.

He was a studied, relentless lover. It was ever something he did to, not with her. Like everything else she could observe him do, he did it well, but for himself only. "I never do anything naked," he said to her. She looked at him questioningly, with a half smile. *So that was not your skin my legs knew?* she thought.

"I always wear my socks," answering her half smile, her unspoken question. And she was plunged in doubt. Skinsocks? Like all her other small confidences, he had taken another one from her. He had never been naked with her—perhaps he had, but his denial was as hurting as any actuality.

He wished he could accept love as she did with a large, child-eyed innocence and joy. Her joy angered him, engaged him. He was repulsed and attracted by her unqualified embraces, city hick, sweet fodder gal. To plunge in her, to play her like she played.

She was hurt. She wondered why, why must there always be pain? This pain just seized her deep. So profound that it ate the tears that might break it up and wash it away; it ate the scream and cries that would shatter it. It grabbed her muscles so that her tremblings were stilled, locking her into an erect posture denying her relief.

I am too strong, she thought. Yet she felt the pain throb deep inside. It moved up her vulva, stabbing toward her womb. Her womb, full of hope, ached from its desire and betrayal. This, then, she sensed, was her loss of virginity. For it happened not with that first entrance, the first being rarely the best, and memorable only because of its novelty. But this pain was the deflowering, the busted cherry, her loss of innocence.

Of course she would share her choosing with Jason, one rare and incredible nighttime before her eighteenth birthday in his apartment overlooking Cenpark. It began wrong, she'd broken her own rule—smoked one of his huge Nigerian imports. It was a vintage crop that year, Bud had told her—a Nigerian nineteen, a true and sweetly somber joint, liquid, calm, false clarity and streetlights burnished in their late sunset hue.

The huge empty room that was Jason's box should have told her something, this was no slave hovel, no artisan's crammed warren, a whole jumpspace of a room, with a tub and water, no portosan.

She reeled with her own great giddiness. "I am choosing. I will be a musician, an artisan! My long-awaited moment shouts me, rumbles me, tumbles me!

"Jason, what a pairbond we have. You'll be my second song after I declare my choice."

"What will be your first?"

"My first will be the choosing."

"You really think choosing's good? What if you did not have to choose? The world holds more than those with options."

"La. Yah. There are them without."

"No, babe. More like, there are those who never have to, at least not like you do, doll. Not either work nor work, neither serve nor serve. No City's Muse. No slavebox."

"You work, Jason."

"Yo, plenty downtime and new ones like you. I made your City's Muse."

"Nah. My folks met the Muse their time and their parents."

"They met another Muse. This Muse knows more . . . knew you from birth. . . . How I sighted you."

"Sighted me?"

"Read you, doll, watched you, waited for you, wanted you, before your choosing, whatever it would be."

"You, a technoman, can sight things? You must have some strange access code."

"Don't be a primitive."

"I'm not, maybe city slowed but not devo."

"O baby one, this is the first smoke you've agreed to share. Laced with my chemist's best, to celebrate your choosing."

"Jason, umm."

He had removed her boot and sock, licked her arch, and sucked her big toe.

"So, what will it be?"

"The horn, Jason, the horn, I love horns, the tenor saxophone."

His fingers swirled around her navel. She felt in a swoon, unable to move. She felt his fingernails dig into her back. But the pain was distant.

"Jason, that hurts."

"It won't sting, babe, this is good-bye, the sweetest, the best."

She felt wildly out of sync. He was manic, awhirl, a plunging, racing, giddy madness. The flashes of discomfort were washed in an orange passion. There were colors that she realized were not drug-induced but were holograms.

She felt a deep fear. He was not waiting for her this time, but driving her. It was a sensory overload, he moved about her, through her in bolts and jolts. Screaming horns wailed, spinning through the air and crashing around her.

She could not see. She felt her insides rush out, a thin slice, warmth at her side. Jason sat beside her caressing a blade.

Every time she was back in Nuyorc, she would remember. How in choosing the horn, she would become one. Ah, they had left her lovely breasts, but between them, the flesh buttons, and below, a swell from her flat abdomen. They were clever about the windpipe, the trachea; she could eat but no longer speak, not without playing herself. And she was a great player, roaming the invisible world that runs the world, avoiding the other freak flesh instruments; avoiding those who wanted to touch. Blowing for those who never have to choose, who never have to Become, but Are.

The Goophered Grapevine

Charles W. Chesnutt

(1887)

Some years ago my wife was in poor health, and our family doctor, in whose skill and honesty I had implicit confidence, advised a change of climate. I shared, from an unprofessional standpoint, his opinion that the raw winds, the chill rains, and the violent changes of temperature that characterized the winters in the region of the Great Lakes tended to aggravate my wife's difficulty, and would undoubtedly shorten her life if she remained exposed to them. The doctor's advice was that we seek, not a temporary place of sojourn, but a permanent residence, in a warmer and more equable climate. I was engaged at the time in grape-culture in northern Ohio, and, as I liked the business and had given it much study, I decided to look for some other locality suitable for carrying it on. I thought of sunny France, of sleepy Spain, of Southern California, but there were objections to them all. It occurred to me that I might find what I wanted in some one of our own Southern States. It was a sufficient time after the war for conditions in the South to have become somewhat settled; and I was enough of a pioneer to start a new industry, if I could not find a place where grape-culture had been tried. I wrote to a cousin who had gone into the turpentine business in central North Carolina. He assured me, in response to my inquiries, that no better place could be found in the South than the State and neighborhood where he lived; the climate was perfect for health, land, in conjunction with the soil, ideal for grape-culture; labor was cheap, and land could be bought for a mere song. He gave us a cordial invitation to come and visit him while we looked into the matter. We accepted the invitation, and after several days of leisurely travel, the last hundred miles of which were up a river on a sidewheel steamer, we reached our destination, a quaint old town, which I shall call Patesville, because, for one reason, that is not its name. There was a red brick market-house in the public square, with a tall tower, which held a four-faced clock that struck the hours, and from which there pealed out a curfew at nine o'clock. There were two or three hotels, a court-house, a jail, stores, offices, and all the appurtenances of a county seat and a commercial emporium; for while Patesville numbered only four or five thousand inhabitants, of all shades of complexion, it was one of the principal towns in North Carolina, and had a considerable trade in cotton and naval stores. This business activity was not immediately apparent to my unaccustomed eyes. Indeed, when I first saw the town, there brooded over it a calm that seemed almost sabbatic in its restfulness, though I learned later on that underneath its somnolent exterior the deeper currents of life—love and hatred, joy and despair, ambition and avarice, faith and friendship—flowed not less steadily than in livelier latitudes.

We found the weather delightful at that season, the end of summer, and were hospitably entertained. Our host was a man of means and evidently regarded our visit as a pleasure, and we were therefore correspondingly at our ease, and in a position to act with the coolness of judgment desirable in making so radical a change in our lives. My cousin placed a horse and buggy at our disposal, and himself acted as our guide until I became somewhat familiar with the country.

I found that grape-culture, while it had never been carried on to any great extent, was not entirely unknown in the neighborhood. Several planters thereabouts had attempted it on a commercial scale, in former years, with greater or less success; but like most Southern industries, it had felt the blight of war and had fallen into desuetude.

I went several times to look at a place that I thought might suit me. It was a plantation of considerable extent, that had formerly belonged to a wealthy man by the name of McAdoo. The estate had been for years involved in litigation between disputing heirs, during which period shiftless cultivation had well-nigh exhausted the soil. There had been a vineyard of some extent on the place, but it had not been attended to since the war, and had lapsed into utter neglect. The vines— here partly supported by decayed and broken-down trellises, there twining themselves among the branches of the slender saplings which had sprung up among them—grew in wild and unpruned luxuriance, and the few scattered grapes they bore were the undisputed prey of the first comer. The site was admirably adapted to grape-raising; the soil, with a little attention, could not have been better; and with the native grape, the luscious scuppernong, as my main reliance in the beginning, I felt sure that I could introduce and cultivate successfully a number of other varieties.

One day I went over with my wife to show her the place. We drove out of the town over a long wooden bridge that spanned a spreading mill-pond, passed the long whitewashed fence surrounding the county fair-ground, and struck into a road so sandy that the horse's feet sank into the fetlocks. Our route lay partly up hill and partly down, for we were in the sand-hill county; we drove past cultivated farms, and then by abandoned fields grown up in scrub-oak and short-leaved pine, and once or twice through the solemn aisles of the virgin forest, where the tall pines, well-nigh meeting over the narrow road, shut out the sun, and wrapped us in cloistral solitude. Once, at a cross-roads, I was in doubt as to the turn to take, and we sat there waiting ten minutes—we had already caught some of the native infection of restfulness—for some human being to come along, who could direct us on our way. At length a little negro girl appeared, walking straight as an arrow, with a piggin full of water on her head. After a little patient investigation, necessary to overcome the child's shyness, we learned what we wished to know, and at the end of about five miles from the town reached our destination.

We drove between a pair of decayed gateposts—the gate itself had long since disappeared—and up a straight sandy lane, between two lines of rotting rail fence, partly concealed by jimson-weeds and briers, to open space where a dwelling-house had once stood, evidently a spacious mansion, if we might judge from the ruined chimneys that were still standing, and the brick pillars on which the sills rested. The house itself, we had been informed, had fallen a victim to the fortunes of war.

We alighted from the buggy, walked about the yard for a while, and then wandered off into the adjoining vineyard. Upon Annie's complaining of weariness I led the way back to the yard, where a pine log, lying under a spreading elm, afforded a shady though somewhat hard seat. One end of the log was already occupied by a venerable looking colored man. He held on his knees a hat full of grapes, over which he was smacking his lips with great gusto, and a pile of grapeskins near him indicated that the performance was no new thing. We approached him at an angle from the rear, and were close to him before he perceived us. He respectfully rose as we drew near, and was moving away, when I begged him to keep his seat.

"Don't let us disturb you," I said. "There is plenty of room for us all."

He resumed his seat with somewhat of embarrassment. While he had been standing, I had observed that he was a tall man, and, though slightly bowed by the weight of years, apparently quite vigorous. He was not entirely black, and this fact, together with the quality of his hair, which was about six inches long and very bushy, except on the top of his head, where he was quite bald, suggested a slight strain of other than negro blood. There was a shrewdness in his eyes, too, which was not altogether African, and which, as we afterwards learned from experience was indicative of a corresponding shrewdness in his character. He went on eating the grapes, but did not seem to enjoy himself quite so well as he had apparently done before he became aware of our presence.

"Do you live around here?" I asked, anxious to put him at his ease.

"Yas, suh. I lives des ober yander, behine de nex' san'-hill, on de Lumberton plank-road."

"Do you know anything about the time when this vineyard was cultivated?"

"Lawd bless you, suh, I knows all about it. Dey ain' na'er a man in dis settlement w'at won' tell you ole Julius McAdoo 'uz bawn en raise' on dis yer same plantation. Is you de Norv'n gemman w'at's gwine ter buy de ole vimya'd?"

"I am looking at it," I replied; "but I don't know that I shall care to buy unless I can be reasonably sure of making something out of it."

"Well, suh, you is a stranger ter me, en I is a stranger ter you, en we is bofe strangers ter one anudder, but 'f I 'uz in yo' place, I wouldn' buy dis vimya'd."

"Why not?" I asked.

"Well, I dunno whe'r you believes in cunj'in'er not—some er de w'ite folks don't, er says dey don't—but de truf er de matter is dat dis yer ole vimya'd is goophered."

"Is what?" I asked, not grasping the meaning of this unfamiliar word.

"Is goophered—cunju'd, bewitch'."

He imparted this information with such solemn earnestness, and with such an air of confidential mystery, that I felt somewhat interested, while Annie was evidently much impressed, and drew closer to me.

"How do you know it is bewitched?" I asked.

"I wouldn' spec' fer you ter b'lieve me 'less you know all 'bout de fac's. But ef you en young miss dere doan' min' lis'nin' ter a ole nigger run on a minute er two w'ile you er restin', I kin 'splain to you how it all happen'."

We assured him that we would be glad to hear how it all happened, and he began to tell us. At first the current of his memory—or imagination—seemed somewhat sluggish; but as his embarrassment wore off, his language flowed more freely, and the story acquired perspective and coherence. As he became more and more absorbed in the narrative, his eyes assumed a dreamy expression, and he seemed to lose sight of his auditors, and to be living over again in monologue his life on the old plantation.

"Ole Mars Dugal' McAdoo," he began, "bought dis place long many year befo' de wah, en I 'member well w'en he sot out all dis yer part er de plantation in scuppernon's. De vimes growed monst'us fas', en Mars Dugal' made a thousan' gallon er scuppernon' wine eve'y year.

"Now, ef dey's an'thing a nigger lub, nex' ter 'possum, en chick'n, en watermillyums, it's scuppernon's. Dey ain' nuffin dat kin stan' up side'n de scuppernon' for sweetness; sugar ain't a suckumstance ter scuppernon'. W'en de season is nigh 'bout ober, en de grapes begin ter swivel up des a little wid de wrinkles er ole age—w'en de skin git sot' en brown—den de scuppernon' make you smack yo' lip en roll yo' eye en wush fer mo'; so I reckon it ain' very 'stonishin' dat niggers lub scuppernon'.

"Dey wuz a sight er niggers in de naberhood er de vimya'd. Dere wuz ole Mars Henry Brayboy's niggers, en ol Mars Jeems McLean's niggers, en Mars Dugal's own niggers; den dey wuz a settlement er free niggers en po' buckrahs down by de Wim'l'ton Road, en Mars Dugal' had de only vimya'd in de naberhood. I reckon it ain' so much so nowadays, but befo' de wah, in slab'ry times, a nigger didn' mine goin' fi' er ten mile in a night, w'en dey wuz sump'n good ter eat at de yuther een'.

"So atter a w'ile Mars Dugal' begin ter miss his scuppernon's. Co'se he 'cuse' de niggers er it, but dey all 'nied it ter de las'. Mars Dugal' sot spring guns en steel traps, en he en de oberseah sot up nights once't er twice't, tel one night Mars Dugal'—he 'uz a monst'us keerless man—got his leg shot full er cow-peas. But somehow er nudder dey couldn' nebber ketch none er de niggers. I dunner how it happen, but it happen des like I tell you, en de grapes kep' on a-goin' des de same.

"But bimeby ole Mars Dugal' fix' up a plan ter stop it. Dey wuz a cunjuh 'oman livin' down 'mongs' de free niggers on de Wim'l'ton Road, en all de darkies fum Rockfish ter Beaver Crick wuz feared er her. She could wuk de mos' powerfulles' kin' er goopher—could make people hab fits, er rheumatiz, er make 'em des dwinel away en die; en dey say she went out ridin' de niggers at night, fer she wuz a witch 'sides bein' a cunjuh 'oman. Mars Dugal' hearn 'bout Aun' Peggy's doin's, en begun ter 'flect whe'r er no he couldn' git her ter he'p him keep de niggers off'n de grapevimes. One day in de spring er de year, ole miss pack' up a basket er chick'n en poun'-cake, en a bottle er scuppernon' wine, en Mars Dugal' tuk it in his buggy en driv ober ter Aun' Peggy's cabin. He tuk de basket in, en had a long talk wid Aun' Peggy.

"De nex' day Aun' Peggy come up ter de vimya'd. De niggers seed her slippin' 'roun', en dey soon foun' out what she 'uz doin' dere. Mars Dugal' had hi'ed her ter goopher de grape vimes. She sa'ntered 'roun' 'mongs' de vimes, en tuk a leaf fum dis one, en a grape-hull fum dat one, en a grape-seed fum anudder one; en den a little twig fum here, en a little pinch er dirt fum dere—en put it all in a big black bottle, wid a snake's toof en a speckle' hen's gall en some ha'rs fum a black cat's tail, en den fill' de bottle wid scuppernon' wine. W'en she got de goopher all ready en fix', she tuk'n went out in de woods en buried it under de root uv a red oak tree, en den come back en tole one er de niggers she done goopher de grapevimes, en a'er a nigger w'at eat dem grapes 'ud be sho ter die inside'n twel' mont's.

"Atter dat de niggers let de scuppernon's 'lone, en Mars Dugal' didn' hab no 'casion ter fine no mo' fault; en de season wuz mos' gone, w'en a strange gemman stop at de plantation one night ter see Mars Dugal' on some business; en his coachman, seein' de scuppernon's growin' so nice en sweet, slip 'roun' behine de smoke-house, en et all de scuppernon's he could hole. Nobody didn' notice it at de time, but dat night, on de way home, de gemman's hoss runned away en kill' de coachman. W'en we hearn de noos, Aun' Lucy, de cook, she up'n say she seed de strange nigger eat'n' er de scuppernon's behine de smoke-house; en den we knowed de gopher had b'en er wukkin'. Den one er de nigger chilluns runned away fum de quarters one day, en got in de scuppernon's, en died de nex' week. W'ite folks say he die' er de fevuh, but de niggers knowed it wuz de goopher. So you k'n be sho de darkies didn' hab much ter do wid dem scuppernon' vimes.

"W'en de scuppernon' season uz ober fer dat year, Mars Dugal' foun' he had made fifteen hund'ed gallon er wine; en one er de niggers hearn him laffin wid de oberseah fit ter kill, en sayin dem fifteen hund'ed gallon er wine wuz monst'us good intrus' on de ten dollars he laid out on de vimya'd. So I 'low ez he paid Aun' Peggy ten dollars fer to goopher de grapevimes.

"De goopher didn' wuk no mo' tel de nex' summer, w'en 'long to'ds de middle er de season one er de fiel' han's died; en ez dat let' Mars Dugal' sho't er han's, he went off ter town fer ter bu anudder. He fotch de noo nigger home wid 'im. He wuz er ole nigger, er de color er a gingy-cake, en ball ez a hoss-apple on de top er his head. He wuz a peart ole nigger, do', en could do a big day's wuk.

"Now it happen dat one er de niggers on de nex' plantation, one er old Mars Henry Brayboy's niggers, had runned away de day befo', en tuk ter de swamp, en ole Mars Dugal' en some er de yuther nabor w'ite folks had gone out wid dere guns en dere dogs fer ter he'p 'em hunt fer de nigger; en de han's on our own plantation wuz all so flusterated dat we fuh-got ter tell de noo han' 'bout de goopher on de scuppernon' vimes. Co'se he smell de grapes en see de vimes, an atter dahk de fus thing he done wuz ter slip off ter de grapevimes 'dout sayin' nuffin ter nobody. Nex' mawnin' he tole some er de niggers 'bout de fine bait er scuppernon' he et de night befo'.

"W'en dey tole 'im 'bout de goopher on de grapevimes, he 'uz dat tarrified dat he turn pale, en look des like he gwine ter die right in his tracks. De oberseah come up en axed w'at 'uz de matter; en w'en dey tole 'im Henry be'n eatin' er de scuppernon's, en got de goopher on 'im, he gin Henry a big drink er w'iskey, en 'low dat de nex' rainy day he take 'im ober ter Aun' Peggy's, en see ef she wouldn' take de goopher off'n him, seein' ez he didn' know nuffin erbout it tel he done et de grapes.

"Sho nuff, it rain de nex' day, en de oberseah went ober ter Aun' Peggy's wid Henry. En Aun' Peggy say dat bein' ez Henry didn' know 'bout de goopher, en et de grapes in ign'ance er de conseq'ences, she reckon she mought be able fer ter take de goopher off'n him. So she fotch out er bottle wid some cunjuh medicine in it, en po'd some out in a go'd for Henry ter drink. He manage ter git it down; he say it tas'e like whiskey wid sump'n bitter in it. She 'lowed dat 'ud keep de goopher off'n him tel de spring: but w'en de sap begin ter rise in de grapevimes he ha' ter come en see her ag'in, en she tell him w'at e's ter do.

"Nex' spring, w'en de sap commence' ter rise in de scuppernon' vime, Henry tuk a ham one night. Whar'd he git de ham? I doan know; dey wa'n't no hams on de plantation 'cep'n' w'at 'uz in de smoke-house, but I never see Henry 'bout de smoke-house. But ez I wuz a-sayin', he tuk de ham ober ter Aun' Peggy's; en Aun' Peggy tole 'im dat w'en Mars Dugal' begin ter prune de grapevimes, he mus' go en take 'n scrape off de sap whar it ooze out'n de cut een's er de vimes, en 'n'int his ball head wid it; en ef he do dat once't a year de goopher wouldn' wuk agin 'im long ez he done it. En bein' ez he fotch her de ham, she fix' it so he kin eat all de scuppernon' he want.

"So Henry 'n'int his head wid de sap out'n de big grapevime des ha'f way 'twix' de quarters en de big house, en de goopher nebber wuk agin him dat summer. But de beatenes' thing you eber see happen ter Henry. Up ter dat time he wuz ez ball ez a sweeten' 'tater, but des ez soon ez de young leaves begun ter come out on de grapevimes, de ha'r begun ter grow out on Henry's head, en by de middle er de summer he had de bigges' head er ha'r on de plantation. Befo' dat, Henry had tol'able good ha'r 'roun' de aidges, but soon ez de young grapes begun ter come, Henry's ha'r begun to quirl all up in little balls, de like dis yer reg'lar grapy ha'r, en by de time de grapes got ripe his head look des like a bunch er grapes. Combin' it didn' do no good; he wuk at it ha'f de night wid er Jim Crow* en think he git it straighten' out, but in de mawnin' de grapes 'ud be dere des de same. So he gin it up, en tried ter keep de grapes down by havin' his hair cut sho't.

"But dat wa'n't de quares' thing 'bout de goopher. When Henry come ter de plantation, he wuz gittin' a little ole an stiff in de j'ints. But dat summer he got des ez spry en libely ez an young nigger on de plantation; fac', he got so biggity dat Mars Jackson, de oberseah, ha'ter th'eaten ter

*A small card, resembling a currycomb in construction, and used by negroes in the rural districts instead of a comb.

whip 'im, ef he didn' stop cuttin' up his didos en behave hisse'f. But de mos' cur'ouses' thing happen' in de fall, when de sap begin ter go down in de grapevimes. Fus', when de grapes 'uz gethered, de knots begun ter straighten out'n Henry's ha'r; en w'en de leaves begin ter fall, Henry's ha'r 'mence' ter drap out; en when de vimes 'uz bar', Henry's head wuz baller'n it wuz in de spring, en he begin ter git ole en so stiff in de j'ints ag'in, en paid no mo' 'tention ter de gals dyoin' er de whole winter. En nex' spring, w'en he rub de sap on ag'in, he got young ag'in, en so soopl en libely dat none er de young niggers on de plantation couldn' jump, ner dance, ner hoe ez much cotton ez Henry. But in de fall er de year his grapes 'mence' ter straighten out, en his j'ints ter git stiff, en his ha'r drap off, en de rheumatic begin ter wrestle wid 'im.

"Now, ef you'd 'a knowed ole Mars Dugal' McAdoo, you'd 'a knowed dat it ha'ter be a mighty rainy day when he couldn' fine sump'n fer his niggers ter do, en it ha' ter be a mighty little hole he could n' crawl thoo, en ha' ter be a monst'us cloudy night when a dollar git by him in de dahkness; en w'en he see how Henry git young in de spring en ole in de fall, he 'lowed ter hisse'f ez how he could make mo' money out'n Henry dan by wukkin' him in de cotton-fiel'. 'Long de nex' spring, atter de sap 'mence' ter rise, en Henry 'n'int 'is head en sta'ted fer ter git young en soopl, Mars Dugal' up 'n tuk Henry ter town, en sole 'im fer fifteen hunder' dollars. Co'se de man w'at bought Henry didn' know nuffin 'bout de goopher, en Mars Dugal' didn' see no 'casion fer ter tell 'im. Long to'ds de fall, w'en de sap went down, Henry begin ter git ole akin same ez yuzhal, en his noo marster begin ter git sheered les'n he gwine ter lose his fifteen-hunder'-dollar nigger. He sent fer a mighty fine doctor, but de med'cine didn' 'pear ter do no good; de goopher had a good holt. Henry tole de doctor 'bout de goopher, but de doctor des laff at 'im.

"One day in de winter Mars Dugal' went ter town, en wuz santerin' 'long de Main Street, when who should he meet but Henry's noo marster. Dey said 'Hoddy,' en Mars Dugal' ax 'im ter hab a seegyar; en atter dey run on awhile 'bout de craps en de weather, Mars Dugal' ax 'im, sorter keerless, like ez ef des thought of it—

"'How you like de nigger I sole you las' spring?'

"Henry's marster shuck his head en knock de ashes off'n his seegyar.

"''Spec' I made a bad bahgin when I bought dat nigger. Henry done good wuk all de summer, but sence de fall set in he 'pears ter be sorter pinin' away. Dey ain' nuffin pertickler de matter wid 'im—leastways de doctor say so—'cep'n' a tech er de rheumatiz; but his ha'r is all fell out, en ef he don't pick up his strenk mighty soon. I spec' I'm gwine ter lose 'im.'

"Dey smoked on awhile, en bimeby ole mars say. 'Well, a bahgin's a bahgin, but you en me is good fren's, en I doan wan' ter see you lose all de money you paid fer dat nigger; en if w'at you say is so, en I ain't 'sputin' it, he ain't wuf much now. I 'spec's you wukked him too he'd dis summer, er e'se de swamps down here don't agree wid de san'-hill nigger. So you des lemme know, en ef he gits any wusser I'll be willin' ter gib yer five hund'ed dollars fer 'im, en take m' chances on his livin'.'

"Sho 'nuff, when Henry begun ter draw up wid de rheumatiz en it look like he gwine ter die fer sho, his noo marster sen' fer Mars Dugal', en Mars Dugal' gin him what he promus, en brung Henry home ag'in. He tuk good keer uv 'im dyoin' er de winter—give 'im w'iskey ter rub his rheumatiz, en terbacker ter smoke, en all he want ter eat—caze a nigger w'at he could make a thousan' dollars a year off'n didn' grow on eve'y huckleberry bush.

"Nex' spring, w'en de sap ris en Henry's ha'r commence' ter sprout, Mars Dugal' sole 'im ag'in, down in Robeson County dis time; en he kep' dat sellin' business up fer five year er mo'. Henry nebber say nuffin 'bout de goopher ter his noo marsters, 'caze he know he gwine ter be tuk good keer uv de nex' winter, w'en Mars Dugal' buy him back. En Mars Dugal' made 'nuff money off'n Henry ter buy anudder plantation ober on Beaver Crick.

"But 'long 'bout de een' er dat five year dey come a stranger ter stop at de plantation. De fus' day he 'uz dere he went out wid Mars Dugal' en spent all de mawnin' lookin' ober de vimya'd, en atter dinner dey spent all de evenin' playin' kya'ds. De niggers soon 'skiver' dat he wuz a Yankee, en dat he come down ter Norf C'lina fer ter l'arn de w'ite folks how to raise grapes en make wine. He promus Mars Dugal' he c'd make de grapevimes b'ar twice't ez many grapes, en dat de noo winepress he wuz a-sellin' would make mo'd'n twice't ez many gallons er wine. En ole Mars Dugal' des drunk it all in, des 'peared ter be bewitch' wid dat Yankee. W'en de darkies see dat Yankee runnin' 'roun' de vimya'd en diggin' under de grapevimes, dey shuk dere heads, en 'lowed dat dey feared Mars Dugal' losin' his min'. Mars Dugal' had all de dirt dug away fum under de roots er all de scuppernon' vimes, an' let 'em stan' dat away fer a week er mo'. Den dat Yankee made de niggers fix up a mixtry er lime en ashes en manyo, en po' it 'roun' de roots er de grapevimes. Den he 'vise Mars Dugal' fer ter trim de vimes close't, en Mars Dugal' tuck 'n done eve'ything de Yankee tole him ter do. Dyoin' all er dis time, mind yer, dis yer Yankee wuz libbin' off'n de fat er de lan', at de big house, en playin' kya'ds wid Mars Dugal' eve'y night; en dey say Mars Dugal' los' mo'n a thousan' dollars dyoin' er de week dat Yankee wuz a-ruinin' de grapevimes.

"W'en de sap ris nex' spring, ole Henry 'n'inted his head ez yuzhal, en his ha'r 'mence' ter grow des de same ez it done eve'y year. De scuppernon' vimes growed monst's fas', en de leaves wuz greener en thicker den dey eber be'n dyoin' my rememb'ance; en Henry's ha'r growed out thicker den eber, en he 'peared ter git younger 'n younger, en soopler 'n soopler; en seein' ez he wuz sho't er han's dat spring, havin' tuk in consid'able noo groun', Mars Dugal' 'cluded he wouldn' sell Henry 'tel he git de crap in en de cotton chop'. So he kep' Henry on de plantation.

"But 'long 'bout time fer de grapes ter come on de scuppernon' vimes, dey 'peared ter come a change ober 'em; de leaves withered en swivel' up, en de young grapes turn' yaller, en bimeby eve'ybody on de plantation could see dat de whole vimya'd wuz dyin'. Mars Dugal' tuk'n water de vimes en done all he could, but 't wa'n' no use: dat Yankee had done bus' de watermillyum. One time de vimes picked up a bit, en Mars Dugal' 'lowed dey wuz gwine ter come out ag'in; but dat Yankee done dug too close under de roots, en prune de branches too close ter de vime, en all dat lime en ashes done burn' de life out'n de vimes, en dey des kep' a-with'in' en a-swivelin'.

"All dis time de goopher wuz a wukkin'. When de vimes sta'ted ter wither, Henry 'mence' ter complain er his rheumatiz; en when de leaves begin ter dry up, his ha'r'mence' ter drap out. When de vimes fresh' up a bit, Henry'd git peart ag'in, en when de vimes wither' ag'in, Henry'd git ole ag'in, en des kep' gittin' mo' en mo' fitten fer nuffin; he des pined away, en pined away, en fine'ly tuk ter his cabin; en when de big vime whar he got de sap ter 'n'int his head withered en turned yaller en died, Henry died too—des went out sorter like a cannel. Dey didn't 'pear ter be nuffin de matter wid 'im, 'cep'n' de rheumatiz, but his strenk des dwinel' away 'tel he didn' hab ernuff lef' ter draw his bref. De goopher had got de under bolt, en th'owed Henry dat time fer good en all.

"Mars Dugal' tuk on might'ly 'bout losin' his vimes en his nigger in de same year; en he swo' dat ef he could git holt er dat Yankee he'd wear 'im ter a frazzle, en den chaw up de frazzle; en he'd done it, too, for Mars Dugal' 'uz a monst'us brash man w'en he once git started. He sot de vimya'd out ober ag'in, but it wuz th'ee er fo' year befo' de vimes got ter b'arin' any scuppernon's.

"W'en de wah broke out, Mars Dugal' raise' a comp'ny, en went off ter fight de Yankees. He say he wuz mighty glad dat wah come, en he des want ter kill a Yankee fer eve'y dollar he los' 'long er dat grape-raisin' Yankee. En I 'spec' he would 'a' done it, too, ef de Yankees hadn' s'picioned sump'n en killed him fus'. Atter de s'render ole miss move' ter town, de niggers all scattered 'way fum de plantation, en de vimya'd ain' be'n cultervated sence."

"Is that story true?" asked Annie doubtfully, but seriously, as the old man concluded his narrative.

"It's des ez tru ez I'm a-settin' here, miss. Dey's a easy way ter prove it: I kin lead de way right ter Henry's grave ober yander in de plantation buryin' groun'. En I tell yer w'at, marster, wouldn' 'vise you to buy dis yer ole vimya'd, 'caze de goopher's on it yit, en dey ain' no tellin' w'en it's gwine ter crap out."

"But I thought you said all the old vines died."

"Dey did 'pear ter die, but a few un 'em come out ag'in, en is mixed in 'mongs' de yuthers. Ain' skeered ter eat de grapes, 'caze I knows de old vimes fum de noo ones; but wid strangers de ain' no tellin' w'at mought happer. I wouldn' 'vise yer ter buy dis vimya'd."

I bought the vineyard, nevertherless, and it has been for a long time in a thriving condition, and is often referred to by the local press as a striking illustration of the opportunities open to Northern capital in the development of Southern industries. The luscious scuppernong holds first rank among our grapes, though we cultivate a great many other varieties, and our income from grapes packed and shipped to the Northern markets is quite considerable. I have not noticed any developments of the goopher in the vineyard, although I have a mild suspicion that our colored assistants do not suffer from want of grapes during the season.

I found, when I bought the vineyard, that Uncle Julius had occupied a cabin on the place for many years, and derived a respectable revenue from the product of the neglected grapevines. This, doubtless, accounted for his advice to me not to buy the vineyard, though whether it inspired the goopher story I am unable to state. I believe, however, that the wages I paid him for his services as coachman, for I gave him employment in that capacity, were more than an equivalent for anything he lost by the sale of the vineyard.

The Evening and the Morning and the Night

Octavia E. Butler

(1987)

When I was fifteen and trying to show my independence by getting careless with my diet, my parents took me to a Duryea-Gode disease ward. They wanted me to see, they said, where I was headed if I wasn't careful. In fact, it was where I was headed no matter what. It was only a matter of when: now or later. My parents were putting in their vote for later.

I won't describe the ward. It's enough to say that when they brought me home, I cut my wrists. I did a thorough job of it, old Roman style in a bathtub of warm water. Almost made it. My father dislocated his shoulder breaking down the bathroom door. He and I never forgave each other for that day.

The disease got him almost three years later—just before I went off to college. It was sudden. It doesn't happen that way often. Most people notice themselves beginning to drift—or their relatives notice—and they make arrangements with their chosen Institution. People who are noticed and who resist going in can be locked up for a week's observation. I don't doubt that that observation period breaks up a few families. Sending someone away for what turns out to be a false alarm. . . . Well, it isn't the sort of thing the victim is likely to forgive or forget. On the other hand, not sending someone away in time—missing the signs or having a person go off suddenly without signs—is inevitably dangerous for the victim. I've never heard of it going as badly, though, as it did in my family. People normally injure only themselves when their time comes—unless someone is stupid enough to try to handle them without the necessary or restraints.

My father had killed my mother, then killed himself. I wasn't home when it happened. I had stayed at school later than usual, rehearsing graduation exercises. By the time I got home, there were cops every-where. There was an ambulance, and two attendants were wheeling someone out on a stretcher—someone covered. More than covered. Al-most . . . bagged.

The cops wouldn't let me in. I didn't find out until later exactly what had happened. I wish I'd never found out. Dad had killed Mom, then skinned her completely. At least that's how I hope it happened. I mean I hope he killed her first. He broke some of her ribs, damaged her heart. Digging.

Then he began tearing at himself, through skin and bone, digging. He had managed to reach his own heart before he died. It was an espe-cially bad example of the kind of thing that makes people afraid of us. It gets some of us into trouble for picking at a pimple or even for day-dreaming. It has inspired restrictive laws, created problems with jobs, housing, schools. . . . The Duryea-Gode Disease Foundation has spent millions telling the world that people like my father don't exist.

A long time later, when I had gotten myself together as best I could, I went to college—to the University of Southern California—on a Dilg scholarship. Dilg is the retreat you try to send your out-of-control DGD relatives to. It's run by controlled DGDs like me, like my parents while they lived. God knows how any controlled DGD stands it. Anyway, the place has a waiting list miles long. My parents put me on it after my sui-cide attempt, but chances were, I'd be dead by the time my name came up.

I can't say why I went to college—except that I had been going to school all my life and didn't know what else to do. I didn't go with any particular hope. Hell, I knew what I was in for eventually. I was just marking time. Whatever I did was just marking time. If people were willing to pay me to go to school and mark time, why not do it?

The weird part was, I worked hard, got top grades. If you work hard enough at something that doesn't matter, you can forget for a while about the things that do.

Sometimes I thought about trying suicide again. How was it I'd had the courage when I was fifteen but didn't have it now? Two DGD par-ents—both religious, both as opposed to abortion as they were to sui-cide. So they had trusted God and the promise of modern medicine and had a child. But how could I look at what had happened to them and trust anything?

I majored in biology. Non-DGDs say something about our disease makes us good at the sciences—genetics, molecular biology, biochemistry. . . . That something was terror. Terror and a kind of driving hopelessness. Some of us went bad and became destructive before we had to—yes, we did produce more than our share of criminals. And some of us went good—spectacularly—and made scientific and medical history. These last kept the doors at least partly open for the rest of us. They made discoveries in genetics, found cures for a couple of rare diseases, made advances against other diseases that weren't so rare—including, ironically, some forms of cancer. But they'd found nothing to help themselves. There had been nothing since the latest improvements in the diet, and those came just before I was born. They, like the original diet, gave more DGDs the courage to have children. They were supposed to do for DGDs what insulin had done for diabetics—give us a normal or nearly normal life span. Maybe they had worked that way for someone somewhere. They hadn't worked that way for anyone I knew.

School was a pain in the usual ways. I didn't eat in public anymore, didn't like the way people stared at my biscuits—cleverly dubbed "dog bicuits" in every school I'd ever attended. You'd think university students would be more creative. I didn't like the way people edged away from me when they caught sight of my emblem. I'd begun wearing it on a chain around my neck and putting it down inside my blouse, but people managed to notice it anyway. People who don't eat in public, who drink nothing more interesting than water, who smoke nothing at all—people like that are suspicious. Or rather, they make others suspicious. Sooner or later, one of those others, finding my fingers and wrists bare, would fake an interest in my chain. That would be that. I couldn't hide the emblem in my purse. If anything happened to me, medical people had to see it in time to avoid giving me the medications they might use on a normal person. It isn't just ordinary food we have to avoid, but about a quarter of a *Physicians' Desk Reference* of widely used drugs. Every now and then there are news stories about people who stopped carrying their emblems—probably trying to pass as normal. Then they have an accident. By the time anyone realizes there is anything wrong, it's too late. So I wore my emblem. And one way or another, people got a look at it or got the word from someone who had. "She *is*!" Yeah.

At the beginning of my third year, four other DGDs and I decided to rent a house together. We'd all had enough of being lepers twenty-four hours a day. There was an English major. He wanted to be a writer and tell our story from the inside—which had only been done thirty or forty times before. There was a special-education major who hoped the handicapped would accept her more readily than the able-bodied, a premed who planned to go into research, and a chemistry major who didn't really know what she wanted to do.

Two men and three women. All we had in common was our disease, plus a weird combination of stubborn intensity about whatever we happened to be doing and hopeless cynicism about everything else. Healthy people say no one can concentrate like a DGD. Healthy people have all the time in the world for stupid generalizations and short attention spans.

We did our work, came up for air now and then, ate our biscuits, and attended classes. Our only problem was housecleaning. We worked out a schedule of who would clean what when, who would deal with the yard, whatever. We all agreed on it; then, except for me, everyone seemed to forget about it.

I found myself going around reminding people to vacuum, clean the bathroom, mow the lawn. . . . I figured they'd all hate me in no time, but I wasn't going to be their maid, and I wasn't going to live in filth. Nobody complained. Nobody even seemed annoyed. They just came up out of their academic daze, cleaned, mopped, mowed, and went back to it. I got into the habit of running around in the evening reminding people. It didn't bother me if it didn't bother them.

"How'd you get to be housemother?" a visiting DGD asked.

I shrugged. "Who cares? The house works." It did. It worked so well that this new guy wanted to move in. He was a friend of one of the others, and another premed. Not bad looking.

"So do I get in or don't I?" he asked.

"As far as I'm concerned, you do," I said. I did what his friend should have done—introduced him around, then, after he left, talked to the others to make sure nobody had any real objections. He seemed to fit right in. He forgot to clean the toilet or mow the lawn, just like the others. His name was Alan Chi. I thought Chi was a Chinese name, and I wondered. But he told me his father was Nigerian and that in Ibo the word meant a kind of guardian angel or personal God. He said his own personal God hadn't been looking our for him very well to let him be born to two DGD parents. Him too.

I don't think it was much more than that similarity that drew us together at first. Sure, I liked the way he looked, but I was used to liking someone's looks and having him run like hell when he found out what I was. It took me a while to get used to the fact that Alan wasn't going anywhere.

I told him about my visit to the DGD ward when I was fifteen—and my suicide attempt afterward. I had never told anyone else. I was surprised at how relieved it made me feel to tell him. And somehow his reaction didn't surprise me.

"Why didn't you try again?" he asked. We were alone in the living room.

"At first, because of my parents," I said. "My father in particular. I couldn't do that to him again."

"And after him?"

"Fear. Inertia."

He nodded. "When I do it, there'll be no half measures. No being rescued, no waking up in a hospital later."

"You mean to do it?"

"The day I realize I've started to drift. Thank God we get some warning."

"Not necessarily."

"Yes, we do. I've done a lot of reading. Even talked to a couple of doctors. Don't believe the rumors non-DGDs invent."

I looked away, stared into the scarred, empty fireplace. I told him exactly how my father had died—something else I'd never voluntarily told anyone.

He sighed. "Jesus!"

We looked at each other.

"What are you going to do?" he asked.

"I don't know."

He extended a dark, square hand, and I took it and moved closer to him. He was a dark, square man—my height, half again my weight, and non of it fat. He was so bitter sometimes, he scared me.

"My mother started to drift when I was three," he said. "My father only lasted a few months longer. I heard he died a couple of years after he went into the hospital. If the two of them had had any sense, they would have had me aborted the minute my mother realized she was

pregnant. But she wanted a kid no matter what. And she was Catholic."
He shook his head. "Hell, they should pass a law to sterilize the lot of us."

"They?" I said.

"You want kids?"

"No, but—"

"More like us to wind up chewing their fingers off in some DGD ward."

"I don't want kids, but I don't want someone else telling me I can't have any."

He stared at me until I began to feel stupid and defensive. I moved away from him.

"Do you want someone else telling you what to do with your body?" I asked.

"No need," he said. "I had that taken care of as soon as I was old enough."

This left me staring. I'd thought about sterilization. What DGD hasn't? But I didn't know anyone else our age who had actually gone through with it. That would be like killing part of yourself—even though it wasn't a part you intended to use. Killing part of yourself when so much of you was already dead.

"The damned disease could be wiped out in one generation," he said, "but people are still animals when it comes to breeding. Still following mindless urges, like dogs and cats."

My impulse was to get up and go away, leave him to wallow in his bitterness and depression alone. But I stayed. He seemed to want to live even less than I did. I wondered how he'd made it this far.

"Are you looking forward to doing research?" I probed. "Do you believe you'll be able to—"

"No."

I blinked. The word was as cold and dead a sound as I'd ever heard.

"I don't believe in anything," he said.

I took him to bed. He was the only other double DGD I had ever met, and if nobody did anything for him, he wouldn't last much longer. I couldn't just let him slip away. For a while, maybe we could be each other's reasons for staying alive.

He was a good student—for the same reason I was. And he seemed to shed some of his bitterness as time passed. Being around him helped me understand why, against all sanity, two DGDs would lock in on each other and start talking about marriage. Who else would have us?

We probably wouldn't last very long, anyway. These days, most DGDs make it to forty, at least. But then, most of them don't have two DGD parents. As bright as Alan was, he might not get into medical school because of his double inheritance. No one would tell him his bad genes were keeping him out, of course, but we both knew what his chances were. Better to train doctors who were likely to live long enough to put their training to use.

Alan's mother had been sent to Dilg. He hadn't seen her or been able to get any information about her from his grandparents while he was at home. By the time he left for college, he'd stopped asking questions. Maybe it was hearing about my parents that made him start again. I was with him when he called Dilg. Until that moment, he hadn't even known whether his mother was still alive. Surprisingly, she was.

"Dilg must be good," I said when he hung up. "People don't usually . . . I mean . . ."

"Yeah, I know," he said. "People don't usually live long once they're out of control. Dilg is different." We had gone to my room, where he turned a chair backward and sat down. "Dilg is what the others ought to be, if you can believe the literature."

"Dilg is a giant DGD ward," I said. "It's richer—probably better at sucking in the donations—and it's run by people who can expect to become patients eventually. Apart from that, what's different?"

"I've read about it," he said. "So should you. They've got some new treatment. They don't just shut people away to die the way the others do."

"What else is there to do with them? With us."

"I don't know. It sounded like they have some kind of sheltered workshop. They've got patients doing things."

"A new drug to control the self-destructiveness?"

"I don't think so. We would have heard about that."

"What else could it be?"

"I'm going up to find out. Will you come with me?"

"You're going up to see your mother."

He took a ragged breath. "Yeah. Will you come with me?"

I went to one of my windows and stared out at the weeds. We let them thrive in the backyard. In the front we mowed them, along with a few patches of grass.

"I told you my DGD-ward experience."

"You're not fifteen now. And Dilg isn't some zoo of a ward."

"It's got to be, no matter what they tell the public. And I'm not sure I can stand it."

He got up, came to stand next to me. "Will you try?"

I didn't say anything. I focused on our reflections in the window glass—the two of us together. It looked right, felt right. He put his arm around me, and I leaned back against him. Our being together had been as good for me as it seemed to have been for him. It had given me something to go on besides inertia and fear. I knew I would go with him. It felt like the right thing to do.

"I can't say how I'll act when we get there," I said.

"I can't say how I'll act, either," he admitted. "Especially . . . when I see her."

He made the appointment for the next Saturday afternoon. You make appointments to go to Dilg unless you're a government inspector of some kind. That is the custom, and Dilg gets away with it.

We left L.A. in the rain early Saturday morning. Rain followed us off and on up the coast as far as Santa Barbara. Dilg was hidden away in the hills not far from San Jose. We could have reached it faster by driving up I-5, but neither of us were in the mood for all that bleakness. As it was, we arrived at one P.M. to be met by two armed gate guards. One of these phoned the main building and verified our appointment. Then the other took the wheel from Alan.

"Sorry," he said. "But no one is permitted inside without an escort. We'll meet your guide at the garage."

None of this surprised me. Dilg is a place where not only the patients but much of the staff has DGD. A maximum security prison wouldn't have been as potentially dangerous. On the other hand, I'd never heard of anyone getting chewed up here. Hospitals and rest homes had accidents. Dilg didn't.

It was beautiful—an old estate. One that didn't make sense these days of high taxes. It had been owned by the Dilg family. Oil chemicals, pharmaceuticals. Ironically, they had even owned part of the late, unlamented Hedeon Laboratories. They'd had a briefly profitable interest in

Hedeonco: the magic bullet, the cure for a large percentage of the world's cancer and a number of serious viral diseases—and the cause of Duryea-Gode disease. If one of your parents was treated with Hedeonco and you were conceived after the treatments, you had DGD. If you had kids, you passed it on to them. Not everyone was equally affected. They didn't all commit suicide or murder, but they all mutilated themselves to some degree if they could. And they all drifted—went off into a world of their own and stopped responding to their surroundings.

Anyway, the only Dilg son of his generation had had his life saved by Hedeonco. Then he had watched four of his children die before Doctors Kenneth Duryea and Jan Gode came up with a decent understanding of the problem and a partial solution: the diet. They gave Richard Dilg a way of keeping his next two children alive. He gave the big, cumbersome estate over to the care of DGD patients.

So the main building was an elaborate old mansion. There were other, newer buildings, more like guest houses than institutional buildings. And there were wooded hills all around. Nice country. Green. The ocean wasn't far away. There was an old garage and a small parking lot. Waiting in the lot was a tall, old woman. Our guard pulled up near her, let us out, then parked the car in the half-empty garage.

"Hello," the woman said, extending her hand. "I'm Beatrice Alcantara." The hand was cool and dry and startlingly strong. I thought the woman was DGD, but her age threw me. She appeared to be about sixty, and I had never seen a DGD that old. I wasn't sure why I thought she was DGD. If she was, she must have been an experimental model—one of the first to survive.

"Is it Doctor or Ms.?" Alan asked.

"It's Beatrice," she said. "I am a doctor, but we don't use titles much here."

I glanced at Alan, was surprised to see him smiling at her. He tended to go a long time between smiles. I looked at Beatrice and couldn't see anything to smile about. As we introduced ourselves, I realized I didn't like her. I couldn't see any reason for that either, but my feelings were my feelings. I didn't like her.

"I assume neither of you have been here before," she said, smiling down at us. She was at least six feet tall, and straight.

We shook our heads. "Let's go in the front way, then. I want to prepare you for what we do here. I don't want you to believe you've come to a hospital."

I frowned at her, wondering what else there was to believe. Dilg was called a retreat, but what difference did names make?

The house close up looked like one of the old-style public buildings—massive, baroque front with a single domed tower reaching three stories above the three-story house. Wings of the house stretched for some distance to the right and left of the tower, then cornered and stretched back twice as far. The front doors were huge—one set of wrought iron and one of heavy wood. Neither appeared to be locked. Beatrice pulled open the iron door, pushed the wooden one, and gestured us in.

Inside, the house was an art museum—huge, high ceilinged, tile floored. There were marble columns and niches in which sculptures stood or paintings hung. There were other sculptures displayed around the rooms. At one end of the rooms there was a broad staircase leading up to a gallery that went around the rooms. There more art was displayed. "All this was made here," Beatrice said. "Some of it is even sold from here. Most goes to galleries in the Bay Area or down around L.A. Our only problem is turning out too much of it."

"You mean the patients do this?" I asked.

The old woman nodded. "This and much more. Our people work instead of tearing at themselves or staring into space. One of them invented the p.v. locks that protect this place. Though I almost wish he hadn't. It's gotten us more government attention than we like."

"What kind of locks?" I asked.

"Sorry. Palmprint-voiceprint. The first and the best. We have the patent." She looked at Alan. "Would you like to see what your mother does?"

"Wait a minute," he said. "You're telling us out-of-control DGDs create art and invent things?"

"And that lock," I said. "I've never heard of anything like that. I didn't even see a lock."

"The lock is new," she said. "There have been a few news stories about it. It's not the kind of thing most people would buy for their homes. Too expensive. So it's of limited interest. People tend to look at what's done at Dilg in the way they look at the efforts of idiots savants. Interesting, incomprehensible, but not really important. Those likely to be interested in the lock and able to afford it know about it." She took a deep breath, faced Alan again. "Oh, yes, DGDs create things. At least they do here."

"Out-of-control DGDs."

"Yes."

"I expected to find them weaving baskets or something—at best. I know what DGD wards are like."

"So do I," she said. "I know what they're like in hospitals, and I know what it's like here." She waved a hand toward an abstract painting that looked like a photo I had once seen of the Orion Nebula. Darkness broken by a great cloud of light and color. "Here we can help them channel their energies. They can create something beautiful, useful, even something worthless. But they create. They don't destroy."

"Why?" Alan demanded. "It can't be some drug. We would have heard."

"It's not a drug."

"Then what is it? Why haven't other hospitals—?"

"Alan," she said. "Wait."

He stood frowning at her.

"Do you want to see your mother?"

"Of course I want to see her!"

"Good. Come with me. Things will sort themselves out."

She led us to a corridor past offices where people talked to one another, waved to Beatrice, worked with computers. . . . They could have been anywhere. I wondered how many of them were controlled DGDS. I also wondered what kind of game the old woman was playing with her secrets. We passed through rooms so beautiful and perfectly kept it was now obvious they were rarely used. Then at a broad, heavy door, she stopped us.

"Look at anything you like as we go on," she said. "But don't touch anything or anyone. And remember that some of the people you'll see injured themselves before they came to us. They still bear the scars of those injuries. Some of those scars may be difficult to look at, but you'll be in no danger. Keep that in mind. No one here will harm you." She pushed the door open and gestured us in.

Scars didn't bother me much. Disability didn't bother me. It was the act of self-mutilation that scared me. It was someone attacking her own arm as though it were a wild animal. It was someone who had torn at himself and been restrained or drugged off and on for so long that he barely had a recognizable human feature left, but he was still trying with what he did have to dig into his own flesh. Those are a couple of the things I saw at the DGD ward when I was fifteen. Even then I could have stood it better if I hadn't felt I was looking into a kind of temporal mirror.

I wasn't aware of walking through that doorway. I wouldn't have thought I could do it. The old woman said something, though, and I found myself on the other side of the door with the door closing behind me. I turned to stare at her.

She put her hand on my arm. "It's all right," she said quietly. "That door looks like a wall to a great many people."

I backed away from her, out of her reach, repelled by her touch. Shaking hands had been enough, for God's sake.

Something in her seemed to come to attention as she watched me. It made her even straighter. Deliberately, but for no apparent reason, she stepped toward Alan, touched him the way people do sometimes when they brush past—a kind of tactile "Excuse me." In that wide, empty corridor, it was totally unnecessary. For some reason, she wanted to touch him and wanted me to see. What did she think she was doing? Flirting at her age? I glared at her, found myself suppressing an irrational urge to shove her away from him. The violence of the urge amazed me.

Beatrice smiled and turned away. "This way," she said. Alan put his arm around me and tried to lead me after her.

"Wait a minute," I said, not moving.

Beatrice glanced around.

"What just happened?" I asked. I was ready for her to lie—to say nothing happened, pretend not to know what I was talking about.

"Are you planning to study medicine?" she asked.

"What? What does that have to do—?"

"Study medicine. You may be able to do a great deal of good." She strode away, taking long steps so that we had to hurry to keep up. She led us through a room in which some people worked at computer terminals and others with pencils and paper. It would have been an ordinary scene except that some people had half their faces ruined or had only one hand or leg or had other obvious scars. But they were all in control now. They were working. They were intent but not intent on self-destruction. Not one was digging into or tearing away flesh. When we had passed through this room and into a small, ornate sitting room, Alan grasped Beatrice's arm.

"What is it?" he demanded. "What do you do for them?"

She patted his hand, setting my teeth on edge. "I will tell you," she said. "I want you to know. But I want you to see your mother first." To my surprise, he nodded, let it go at that.

"Sit a moment," she said to us.

We sat in comfortable, matching upholstered chairs—Alan looking reasonably relaxed. What was it about the old lady that relaxed him but put me on edge? Maybe she reminded him of his grandmother or something. She didn't remind me of anyone. And what was that nonsense about studying medicine?

"I wanted you to pass through at least one workroom before we talked about your mother—and about the two of you." She turned to face me. "You've had a bad experience at a hospital or a rest home?"

I looked away from her, not wanting to think about it. Hadn't the people in that mock office been enough of a reminder? Horror film office. Nightmare office.

"It's all right," she said. "You don't have to go into it, just outline it for me."

I obeyed slowly, against my will, all the while wondering why I was doing it.

She nodded, unsurprised. "Harsh, loving people, parents. Are they alive?"

"No."

"Were they both DGD?"

"Yes, but . . . yes."

"Of course, aside from the obvious ugliness of your hospital experience and its implications for the future, what impressed you about the people in the ward?"

I didn't know what to answer. What did she want? Why did she want anything from me? She should have been concerned with Alan and his mother.

"Did you see people unrestrained?"

"Yes," I whispered. "One woman. I don't know how it happened that she was free. She ran up to us and slammed into my father without moving him. He was a big man. She bounced off, fell, and . . . began tearing at herself. She bit her own arm and . . . swallowed the flesh she'd bitten away. She tore at the wound she'd made with the nails of her other hand. She . . . I screamed at her to stop." I hugged myself, remembering the young woman, bloody, cannibalizing herself as she lay at our feet, digging into her own flesh. Digging. "They try so hard, fight so hard to get out."

"Out of what?" Alan demanded.

I looked at him, hardly seeing him.

"Lynn," he said gently. "Out of what?"

I shook my head. "Their restraints, their disease, the ward, their bodies . . ."

He glanced at Beatrice, then spoke to me again. "Did the girl talk?"

"No. She screamed."

He turned away from me uncomfortably. "Is this important?" he asked Beatrice.

"Very," she said.

"Well . . . can we talk about it after I see my mother?"

"Then and now." She spoke to me. "Did the girl stop what she was doing when you told her to?"

"The nurses had her a moment later. It didn't matter."

"It mattered. Did she stop?"

"Yes."

"According to the literature, they rarely respond to anyone," Alan said.

"True." Beatrice gave him a sad smile. "Your mother will probably respond to you, though."

"Is she? . . ." He glanced back at the nightmare office. "Is she as controlled as those people?"

"Yes, though she hasn't always been. Your mother works with clay now. She loves shapes and textures and—"

"She's blind," Alan said, voicing the suspicion as though it were fact. Beatrice's words had sent my thoughts in the same direction. Beatrice hesitated. "Yes," she said finally. "And for the usual reason. I had intended to prepare you slowly."

"I've done a lot of reading."

I hadn't done much reading, but I knew what the usual reason was. The woman had gouged, ripped, or otherwise destroyed her eyes. She would be badly scarred. I got up, went over to sit on the arm of Alan's chair. I rested my hand on his shoulder, and he reached up and held it there.

"Can we see her now?" he asked.

Beatrice got up. "This way," she said.

We passed through more workrooms. People painted; assembled machinery; sculpted in wood, stone; even composed and played music. Almost no one noticed us. The patients were true to their disease in that respect. They weren't ignoring us. They clearly didn't know we existed. Only the few controlled DGD guards gave themselves away by waving or speaking to Beatrice. I watched a woman work quickly, knowledgeably, with a power saw. She obviously understood the perimeters of her body, was not so dissociated as to perceive herself as trapped in something she needed to dig her way out of. What had Dilg done for these people that other hospitals did not do? And how could Dilg withhold its treatment from the others?

"Over there we make our own diet foods," Beatrice said, pointing through a window toward one of the guest houses. "We permit more variety and make fewer mistakes than the commercial preparers. No ordinary person can concentrate on work the way our people can."

I turned to face her. "What are you saying? That the bigots are right? That we have some special gift?"

"Yes," she said. "It's hardly a bad characteristic, is it?"

"It's what people say whenever one of us does well at something. It's their way of denying us credit for our work."

"Yes. But people occasionally come to the right conclusions for the wrong reasons." I shrugged, not interested in arguing with her about it.

"Alan?" she said. He looked at her.

"Your mother is in the next room."

He swallowed, nodded. We both followed her into the room.

Naomi Chi was a small woman, hair still dark, fingers long and thin, graceful as they shaped the clay. Her face was a ruin. Not only her eyes but most of her nose and one ear were gone. What was left was badly scarred. "Her parents were poor," Beatrice said. "I don't know how much they told you, Alan, but they went through all the money they had, trying to keep her at a decent place. Her mother felt so guilty, you know. She was the one who had cancer and took the drug. . . . Eventually, they had to put Naomi in one of those state approved, custodial-care places. You know the kind. For a while, it was all the government would pay for.

Places like that . . . well, sometimes if patients were really trouble-
some—especially the ones who kept breaking free—they'd put them in
a bare room and let them finish themselves. The only things those
places took good care of were the maggots, the cockroaches, and the
rats."

I shuddered. "I've heard there are still places like that."

"There are," Beatrice said, "kept open by greed and indifference."
She looked at Alan. "Your mother survived for three months in one of
those places. I took her from it myself. Later I was instrumental in having that particular place closed."

"You took her?" I asked.

"Dilg didn't exist then, but I was working with a group of controlled
DGDs in L.A. Naomi's parents heard about us and asked us to take her.
A lot of people didn't trust us then. Only a few of us were medically
trained. All of us were young, idealistic, and ignorant. We began in an
old frame house with a leaky roof. Naomi's parents were grabbing at
straws. So were we. And by pure luck, we grabbed a good one. We were
able to prove ourselves to the Dilg family and take over these quarters."

"Prove what?" I asked.

She turned to look at Alan and his mother. Alan was staring at
Naomi's ruined face, at the ropy, discolored scar tissue. Naomi was shap-
ing the image of an old woman and two children. The gaunt, lined face
of the old woman was remarkably vivid—detailed in a way that seemed
impossible for a blind sculptress.

Naomi seemed unaware of us. Her total attention remained on her
work. Alan forgot about what Beatrice had told us and reached out to
touch the scarred face.

Beatrice let it happen. Naomi did not seem to notice. "If I get her attention for you," Beatrice said, "we'll be breaking her routine. We'll
have to stay with her until she gets back into it without hurting herself.
About half an hour."

"You can get her attention?" he asked.

"Yes."

"Can she?" Alan swallowed. "I've never heard of anything like this.
Can she talk?"

"Yes. She may not choose to, though. And if she does, she'll do it
very slowly."

"Do it. Get her attention."

"She'll want to touch you."

"That's all right. Do it."

Beatrice took Naomi's hands and held them still, away from the wet clay. For several seconds Naomi tugged at her captive hands, as though unable to understand why they did not move as she wished.

Beatrice stepped closer and spoke quietly. "Stop, Naomi." And Naomi was still, blind face turned toward Beatrice in an attitude of attentive waiting. Totally focused waiting.

"Company, Naomi."

After a few seconds, Naomi made a wordless sound.

Beatrice gestured Alan to her side, gave Naomi one of his hands. It didn't bother me this time when she touched him. I was too interested in what was happening. Naomi examined Alan's hand minutely, then followed the arm up to the shoulder, the neck, the face. Holding his face between her hands, she made a sound. It may have been a word, but I couldn't understand it. All I could think of was the danger of those hands. I thought of my father's hands.

"His name is Alan Chi, Naomi. He's your son." Several seconds passed.

"Son?" she said. This time the word was quite distinct, though her lips had split in many places and had healed badly. "Son?" she repeated anxiously. "Here?"

"He's all right, Naomi. He's come to visit."

"Mother?" he said.

She reexamined his face. He had been three when she started to drift. It didn't seem possible that she could find anything in his face that she would remember. I wondered whether she remembered she had a son.

"Alan?" she said. She found his tears and paused at them. She touched her own face where there should have been an eye, then she reached back toward his eyes. An instant before I would have grabbed her hand, Beatrice did it.

"No!" Beatrice said firmly.

The hand fell limply to Naomi's side. Her face turned toward Beatrice like an antique weather vane swinging around. Beatrice stroked her hair, and Naomi said something I almost understood. Beatrice looked at Alan, who was frowning and wiping away tears.

"Hug your son," Beatrice said softly.

Naomi turned, groping, and Alan seized her in a tight, long hug. Her arms went around him slowly. She spoke words blurred by her ruined mouth but just understandable.

"Parents?" she said. "Did my parents . . . care for you?" Alan looked at her, clearly not understanding.

"She wants to know whether her parents took care of you," I said.

He glanced at me doubtfully, then looked at Beatrice.

"Yes," Beatrice said. "She just wants to know that they cared for you."

"They did," he said. "They kept their promise to you, Mother."

Several seconds passed. Naomi made sounds that even Alan took to be weeping, and he tried to comfort her.

"Who else is here?" she said finally.

This time Alan looked at me. I repeated what she had said.

"Her name is Lynn Mortimer," he said. "I'm . . ." He paused awkwardly. "She and I are going to be married."

After a time, she moved back from him and said my name. My first impulse was to go to her. I wasn't afraid or repelled by her now, but for no reason I could explain, I looked at Beatrice.

"Go," she said. "But you and I will have to talk later."

I went to Naomi, took her hand.

"Bea?" she said.

"I'm Lynn," I said softly.

She drew a quick breath. "No," she said. "No, you're . . ."

"I'm Lynn. Do you want Bea? She's here."

She said nothing. She put her hand to my face, explored it slowly. I let her do it, confident that I could stop her if she turned violent. But first one hand, then both, went over me very gently.

"You'll marry my son?" she said finally.

"Yes."

"Good. You'll keep him safe."

As much as possible, we'll keep each other safe. "Yes," I said.

"Good. No one will close him away from himself. No one will tie him or cage him." Her hand wandered to her own face again, nails biting in slightly.

"No," I said softly, catching the hand. "I want you to be safe, too."

The mouth moved. I think it smiled. "Son?" she said.

He understood her, took her hand.

"Clay," she said. Lynn and Alan in clay. "Bea?"

"Of course," Beatrice said. "Do you have an impression?"

"No!" It was the fastest that Naomi had answered anything. Then, almost childlike, she whispered, "Yes."

Beatrice laughed. "Touch them again if you like, Naomi. They don't mind."

We didn't. Alan closed his eyes, trusting her gentleness in a way I could not. I had no trouble accepting her touch, even so near my eyes, but I did not delude myself about her. Her gentleness could turn in an instant. Naomi's fingers twitched near Alan's eyes, and I spoke up at once, out of fear for him.

"Just touch him, Naomi. Only touch."

She froze, made an interrogative sound.

"She's all right," Alan said.

"I know," I said, not believing it. He would be all right, though, as long as someone watched her very carefully, nipped any dangerous impulses in the bud.

"Son!" she said, happily possessive. When she let him go, she demanded clay, wouldn't touch her old-woman sculpture again. Beatrice got new clay for her, leaving us to soothe her and ease her impatience. Alan began to recognize signs of impending destructive behavior. Twice he caught her hands and said no. She struggled against him until I spoke to her. As Beatrice returned, it happened again, and Beatrice said, "No, Naomi." Obediently Naomi let her hands fall to her sides.

"What is it?" Alan demanded later when we had left Naomi safely, totally focused on her new work—clay sculptures of us. "Does she only listen to women or something?"

Beatrice took us back to the sitting room, sat us both down, but did not sit down herself. She went to a window and stared out. "Naomi only obeys certain women," she said. "And she's sometimes slow to obey. She's worse than most—probably because of the damage she managed to do to herself before I got her." Beatrice faced us, stood biting her lip and frowning. "I haven't had to give this particular speech for a while," she said. "Most DGDs have the sense not to marry each other and produce children. I hope you two aren't planning to have any—in spite of our need." She took a deep breath "It's a pheromone. A scent. And it's sex-linked. Men who inherit the disease from their fathers have no trace of the scent. They also tend to have an easier time with the disease. But they're useless to us as staff here. Men who inherit from their mothers have as much of the scent as men get. They can be useful here because the DGDs can at least be made to notice them. The same for women who inherit from their mothers but not their fathers. It's only when two irresponsible DGDs get together and produce girl children like me or Lynn that you get someone who can really do some good in a place like this." She looked at me. "We are very rare commodities, you and I. When you finish school you'll have a very well-paying job waiting for you."

"Here?" I asked.

"For training, perhaps. Beyond that, I don't know. You'll probably help start a retreat in some other part of the country. Others are badly needed." She smiled humorlessly. "People like us don't get along well to-gether. You must realize that I don't like you any more than you like me."

I swallowed, saw her through a kind of haze for a moment. Hated her mindlessly—just for a moment.

"Sit back," she said. "Relax your body. It helps."

I obeyed, not really wanting to obey her but unable to think of any-thing else to do. Unable to think at all. "We seem," she said, "to be very territorial. Dilg is a haven for me when I'm the only one of my kind here. When I'm not, it's a prison."

"All it looks like to me is an unbelievable amount of work," Alan said.

She nodded. "Almost too much." She smiled to herself. "I was one of the first double DGDs to be born. When I was old enough to under-stand, I thought I didn't have much time. First I tried to kill myself. Fail-ing that, I tried to cram all the living I could into the small amount of time I assumed I had. When I got into this project, I worked as hard as I could to get it into shape before I started to drift. By now I wouldn't know what to do with myself if I weren't working."

"Why haven't you . . . drifted?" I asked.

"I don't know. There aren't enough of our kind to know what's nor-mal for us."

"Drifting is normal for every DGD sooner or later."

"Later, then."

"Why hasn't the scent been synthesized?" Alan asked. "Why are there still concentration-camp rest homes and hospital wards?"

"There have been people trying to synthesize it since I proved what I could do with it. No one has succeeded so far. All we've been able to do is keep our eyes open for people like Lynn." She looked at me. "Dilg scholarship, right?"

"Yeah. Offered out of the blue."

"My people do a good job keeping track. You would have been contacted just before you graduated or if you dropped out."

"Is it possible," Alan said, staring at me, "that she's already doing it? Already using the scent to . . . influence people?"

"You?" Beatrice asked.

"All of us. A group of DGDs. We all live together. We're all controlled, of course, but . . ." Beatrice smiled. "It's probably the quietest house full of kids that anyone's ever seen."

I looked at Alan, and he looked away. "I'm not doing anything to them," I said. "I remind them of work they've already promised to do. That's all."

"You put them at ease," Beatrice said. "You're there. You . . . well, you leave your scent around the house. You speak to them individually. Without knowing why, they no doubt find that very comforting. Don't you, Alan?"

"I don't know," he said. "I suppose I must have. From my first visit to the house, I knew I wanted to move in. And when I first saw Lynn, I . . ." He shook his head. "Funny, I thought all that was my idea."

"Will you work with us, Alan?"

"Me? You want Lynn."

"I want you both. You have no idea how many people take one look at one workroom here and turn and run. You may be the kind of young people who ought to eventually take charge of a place like Dilg."

"Whether we want to or not, eh?" he said.

Frightened, I tried to take his hand, but he moved it away. "Alan, this works," I said. "It's only a stopgap, I know. Genetic engineering will probably give us the final answers, but for God's sake, this is something we can do now!"

"It's something you can do. Play queen bee in a retreat full of workers. I've never had any ambition to be a drone."

"A physician isn't likely to be a drone," Beatrice said.

"Would you marry one of your patients?" he demanded. "That's what Lynn would be doing if she married me whether I become a doctor or not."

She looked away from him, stared across the room. "My husband is here," she said softly. "He's been a patient here for almost a decade. What better place for him . . . when his time came?"

"Shit!" Alan muttered. He glanced at me. "Let's get out of here!" He got up and strode across the room to the door, pulled at it, then realized it was locked. He turned to face Beatrice, his body language demanding she let him out. She went to him, took him by the shoulder, and turned him to face the door. "Try it once more," she said quietly. "You can't break it. Try."

Surprisingly, some of the hostility seemed to go out of him. "This is one of those p.v. locks?" he asked.

"Yes."

I set my teeth and looked away. Let her work. She knew how to use this thing she and I both had. And for the moment, she was on my side.

I heard him make some effort with the door. The door didn't even rattle. Beatrice took his hand from it, and with her own hand flat against what appeared to be a large brass knob, she pushed the door open.

"The man who created that lock is no one in particular," she said. "He doesn't have an unusually high I.Q., didn't even finish college. But sometime in his life he read a science-fiction story in which palmprint locks were a given. He went that story one better by creating one that responded to voice or palm. It took him years, but we were able to give him those years. The people of Dilg are the problem solvers, Alan. Think of the problems you could solve!"

He looked as though he were beginning to think, beginning to understand. "I don't see how biological research can be done that way," he said. "Not with everyone acting on his own, not even aware of other researchers and their work."

"It is being done," she said, "and not in isolation. Our retreat in Colorado specializes in it and has—just barely—enough trained, controlled DGDs to see that no one really works in isolation. Our patients can still read and write—those who haven't damaged themselves too badly. They can take each other's work into account if reports are made available to them. And they can read material that comes in from the outside. They're working, Alan. The disease hasn't stopped them, won't stop them." He stared at her, seemed to be caught by her intensity—or her scent. He spoke as though his words were a strain, as though they hurt his throat. "I won't be a Puppet. I won't be controlled . . . by a goddam smell!"

"Alan—"

"I won't be what my mother is. I'd rather be dead!"

"There's no reason for you to become what your mother is."

He drew back in obvious disbelief.

"Your mother is brain damaged—thanks to the three months she spent in that custodial-care toilet. She had no speech at all when I met her. She's improved more than you can imagine. None of that has to happen to you. Work with us, and we'll see that none of it happens to you."

He hesitated, seemed less sure of himself. Even that much flexibility in him was surprising.

"I'll be under your control or Lynn's," he said.

"Not even your mother is under my control. She's aware of me. She's able to take direction from me. She trusts me the way any blind person would trust her guide."

"There's more to it than that."

"Not here. Not at any of our retreats."

"I don't believe you."

"Then you don't understand how much individuality our people retain. They know they need help, but they have minds of their own. If you want to see the abuse of power you're worried about, go to a DGD ward."

"You're better than that," I admitted. "Hell is probably better than that. But . . ."

"But you don't trust us."

He shrugged.

"You do, you know." She smiled. "You don't want to, but you do. That's what worries you, and it leaves you with work to do. Look into what I've said. See for yourself. We offer DGDs a chance to live and do whatever they decide is important to them. What do you have, what can you realistically hope for that's better than that?"

Silence. "I don't know what to think," he said finally.

"Go home," she said. "Decide what to think. It's the most important decision you'll ever make."

He looked at me. I went to him, not sure how he'd react, not sure he'd want me no matter what he decided.

"What are you going to do?" he asked.

The question startled me. "You have a choice," I said. "I don't. If she's right . . . how could I not wind up running a retreat?"

"Do you want to?"

I swallowed. I hadn't really faced that question yet. Did I want to spend my life in something that was basically a refined DGD ward? "No!"

"But you will."

"Yes." I thought for a moment, hunted for the right words. "You'd do it."

"What?"

"If the pheromone were something only men had, you would do it."

That silence again. After a time he took my hand, and we followed Beatrice out to the car. Before I could get in with him and our guard-escort, she caught my arm. I jerked away reflexively. By the time I caught myself, I had swung around as though I meant to hit her. Hell, I did mean to hit her, but I stopped myself in time. "Sorry," I said with no attempt at sincerity.

She held out a card until I took it. "My private number," she said. "Before seven or after nine, usually. You and I will communicate best by phone."

I resisted the impulse to throw the card away. God, she brought out the child in me.

Inside the car, Alan said something to the guard. I couldn't hear what it was, but the sound of his voice reminded me of him arguing with her—her logic and her scent. She had all but won him for me, and I couldn't manage even token gratitude. I spoke to her, low voiced.

"He never really had a chance, did he?"

She looked surprised. "That's up to you. You can keep him or drive him away. I assure you, you *can* drive him away."

"How?"

"By imagining that he doesn't have a chance." She smiled faintly. "Phone me from your territory. We have a great deal to say to each other, and I'd rather we didn't say it as enemies."

She had lived with meeting people like me for decades. She had good control. I, on the other hand, was at the end of my control. All I could do was scramble into the car and floor my own phantom accelerator as the guard drove us to the gate. I couldn't look back at her. Until we were well away from the house, until we'd left the guard at the gate and gone off the property, I couldn't make myself look back. For long, irrational minutes, I was convinced that somehow if I turned, I would see myself standing there, gray and old, growing small in the distance, vanishing.

Afterword

"The Evening and the Morning and the Night" grew from my ongoing fascinations with biology, medicine, and personal responsibility.

In particular, I began the story wondering how much of what we do is encouraged, discouraged, or otherwise guided by what we are genetically. This is one of my favorite questions, parent to several of my novels. It can be a dangerous question. All too often, when people ask it, they mean who has the biggest or the best or the most of whatever they see as desirable. Genetics as a board game, or worse, as an excuse for the social Darwinism that swings into popularity every few years. Nasty habit.

And yet the question itself is fascinating. And disease, as grim as it is, is one way to explore answers. Genetic disorders in particular may teach us much about who and what we are.

I built Duryea-Gode disease from elements of three genetic disorders. The first is Huntington's disease—hereditary, dominant, and thus an inevitability if one has the gene for it. And it is caused by only one abnormal gene. Also Huntington's does not usually show itself until its sufferers are middle-aged.

In addition to Huntington's, I used phenylketonuria (PKU), a recessive genetic disorder that causes severe mental impairment unless the infant who has it is put on a special diet.

Finally, I used Lesh-Nyan disease, which causes both mental impairment and self-mutilation.

To elements of these disorders, I added on my own particular twists: a sensitivity to pheromones and the sufferers' persistent delusion that they are trapped, imprisoned within their own flesh, and that that flesh is somehow not truly part of them. In that last, I took an idea familiar to us all—present in many religions and philosophies—and carried it to its terrible extreme.

We carry as many as fifty thousand different genes in each of the nuclei of our billions of cells. If one gene among the fifty thousand, the

Huntington's gene, for instance, can so greatly change our lives—what we can do, what we can become—then what are we?

What, indeed.

For readers who find this question as fascinating as I do, I offer a brief, unconventional reading list: *The Chimpanzees of Gombe: Patterns of Behavior* by Jane Goodall, *The Boy Who Couldn't Stop Washing: The Experience and Treatment of Obsessive-Compulsive Disorder* by Judith L. Rapoport, *Medical Detectives* by Berton Roueché, *An Anthropologist on Mars: Seven Paradoxical Tales* and *The Man Who Mistook His Wife for a Hat and Other Clinical Tales* by Oliver Sacks.

Enjoy!

TWICE, AT ONCE, SEPARATED

Linda Addison

(2000)

> The shamans came together to find a cure for the sickness in the people's souls that caused children to be born sick. They changed into strong hekura—jaguar, ocelot, puma—and climbed the ladder of the earth to search for the soul-eater's path. The only way to save their children's souls was to leave the poisoned place, go beyond the sky layer. The people entered Ship to follow the path to the demon's birthplace, where they will once again change into strong hekura and destroy the demon's nest, releasing the captured souls so children can again be born strong and healthy.
>
> —chant taught to every Yanomami shaman

The artificial sunlight of Ship drew sharp shadows around the men sitting in the dirt of the central plaza of Bataasi-teri village. The scent of roasted plantains, from the communal fire, filled the air. Xotama stood in the shade of the circular village and listened to the wedding contract play out. Mayomi, her grandmother, sat within listening distance, nodding at their shaman, Hurewa, when an acceptable number of valuable items was mentioned. They were haggling about woven baskets. Hurewa, with his usual calm, simply shook his head at the numbers they proposed.

Mayomi had spent a long time, the night before, talking to Xotama about the planned marriage. No matter what she said, Xotama felt sick inside. A restless night made her feel no better today. Her life was haunted by a sense of being splintered. She had gone through the cleansing ceremony to remove the pain left by her mother's death, but no amount of meditation or rituals helped. Only her dreams gave her temporary comfort. Dreams of being with someone she didn't know, someone whose face she never saw.

"Tutewa will be a good husband," Rahimi, her best friend, said. "He's generous and not bad to look at. He's moving here to look after your grandmother, so we'll still see each other."

Xotama found his round face and deep brown eyes attractive. He had meticulously painted circles and bands of red ochre over his entire body.

She turned the slender white stick that pierced her nasal septum. "I know. It's not him, it's me. I'm not—" The expected path of her life caught in her throat.

Rahimi put her arm around Xotama's waist. "Is it the dreams again?" she whispered.

Xotama nodded. "I've tried to forget them, but she came to me again last night. I can't do this." She pulled away from Rahimi and walked into the central plaza. The conversation stopped.

"What is this, does the bride need a closer look at her husband-to-be?" Tutewa's father said. "Stand up, son, let her see how strong you are. There will be no empty bellies in your hammock. We are good hunters." He prodded Tutewa.

He started to stand, but Xotama gestured for him to sit. "No, I'm sorry, this isn't . . ." Her voice faded under their stares.

Mayomi rushed over to her. "Forgive my granddaughter. She's not herself today."

"She seems very much herself today, Grandmother," Hurewa said. "What are you trying to say, Xotama?"

"I'm sorry, but I'm not ready to marry," Xotama said. She saw Rahimi put her hands over her mouth.

Everyone started shouting at once.

Above the shabonos and forest, beyond the sky created by technology, a meta-plasmic layer contained the neural web called Ship. A Watcher let her mind roam the forest quadrant of the hollowed-out, terra-formed asteroid where Xotama stood. Their minds touched through the bio-implants all Yanomami carried in their brains. The Watcher's real body was in slow stasis, growing old a hundred times slower than those who inhabited the forests. Her mind lived in the virtual world sustained by Ship.

Today she worked in navigation, in the form of a green-furred monkey with four arms. Long fingers moved quickly over a multicolored ball of writhing vines, tapping any ends that snaked out. Each touch generated a bright spark of light, making the end flow back into the center of the vines. The echo of dreams shared with Xotama sang back at her, just as they haunted Xotama.

She drank in Xotama's turmoil, smoothed it over her virtual face, breathing in the sharp, sweet flavor of discontent. There was a corresponding hunger in her, a breach. Though she knew more than Xotama, the knowledge did little to feed the unsettling emptiness.

. . . tell me, what troubles you? . . . Ship asked, a gentle whisper in her mind.

Talking with Ship was like floating underwater. She surrendered to the smothering, reminding herself there was no body to suffocate, just a sensation in the mind, to treat it like a dream and enter gently, as if falling asleep.

(I can not find the words) she thought to it.

. . . what does it look like? . . .

She let the hunger take shape: a dark circle broken in two, one jagged piece disappears, the other grows larger, one eye appears in the center, tears of light slowly fall from the eye, the dark half becomes a tattered sail, beating wildly in a firestorm that consumes the light, the eye begins to close.

. . . enough . . . Ship said, dissolving the images.

In navigation, tendrils of vine whipped through the air. She worked rapidly to get the vines back in control. An otter with orange skin and three pairs of arms swam into navigation. He licked her face, transmitting his genetic designation, and began to work over the vines.

. . . i have tasted your discomfort for a long time but hoped you would settle it on your own . . . Ship said. . . . she can not heal without you . . . you must find a way or you will both be lost . . .

She thought the word "home" and was in her virtual hammock, in the vast circular shabono that housed all the Watchers. A neighbor in the shape of a golden panther nudged her with his shoulder. His touch was like an early morning breeze. He asked, (why are you afraid?)

(I am broken and I don't know how to become whole) she said.

Mayomi grabbed Xotama's arm to pull her away. Hurewa stood and gently moved the grandmother aside. He cupped Xotama's face in his hands, stared hard into her eyes. After caressing the moon-shaped birthmark on her left cheek, he clapped his hands to get everyone's attention.

Xotama looked at Tutewa and felt a flutter of desire mixed with sadness.

"What is wrong with this girl?" Tutewa's father said, pointing at her. "Does she think my son is not good enough?"

"Let her be, Father," Tutewa said. "I want to hear what she has to say."

Xotama fought back tears, wanting to give some explanation, but she didn't know where to start.

"Let me tell you about a dream I had last night," Hurewa said. "I saw Xotama's birthmark on the beak of a golden toucan surrounded by other birds, with bright red and blue feathers, perched on white rocks. They rose into the sky as one, leaving the golden bird on the ground. A hekura in the shape of a young leopard crept into the circle of rocks. Its eyes glowed red. I recognized it as my hekura and stood in front of her as it leapt. I took it into my chest and saw her true form through its eyes. A young girl, staring at her shadow on the ground, drawn by bright moonlight. Her shadow stepped off the ground and stood next to her. The moon came closer until it was so bright I had to run into the forest.

"What do you see in your dreams, Xotama?"

She took a deep breath and said, "There is another in my dreams, someone I never see but can sense. She has shown me many things. Last night we flew high above a green forest, dotted sparsely with villages, brown circular pots, their edges stretched inward to a flickering center. I wasn't afraid because she was with me. I don't know who she is or what the dreams mean. When I wake I feel like half a person.

"I think only Ship can help me understand what these dreams mean."

A young man from Tutewa's village said, "Women are not allowed to talk to Ship."

"There are women Watchers," Xotama said. "There are stories of women shamans. I don't think Ship cares that I have a womb."

This started the yelling again. Hurewa had to bang two gourds to get everyone's attention. "We live inside Ship, not unlike a womb. Without Ship we would spill into the airless trail we follow, our souls eaten by the Soul Killer. I'm not going to judge for Ship. Which of you think you can?" No one said a word.

"When I woke this morning, the air was full of big and small magic," the shaman said. "Xotama must walk the path of the spirits before we have any more discussions of marriage. Important dreams have to be honored."

Tutewa walked over to Xotama and spit on the ground in front of her to signify the path was clear between them. "I accept that you need to settle this storm inside. I will wait ten days for a message from you. If I hear nothing, I'll consider our marriage bond dissolved."

He walked away, followed by his father and the three other men from his shabono. They ducked out the narrow opening of the walled village, into the forest.

Part of her didn't want him to go. If only she could push this pain away and be happy in her life. She balled up her fists. What was wrong with her?

Hurewa took Xotama's hand and led her across the center court to a shaded area. Mayomi followed. They sat out of earshot of everyone else. More people drifted into the shabono. Men, women, and children gathered on the far side of the center fire, keeping a cautious distance between themselves and Xotama.

"A path of fire waits in front of you before your journey ends," Hurewa said. "The end is the beginning. Enter the circle."

"The circle?" Xotama asked.

"You'll understand when the time comes. It will take all your courage to heal this breach. The flow of this day has been changed by your words and my dream messenger. It wouldn't be wise to stop now. Are you ready to begin?"

Xotama took a quick breath. She hadn't thought beyond the aching need to stop today's events. "I don't know. Will you come with me?"

"No. You must do this alone. It will be dangerous. Not everyone who seeks Ship returns."

"There must be another way," Mayomi pleaded. "I've taken care of her since her mother died giving birth to her. Her father entrusted me with her life when he moved to another shabono to marry. I fear her mother's spirit lingers nearby, pulling at her."

"Someone lingers near, but it's not her mother," the shaman said.

Mayomi looked stricken, opened her mouth as if to speak, but put her fist over it instead.

"You will follow the river to the place where no one lives." Hurewa held Xotama's hands. "There, if Ship is agreeable, you may be returned to the shadow in your dreams. We will sit vigil for you."

Tears fell from Mayomi's eyes, but she said nothing.

"Let's go," he said.

They stood and walked to the shabono's exit. No one approached them. Rahimi looked like she wanted to go to her, but her mother was holding her arm.

"What about supplies?" Mayomi asked.

"Ship will give her what she needs," he said. "We should go from here alone, Mayomi."

"Remember that I love you," Mayomi whispered in Xotama's ear.

They walked to the river down a rarely used path. The thick, sweet scent of flowering vines lifted her soul; their red blossoms made her smile. The hōrema bird began its afternoon song: "were, were, were . . ." A little of her fear dissipated in the air of the forest. This could be just another day if not for the fact that she was leaving everyone she knew to search for an unknown person in a place she'd never been before.

A freshly carved canoe waited on the bank.

"This is my personal canoe. It will carry you to the next place," the shaman said. He mixed some earth with spit in his hands and smoothed the mixture over the bow of the canoe, working a spell of protection into the wood.

"Thank you for believing me," she said.

"There is strong magic in you. I wouldn't be a good shaman if I ignored it." He helped her into the canoe, handed her a paddle, and pushed the canoe toward the center of the river.

She waved at him as the canoe carried her away. The current moved well enough that she only used the paddle to push away from rocks or fallen tree trunks. Light from the afternoon sky, and the water's rocking motion, made her sleepy. Her hand slipped over the edge of the canoe, trailing in the current.

Xotama dreamed she changed into an eel and slid into the river. The other was also there as an eel. They danced in the water, slithering around each other, over and under thick tree roots. There were no words between them, just a perfect dance. Their tails and heads wrapped together to make a wing shape that lifted into the sky as, below, the canoe filled with water.

Xotama woke to water flooding the canoe. She tried using her cupped hands to bail it out, but the canoe tipped over, dumping her into the foaming waves. Underwater, a tangle of tree roots threatened to hold her. She kicked up to the surface before she got too snarled in the roots, and swam to the bank.

She sat on the muddy edge, catching her breath. Now what? The river had carried her away from known territory, and without a canoe she had no idea where to go next. The ground rose, not far from the river, to a hill dense with growth. Trapped between the water and the thick bush, she reasoned that, if this was as far as the canoe took her, the rest of her journey would have to be on foot. She worked her way up the hill, away from the wetland.

In the overgrown bush, little sunlight passed through the thick canopy. Scrub brush and thick vines, in shades of gray, covered the ground, making walking difficult. There was no sign anyone had ever walked this way, not even an overgrown trail. Pushing through whatever vegetation yielded, she heard a rumble overhead, like a coming storm.

She tried not to think about the snakes and rodents living under the tangle of vines and rotting leaves. Twice, Xotama stopped to dig a thorn out of her foot. By the time she reached dry ground, she was limping, her body covered with bleeding scratches. Despite eating a couple of tangerine-colored ediweshi on the way, she was dizzy from lack of food. The palm fruit took the edge off her thirst, but left her hungry and weak. The rumbling above grew louder. Nausea twisted her stomach, but she pushed on until she found a small opening in the hillside. She picked up a stick in case snakes lived in the cave; it would be safer there than in the dark jungle if a storm broke.

Just as she squeezed into the cave, a palm tree crashed down at the entrance. Her scream was swallowed by the thunder of a summer storm. Unable to hold back the nausea, she vomited. Choking on bile, Xotama squeezed deeper into the cave. She listened for sounds of something alive in the cave besides her, but could hear nothing over the roar of the storm.

Too weak to go on, she crouched with her back against the stone wall. She would die here. Alone, with no songs or rituals to take care of her decaying body, her spirit lost forever. She cried softly, curling into a ball.

What made her think Ship would talk to her, even let her enter its sacred space to answer her questions? What place did her small lost life have in Ship's larger existence; in the journey of the people? Drifting into unconsciousness, her last thought was that she had no one to blame except herself.

Xotama stood outside the cave. Wind and rain threw tree branches at her, ripping flesh from her body. She felt no pain. In a flash of lightning, she saw the cave opening was almost completely covered with debris. She looked down at her hands. Bone peeked through the raw flesh that remained. Under the roar of the storm, she heard her grandmother chanting. The ground became very hot, blistering what little skin was left on her feet.

Without taking a single step, she moved down the hill, back to the river. Standing at the spot where she had climbed out of the river, she looked across the whitecaps and saw her canoe rise out of the water. Shoro, dark-feathered birds with long tails, were lifting it. Her grandmother's singing grew louder. It was a chant of protection from the water demons.

Xotama looked down at her arms and legs. The burning had stopped, and her limbs transformed themselves into wings and claws, like the shoro. The lost feeling she had carried her whole life became a single stabbing pain inside her chest. A ring of fire blazed in the sky. Was this the circle in Hurewa's warning? Trembling, she rose on her new wings and flew toward the flames.

She skimmed through the center of the ring. Her feathers burned away. She fell, not down but up, hurtling through a tunnel of colors, to land on a soft pile of leaves. When she opened her eyes, she was an infant being picked up by her grandmother, younger in years but with the same eyes. A woman, the mother she never knew, squatted against a large tree, grimacing in pain as blood ran down her thighs.

Mayomi lay Xotama carefully on the ground. An infant cried. Not her, Xotama realized, but another baby, coming out of their mother.

Twins.

Her mother collapsed as the placenta was delivered. Mayomi cut the umbilical cord and tried to revive Xotama's mother, but she was dead. Mayomi's cries mixed with the hungry newborns' wail.

Twins. Everything made sense now. The dreams, the feeling of being broken in two. Relief mixed with anger. Mayomi knew all along that Xotama was a twin, and never said anything. All the years of pain explained in one word. Twins.

Their grandmother picked the babies up and ran crying into the forest. She stopped at an opening in a hill, laid both babies down to examine them. They were exactly the same, except for the sliver of a moon birthmark on Xotama's face. Mayomi touched the birthmark, kissed the other baby, picked up Xotama, and rushed away from the cave.

Inexplicably, Xotama floated above her abandoned sister, helpless. An old man came out of the cave and picked up the baby. A Watcher, his skin was iridescent blue, like the evening sky, covered with the curling patterns every Yanomami knew as Ship's design. He carried her sister into the cave.

The cries faded. Xotama was on her knees, weeding in her grandmother's tobacco garden. A reflection of Xotama pulled weeds to her left. Xotama shrieked in joy and grabbed her sister, pulling them both to the ground.

"It's you! I can't believe I've found you." Xotama held her sister's face in her hands. She kissed and hugged her tightly.

"Yes, my sister," she answered, embracing her.

Xotama pulled away, looked around. "But how can we be here? Am I dead?"

"You are very much alive." She smiled. "I wanted a familiar place for us to meet. You have happy memories of this garden."

"You can make a place out of memories?"

"Anything imagined can take form here. Is there another place you would like to be?"

Xotama looked around. Everything seemed so real, she expected Mayomi to walk out of the forest. "This is fine. I didn't know Watchers could do this. I guess there's a lot I don't know about Ship and Watchers. Before this day I didn't know I had a sister. I—I thought I was losing my mind."

"I know. I haven't been doing well myself." Her sister wiped Xotama's tears away. "Even though I knew you lived, I needed to touch you."

"But if we aren't really here, how can you touch me?"

She took Xotama's hand. "Doesn't this feel real? As real as any two bodies. More real than dreams."

"Except in my dreams I never saw your face. Didn't know you were my sister. I don't even know your name."

"I don't have a name like you do. Here we know each other by touch."

Xotama thought for a moment. "Can I call you Notama?"

She smiled. "I would like that."

"This is unbelievable. There's so much I don't understand, " Xotama said.

"Do you trust me?"

Xotama looked into the copy of her face, without the birthmark, and nodded.

Notama reached up, her arm stretching until it touched the sky. Xotama looked down at where her sister held her hand. Their flesh melted together. Xotama's eyes closed. She felt as if she were falling asleep.

They were a wind moving over forests, flowing up into the false sky, swiftly passing through a thick wall until they were beyond the asteroid's shell and into outer space. Points of light shimmered around them. Below, a long, dark sliver laid against the starry background: the rough rock that contained everyone Xotama loved, everything she knew of life. They plummeted down, through the vessel's strata of protective minerals, into its meta-plasmic web, caught like insects in the immense memory banks of the intelligence called Ship. It existed in the living plasma that flowed through the outer shell, under the forest ground. It was more than a machine and less than human.

Images from Ship's memory rushed past: First Earth, twisted, dying infants born to sick mothers, poison in the air, in the ground, in many humans: DNA spirals mangled into broken, twisted puzzle pieces: another memory bank filled with an endless stream of undamaged genetic codes, tagged and indexed, the genes of the Yanomami living inside the rock as it hurtled through space. Each new marriage, each new infant produces another flow of genetic possibilities. Xotama and Notama's genetic history undulated from First Earth and extrapolated into patterns that exploded into data streams that even Notama had not experienced.

More and more information poured into their minds. They saw the debates that led to the decision to maintain the forest society among the villages; to keep the people safe and sane during a long journey that would see the birth and death of generations. They saw the bodies of Watchers in stasis pods, clustered like peas throughout the asteroid. Notama's body curled in a pod: still the size of a child. Older Watchers in gleaming blue body suits in the forests, observing the villages, taking samples from the water, ground, plants; surveying animals: wild pigs, tapir, giant anteaters; giant rodents, snakes, armadillos, tortoises, monkeys.

Xotama's mind was stripped down by the waves of information. Each new concept carried countless layers of explanation, information to explain data to explain information. Images slipped and slid into forms she couldn't comprehend. She wanted to tear her eyes out, rip her ears off, anything, anything to stop the roar, but she had no body. Notama was near her, also terrified by the images.

They had unlocked something immense and it was consuming them.

(stopstopstopstop) Notama screamed in images: white lightning, bitter hot freezing decaying piercing gnawing . . .

Xotama was losing words, her thoughts tumbled into ragged sounds, tastes, colors . . .

green

pounding

sweet

red

wet

screech . . .

An old woman's face formed in the deluge of sensations, older than any Yanomami either of them had seen.

(Stop data retrieval, repair memory break, restore previous visualization) Her voice was soothing.

The storm slowed and dissipated like morning mist. They were back in the garden of Notama's making. The pain and chaos faded rapidly.

"Who was that?" Xotama asked.

"One of the first Watchers. Someone who's been with Ship from the early days," Notama said.

They helped each other stand.

"I'm sorry, Xotama. I made a terrible mistake." Notama shook her head. "I thought if I showed you what this was, Ship, the world I live in, that maybe you could stay here. But I took us into the neural web too quickly, I almost—"

"No, don't apologize," Xotama interrupted. "I had the same hope when I found you. For us to be together. But I couldn't live with things shifting around me, or these odd words and things. I need to walk through the forests every day on legs. I need to hold people. I saw your body, it's too young, and your mind too grown to live in a world you couldn't fly in or change whenever you choose."

They held each other. "It's time you returned," Notama said. "I wouldn't want Grandmother to worry too long about you. What will you do with the information you have?"

"Keep it close to my heart," Xotama said. "I see that knowing too much, too soon, is not wisdom."

"Yes, my arrogance has shown me I have a lot to learn," Notama said.

"Will we dream together again?" Xotama asked.

"I believe we will, but without the confusion. Are you ready to go?"

"Yes. You are forever in my heart and my 'genes.'" Xotama smiled at using the new word.

Notama kissed her forehead.

Xotama blinked. She stood in the mouth of a cave. Sunlight spilled over the forest. Other than some scratches, she was uninjured. This was not the cave she hid in from the storm. She had been returned to the cave her sister had been carried into as a newborn.

Her sister. Tears ran down her face and she laughed. She had a sister.

This cave was not far from her village. She took her time walking back, enjoying every sound and scent along the way. She had seen many things with Notama. It would take a long time for her to understand even a small part of it. Maybe a lifetime.

For the first time, she looked forward to the future. She and Tutewa would marry, have children. Perhaps one of them would be a Watcher. Xotama wouldn't see the end of their journey, nor her children's children, but one day Yanomami would see the end of this path, and the beginning of something she could only taste at the back of her mind. Perhaps some of these Yanomami would carry her genes.

Xotama entered her village as the sky began to dim. The smell of roasted armadillo and plantains filled the air. Many people feasted around the center fire. Conversation stopped as she walked across the dusty space.

Rahimi ran up and grabbed her in a tight hug. "I'm so happy you're safe."

Xotama pulled away, looking past Rahimi to her grandmother, who stood transfixed at the edge of her hammock.

"What's wrong?" her friend asked.

"Nothing. Everything is fine. I'm going to be okay." She hugged Rahimi back. "I have to talk to Mayomi."

She walked to her grandmother. Hurewa signs of protection were painted in red over Xotama's hammock. She smiled. When she left the village, the shaman knew more than anyone about Ship, but now she returned with so much more knowledge.

Mayomi met her gaze. Tears began to fall from her eyes. She sat on the ground. Xotama sat next to her.

"You know?" Mayomi whispered.

"Yes, everything. I found her. She's not a dream, any more than I am. Why didn't you tell me?"

"It's hard enough making a place for one child without a mother. I had just lost a daughter, and held two babies in my arms. On First Earth, one of you would have had to die. Here, I knew the Watchers would take care of the one I left behind. It was the only way both could have a life not filled with burden.

"I couldn't tell you what had happened." Mayomi looked down. "It's not permitted to speak of these things. Your mother's spirit might have been pulled back by my words, to haunt us."

Xotama shook her head. "You and I will not speak of this again." She took her grandmother's hand and kissed it. "I've found my lost self. I can be whole. Now we are both here." Xotama cupped her hands over her chest.

They stood and held each other. Xotama closed her eyes and saw the rock, their world, hurtling through space toward an unknown future. She would marry and have children and, in spite of the taboos, teach them about their aunt and what she learned from Ship during that time of almost-madness.

Gimmile's Songs

Charles R. Saunders

(1984)

The banks of the Kambi River were low and misty, crowded with waterbucks and wading birds and trees draped in green skeins of moss. Dossouye, once an *ahosi*—a woman soldier of the Kingdom of Abomey—rode toward the Kambi.

Slowly the *ahosi* guided her war-bull to the riverbank. She knew the Kambi flowed through Mossi, a sparsely populated kingdom bordering Abomey. Between the few cities of Mossi stretched miles of uninhabited bushland speckled with clumps of low-growing trees. Dossouye watched sunlight sparkle through veils of humid mist rising from the Kambi.

"Gbo—stop," she commanded when the war-bull came to the edge of the river. At the sight of the huge, horned mount, the birds fled in multicolored clouds and the waterbucks stampeded for the protection of the trees.

The war-bull halted. Dossouye gazed across the lazily flowing river.

"What do we do now, Gbo?" she murmured. "Cross the river, or continue along the bank?"

The war-bull snorted and shook its curving horns. In size and form, Dossouye's mount differed little from the wild buffalo from which its ancestors had been bred generations ago. Although the savage disposition of its forebears was controllable now, a war-bull was still as much weapon as mount. Dossouye had named hers "Gbo," meaning "protection."

With a fluid motion, the *ahosi* dismounted. Her light leather armor stuck uncomfortably to her skin. Days had passed since her last opportunity to bathe. Glancing along the banks of the Kambi, she saw no creature larger than a dragonfly. The prospect of immersing herself in the warm depths of the Kambi hastened her decision.

"We will cross the river, Gbo," she said, speaking as though the beast could understand her words. "But first, we'll enjoy ourselves!"

So saying, she peeled the leather armor from her tall, lean frame and laid it on the riverbank alongside her sword, shield, and spear. Knowing Gbo would also prefer to swim unencumbered, she removed the war-bull's saddle and bridle.

Naked, she was all sinew and bone, with only a suggestion of breast and hip. Her skin gleamed like indigo satin, black as the hide of her war-bull: When she pulled off her close-fitting helmet, her hair sprung outward in a kinky mane.

She waded into the warm water. Gbo plunged in ahead of her, sending spumes of the Kambi splashing into her face. Laughing, Dossouye dove deeper into the river. The water flowed clear enough for her to see the silvery scales of fish darting away from her sudden intrusion. Dossouye surfaced, gulped air, and resubmerged, diving toward the weed-carpeted floor of the Kambi. When her feet touched bottom, she kicked upward to the bright surface. Suddenly she felt a nudge at her shoulder, gentle yet possessed of sufficient force to send her spinning sideways.

For a moment, Dossouye panicked, her lungs growing empty of air. Then she saw a huge, dark bulk floating at her side. Gbo! she realized. Shifting in the water, she hovered over the war-bull's back. Then she grasped his horns and urged him toward the surface. With an immense surge of power, Gbo shot upward, nearly tearing his horns from Dossouye's grip.

In a sun-dazzling cascade, they broke the surface. Still clinging to the war-bull's horns, Dossouye laughed. For the first time, she felt free of the burden of melancholy she had borne since her bittter departure from Abomey. Lazily she stretched across the length of Gbo's back as the war-bull began to wade shoreward.

Abruptly Gbo stiffened. Dossouye felt a warning tremor course through the giant muscles beneath her. Blinking water from her eyes, she looked toward the bank—and her own thews tensed as tautly as Gbo's.

There were two men in the riverbank. Armed men, mounted on horses. The spears of the intruders were leveled at Dossouye and Gbo. The men were clad in flowing trousers of black silk-cotton. Turbans of the same material capped their heads. Above the waist, they wore only brass-studded baldrics to which curved Mossi swords were sheathed.

Along with their swords, they carried long-bladed spears and round shields of rhinoceros hide bossed with iron.

One rider was bearded, the other smooth-chinned. In their narrow, umber faces, Dossouye discerned few other differences. Their dark eyes stared directly into hers. They sat poised in their saddles like beasts of prey regarding a victim.

Dossouye knew the horsemen for what they were: *daju*, footloose armsmen who sometimes served as mercenaries, though they were more often marauding thieves. The *daju* roamed like packs of wild dogs through the empty lands between the insular Mossi cities.

Through luck and skill, Dossouye had until now managed to avoid unwelcome encounters with the *daju*. Now . . . she had run out of luck. Her weapons and armor lay piled behind the horsemen.

Her face framed by Gbo's horns, Dossouye lay motionless, sunlight gemming the water beaded on her bare skin. The two *daju* smiled. . . .

Dossouye pressed her knees against Gbo's back. Slowly the war-bull waded up the incline of the riverbottom. The bearded *daju* spoke sharply, his Mossi words meaningless to Dossouye. But the eloquence of the accompanying gesture he made with his spear was compelling. His companion raised his own weapon, cocking his elbow for an instant cast.

Gbo continued to advance. Dossouye flattened on his back, tension visible in the long, smooth muscles of her back and thighs. As the war-bull drew closer, the bearded *daju* repeated his gesture. This time he spoke in slurred but recognizable Abomean, demanding that Dossouye dismount immediately.

Whispering a command, Dossouye poked a toe into Gbo's right flank. Together they moved with an explosive swiftness that bewildered even the cunning *daju*.

Hoofs churning in the mud of the bank the war-bull shouldered between the startled horses. Then Gbo whirled to the left, horned head swinging like a giant's bludgeon and smashing full into the flank of the bearded *daju's* mount. Shrieking in an almost human tone, the horse collapsed, blood spouting from a pair of widely spaced punctures. Though the *daju* hurled himself clear when his horse fell, he landed clumsily and lay half-stunned while Gbo gored his screaming, kicking steed.

At the beginning of Gbo's charge, Dossouye had slid downward from the war-bull's back. When Gbo hit the *daju*'s horse, she clung briefly to her mount's flank, fingers and toes her only purchase against water-slick hide. Dossouye was gambling, hoping the unexpected attack would unnerve the *daju* sufficiently long for her to reach a weapon.

When the horse crashed to the ground, Dossouye leaped free, hitting the riverbank lightly like a cat pouncing from a tree. Her luck returned; the second *daju*'s horse was rearing and pawing the air uncontrollably, its rider cursing as he hauled savagely on the reins. A swift scan showed Dossouye that nothing stood between her and her weapons. As she darted toward them, she shouted another command over her shoulder to Gbo.

Hoofbeats drummed behind her. Still running, Dossouye snatched up her spear. Then she whirled to face the onrushing *daju*.

The beardless warrior charged recklessly, Mossi oaths spilling from his lips. Without hesitation, Dossouye drew back her arm and hurled her weapon full into the breast of the oncoming horse. Though the distance of the cast was not great, the power of the *ahosi*'s whiplike arm drove the spearpoint deep into the flesh of the *daju*'s steed. In the fraction of a moment she'd had to decide, Dossouye had chosen the larger target. Had she aimed at the man, he could have dodged or deflected the spear, then easily slain her.

With a shrill neigh of pain, the horse pitched to its knees. The sudden stop sent the *daju* hurtling through the air. He landed only a few paces from Dossouye. As the *ahosi* bent to retrieve her sword, she thought she saw a bright yellow flash, a spark of sunlight from something that flew from the *daju*'s body when he fell.

Dossouye's curiosity concerning that flash was only momentary. To save her life now, she must move as swiftly as ever on an Abomean battlefield. Sword hilt firmly in hand, she reached the fallen *daju* in two catlike bounds. His spear had flown from his hand—he was struggling frantically to pull his sword from its scabbard when Dossouye's point penetrated the base of his skull, killing him instantly.

Turning from the *daju*'s corpse, Dossouye surveyed the scene of sudden slaughter. The horse she'd speared had joined its rider in death. Its own fall had driven Dossouye's spearpoint into its heart. The bearded *daju*'s steed was also dead, blood still leaking from gaping horn wounds.

The bearded *daju* lay face-down in the mud. Gbo stood over him, one red-smeared horn pressing against the marauder's back. The *daju* trembled visibly, as if he realized he lived only because of the command Dossouye had earlier flung at the war-bull. Because the *daju* spoke Abomean Dossouye wished to question him. Without the *ahosi's* word, Gbo would have trampled the man into an unrecognizable pulp.

Like a great, lean panther, Dossouye stalked toward the prone *daju*. Anger burned hot within her; the high spirits she had allowed herself earlier were gone now, leaving her emotions as naked as her body. Reaching Gbo, Dossouye stroked his side and murmured words of praise in his ear. Once again, the war-bull had lived up to the meaning of his name. Dossouye spoke another command, and Gbo lifted his horn from the *daju's* back . . . but only slightly. When the man attempted to rise, his spine bumped against Gbo's horn. Instantly he dropped back into the mire. He managed to turn his head sufficiently far to gaze one-eyed at the *ahosi* standing grimly at the side of her mount.

"Spare . . . me," the *daju* croaked.

Snorting in contempt, Dossouye knelt next to the *daju's* head.

"Where are the rest of your dogs?" she demanded. "From what I've heard, you *daju* travel in packs."

"Only . . . Mahadu and me," the *daju* replied haltingly. "Please . . . where is the *moso*? Mahadu had it. . . ."

"What is a '*moso*'?"

"*Moso* is . . . small figure . . . cast from brass. Very valuable . . . will share . . . with you."

"I know exactly what you wanted to 'share' with me!" snapped Dossouye. Then she remembered the bright reflection she had spotted when the beardless *daju* fell from his horse. Valuable?

"I saw no '*moso*,'" she said. "Now I'm going to tell my war-bull to step away from you. Then I want you to get up and run. Do not look back; do not even think about recovering your weapons. I want you out of my sight very quickly. Understand?"

The *daju* nodded vigorously. At a word from Dossouye, Gbo backed away from the prone man. Without further speech, the *daju* scrambled to his feet and fled, not looking back. Swiftly he disappeared in a copse of mist-clad trees.

Gbo strained against Dossouye's command as though it were a tether immobilizing him. Dossouye trailed her hand along his neck and ears, gentling him. She could not have explained why she spared the *daju*. In the Abomean army, she had slain on command, as well-trained as Gbo. Now, she killed only to protect herself. She felt no compunctions at having dispatched the *daju* named Mahadu from behind. Yet she had just allowed an equally dangerous foe to live. Perhaps she had grown weary of dealing death.

Impatiently she shook aside her mood. Again she recalled the fleeting reflection she had seen only moments ago. A *moso*, the *daju* had said. Valuable. . . .

It was then that she heard four sharp, clear musical notes sound behind her.

As one, Dossouye and Gbo spun to confront the latest intruder. A lone man stood near the bodies of Mahadu and his horse. But this one did not look like a *daju*. Indeed, never before had Dossouye encountered anyone quite like him. He was a composition in brown: skin the rich hue of tobacco; trousers and open robe a lighter, almost russet shade; eyes the deep color of fresh-turned loam. His hair was plaited into numerous braids of shoulder length, each one sectioned with beads strung in colorful patterns. Beneath the braids, his oval face appeared open, friendly, dominated by warm eyes and a quick, sincere smile. A black mustache grew on his upper lip; wisps of beard clung to his chin and cheeks. His was a young face; he could not have been much older than Dossouye's twenty rains. He was as lean in build as Dossouye, though not quite as tall.

In his hand, the stranger bore the instrument that had sounded the four notes. It was a *kalimba*, a hollow wooden soundbox fitted with eight keys that resonated against a raised metal rim. Held in both hands, the small instrument's music was made by the flicking of the player's thumbs across the keys.

No weapons were evident to Dossouye's practiced gaze. More than one blade, however, could lie hidden in the folds of the stranger's robe. As if divining that thought, the stranger smiled gently.

"I did not mean to alarm you, *ahosi*," he said in a smooth, soft voice. His Abomean was heavily accented, but his speech was like music.

"I heard the sounds of fighting as I passed by," he continued. His thumb flicked one of the middle keys of the *kalimba*. A deep note arrowed across the riverbank—*blood, death.*

Gbo bellowed and shook his blood-washed horns. Dossouye's hand tightened on the hilt of her carmined sword.

"Now I see the battle is over. And you certainly have nothing to fear from me."

He touched another key. A high, lilting note floated skyward like a bird—*peace, joy*. Gbo lowed softly as a steer in a pasture. Dossouye smiled and lowered her blade. Rains had passed since she had last known the serenity embodied in that single note.

But she had been deceived before.

"Who are you?" she demanded.

"I am Gimmile, a *bela*—a song-teller," he replied, still smiling. "You can put down your sword and get dressed, you know. I will not harm you. Even if I wanted to, I don't think I could. One Abomean *ahosi*, it seems, is worth at least two *daju*—and I am certainly no *daju*."

Dossouye felt his eyes appraising her unclad form. She knew she was bony, awkward . . . but that was not what Gimmile saw. He had watched her move, lithe and deadly as a great cat. He noted the strong planes of her face, the troubled depths of her eyes.

Dossouye did not trust Gimmile. Still, he had spoken truth when he said he could not harm her. Not while she had a sword in her hand and Gbo at her side.

"Watch him," she told the war-bull.

As Dossouye walked to her pile of armor, Gbo confronted the *bela*. Gimmile did not flinch at the size and ferocity of Dossouye's mount. Instead, he reached out and touched the snout of the war-bull.

Seeing the *bela*'s danger, Dossouye opened her mouth to shout the command that would spare Gimmile from the goring he unwittingly courted. But Gbo did nothing more than snort softly and allow Gimmile to stroke him.

Never in Dossouye's memory had a war-bull commanded to guard allowed itself to be touched by a stranger. She closed her mouth and began to don her armor.

"Were you about to cross the Kambi when the *daju* attacked, *ahosi*?" Gimmile asked, his hands pulling gently at Gbo's ears.

"The name is Dossouye. And the answer is 'Yes.'"

"Well, Dossouye, it seems I owe you a debt. I think those *daju* might have been a danger to me had you not come along."

"Why a danger?" Dossouye asked, looking sharply at him while she laced her leather cuirass.

"A *bela's* songs can be . . . valuable," Gimmile replied enigmatically. "Indirectly, you may have saved my life. My dwelling is not far from here. I would like to share my songs with you. I also have food. I—I have been alone for a long time."

He plucked another key on his *kalimba* . . . a haunting, lonely sound. And Dossouye knew then that her feeling echoed Gimmile's. Her avoidance of human contact since she had left Abomey had worn a cavity of loneliness deep within her. Her soul was silent, empty.

She looked at the *bela*; watched Gbo nuzzle his palm. Gbo trusted Gimmile. But suspicion still prowled restlessly in Dossouye's mind. Why was Gimmile alone? Would not a song-teller need an audience in the same way a soldier needed battle? And what could Gimmile possess that would be of value to thieves? Surely not his songs or his *kalimba*, she told herself.

Suddenly Dossouye wanted very badly to hear Gimmile's songs, to talk with him, to touch him. Weeks had passed since she last met a person who was not a direct threat to her life. Her suspicions persisted. But she decided to pay them no heed.

"I will come with you," she decided. "But not for long."

Gimmile removed his hand from Gbo's muzzle and played a joyous chorus on the *kalimba*. He sang while Dossouye cinched the saddle about the massive girth of the war-bull. She did not understand the Mossi words of the song, but the sound of his voice soothed her as she cleaned *daju* blood from her sword and Gbo's horns.

Then she mounted her war-bull. Looking down at Gimmile, who had stopped singing, Dossouye experienced a short-lived urge to dig her heels into Gbo's flanks and rush across the river. . . .

Gimmile lifted his hand, waiting for Dossouye to help him onto the war-bull's back. There was tranquility in his eyes and a promise of solace in his smile. Taking his hand, Dossouye pulled him upward. He settled in front of her. So lean were the two of them that there was room in the saddle for both. His touch, the pressure of his back against her breast, the way he fit in the circle of her arms as she held Gbo's reins—the *bela's* presence was filling an emptiness of which Dossouye had forced herself to remain unaware, until now.

"Which way?" she asked.

"Along the bank toward the setting of the sun," Gimmile directed.

For all the emotions resurging within her, Dossouye remained aware that the *bela* had indicated a direction opposite the one the fleeing *daju* had taken. Yet as she urged Gbo onward, her suspicions waned. And the memory of the flashing thing the beardless *daju* had dropped faded like morning mist from her mind.

A single pinnacle of stone rose high and incongruous above the tree-tops. It was as though the crag had been snatched by a playful god from the rocky wastes of Axum and randomly deposited in the midst of the Mossi rain forest. Creepers and lianas festooned the granite-gray peak with traceries of green.

This was Gimmile's dwelling.

Dossouye sat in a cloth-padded stone chair in a chamber that had been hollowed from the center of the pinnacle. Its furnishings were cut from stone. Intricately woven hangings relieved the grayness of the walls. Earlier, Dossouye had marveled at the halls and stairwells honey-combing the rock.

As she finished the meal of boiled plantains Gimmile had prepared, Dossouye recalled stories she had heard concerning the cliff-cities of the Dogon. But Dogon was desert country; in a land of trees like Mossi, a spur of stone such as Gimmile's tower was anomalous.

Little speech had passed during the meal. Gimmile seemed to communicate best with his *kalimba*. The melodies that wafted from the eight keys had allayed her misgivings, which had been aroused again when the *bela* had insisted Gbo be penned in a stone corral at the foot of the pinnacle.

"You wouldn't want him to wander away," Gimmile had warned.

Dossouye knew it would take an elephant to dislodge Gbo once she commanded him to remain in one place. But Gimmile had sung his soothing songs and smiled his open smile, and Dossouye led Gbo into the enclosure and watched while Gimmile, displaying a wiry strength not unlike her own, wrestled the stone corral bar into place.

He played and smiled while leading Dossouye up the twisting stair-wells through which thin streams of light poured from small ventilation holes. He sang to her as he boiled the plantains he had obtained from a storage pot. When she ate, he plucked the *kalimba*.

Gimmile ate nothing. Dossouye had meant to question him about that; but she did not, for she was happy and at peace.

Yet . . . she was still an *ahosi*. When Gimmile took away the wooden bowl from which she had eaten, Dossouye posed an abrupt question:

"Gimmile, how is it that you, a singer of songs, live in a fortress a king might envy?" Gimmile's smile faded. For the first time, Dossouye saw pain in his eyes. Contrition stabbed at her, but she could not take back her question.

"I am sorry," she stammered. "You offer me food and shelter, and I ask questions that are none of my concern."

"No," the *bela* said, waving aside her apology. "You have a right to ask; you have a right to know."

"Know what?"

Gimmile sat down near her feet and looked up at her with the eyes of a child. But the story he told was no child's tale.

As a young *bela*, new to his craft, Gimmile had come to the court of Konondo, king of Dedougou, a Mossi city-state. On a whim, the king had allowed the youthful *bela* to perform for him. So great was Gimmile's talent with voice and *kalimba* that the envy of Bankassi, regular *bela* to the court, was aroused. Bankassi whispered poison into the ear of the king, and Konondo read insult and disrespect into the words of Gimmile's songs, though in fact there was none. When Gimmile asked the king for a *kwabo*, the small gift customarily presented to *belas* by monarchs, Konondo roared:

"You mock me, then dare to ask for a *kwabo*? I'll give you a *kwabo*! Guards! Take this jackal, give him fifty lashes, and remove him from Dedougou!"

Struggling wildly, Gimmile was dragged from the throne room. Bankassi gloated, his position at Konondo's court still secure.

Another man might have died from Konondo's cruel punishment. But hatred burned deep in Gimmile. Hatred kept him alive while the blood from his lacerated back speckled his stumbling trail away from Dedougou. Hatred carried him deep into a forbidden grove in the Mossi forest, to the hidden shrine of Legba. . . .

(Dossouye's eyes widened at the mention of the accursed name of Legba, the god of apostates and defilers. His worship, his very name, had long ago been outlawed in the kingdoms bordering the Gulf of Otongi. At the sound of Legba's name, Dossouye drew away from Gimmile.)

In a single bitter, blasphemous night, Legba had granted Gimmile's entreaty. *Baraka*, a mystic power from the god's own hand, settled in Gimmile's *kalimba* . . . and invaded Gimmile's soul. Wounds miraculously healed, mind laden with vengeance, Gimmile had emerged from the shrine of evil. He was more than a *bela* now. He was a bearer of *Baraka*, a man to be feared.

On a moonless night, Gimmile stood outside the walls of Dedougou. Harsh notes resounded from his *kalimba*. And he sang . . .

> The king of Dedougou is bald as an egg.
> His belly sags like an elephant's,
> His teeth are as few as a guinea fowl's,
> And his *bela* has no voice. . . .

In the court of Konondo, the people cried out in horror when every strand of the king's hair fell from his head. Konondo shrieked in pain and fear as his teeth dropped from his mouth like nuts shaken from a tree. The pain became agony when his belly distended, ripping through the cloth of his regal robes. Only the *bela* Bankassi's voice failed to echo the terror and dismay that swiftly became rampant in Dedougou. Tortured, inhuman mewlings issued from Bankassi's throat, nothing more.

Gimmile had his vengeance: Soon, however, the *bela* learned he had not been blessed by Legba's gift of *Baraka*. For Legba's gifts were always accompanied by a price, and Legba's price was always a curse.

Gimmile could still sing about the great deeds of warriors of the past, or about gods and goddesses and the creation of the world, or about the secret speech of animals. But the curse that accompanied Gimmile's *Baraka* was this: The songs he sang about the living, including himself, came true!

"And it is a curse, Dossouye," Gimmile said, his tale done, his fingers resting idly on the *kalimba*'s keys.

"Word of what I could do spread throughout Mossi. People sought me out as vultures seek out a corpse. They wanted me to sing them rich, sing them beautiful, sing them brave or intelligent. I would not do that. I had wanted only to repay Konondo and Bankassi for what they had done to me. Still, the *Baraka* remained within me . . . unwanted, a curse. Men like the *daju* you killed surrounded me like locusts, trying to force me to sing them cities of gold. Instead, I sang myself away from them all."

"And you—*sang* this rock, where no such rock has a right to be?" Dossouye asked, her voice tight with apprehension.

"Yes," Gimmile said. "I sing, and Legba provides."

"Legba sent you this tower," Dossouye said slowly, realization dawning as Gimmile rose to his feet. Gimmile nodded.

"And Legba has also sent—"

"You," Gimmile confirmed. His smile remained warm and sincere; not at all sinister as he flicked the keys of his *kalimba* and began to sing. . . .

Dossouye's hand curled around her swordhilt. She meant to smash the *kalimba* and silence its spell . . . but it was too late for that. Gimmile's fingers flew rapidly across the keys. Dossouye's fingers left her swordhilt. She unfastened the clasp of the belt that secured the weapon to her waist. With a soft thump, the scabbard struck the cloth-covered floor.

Gimmile placed the *kalimba* on a nearby table and spoke to it in the same manner Dossouye spoke when issuing a command to Gbo. As he walked toward her, the instrument continued to play, even though Gimmile no longer touched it.

Scant heed did Dossouye pay to this latest manifestation of Gimmile's *Baraka*. Taking her hands, Gimmile raised the *ahosi* to her feet. She did not resist him. Gimmile sang his love to her while his fingers tugged at the laces of her cuirass.

He sang a celebration to the luster of her onyx eyes. She stopped his questing hands and removed her armor for the second time that day. He shaped her slender body with sweet words that showed her the true beauty of her self; the beauty she had hidden from herself for fear others might convince her it was not really there.

Gimmile's garments fell from him like leaves from a windblown tree. Spare and rangy, his frame was a male twin of Dossouye's. He sang her into an embrace.

While Gimmile led her to a stone bed softened by piles of patterned cloth, the *ahosi* in Dossouye protested stridently but ineffectively. She had known love as an *ahosi*; but always with other women soldiers, never a man. To accept the seed of a man was to invite pregnancy, and a pregnant *ahosi* was a dead one. The *ahosi* were brides of the King of Abomey. The King never touched them, and death awaited any other man who did. Such constraints meant nothing now, as Gimmile continued to sing.

Dossouye's fingers toyed with the beads in Gimmile's braids. Her mouth branded his chest and shoulders with hot, wet circles. Only when Gimmile drew her down to the bed did he pause in his singing. Then the song became theirs, not just his, and they sang it together. And when their mouths and bodies met, Gimmile had no further need for the insidious power of Legba's *Baraka*. But the *kalimba* continued to play.

Abruptly, uncomfortably, Dossouye awoke. A musty odor invaded her nostrils. Something sharp prodded her throat. Her eyelids jarred open.

The light in Gimmile's chamber was dim, Dossouye lay on her back, bare flesh abrading against a rough, stony surface. Her gaze wandered upward along a length of curved, shining steel—a *sword*! Her vision and her mind snapped into clear focus then, the lingering recall of the day and night before thrust aside as she gazed into the face of the bearded *daju*, the attacker whose life she had spared.

"Where is . . . *moso*?" the *daju* demanded. "You have it . . . I know."

Dossouye did not know what he meant. She shifted her weight, reflexively moving away from the touch of the swordpoint at her throat. Something sharp dug at her left shoulderblade.

Ignoring the *daju* she turned, slid her hand beneath her shoulder; and grasped a small, sharp-edged object. She raised herself on one elbow and intently examined the thing she held in her hand.

It was a figurine cast in brass, no more than three inches high, depicting a robed *bela* playing a *kalimba*. Beaded braids of hair; open, smiling face . . . every detail had been captured perfectly by the unknown craftsman. The joy she had experienced the night before and the fear she was beginning to feel now were both secondary to the sudden pang of sadness she experienced when she recognized the tiny brass face as Gimmile's.

"That is . . . *moso*!" the *daju* shouted excitedly. Eagerly he reached for the figurine. Ignoring the *daju*'s sword, Dossouye pulled the *moso* away from the thief's grasp. Her eyes swiftly scanned the chamber. With a tremor of horror, she realized she was lying on a bare stone floor next to a broken ruin of a bed.

"Hah!" spat the *daju*. "You know how . . . to bring *moso* to life. Legba made . . . Gimmile into *moso* to pay for *Baraka*. But *moso* can . . . come to life . . . and sing wishes true. Mahadu and I . . . found *moso* near here. Could not . . . bring to life. We were taking *moso* . . . to *Baraka*-man . . . when we saw you. Now . . . you tell . . . how to bring *moso* to life. Tell . . . and might . . . let you live."

Dossouye stared up at the *daju*. Murder and greed warred on his vulpine face. His swordpoint hovered close to her throat. And she had not the slightest notion how Gimmile could be made to live.

With blurring speed, she hurled the *moso* past the broken bed. The figurine bounced once off jagged stone, then disappeared. With a stran-gled curse, the *daju* stared wildly after the vanished prize, momentarily forgetting his captive. Dossouye struck aside the *daju*'s swordarm and drove her heel into one of his knees. Yelping in pain, the *daju* stumbled. His sword dropped from his hand. Dossouye scrambled to her feet.

Twisting past the *daju*, Dossouye dove for his fallen sword. And a galaxy of crimson stars exploded before her eyes when the booted foot of the *daju* collided with the side of her head.

Dossouye fell heavily, rolled, and lay defenseless on her back, waves of sick pain buffeting her inside her skull. Recovering his blade, the *daju* limped toward her, his face contorted with hate.

"I will . . . bring *moso* to life . . . without you," he grated. "Now . . . Abomean bitch . . . *die!*"

He raised his curved blade. Dossouye lay stunned, helpless. Without a weapon in her hand, not even her *ahosi*-trained quickness could save her now. She tensed to accept the blow that would slay her.

The *daju* brought his weapon down. But before it reached Dossouye's breast, a brown-clad figure hurled itself into the path of the blade. Metal bit flesh, a voice cried out in wrenching agony, and Gimmile lay stretched between Dossouye and the *daju*. Blood welled from a wound that bisected his side.

The *daju* stared down at Gimmile, mouth hanging open, eyes white with dread and disbelief. Dossouye, consumed with almost feral rage, leaped to her feet, tore the *daju*'s sword from his nerveless grasp, and plunged the blade so deeply through his midsection that the point ripped in a bloody shower through the flesh of his back.

Without a sound, without any alteration of the expression of shock frozen on his face, the *daju* sank to the floor. Death took him more quickly than he deserved.

Dossouye bent to Gimmile's side. The *bela* sprawled face-down, unmoving. Gently Dossouye turned him onto his back and cradled his braided head in her lap. Though his life leaked in a scarlet stream from his wound, Gimmile's face betrayed no pain. His hands clutched his *kalimba,* but the instrument was broken. It would never play again.

"I never lied to you, Dossouye," Gimmile said, his voice still like music. "But I did not tell you everything. The king of Dedougou has been dead three hundred rains. So have I. After I sang my vengeance against Konondo and Bankassi, after I sang this tower to escape those who wanted to use me, the truth of Legba's curse became clear. I would forever be a *moso,* a unifying thing of metal. Only great emotions—love, hate, joy, sorrow—can restore me to life. But such life never lasts long.

"It was your rage at the *daju* who stole me that brought me to life by the river. I saw you . . . wanted you, even as the *daju* did. The *Baraka* of Legba gave you to me. I wish . . . I had not needed the *Baraka* to gain your love. Now . . . the *kalimba* is broken; the *Baraka* is gone from me. I can feel it flowing out with my blood. This time, I will not come back to life."

Dossouye bowed her head and shut her eyes. She did not want to hear more or see more; she wished never to hear or see again.

"Dossouye."

The *bela's* voice bore no sorcerous compulsion now. Still, Dossouye opened her eyes and looked into those of Gimmile. Neither deceit nor fear of death lay in those earth-brown depths. Only resignation—and peace.

"I know your thoughts, Dossouye. You bear the seed of a—ghost. There will be no child inside you. Now, please turn from me, Dossouye. I do not want you to see me die."

He closed his eyes. Dossouye touched his cheeks, his lips. Then she rose and turned away. His blood smeared her bare thighs.

Memories diverted by the fight with the *daju* returned in a rush of pain. Even as she gazed sorrowfully at the dust-laden remnants of the accouterments of Gimmile's chamber, Dossouye remembered his warmth, his kindness, the love they had shared too briefly. The memories scalded her eyes.

*   *   *

Dossouye and Gbo stood quietly by the bank of the Kambi. The sun had set and risen once since they last saw the heat-mist rise from the river. Dossouye stroked Gbo's side, thankful that Gimmile had penned him the day before. Formidable though the war-bull was, there was still a chance the *daju* might have brought him down with a lucky thrust of sword or spear. In her swordhand, Dossouye held a brass figurine of a *bela* with a broken *kalimba*. Tarnish trickled like blood down the metal side of the *moso*.

"You never needed Legba, Gimmile," Dossouye murmured sadly. "You could have sung your vengeance in other cities, and all the kings of Mossi would have laughed at Konondo's pettiness, and the laughter would have reached Dedougou. The sting of your songs would have long outlived the sting of his lash."

She closed her fist around the *moso*.

"You did not need Legba for me, either, Gimmile."

Drawing back her arm, Dossouye hurled the *moso* into the Kambi. It sank with a splash as infinitesimal as the ranting of woman and man against the gods.

Mounting Gbo, Dossouye urged him into the water. Now she would complete the crossing that had been interrupted the day before. Her road still led to nowhere. But Gimmile sang in her soul. . . .

AT THE HUTS OF AJALA

Nisi Shawl

(2000)

They all keep calling her a "two-headed woman." Loanna wants to know why, so after the morning callers leave, she decides on asking her Iya. When she was little, the other kids used to call her "four-eyes." But this is different, said with respect by grown adults.

She finds the comb and hair grease on the bureau in the room where she's been sleeping. When she left Cleveland three days ago, it was winter. Now she steps out onto the wrought-iron balcony, and it's spring. Her first visit, on her own, to the Crescent City, New Orleans, drowning home of her mother's kin.

Iya sits in her wicker chair, waiting. She is a tall woman, even seated, and she's dressed all in white: white head scarf, white blouse, white skirt with matching belt, white stockings and tennis shoes, and a white cardigan, too, which she removes now that the day has warmed. She shifts her feet apart, and Loanna drops to sit between them.

Certainly Loanna is old enough to do her own hair, but Iya knows different ways of braiding, French rolls and cornrows, special styles suitable for the special occasion of a visit to Mam'zelle La Veau's grave. Besides, it's nice to feel Iya's hands, her long brown fingers gently nimble, swiftly touching, rising along the length of Loanna's wiry tresses and transforming them into neat, uniformly bumpy braids. Relaxed by the rhythm and intimacy, she asks, "Why all you friends call me that?"

"Call you what, baby?" Iya's voice is rough but soft, like a terrycloth towel. "Hand me up a bobby pin."

"Two-headed," says Loanna. She lifts the whole card full of pins and feels the pressure as her Iya chooses one and pulls it free.

"Two-headed? It means like you got the second sight, sorta. Like Indian mystics be talkin' about openin' they third eye. Only more so."

"But why say it like that?" Loanna asks, persisting. Some odd things have gone on since she got here: folks dropping on one knee, saying prayers in African to the dry, exacting sound of rattling gourds. Tearful entrances and laughing retreats, gifts of honey, candles, and coconuts. Not every question gets her an answer, but she's here to learn, so she always tries again. "Why call it two-headed, and why say that about me?"

"Oooh, now, that's a story." Iya pauses for a moment, finishing off a row, and the murmur of a neighbor's voice rises through slow rustling trees and over the courtyard wall, light and indistinct. Iya sections off another braid and repeats herself. "That is *truly* a *story*, baby. You wanna hear it now?"

Loanna nods, then winces from the pain of pulling her own hair. "Ow! I mean, yeah," she says.

"Ty to sit still, then, so I can concentrate. Lessee. This story started before you were born, Loanna, 'bout fifteen years ago. The night before you were born, actually, to be exact. You remember that night?"

"Naww," says Loanna, giggling.

"Your mama sure do. But she ain't the only one. I was *there*, and what I can't tell you, ain't nobody can. Here, shift yourself this way so I can reach the back. You comfortable?"

Loanna scoots the pillow forward. "Mmm-hmm." She faces a peach stucco wall now, not so interesting as the view she had of the garden. So Loanna closes her eyes, lets her Iya's words form pictures in her mind. This is what she sees:

She sees herself. She sees Loanna-that-was, Loanna-to-come, Loanna-she-who-will-always-be. She can tell by her feet, large like her mama's, by her strong, long legs. She can tell by her milk-and-honey skin. (How'd she get to be so fair? No white folks, counting back for five generations . . . but that's another story.) She recognizes her flat butt that reminds her daddy of Aunt Fiona, and there's the mark like two lips above it; Aunt Nono calls that an Angel's Kiss. Her back looks funny; maybe that's because she never really gets to see it. Her breasts look bigger. She can see them swaying in and out of sight as she walks away from her own disembodied point of view, down some sort of path.

But her breasts aren't the *main* difference. The *main* difference is her head. Or the lack of it; her head is not there. In its place are rays of shimmering light that stream down from a luminous ball floating nearly a foot above the stem of her graceful neck. The ball of light itself is colorless, but as Loanna's viewpoint follows it she sees it sending flares of color in all directions. She understands from her Iya that this is her *ori*, which contains instructions and wisdom from the ancestors. With the guidance of her *ori*, she has left the heavenly city, on her way to choose a head. It is a very important decision.

Coming too quickly around a turn in the path, she catches up with herself, suddenly merging with the ball of light. All at once, it is as if she had a thousand eyes. Each beam of light absorbs the significance of what it touches, and in a depth and detail Loanna has difficulty handling. Images spin into her out of the formerly indistinguishable darkness: The stern trunks of trees stand in meaningful positions; their beckoning branches droop with leaves, each leaf a poem, waiting to fall with a sigh, reciting itself as it drifts free. But the piercing rays need not wait as they caress each layer of cellular structure, reading the secrets of greenness and sugar, tasting chlorophyll and acknowledging Loanna's part in its manufacture, her gaseous contribution to its growth. Then there is the throb and rustle of waves of wind, then the shift to shooting through the soil beneath her feet, which is alive: warm and changing with worms, and damp and seething with nameless hungers which are hers, it's all hers, all herself.

Somehow, she adjusts. She swims in the sea of the knowledge of everything around her. She wears an apron of fine cowrie shells (caressing tides of food; soft, sucking feet), a skirt of grass (dry whispers of a burning sun), a leather pouch—she tries to absorb it all. Directed by her *ori*, she even manages to move forward, toward her destiny. Wonders around her part and let her pass.

There is sand beneath her feet (silica, each grain a window in a castle on another world), and a curtain of vines before her (twisting, the eternal spiral up, and drinking from a hidden well) when she reaches the place to which she has been led. She peers through the leaves and *sees* a firelit clearing (the shape of a spicy scent in the wood burning, a curl of smoke—the eternal spiral up). Over the fire hangs a kettle (the song of its making rings like a silent gong in the play of her vision) filled with bubbling stew (reluctant roots dug and diced apart, farewells from the nervous forager which gave its body, its blood).

Ajala, the maker of heads, enters the clearing. He is like a man. A drunk man, Loanna perceives. A mean drunk. He has lost, gambling.

Lost to the King, a spirit of swords and justice. The cowries clicked and fell, clicked and fell, all day, till he was without a shell to pay. This is all Loanna can tell from a single "glance." Another ray streams out in his direction—and Ajala seizes it as it lands! He is no man, but a god! He pulls her forward by the ray of her perception.

She stands in front of Ajala. He is dark and crooked (the better to become lost in) and not at all in a happy mood (a woman wrapped her goods in white cloth and walked away). He *speaks* to her, laying heavy slabs of speech upon her mind. He gives her anger, wet and cynically cold, which would mean this in words: "Ha, you come too late! You seek a head? I have ceased to make heads. What is the use, when they will all eventually belong to the King? Not even those already made will I sell to you, for with the rise of the sun all will belong to him, to Kabio Sile. And I am too drunk to bring you to them now. Besides, I want my stew. You are welcome to join me—except, of course, you have no mouth!"

Unkind laughter fills the clearing. Loanna turns to go, switching her hips angrily, which causes her cowrie-shell apron to clatter. Ajala stops her with one hand on her shoulder and swings her back around.

"But what is *this?*" says Ajala. "You are *very* rich! With these beautiful shells I could cancel my debt! Very well, I will take you. But just to the F hut, no farther."

The F hut . . . this is where he stores those heads barely worthy of the name. Loanna is sure the ancestors have provided her with enough goods for a C, the next grade up. But even an F is better than nothing, she figures. So she removes the apron and he receives it, and they are off.

Stars have appeared above them. The *ori* touches their colors with its own and brings to Loanna their distance, their magnificently pure combustion and their blazing bravery of the void. Then she is at the F hut, and it is time to choose.

These heads are made of mud, and they are really pretty bad. Some of them aren't even dry yet. The features are all rough, and mostly irregular in size and shape. As she squats to turn the mud heads over and pick the best, the leather pouch swings out on its cord, then bangs against her belly. It sobs of lost herdmates, of running open-nosed, into the wind—but what's within?

Curious, she pulls it open, puts in her fingers, and draws out a pinch of salt (longing for the cresting waves, shh, the hissing of the sea, exposed before the sun now, but once, what is it that lies at the bottom of the ocean?). Ah, here is the rest of her fortune! Perhaps she can obtain a C head after all.

Ajala waits impatiently for her decision—too impatiently, it seems to Loanna. She picks an F at random, lifts it, makes as though to put it on. There is an angle, a hidden aspect to Ajala's waiting that is somehow wrong. His eyes are growing strangely larger as he watches her lower the head. They are almost all he has now for a face: huge eyes watching as she lowers the head over her *ori*. But what is this terrible blankness descending upon her mind? The telling colors cannot penetrate the thick mud of her head—it is a trap! Quickly she raises the F back up and sets it to the side. Ajala leans over her, silent yet threatening. She throws her hands up in defense, and two grains of salt fly from her fingers to his face. Of course they land in his enormous eyes. Tears spill from them and fall upon the ground. Ajala cries (no love, alone, alone, no one, no love). When he is finished, he sighs wistfully. His sigh says, "It is too long since I've had the salt to spare for tears. Is there more?"

Loanna shows him the pouchful. Good. In exchange for the salt, he will take her to choose a C head. Through the songs of insects (brief, brief, but sharp and fleet is our short leap, bright, sweet, the glittering of our span) and the heavy dew they go, to come at last to the C hut.

These heads are made of woven wood. There is a certain uniformity of feature. They're better than the F heads, but there's nothing spectacularly exciting about any of them. Because she sees no real differences, Loanna chooses quickly. Before putting on her C head, she checks out Ajala. He is withdrawn, brooding over his many ancient wrongs and sorrows. No trick this time, it seems. The head fits smoothly into place.

She can't see. It is dark. She can smell the soil, hear the crickets, but it is all filtered, lessened to the trickle of experience that she used to be used to. The rays of her *ori* tease her with flickering glimpses of the essence. She turns, blinks her eyelids, parts her lips experimentally. "I—" she says, a creaking in the night. The crickets silence themselves. "I want—" She wants an A head. An A. But she doubts this bitter god will grant her wish for the asking. And she has used up all the trade goods the ancestors gave her, just to reach the point where she realizes that what she wants is *more*.

She'll have to use what she's been given to get what must be gotten, then.

There. That darker darkness must be he. She addresses it. "I want—to thank you from the bottom of my heart. I mean, like, this is so completely swollen! I thought you said you were only gonna give me a C head. But this A is—is—it's—"

The god appears clearly before her, shining with anger. It lights him as though it were a fire, and he glows like a maddened furnace. "IT IS A C! A C HEAD IS WHAT YOU HAVE AND NOTHING BUT A C!"

Loanna fears the heat of Ajala's anger will ignite her poor wooden head. Also she feels something she's never felt before, a sort of . . . tugging . . . at the top. But she persists. "Oh, chill, it's all right," she says. "I'll let everybody know what a deal I got. Unless . . ."—holding up a hand to forestall further wrath—"unless you don't want me to. No, okay, I won't tell. You made some kinda mistake, dincha?"

Ajala strives to control his anger. He succeeds in subduing himself to a dull red glow. "This is the C hut. It contains nothing but C heads!"

"Uhh, yeah. Sure. I understand. I won't tell anybody. Except if they notice and ask me how I got it, okay?"

"AARRGH!" bellows Ajala. "COME!" He grabs her with one hot hand and drags her into the forest.

There is no path to the A hut; at least none that Loanna can detect. The way is a lot more difficult and a lot less interesting than the last two trips. Just stumbling through the dark, her hand sweating in the hot grip of the god's. She'd probably be a little steadier on her feet if it wasn't for the insistent tugging at her scalp, pulling her constantly off course.

After a while, the darkness lessens. This seems to increase Ajala's fury. Without warning he stops, picks Loanna up by the waist, and flings her over his shoulder. Then he's off again, at a very uncomfortable trot.

"What's—the big—hurry?" she manages to whuff out between the god's jolting strides.

"Dawn," he explains. Between panting breaths he adds, "I must—return soon—to pay my debt—to the King—or lose my heads. But first—you will see—you are wrong. Not far now," he ends.

By the time they reach the A hut, Loanna's neck is sore from the odd tugging, which has been perpendicular to their path, for the most part. The rest of her feels a little rough as well. And she feels even worse when she sees the A heads.

These heads are made of jewels.

Amethyst, rose quartz, aventurine, and other stones she cannot name, they glow with living light. Each is perfect, each unique. There is no way to pretend that what she wears is one of these. So much for deceit.

What else does she have? She has spent her inheritance. She has used her head, such as it is. She kneels before the luminous beauty of the A's, but she's being pulled away by this unaccountable vacuum. What is it?

"Mama!" she screams in fear and frustration. "Maa-maa!" And that's when she gets it: the answer to her question and the solution to her problem, too, all at once, all in one. Where she's going, where she'll soon be coming from. The door, the gate, the entranceway for everything that ever was in the world.

"Wait," she pleads to the unseen force. "Mama, wait just a minute. I got a idea." Her mother must hear her, or somebody must, for the compelling pressure to be born lessens just a little.

"Ajala," she says. "You got the cowries. You got the salt. But you'd like more, right? Course you would. For an A head I—"

"You admit you have only a C head?"

"Yeah, well, I guess I did try to jack you around a little. Sorry. But now, if you let me choose an A head, I can lead you to the source. Where I got the shells and cowries from. Take away as much as you can carry!"

"Is it far? I don't have much time. . . ."

"No, no, it's really close. It'll only take a few minutes, okay? Can I pick one?"

Ajala nods. Breathlessly, she selects a large, round head of pale blue celestite. There is a moment of disorientation as she removes her C and is flooded by the universe (the turning, rising rightly, the eternal spiral up). But then the celestite is over her ori, focusing and altering her perceptions, directing and filtering the rays of light that connect her to the world: her awareness of that connection. Plus she has her other senses: eyes, ears, nose; all working very well. Is that faint odor fish?

Ajala looks different through these eyes. Loanna decides that she now finds him cooler. She stands, and beckons him to come and kneel before her. Parting her skirt, she brings him gently to the source.

The god is reverent. He prays to the source, mouthing soundless words. He speaks skillfully, with a silver tongue.

Loanna sags against him, pliable with pleasure. She is pulled taut again, stretched between these two irresistible forces: one between her legs, the other somewhere over her shoulders.

At last she can stand no more. "I like your approach," she says softly. "Now let's see your retreat." To her surprise, he backs away without protest. He looks up at her, smiling happily. A huge pearl falls from his lips; his reward.

She has to go. She really must. But as she is drawn away from the A hut, out into her life, Ajala places the C head into her hands (long fingers like her grandfather's, but they don't look a bit artistic on top of Uncle Donald's square palms).

She is confused by the god's offering. "Put it on," he says in a receding shout. "Put it on, wear it over your A. You can always take it off again. And you may find it necessary, sometimes, to be less than you are capable of being. I know—" His last words are lost as she is born.

Loanna opens her eyes. Now shadows sway on the stucco wall, struck by the lowering sun. The lingering sweetness of the god's homage spreads like syrup through the afternoon air, mingling with the golden light. Her dream of the story is over, though Iya's voice continues, twisting its ends together, pulling them up and into the eternal spiral.

"Yeah, we finally got you to make up your mind to honor us with your presence, and you came all in a rush into this world," Iya finishes. "I was hot and dizzy from all that bendin' up and down, all that runnin' back and forth. Didn't nobody offer *me* no ice chips. But I got to see you first and right away, and I knew you were special. A caul, yeah, but that don't automatically mean that much." Iya pauses. Her swift fingers lie still in her lap, their task long done. "It was your eyes told me. Told me everything I just told you—and then some. I can't remember everything your eyes told me on the day that you was born."

"So then was when you decided you were gonna teach me?"

"When you was old enough, right," Iya says. "So let's get on off this balcony and go visit Mam'zelle La Veau. You got the coins? Your gele's on the bed, with the rest of your outfit. We'll pick us some flowers for the grave site on the way. Anything else your *ori*'s tellin' you to bring, baby?"

Loanna's eyes close again, enabling her to focus on the resonance within, the quiet bell of her consciousness. "A—a egg? A *blue* egg? Iya, how we supposed to get that?"

Iya rolls her eyes. "Honey, I don' know. But if the ancestors tellin' you Mam'zelle need a blue egg, we gone get her a blue egg."

"But, Iya, don't you think it might—"

"Loanna!" Iya's voice is sharp and stern. "Here's the first thing you gotta learn: When your head tells you somethin', *listen*. 'Specially if you askin' a question. You get an answer, accept that answer." She rises, and holds out her hands to help her student stand.

"Today you prayin' for the help and guidance of a woman who was famous for not takin' nothin' off nobody, the original Voodoo Queen. So you gotta be sincere, and you gotta stand firm for yourself. Like when we buy our flowers and you give the man a twenty-dollar bill, and if he only give you change back for a ten, what you gonna do?"

Loanna's fingers trace the braids curving above her ears. "Ask him where's the rest. 'Cause I know I'm not stupid. I can count."

"That's right. Same way with this. You know. You not stupid. That's what you gotta learn to believe, honey, you wanna live up to your potential. After all," Iya concludes, as Loanna follows her inside, "what's the good of havin' two heads unless you use 'em?"

THE WOMAN IN THE WALL

Steven Barnes

(2000)

The Swiss ambassador's round ruddy face radiated sincerity, competence, intelligence—and, at the moment, worry. "Have you been treated well?" Johanna Krohn asked.

"Yes, thank you." Shawna Littleton glanced down at her arms, covered to the elbow by an umber cotton smock barely half a shade darker than her own skin. Frayed white slippers covered her feet. Her hair was drawn back in a bun. Her delicate artist's fingers were folded carefully in her lap. She fought to keep her face placid, unreadable. She might have been thinking of clouds: blue-white, perhaps, and drifting against an azure sky.

The interview site was a cupboard of a room crowded with rude wooden furniture. A glowering gilt-framed image of General Zanga's stern black face was the only decoration. "And your daughter?" Mrs. Krohn asked.

"Stepdaughter," Shawna corrected. "She came to live with us just last year, when her mother died."

"I see. Is she well?"

"Lizzie wants to go home."

"Of course. Do you have any complaints? I mean, about your treatment."

On the far side of the room's single door, a soldier coughed. Shawna shook her head once, side to side. Her smile was polite.

"Do you have all of your possessions? Your paintings and photographs?" the ambassador asked. Beneath her right hand lay a portfolio, a thin sheaf of photographs, a biographical sheet, interviews with the famous Shawna Littleton.

"No. Most of our possessions were destroyed when our plane crashed.

I salvaged some jewelry." Shawna paused, her lips pursed. "We traded it for food and water in the camp."

"Which camp was this?" Mrs. Krohn asked. Her voice was neutral.

"Camp Eight," Shawna Littleton answered carefully.

The Swiss woman chewed at her damp, slightly protuberant lower lip. "Our doctors will examine you. For your own safety, of course."

Of course. Shawna straightened in her chair. "Is there a problem of some kind?"

"Mrs. Littleton, there is an enormous difference between camps Seven and Eight. Camp Eight is the compound for political prisoners, where you were kept?" There was an implied question at the end of the sentence. "We are attempting to free as many prisoners as possible. General Zanga's new government, in a humanitarian spirit of cooperation"—she lifted and cleared her voice, almost as if speaking for hidden microphones—"is helping us. However, the process is a slow one."

"And the other encampment?" Shawna allowed only the barest trace of emotion into her question.

"A quarantine area. As you know, there have been . . ."—Mrs. Krohn searched for the appropriate words—"considerable problems with communicable diseases in the Republic. We face rampant parasitism, typhus, polio, syphilis—" Again, that odd inflection. Something left unsaid.

Mrs. Krohn cleared her throat. "We have also detected nine variants of HIV in the area. The refugee camps are what the scientists call a 'forcing ground.'" The two women locked eyes. Shawna's gaze was hard, almost lifeless, like an image stamped onto a copper coin. The Swiss woman's face grew redder. She lost the contest of wills and looked away.

At a fly buzzing against the windowpane.

Shawna followed her gaze.

A fly.

It rubbed its forelegs, took flight in a loop, landed again. It buzzed. Shawna rubbed her fingers against her temples. She shifted her eyes back to Mrs. Krohn's, locked them there. Only then, at that moment, did Mrs. Krohn see what she had expected: nervousness. A touch of something near panic, held down very tightly.

Triggered by the sight and sound of a fly.

* * *

Even after nightfall, Camp Seven's stench was a syrup of dead flies and rotting human flesh, a wafting wall of acid. Gas-masked soldiers roved the perimeter, wetting the dirt with disinfectant and deodorant.

Camp Seven was nearly a square kilometer of clustered ramshackle cabins, tents, and makeshift huts. The spaces between them were dotted with cook fires and outhouses, roving knots of starving refugees, and armed guard patrols.

Concentric rings of concertina and razor wire walled the entire camp. Between the rings was a prowl space for the guard dogs, mongrel mixtures of shepherd and rottweiler bred for strength and aggression. Spotlights slid sinuously along the prowl space, crisscrossing every few seconds.

Four central checkpoints breached the fence, each guarded by armed soldiers. At the northeast gate the soldiers laughed raucously and strutted, saluting each other cockily as if still part of a glorious foreign empire. They turned serious as a Klaxon's shriek split the night, and their flagged gates lifted. A tarp-covered, stake-bed Chevrolet truck rumbled in.

The black wraiths roaming the camp craned toward the gate, eyes hopeful. They looked like refugees anywhere on this blighted continent, with one exception: Each wore a blue plastic collar. Within each collar was a radio device keyed to transceivers around the camp perimeter.

The Chevy's engine shook and belched smoke for a full minute after the wheels stopped turning. Soldiers unlatched the back of the truck, barking orders in their native tongue.

Men and women tumbled from the back. They were as dark as the night itself, cloaked only in rags and despair, both garments grown shiny with wear.

When the inmates realized that the truck carried not food but more miserable refugees, their malnourished attention broke and they resumed their numb and endless perambulation.

Jabbing with rifle butts, the soldiers prodded the newcomers into a line. As one guardsman peered into the back of the truck, a grin creased his broad face. He forced a tall, bespectacled, very dark man from the back. "All right, we're coming. Please," the tall man protested in English, and was pushed roughly aside. From within the truck came a woman's voice. "Please," she said in English. "Just give us a minute. You're scaring the child."

Shawna Littleton crawled over the gate on hands and knees. Nearly as dark as the other prisoners, she wore snug Levi's and a soot-stained cotton blouse. She was tall, thin, and exquisitely sculpted. Her cheekbones were only a breath from the surface, but her flawless skin declared this to be the result of exercise and diet, not starvation.

The true surprise was still to come. A tiny girl lay curled in a dark corner of the truck. She was perhaps nine years old, but small for her age. She wore a soot-smudged white cotton dress. The girl stared out at them, her eyes wide and liquid. Thin arms clutched her knees against her chest.

The soldier grabbed Shawna's slender arm roughly, yanking her down from the truck. She spilled onto her knees in the dirt and glared at them, her beautiful face twisted with rage. "You bastards!"

The bespectacled man went very rigid. He yelled at the soldier in his own language and pushed him away from Shawna.

The soldier looked at him calmly, as if examining a mosquito that had alighted on his arm. He drew his pistol and, at point-blank range, calmly fired two bullets into the tall man's stomach.

Shock distorted Shawna's face. Her mouth worked without producing words. Then she screamed, "Mitch!"

Clasping his belly, the tall man staggered away from the truck. As the echoes washed away, they seemed to draw all other sound away with them. The eerie silence was broken only by scratching sounds as the tall man stumbled like a drunk, toes scuffing up little clouds of dust. He took three steps, four, crumpled to his knees, then staggered up again. He lurched blindly toward the northernmost guard gate.

There, against nearly a kilometer of concertina wire, stood a makeshift wall six feet high and almost two hundred meters long, composed of shells and rocks, rags and pieces of board, splashes of paint and twists of clay.

The faces of Africa stared out from the wall. Kwanta faces carved of wood and Adansi images of bone. A hundred different animals lived there, including Chi Wara antelopes and Gato lion spirits. A thousand symbols, a dozen tribal patterns on display: broad lips and high cheekbones, strong hands and kinky hair. Pende house mothers, Masai giraffes wrought from truck bumpers, firewood gorillas and wire-frame crocodiles. Oil-painted antelope and a scrap-iron vulture with a missing lower mandible. Exquisite Zulu beadwork.

Here were artistic styles and animals from every corner of Sub-Saharan Africa. The only common element was infection.

The tall man tottered along the wall, fingers tracing the countless faces and figures tightly fitted together by a thousand hands. He almost seemed to be searching for his own face, perhaps wondering if it was concealed somewhere there, within the wall.

Then, as if finally realizing that the time for life had passed, he slid to the ground. Blood smeared a glass mosaic chimp. He stared up at the ape, something very like a sad smile shading his lips. His eyes closed.

Shawna Littleton stared, trembling in the grip of shock so great it threatened her sanity. The girl child crawled out of the truck. Her small, dark face was blistered, her hair singed and then clipped away almost to the scalp. Her dress stank of smoke. "Daddy . . . ?" Her voice was disbelieving.

She started toward the dead man, but the soldiers pushed her away. She made a clucking sound in the back of her throat, then again the question: "Daddy?"

She began to scream. Shawna overcame her own paralysis and ran toward the girl. A soldier backhanded her hard across the mouth. Her head snapped back and she tumbled to the ground, lips split. He hauled her up and shoved her roughly back into line.

The girl never stopped screaming, but flinched back before the soldier could strike her. The guards prodded them both toward a line of stinking shacks.

Shawna Littleton fought to keep her voice steady. "His name is Mitch Littleton," she said urgently, repeating the same frantic words to everyone she passed. "A very famous man. Artist." She was shivering. "Many friends. Help him, please. President Chimbey brought us here—"

A mistake. Rifles clinked, the soldiers bristled at the hated name. Even in her excited state, the slender woman realized her error, tried to correct it. "Someone has to help him. Please." She repeated the words, over and over again. "This is my stepdaughter, Elizabeth. Somebody help us. You don't understand." Her voice almost broke. "It not our war. We don't belong here."

A hundred small campfires misted the night stars. Men, women, and scrawny children hunched around smoking oil drums. Open latrine trenches boiled with the odors of sour stomachs, diseased kidneys.

Even worse than the toilet stench was the impossibly fetid and om-
nipresent bleach-and-buttermilk miasma of stale semen. In the darkness
to the left, someone squealed. Shawna squinted, eyes struggling to
pierce the shadows. In the hollow between two shacks, three men huddled tightly around a fourth. The fourth crouched on hands and knees,
grunting in a thick, furry voice.

She covered Elizabeth's eyes.

They were led between the rows of lean-tos and tents, blankets
strung over lines of cord, cardboard shanties and tattered bungalows.
Dark, gaunt figures studied them. The impact of their raw and urgent
need seared Shawna like air vented from a kiln.

She heard herself murmuring, "Oh God, Oh God . . ."

The agony of Mitchell's death was nothing, less than nothing, completely supplanted by the unknown horrors of her future. There would
be time for grief later.

If there *was* a later.

Their guide pushed a heavy blanket from the doorway of a corrugated
tin shack and shoved them in. The shack held four beds, one unoccu-
pied. Three hollow-eyed women crouched within like ferrets huddled in
a cage. One was tall and skeletally thin. The third and eldest was of
medium height. The eldest's bunk was concealed in deep shadows, in
the darkest corner of the shack. Once, she had been short and fat. Now,
folds of flesh hung around her like a dark shroud. From the curdled yellow deposits in her eyes and the pronounced tremor of her hands,
Shawna thought her gravely ill.

The soldier spoke to Shawna in a language she didn't understand.

"I . . . am . . . American," she stuttered again, sounding stupid even
to herself. He said something else, jabbering. For a dreadful moment, his
gaze raped her. He grinned at the swelling of her breasts and hips. He
made a crude gesture with a stiffened thumb and cupped palm, then
laughed and left.

Shawna Littleton stood in the doorway for a long moment, an arm
around Elizabeth the entire time. "It's all right," she said. "Don't worry.
Everything will be all right."

Her new roommates studied her as if she were festooned with prime
rib. Not for the first time she realized how utterly alien she had to appear, with her American clothes, her polished fingernails, and her
American flesh upon her American bones. Some percentage of her was

the same basic genetic stock as these women, perhaps, but they weren't the same. Not at all.

She was American, and they were . . . well, they were unfortunate.

"Littleton," she said, pointing at herself. They rattled unintelligible words at her.

Perhaps there were names in there somewhere. Perhaps not. Without realizing she had done so consciously, she ordered them short, tall, and fat, and named them after the three Gorgon sisters: *Stheno, Euryale,* and *Medusa.* It was either that or Larry, Moe, and Curly, and at the moment, Shawna Littleton didn't have the strength to smile.

"*Tu parles français?*" she asked hesitantly. Medusa, the eldest, looked at her shrewdly. In her former plumpness, Medusa might have been pretty. Even beautiful. Now, she was a hag.

"You are the American?" Medusa asked in halting French.

Frightened, Shawna nodded her head. They circled her. The three women smelled like rancid fat.

Shawna held her stepdaughter close against her.

Medusa spoke again, in French. "Soldiers burn my farm. Kill my man. I end here, like you." She smiled, exposing swollen, diseased gums. "Like you. Not so much difference between us now, American."

Shawna understood, but couldn't find words to reply.

"You want food, you earn it." Medusa laughed, mouth wide. "They like you! They like you fine!" Something cruel burned in her eyes. "Your man, he died to help you. This is his child?"

Shawna nodded.

"He died to protect you. What you do to feed his child, eh?" And she laughed uproariously. Medusa said something to Stheno and Euryale, and they laughed as well.

Shawna gripped Lizzie and backed away from them, holding the sobbing girl as tightly as she could. Shawna whispered comfort to her, stroking and kissing gently. After a long time, Lizzie stopped crying and slept. Shawna rocked her, numb, not daring to let herself feel the shock of Mitchell's death. Not now. Later, perhaps. She had to be strong, if they were going to have any chance at all.

She smoothed Lizzie's hair with her fingers, hoping to God that strokes and whispers and kisses would be enough.

* * *

Perhaps two hours passed. The camp was dark, and silent save for distant mechanical rumblings, and a wet, gargling, persistent cough from someplace closer. Shawna guessed that both Lizzie and the Gorgon sisters were asleep. She was about to slip her arm from beneath the child's head when her stepdaughter's eyes opened. Lizzie sat up, almost completely awake, and folded her small hands in her lap. Her eyes were very cold. "I'm hungry," she said.

"I'll try to find some food in the morning. I'm sure there must be food."

"I'm hungry *now*."

"I don't have any food now." Shawna was dismayed to hear the petulance creeping into her own voice. "I said I'd find some food. I will."

From the other side of the tent came a sour laugh. Medusa's laugh. "Food," Medusa said mockingly in French.

"You *said* you would?" Lizzie screamed it. "You said the plane would be safe. That we'd be all right. You said we could stay out of the war. And now my daddy is *dead*."

A sudden headache sprang to life, so violent and painful that it seemed to have hatched in Shawna's skull full-grown. *Mitchell's gone. Mitchell's gone . . . .*

Lizzie's words had torn the fragile scar tissue away, and the grief was almost unbearable. "I loved him too, dammit," she whispered harshly.

Lizzie stiffened, and tried to tear herself out of Shawna's grasp. She sobbed and scratched, hissing, "Hate you, *hate* you. Killed my daddy . . ." over and over again, so choked by pain she was unable even to scream the words.

"I'm sorry," Shawna whispered. "I'm so damned sorry. What can I do?"

For a moment the child fought with her, and then stopped, tiny brown eyes bright with hate. "You can ask Jesus to kill you and *bring back my daddy*."

Shawna stared numbly. Before she could even begin to reply, someone laughed boisterously in the doorway behind her.

"Nice little girl." A man's voice, speaking English clumsily. She turned and faced a giant.

He was well over six feet tall, perhaps two hundred and forty pounds, dressed in rumpled military fatigues. He was mocha-colored with disturbingly pale eyes. His shaven pate was scarred and lumped enough to obscure whatever masculine beauty he might once have possessed. He wore a pistol on the right side of his belt, a foot-long knife on the left. He drew the knife and began to clean his flat thick fingernails. "Nice little girl. Nice *big* girl," he observed.

His pale gaze lingered on Lizzie. "Like big *and* little girls," he said. "Like very much." Lizzie had stopped struggling the moment the big man appeared, and pressed tightly against Shawna.

Shawna quashed her flash of revulsion. "I'm Shawna Littleton. My husband and I were in the capital, painting a mural for President Chimbey."

"He gone now," the big man said. "They blew him up. On Tee Vee. Saw it. He wasn't dead. He wet himself before he died. Now we have real man. General Zanga. He crush rebels." The big man smiled broadly.

"That has nothing to do with me or the girl. Can you get a message out for us?"

"I am Sergeant Juta. You American?" His English was heavily accented but clear. "Identification papers?"

"Lost when our plane went down."

"Husband . . . died?"

"Not 'died,'" she snapped. "Murdered."

"He struck a guard."

"But—"

"No excuse." His eyes were flat cool holes, deep as the night sea.

She squeezed her eyes tight, fighting a resurgence of pain. "Please. Help us get in touch with the American Consulate."

"We not . . . have talk with Americans. Americans arm rebels." He smiled thickly. "Rebels shoot your plane. You should hate Americans. I do."

"Then, please . . . the Swiss Consulate."

"We are busy. You will be taken care of. Fed and sheltered." Great white teeth spread grinning in the brown face. "We are very civilized." He leaned close to Lizzie. "Would you like to have better food?"

Lizzie tried to curl herself into a ball, to make herself as tiny as possible.

Shawna bit her lip, fought her urge to claw his eyes down to the bloody root. "I need to see someone in charge."

"Commandant very busy." Juta grinned. "His English not good, like mine."

"Perhaps you could translate for us," she said.

His odd, pale eyes flamed at her. "Yes," he said. "Me could. But why?"

Shawna's hands shook as she shook a tiny gold stud earring out of her pocket and handed it to him. Thank God for sufficient presence of mind to take them off before the soldiers picked her up.

"Help me," she said. "Just let me talk to him."

He walked to the doorway and examined it in the oblique firelight. The workmanship was exquisite, she knew—she had created it herself, modeled the little wolf's head after a Kotsebue Indian design she and Mitchell had admired in Alaska, a lifetime ago. That had been for . . . what? Their third book together?

Damn.

Juta dropped the earring into a breast pocket and grinned at her. "Sure, lady. You talk all you want. Maybe two, three day."

Shawna Littleton sat in the high-backed chair Juta provided her, back straight, face composed, fingers folded carefully in her lap. She had washed her hair in harsh, hard water and had scraped what dirt she could from her clothes.

Juta stood next to a desk at which a small, dark wrinkled man struggled with a stack of papers. An ancient fan revolved in creaking overhead circuits. Shawna waited. Outside the window, camp inmates wandered in their endless rounds, speaking in indecipherable tongue, lost in a living purgatory. She pressed at her pants with her hands, imagining that she was smoothing away wrinkles.

Finally the little man looked up at her. He smiled warmly, but with a deep sense of fatigue. Something inside her relaxed. He spoke in rapid fire for a minute.

"This is Webi Shebeli Relocation Camp. Camp Number Seven," Juta translated. "We give you . . . good quarters as soon as possible."

She swallowed hard. "Many of the people here are diseased. I am worried about my health, and the health of my . . . daughter. There hasn't been much food, and the water is bad. She is getting sick."

Juta spoke harshly. She wasn't certain why, but a brief, sharp chill brushed the back of her scalp.

The commandant replied. Juta translated. "We are a poor country. We fight to save our country. We sorry we cannot offer more."

She wiped her face, nerves screaming that the interview was going wrong somehow, even if she wasn't certain how or why. "I am American. My husband and I traveled around the world, learning the art of different indigenous . . ." She paused, and rephrased. "Native peoples. Our plane's engine died. We had to land. The soldiers brought us here. My husband was killed four days ago." Against her best efforts, a bright bubble of pain wormed its way to the surface. "You have to help us. If you could just get word to my father. He has money, and many friends. He could help you in your struggle, and would, to help us. Please."

Juta spoke. The commandant spoke. Juta turned to her. "We do everything we can. Please accept our hospitality."

She looked at the commandant's bland, weary expression. And suddenly, horrifically, she understood. Juta had only translated a portion of her message. The commandant would never know of her father unless it served Juta's purpose. Unless it served the giant's ends.

Juta grinned at her.

"English," she said over and over again to the inmates as she passed them. Lizzie clung pitifully to her side. She was afraid to leave the child alone now. "Isn't there someone who speaks English?"

One of the grinning faces broke into a kind of smile. "*Français?*" one said.

She struggled. "*Tu parles anglais.*"

The last produced a flurry of bastard French. Shawna was lost again.

A small man approached them. He was cocooned in filthy, oil-stained rags. Tufts of hair grew from his cheeks like clumps of cactus. He seemed animated by a kind of twitchy, jumpy energy. "English?" he said. "American?"

She was almost dizzy with gratitude. "Yes! Is there someone who speaks it?"

He spoke his own language again, then stopped, screwed his face and made a little hopping step, and said, "The King."

Lizzie looked up at her stepmother and whispered, "He's like a monkey."

"That's not nice," Shawna said. Shawna kept her own image to herself: The little man looked like a jester wrapped in a mummy's shroud.

"The King," Jester said again. He made a scrabbling motion with his arm, asking her to follow. "The King."

Jester led them past the wall. Shawna had seen it from a distance, had walked past it once, but had never slowed to really *see* it. There were so many different images, so densely packed, that it deserved a close-range appreciation. But the wall's association with Mitchell's death made her want to blot the damned thing from her mind.

It was Lizzie who tugged at her arm, slowing them down.

For the first four days in the camp, except for several outbursts of tears and accusations, the child had been almost catatonic. But now something had snared her attention for the first time since entering Camp Seven. "Look, Shawna," she said. "A mural. Like the one you and Daddy painted?"

"Something like that." She could distinguish bestial forms, most of them highly abstracted. "How many animals can you name?"

Lizzie's lips twitched as the child attempted to smile. "'A,' my name is antelope. 'B,' my name is . . . bear?"

"I think it's an anteater." Shawna peered closer at a long-nosed beast carved from dark wood. "Hard to say." For a moment, she studied it, noted the careful knife strokes, and the way the artist had found a way to blend with the gnarled wood grain. Then she recoiled, almost ashamed of herself that she had forgotten, even for a moment, the danger they were in, and the loss they had suffered.

Then she saw Lizzie's face, so small and round, and the almost desperate way she had focused on the carving, and knew that the girl was struggling for some kind of balance, some tiny place to stand emotionally. *Good girl, Lizzie*, she thought, and pressed her stepdaughter's hand.

"Bears eat ants," Lizzie said defensively. "'C,' my name is cat. It *is* some kind of cat, isn't it?"

Shawna nodded, trying desperately to get into the game, just a little. She found the right angle, and the third object was indeed a cat, rendered in bunches of string.

There were dozens of animals in the wall, but also tiny automobiles, and trees, and human faces by the hundreds. Lizzie's fingers traced one especially striking image, a laughing man, an Ashanti-style mask rendered in what might have once been a plastic canopy. The planes and facial curves were burned in, so that the image was expressed in the concavity. She had never seen anything quite like it—the negative-image aspect immediately set her creative mind buzzing.

If she got out of here . . . (she corrected herself. She couldn't allow herself to think like that. *When* she got out) she would try the technique, maybe finish one of the jobs she and Mitchell had begun together. . . .

Her thoughts wound to a halt.

A hollow-eyed woman knelt in the dirt before the wall. Her fingers bled. At first Shawna wasn't certain what the woman was doing. Then Shawna focused on the woman's papooska backpack, and the dead infant cradled within. The woman's face was streaked with dust and tears. With her own blood, she was finger-painting a screaming child on a ragged piece of plywood. An oval within an oval. Smudges for eyes. Just a bare few lines, *Sum-i* style, a somber minimalism, almost impossibly eloquent.

In that instant, Shawna knew what the wall was. It was a tapestry of loss, a mosaic of human pain. Memories of freedoms and childhood wonders, a collage of dead dreams. She wondered how many human souls had passed through Camp Seven. How many of them knew they would never leave alive, were making a last desperate attempt to leave something, anything, of themselves of the wall.

I was here, each disjointed effort said. *I lived. I saw living things, and shared their world for a time. And then I died.*

The woman knelt there, consumed by her pain and memories. Shawna felt almost voyeuristic to witness her moment of revelation and anguish, but was too hypnotized even to blink as Jester led them away.

The little man guided Shawna and Lizzie through the camp's twisting, narrow byways. As they walked the perimeter clockwise from the northern gate, the cramped confines shifted in perspective, seemed more like the spaces defined by the spokes of a wheel. Everything radiated from a central hub. Here, there seemed to be some kind of order, and even a quality of organic design.

Here, they saw more female prisoners, women wasted into wraiths. The refugees extended hands, begged for food and water, too weak and sick to crawl out to the food trucks.

This inner area was a hospice, a storage facility for the dying. Lizzie was wrong: Their guide wasn't a Jester, he was Charon, their personal escort on a visit to the underworld.

A dwelling in the very center was more than a mere tent, but less than a formal structure, as if over the months someone had cobbled together a makeshift palace from truck parts and scrap lumber.

Jester stood in the doorway, sweeping a fall of carpet aside with his arm.

"King," the little man said.

The ceilings and walls were covered with rugs and statues and carvings. Some were capped with silver and what might have been very weathered gold.

An elaborate bed dominated the center of the room, propped up on truck tires to make a kind of throne. On three sides it was veiled by a barely translucent white curtain.

"Approach." The voice was thickly accented but cultured, and heavy with self-amusement.

Shawna pushed her stepdaughter behind her, then cautiously stepped forward. The man on the bed had once been large, muscular. Now he was all but wasted away, a whisper of his former self.

"Do you . . . speak English?" she asked.

"And French. And Portuguese." He puffed on a hookah pipe, then exhaled a sweet languid cloud of hashish. She was shocked to feel the depth of her response, the sudden strong desire for intoxication. Hashish, yes. Cannabis. Or alcohol. God, yes, a drink. Anything.

"Your plane crashed."

"How did you know that?"

"I hear many things," he said calmly. "The whole camp has heard of the black American artist. Your husband tried to defend you. The soldiers shot him."

Lizzie shuffled her feet. "We don't belong here."

"Where do you belong, Shawna Littleton? I read one of your books once. *A to Z with primitive art of the world?* **A** I am an Abo. **B** I am a Bantu. **C** I am Ceremese. A very funny book."

"Funny?" She tamped down her automatic flare of anger.

"Funny. With your American wealth, you travel the world searching for other people's souls. Where is yours?"

"I meant no disrespect. But I . . . I need help. Please. My presence here is a mistake."

"Yes," he said. "A mistake. I, of course, belong here."

"I didn't mean it like that."

He exhaled a long, sweet stream of smoke, but said nothing.

"Who are you?" Shawna asked.

From the bed he bowed to them without a trace of irony. "My name is Kampala. I owned the largest trading empire in Central Africa."

"How did you end here?"

He shrugged. "Bad timing. Arranging for local goods to be sold and converted to hard currencies. It was then that the rebels tried to overthrow the remnants of the Republic's colonial government. Alas, I am afraid that, while most of my goods are safe, I myself am not." He chuckled, pleased with his own sense of humor. "Poor sanitation, tribal scarring, and anal sex spread this contagion across this continent, and no one spoke the truth in time to save my people. These camps are a final, desperate attempt to stop the death. In the end, my life, your life, the girl's life do not matter. The continent must survive."

"The child is sick," Shawna said.

"She is your daughter."

"Stepdaughter," Lizzie said. "She married my daddy."

"Your father died in her defense," Kampala said. "How do you feel about that?"

I feel like I'm dying, Shawna thought. *Please, God, don't let me die.*

Lizzie said nothing.

After almost a minute, he said, "What do you wish of me?"

"You seem to have resources." Shawna despised the weakness in her voice, the way she rushed the words out. "Do you know a way out of here?"

"Do you think I would have remained here if I did?" He leaned forward until his mouth was against the curtain. His face was as rutted as a storm-washed dirt road. "If you find a way to take your stepdaughter from this place, do it. And quickly. No, I cannot help you. I have access to a few simple conveniences. My money can buy courtesies. But I cannot escape." He pointed to his mouth, around which a thin, skin-tight blue collar was affixed. "So you see the necklace? It cannot be cut. It contains a radio device. They track the sick ones with these."

He laughed bitterly. "So! After so many years of making the rules play my game, I am caught. And if you do not find a way out, you will be caught. But if you stay . . ." His ruined lips twisted into a smile. "In many ways a woman like you could ease her life here."

The breath thickened in her throat. "What do you mean?"

"You wish for better food for your child? Medicine? And believe me, you will need medicine. Perhaps I can help."

The room darkened, contracted. "Oh, God."

"Why not? You are the most beautiful woman in Camp Seven. I am still a man. Such favors would not go unrewarded."

Although she stood still, the room revolved around her. She backed out of the room, pulling Lizzie with her, her eyes on Kampala. He rose and stepped through the curtain, and for the first time she saw him clearly. He was deeply wrinkled. Most of his hair was gone, and his eyes glistened with mucus. His fingers were mere sticks, his belly protuberant beneath rich robes. His lips pulled back in a fleshy smile. Half of his teeth were gone.

Then she was out of the tent, fleeing toward the main camp.

She pulled Lizzie onto the bed. The child trembled, her skin damp and sticky.

"Shawna," Lizzie whispered, the first word she had spoken since Kampala's tent. Shawna pulled her face so close that their noses touched. She could smell her stepdaughter's breath, a sour, fearful scent. Lizzie's eyes were huge. "I'm sorry for the things I said. I don't hate you. Shawna?"

"Yes, Lizzie?"

"Don't leave me." She shivered uncontrollably. "Don't leave me here. Shawna . . . don't . . ." Lizzie buried her face against Shawna's chest, muffling the rest of her words.

Shawna stared into the darkness, seeing nothing. Imagining everything.

Shawna promised herself that it wouldn't happen. That somehow, they would survive without . . . without having to . . .

Such favors would not go unrewarded.

Twice a day, cans of food and water were trucked into Camp Seven. The camp bosses, men like Juta with arms the size of legs, managed the lines. They barked in high, fast, indecipherable strings of words, decided via arcane formulae those who would eat, drink, or die.

At night she dreamed of running sores, broken skulls, and stolen food wrenched from twitching, bloodied hands. During the day she waited six hours in the sun for a cup of brown, brackish water.

Without enough food to fill the child's aching belly, Lizzie began to weaken. Shawna boiled their water, then strained the stinking stuff through her shirt to produce something decent for Lizzie to drink.

Camp Seven seethed with flies, with the constant low sounds of misery, with a repellent, low-level sexual tension. In shadowed alcoves between the huts, thin, fierce-eyed boys traded five minutes with rump or mouth for a cup of thin soup. From those nooks fire-eyed, grizzled dark men grabbed at her, waving packs of cigarettes or pieces of maggoty beef.

Shawna waited from dawn to dusk, standing in the sun to get a can of tinned meat. Lizzie was too weak to wait with her, and wandered away to sit in a patch of shadow, watching as Shawna inched toward the back of the food truck.

Three people remained ahead of her when the man on the back of the truck threw the tarp down. Without a word, he drove away.

Shawna stood in the middle of the camp grounds, dumbfounded, speechless, and unmoving. Finally she scooped Lizzie into her arms and staggered away. The child burned with fever and moaned softly. "I hurt everywhere," she whispered. Shawna counted the steps until they were safe in the stinking heat of their hut.

As gently as she could, Shawna laid the child on her bed, doing what little she could to make Lizzie comfortable. In a sliver of moonlight through a slit of window above them, Lizzie was silvered with perspiration. Another finger of panic pried at Shawna's control. The girl was sweating too much. There wasn't enough drinking water to replace the fluid.

Medusa clucked. The grotesque woman sat in the darkness on the edge of her cot, sighing as her sister massaged her calves. While the flesh hung loose on her upper body, her legs were as swollen as rotten sausages. She watched them both, and then barked out in French, "Your man die for you! What you do for his child, American, hey?"

Shawna fled the shack. She pressed her face against the barbed-wire fence, arms outstretched to the strutting, khaki-clad black soldiers, their carbines slung across brawny shoulders, and she begged them:

"Food," she screamed. "Just a little food. My daughter." They ignored her.

"My daughter." She sank to her knees, lost.

The guards laughed at her.

She cried, and struggled to find a prayer that would not catch in her throat, to a God she was more tempted to curse than implore.

*   *   *

Shawna spent three hours kneeling at the fence, and four more at Lizzie's bedside. Praying for food, praying for water, praying for the strength to pray, to believe in anything except the inevitability of death.

The sun was still below the horizon. Oily fires flickered in metal drums, bathing the entire camp in a dank, yellowish glow, broken only by the steady, gliding searchlights.

Shivering in the cold, Shawna hauled debris to the north gate, under the guard tower. Next to the wall.

All day and into the night she worked. Refugees shambled past her, nattering in their singsong as the pieces of metal and rubber evolved. She could identify at least five distinctly different languages, but spoke none of them. It seemed every human being in the camp had someone so share their misery with, to touch, perhaps to share a grim and desperate joke.

She felt utterly alone.

That night it rained, a hot, slick downpour. She set a pot out to catch water as she huddled in the downpour, continuing to bend and twist metal and plastic. Her fingers slipped, slashed themselves on bits of wire.

Feverishly, focused, she worked. Every detail, every inch of wire, every bend of tubing, every molded bit of paper fit together with precise attention to detail.

After almost twenty hours at the wall, she staggered back to their hut. The rain had turned the ground into a slurry of mud. She pushed her way past the hanging blanket that was their only door, and went to Lizzie's bedside. The fever was worse, and the girl's skin had a shiny, papery quality. Her eyes would barely focus as Shawna fed her one precious spoonful of water at a time. Lizzie blinked, then croaked, "Where's Daddy?"

"Shhh," Shawna said, and stroked the girl's hair softly.

"Are we going soon? Is your work finished yet?"

Shawna nodded.

Lizzie looked away from her. "Daddy said you shouldn't have come. That you shouldn't have made the painting for the bad man."

Shawna leaned closer. "Don't talk about that." That whole life seemed very far away.

Lizzie stared into her stepmother's eyes almost placidly. "Am I going to die?"

Shawna didn't answer. She felt as if the ground had opened up beneath her.

"We shouldn't have come," Lizzie said, then closed her eyes and slept.

Shawna awoke four hours later, weighing a thousand pounds. Concrete had set in her joints. Laboriously, she rolled to her side and sat up. She checked on Lizzie. The child was curled on her side, right thumb in her mouth, her sunken cheeks a bit fuller. Her eyelashes trembled as if she were dreaming, a curl of hair plastered to one dark cheek.

Shawna girded herself, wrapped a blanket around her shoulders, and went outside.

The morning world was framed in darkness, lit only by pain. It was no longer raining. Wet, heavy clouds shrouded the sun. A crowd had gathered up by the wall. They seemed to be . . . inspecting her handiwork.

She began to feel the faintest ray of hope.

The crowd parted for her as she approached. They looked from Shawna to the sculpture, and nodded approval. Tall and thin, short with sagging flesh, men and women, young and old, dark as Shawna and darker they were, but they seemed to include her in their number now, and in that new inclusion she found comfort.

Rendered in stick, in bits of wood and plastic and paper, was Shawna Littleton. The profile was hers, caught there in a curve of wire. Hair was suggested by a knot of string. Her arms were outstretched fragments of particle board. Shawna's plastic face was drawn, anguished. Her pottery-shard lips were frozen open, locked in an eternal scream for help.

"Please," Shawna said desperately. "Listen to me. I am one of you. I am a refugee like you are. This isn't my country. Please. My daughter will die if we don't get out of here." The stolid indifference was gone from the crowd—if, indeed, it had ever existed. Some nodded their comprehension and empathy. A round, short woman patted her arm.

Then there was a nasty laugh from the back of the crowd. "Many of their daughters will die." The voice was terribly familiar. "Have already died." Juta's voice. He shouldered his way forward.

She tried not to look at him. "Please."

He barked laughter. "You think you become part of them by *this*?" He waved deprecatingly at her sculpture, at the woman in the wall. "Not one of them. You are . . . American mongrel. You they color, but not they *heart*."

The crowd began to disperse. Although each was hurt in her own way, crippled and torn by war and disease, they had been prepared to reach out to her. None would stand against the guards.

"Please," she whispered. "It's not my fault." No one listened to her. "I didn't ask to be born in America." The rain hammered against the ground, muddying their footprints. "I didn't ask to be born," she said. A tall woman clutching a bony, huge-eyed child clucked at her sympathetically. "Damn it. Help me. Help us." And finally she said, *"I'm not sick!"*

And then, the last of her strength spent, she sagged to her knees in the mud and tried to sob.

No tears would come.

The Jester found her curled at the door of her shack. He stood without speaking. Rain drizzled down his blunt features.

At length she looked up at him. "I'm going to die here," she said, her voice as flat and cold as a tin roof. "My daughter and I will both die here." She paused, turned her face up to the rain. "We'll all die here."

"You have friends?" Jester said. "Friends outside?"

She nodded glumly, then caught herself. "How much English do you speak?"

"I have English," he said proudly. "Not so good as King, but I have."

She nodded again. "I can reach my friends," she said. "What difference does it make?"

"There is way you could . . . escape, yes?"

She looked at him as if he had suddenly sprouted antennae. Hope flared within her, and she feared it. Hope could shatter, could kill more certainly than AIDS or starvation. "With a sick eight-year-old?"

"No," he said. "By yourself, yes?"

"By . . . myself?"

He nodded. For a long moment the only sound in the camp was the distant yap of dogs and the steady drum of the rain. "I couldn't leave her."

"You find your friends, yes? Bring help. Yes?"

She held his eyes steadily, knew the comforting lie that was being offered. "Yes."

"You help her here?"

"No," she said softly.

"Is she your blood?" Jester said softly.

"No," Shawna whispered. The rain beat harder.

"You find your friends, yes?" he said quickly. "Follow the river. Four, five days down river. Red Cross people."

"How do you know that?" she asked.

"I know. Caught stealing there," he said proudly.

"Four or five days," she whispered.

"You reach it, maybe week the little girl could be out."

"A week," she said numbly.

She listened to her heartbeat.

"Lady," he said. "I watch her for you. Trust me."

She studied him, and shuddered. "You know things," she said. "Do you know . . . is there medicine here? Penicillin?"

"Only King have medicine." Jester wiped the rainwater from his face. "You be at north fence, after midnight."

"Why would you do this?"

"You rich American. Have friends. When you come for the girl, take me with you." He fingered the necklace. "There is no place I can go."

She nodded. "I know that place," she said.

"Shawna?" Lizzie asked feebly. "Where are you going?"

Shawna spooned rainwater between the child's lips. No more tears streamed down Lizzie's fever-swollen cheeks. Dehydration was nearly complete. It would take more than water now—the fever had taken hold, and Lizzie's eyes were like frying glass marbles in her sunken face. "I may be able to get us help," Shawna whispered.

The little girl looked through Shawna. There was little in those eyes now, save pain and fear. "Shawna? Where's Daddy?"

"Daddy will be here soon." Shawna bent close, running a hand over Lizzie's brow. "Soon."

There was a rustle of cloth behind her. She turned. The Gorgons stared at her. Two of them turned away, rolled back beneath their blankets, but Medusa met her eyes squarely. From her shadowed corner, her haggard face blazed with contempt.

Shawna Littleton closed her heart, hardened her mind, and walked out toward the rain. Just before she reached the door, Lizzie said, "Shawna?"

She stopped in the doorway without turning. "Yes?"

"Are you my mommy?"

Shawna stumbled, then caught her balance and ran. Lizzie's last words reverberated in her mind in an endless, rolling echo. She ran in an uncoordinated, animal gallop, making terrible, wet sounds in her throat.

Oncoming footsteps.

She shrank back into a shadow, away from the muddy walkway as the gigantic Juta stalked by. He seemed to stride in slow motion. He smiled and whistled tunelessly, one with the storm.

Shawna Littleton hurried through the darkness, toward damnation.

Jester met her in the shadows. He pointed toward the wall. "Near end. Face of laughing woman. Take lip, pull up. Crawl through. Grab thread, and follow."

"Why can't you go—" she started to say, and then remembered the collars.

"Follow thread to other side. Pull up. You be safe."

She nodded dumbly. Then gripped his shoulder. "Why didn't you tell me about this before? I could have taken the girl with me."

He shrugged and looked at her shrewdly. "More money selling you to King." Then he disappeared.

Shawna waited for the searchlights to slide past, then ran across the yard, dropping into a crouch as another glaring oval crossed her path. The sky above her crackled with lightning.

She knew which sculpture to seek: the Ashanti mask, the laughing woman. A flash of lightning revealed the woman to her, frozen forever in the plastic canopy. She seemed to be staring at Shawna. The unknown artist was surely dead by now—other artwork overlapped this one, making Shawna consider this one of the oldest works. The woman's face was long and thin, abstracted. But even in the poor light she could see that it was riven with care and deprivation.

Why was she laughing? She looked closer. Barely visible, and arrayed about the woman's face like satellites circling a planet, were tiny human faces, plump and healthy.

Children.

For a moment Shawna understood the laughter, then lightning flashed again, and she reflexively pulled the lower lip. The mask slid down, and a two-foot section of the wall came away, exposing a tunnel. An almost invisible fishing line filament was anchored to the underside of the mask. If she followed it, it would take her safely to the escape hatch on the other side.

A sour bubble of hysterical laughter welled in her throat, swiftly quashed. Before she crawled through, she glanced along the wall, where it curved around toward the west gate. Almost two hundred feet away, she thought she could make out her own sculpture, highlighted starkly by lightning and searchlights.

The women in the wall screamed, lightning their eyes, thunder in their silent throats.

Shawna dropped to her belly and crawled through the mud, knee-elbow, knee-elbow, an inch at a time, feeling her way along the filament.

The wind howled. If she strained, she heard within it a child's voice, a cry of terror, of abject betrayal.

She squeezed her eyes shut. It wasn't fair. *Everyone is alone in the world*, she said to herself. Everyone. Besides, if she could just reach the camp, the Red Cross camp, eventually, maybe in a few days . . .

It wasn't fair.

Are you my mommy?

Lightning coiled and thrust above her like a striking serpent.

Suddenly she knew why Medusa hated her. Knew why Juta mocked her. Why the laughing woman laughed. Why her own sculpture screamed.

Another twist of fire in the sky above her, and the insight was gone again, leaving only a cold and lonely certainty.

Shawna turned and crawled back into the camp.

Back in the shack, Shawna rinsed her face and body with rainwater. Her clothes were filthy. There was nothing to be done about that, and the more she thought about it, the less it mattered.

She peered into a shard of mirror. She tried to smile. The sight of her own cracked, demented leer was almost enough to send her careening over the edge.

Shawna kissed her stepdaughter's burning forehead. Lizzie made a weak mewling sound and stretched out a tiny fevered hand. Shawna held it to her cheek.

Lizzie's lips moved without producing audible words. Then: "Mommy."

Her eyes ached to cry, but cleansing tears refused to fall. *Mitch*, she begged, *help me*.

Shawna turned and stood to face Medusa, who lay unmoving, watching her. She searched to find the right words in French. "The King," she said finally. "Can I trust him?"

Medusa didn't blink. "Do you have a choice?" she replied.

The darkness in Kampala's palace was eased by a dozen candles, flickering in silver holders. Kampala sat, watching the entrance as she entered. "You will wear a condom," she said.

"We have them." Even through the hanging veils, the hunger blazed from his eyes.

"I want medicine for my child," she said. Again, he agreed.

"And food. Decent food. She can't keep down the garbage they feed her."

She paused. He waited. The silence lengthened between them.

Kampala asked, "And nothing else? Nothing for yourself?"

She approached his bed, pinching out the candles as she went. Darkness swallowed her, leaving only the dim outline of a woman slipping from her clothes. "Yes," she said, climbing between his sheets. And before they began, she told him.

She stumbled back to her hovel in the morning, her tins of meat and soup enfolded in arms almost too weak to hold them.

She gave Lizzie several capsules of penicillin, followed by a sip of broth.

When Lizzie vomited broth and caplets up, Shawna dug through the filth to find the precious medication. She helped her stepdaughter swallow them again.

This time they stayed down. Shawna sat by the bedside, lost in herself. All she knew, all she cared about, was that Lizzie was alive, *alive*. That each day had to be lived a minute at a time. If she thought about more than that, she would go insane.

Medusa and her sisters watched, all laughter and mockery gone from their faces. Hot with fever, Lizzie's small hand stole into hers, tightened, and then relaxed as healing sleep took her.

Shawna curled up next to Lizzie and closed her eyes, her own hands clutched around the bauble King had given her.

It was nothing fancy, nothing she would have noticed twice in her former life. It was only the wedding ring Mitch had worn, sawed from his finger by scavengers and, as she suspected, sold to the King.

Are you my mommy? Lizzie had asked, as might any child, even one not teetering on the brink of hell itself. *Are you my mommy?*

"I am now," Shawna whispered. And finally, at long last, she cried.

ARK OF BONES

Henry Dumas

(1974)

Headeye, he was follable followin me. I knowed he was followin me. But I just kept goin, like I wasn't payin him no mind. Headeye, he never fish much, but I guess he knowed the river good as anybody. But he ain't know where the fishin was good. Thas why I knowed he was followin me. So I figured I better fake him out. I ain't want nobody with a mojo bone followin me. Thas why I was goin along downriver stead of up, where I knowed fishin was good. Headeye, he hard to fool. Like I said, he knowed the river good. One time I rode across to New Providence with him and his old man. His old man was drunk. Headeye, he took the raft on across. Me and him. His old man stayed in New Providence, but me and Headeye come back. Thas when I knowed how good of a river-rat he was.

Headeye, he o.k., cept when he get some kinda notion in that big head of his. Then he act crazy. Tryin to show off his age. He older'n me, but he little for his age. Some people say readin too many books will stunt your growth. Well, on Headeye, everything is stunted cept his eyes and his head. When he get some crazy notion runnin through his head, then you can't get rid of him till you know what's on his mind. I knowed somethin was eatin on him, just like I knowed it was *him* followin *me*.

I kept close to the path less he think I was tryin to lose him. About a mile from my house I stopped and peed in the bushes, and then I got a chance to see how Headeye was movin along.

Headeye, he droop when he walk. They called him Headeye cause his eyes looked bigger'n his head when you looked at him sideways. Headeye bout the ugliest guy I ever run upon. But he was good-natured. Some people called him Eagle-Eye. He bout the smartest nigger in that raggedy school, too. But most time we called him Headeye. He was always findin things and bringin em to school, or to the cotton patch. One time he found a mojo bone and all the kids cept me went round talkin bout him puttin a curse on his old man. I ain't say nothin. It wont none of my business. But Headeye, he ain't got no devil in him. I found that out.

So, I'm kickin off the clay from my toes, but mostly I'm thinkin about how to find out what's on his mind. He's got this notion in his head about me hoggin the luck. So I'm fakin him out, lettin him droop behind me.

Pretty soon I break off the path and head for the river. I could tell I was far enough. The river was gettin ready to bend.

I come up on a snake twistin toward the water. I was gettin ready to bust that snake's head when a fox run across my path. Before I could turn my head back, a flock of birds hit the air pretty near scarin me half to death. When I got on down to the bank, I see somebody's cow lopin on the levee way down the river. Then to really upshell me, here come Headeye droopin long like he had ten tons of cotton on his back.

"Headeye, what you followin me for?" I was mad.

"Ain't nobody thinkin bout you," he said, still comin.

"What you followin long behind me for?"

"Ain't nobody followin you."

"The hell you ain't."

"I ain't followin you."

"Somebody's followin me, and I like to know who he is."

"Maybe somebody's followin me."

"What you mean?"

"Just what you think."

Headeye, he was gettin smart on me. I give him one of my looks, meanin that he'd better watch his smartness round me, cause I'd have him down eatin dirt in a minute. But he act like he got a crazy notion.

"You come this far ahead me, you must be got a call from the spirit."

"What spirit?" I come to wonder if Headeye ain't got to workin his mojo too much.

"Come on."

"Wait." I grabbed his sleeve.

He took out a little sack and started pullin out something.

"You fishin or not?" I ask him.

"Yeah, but not for the same thing. You see this bone?" Headeye, he took out that mojo, stepped back. I wasn't scared of no ole bone, but everybody'd been talkin bout Headeye and him gettin sanctified. But he never went to church. Only his mama went. His old man only went when he sober, and that be about once or twice a year.

So I look at that bone. "What kinda voodoo you work with that mojo?"

"This is a keybone to the culud man. Ain't but one in the whole world."

"And *you* got it?" I act like I ain't believe him. But I was testin him. I never rush upon a thing I don't know.

"We got it."

"We got?"

"It belongs to the people of God."

I ain't feel like the people of God, but I just let him talk on.

"Remember when Ezekiel was in the valley of dry bones?"

I reckoned I did.

". . . And the hand of the Lord was upon me, and carried me out in the spirit to the valley of dry bones.

"And he said unto me, 'Son of man, can these bones live?' and I said unto him, 'Lord, thou knowest.'

"And he said unto me, 'Go and bind them together. Prophesy that I shall come and put flesh upon them from generations and from generations.'

"And the Lord said unto me, 'Son of man, these bones are the whole house of the brothers, scattered to the islands. Behold, I shall bind up the bones and you shall prophesy the name.'"

He walked on pass me and loped on down to the river bank. This here old place was called Deadman's Landin because they found a dead man there one time. His body was so rotted and ate up by fish and craw dads that they couldn't tell whether he was white or black, just a dead man.

Headeye went over to them long planks and logs leanin off in the water and begin to push them around like he was makin somethin.

"You was followin me." I was mad again.

Headeye acted like he was iggin me. He put his hands up to his eyes and looked far out over the water. I could barely make out the other side of the river. It was real wide right along there and take couple hours by boat to cross it. Most I ever did was fish and swim. Headeye, he act like he iggin me. I began to bait my hook and go down the bank to where he was. I was mad enough to pop him side the head, but I shoulda been glad. I just wanted him to own up to the truth. I walked along the bank. That damn river was risin. It was lappin up over the planks of the landin and climbin up the bank.

Then the funniest thing happened. Headeye, he stopped movin and shovin on those planks and looks up at me. His pole is layin back under a willow tree like he wan't goin to fish none. A lot of birds were still flyin over and I saw a bunch of wild hogs rovin along the levee. All of a sudden Headeye, he say:

"I ain't mean no harm what I said about you workin with the devil. I take it back."

It almost knocked me over. Me and Headeye was arguin a while back bout how many niggers there is in the Bible. Headeye, he know all about it, but I ain't give on to what I know. I looked sideways at him. I figured he was tryin to make up for followin me. But there was somethin funny goin on as I held my peace. I said "huh-huh," and I just kept on lookin at him.

Then he points out over the water and up in the sky wavin his hand all round like he was twirlin a lasso.

"You see them signs?"

I couldn't help but say "yeah."

"The Ark is comin."

"What Ark?"

"You'll see."

"Noah's Ark?"

"Just wait. You'll see."

And he went back to fixin up that landin. I come to see what he was doing pretty soon. And I had a notion to go down and pitch in. But I knowed Headeye. Sometimes he gets a notion in his big head and he act crazy behind it. Like the time in church when he told Rev. Jenkins that he heard people moanin out on the river. I remember that. Cause papa went with the men. Headeye, his old man was with them out in that boat. They thought it was somebody took sick and couldn't row ashore. But Headeye, he kept tellin them it was a lot of people, like a multitude.

Anyway, they ain't find nothin and Headeye, his daddy hauled off and smacked him side the head. I felt sorry for him and didn't laugh as much as the other kids did, though sometimes Headeye's notions get me mad too.

Then I come to see that maybe he wasn't followin me. The way he was actin I knowed he wasn't scared to be there at Deadman's Landin. I threw my line out and made like I was fishin, but I wasn't, cause I was steady watchin Headeye.

By and by the clouds started to get thick as clabber milk. A wind come up. And even though the little waves slappin the sides of the bank made the water jump around and dance, I could still tell that the river was risin. I looked at Headeye. He was wanderin off along the bank, wadin out in the shallows and leanin over like he was lookin for somethin.

I comest to think about what he said, that valley of bones. I comest to get some kinda crazy notion myself. There was a lot of signs, but they weren't nothin too special. If you're sharp-eyed you always seem somethin along the Mississippi.

I messed around and caught a couple of fish. Headeye, he was wadin out deeper in the Sippi, bout hip-deep now, standin still like he was listenin for somethin. I left my pole under a big rock to hold it down and went over to where he was.

"This ain't the place," I say to him.

Headeye, he ain't say nothin. I could hear the water come to talk a little. Only river people know how to talk to the river when it's mad. I watched the light on the waves way upstream where the old Sippi bend, and I could tell that she was movin faster. Risin. The shakin was fast and the wind had picked up. It was whippin up the canebrake and twirlin the willows and the swamp oak that drink themselves full along the bank.

I said it again, thinkin maybe Headeye would ask me where was the real place. But he ain't even listen.

"You come out here to fish or fool?" I asked him. But he waved his hand back at me to be quiet. I knew then that Headeye had some crazy notion in his big head and that was it. He'd be talkin about it for the next two weeks.

"Hey!" I hollered at him. "Headeye, can't you see the river's on the rise? Let's shag outa here."

He ain't pay me no mind. I picked up a coupla sticks and chunked them out near the place where he was standin just to make sure he ain't

fall asleep right out there in the water. I ain't never knowed Headeye to
fall asleep at a place, but bein as he is so damn crazy, I couldn't take the
chance.

Just about that time I hear a funny noise. Headeye, he hear it too,
cause he motioned to me to be still. He waded back to the bank and ran
down to the broken planks at Deadman's Landin. I followed him. A couple drops of rain smacked me in the face, and the wind, she was whippin
up a sermon.

I heard a kind of moanin, like a lot of people. I figured it must be in
the wind. Headeye, he is jumpin around like a perch with a hook in the
gill. Then he find himself. He come to just stand alongside the planks.
He is in the water about knee deep. The sound is steady, not gettin any
louder now, and not gettin any lower. The wind, she steady whippin up
a sermon. By this time, it done got kinda dark, and me, well, I done got
kinda scared.

Headeye, he's all right though. Pretty soon he call me.

"Fish-hound?"

"Yeah?"

"You better come on down here."

"What for? Man, can't you see it gettin ready to rise?"

He ain't say nothin. I can't see too much now cause the clouds done
swole up so big and mighty that everything's gettin dark.

Then I sees it. I'm gettin ready to chunk another stick out at him,
when I see this big thing movin in the far off, movin slow, down river,
naw, it was up river. Naw, it was just movin and standin still at the same
time. The damnest thing I ever seed. It just about a damn boat, the
biggest boat in the whole world. I looked up and what I took for clouds
was sails. The wind was whippin up a sermon on them.

It was way out in the river, almost not touchin the water, just rockin
there, rockin and waitin.

Headeye, I don't see him.

Then I look and I see a rowboat comin. Headeye, he done waded out
about shoulder deep and he is wavin to me. I ain't know what to do. I
guess he bout know that I was gettin ready to run, because he holler out.
"Come on, Fish. Hurry! I wait for you."

I figured maybe we was dead or somethin and was gonna get the
Glory Boat over the river and make it on into heaven. But I ain't say it
aloud. I was so scared I didn't know what I was doin. First thing I know

I was side by side with Headeye, and a funny-lookin rowboat was drawin alongside of us. Two men, about as black as anybody black wants to be, was steady strokin with paddles. The rain had reached us and I could hear that moanin like a church full of people pourin out their hearts to Jesus in heaven.

All the time I was tryin not to let on how scared I was. Headeye, he ain't payin no mind to nothin cept that boat. Pretty soon it comest to rain hard. The two big black jokers rowin the boat ain't say nothin to us, and everytime I look at Headeye, he poppin his eyes out tryin to get a look at somethin far off. I couldn't see that far, so I had to look at what was close up. The muscles in those jokers' arms was movin back an forth every time they swung them oars around. It was a funny ride in that row-boat, because it didn't seem like we was in the water much. I took a chance and stuck my hand over to see, and when I did that they stopped rowin the boat and when I looked up we was drawin longside this here ark, and I tell you it was the biggest ark in the world.

I asked Headeye if it was Noah's Ark, and he tell me he didn't know either. Then I was scared.

They was tyin that rowboat to the side where some heavy ropes hung over. A long row of steps were cut in the side near where we got out, and the moanin sound was real loud now, and if it wasn't for the wind and rain beatin and whippin us up the steps, I'd swear the sound was comin from someplace inside the ark.

When Headeye got to the top of the steps I was still makin my way up. The two jokers were gone. On each step was a number, and I couldn't help lookin at them numbers. I don't know what number was on the first step, but by the time I took notice I was on 1608, and they went on like that right on up to a number that made me pay attention: 1944. That was when I was born. When I got up to Headeye, he was standin on a number, 1977, and so I ain't pay the number any more mind.

If that ark was Noah's, then he left all the animals on shore because I ain't see none. I kept lookin around. All I could see was doors and cab-ins. While we was standin there takin in things, half scared to death, an old man come walkin toward us. He's dressed in skins and his hair is gray and very woolly. I figured he ain't never had a haircut all his life. But I didn't say nothin. He walks over to Headeye and that poor boy's eyes bout to pop out.

Well, I'm standin there and this old man is talkin to Headeye. With the wind blowin and the moanin, I couldn't make out what they was sayin. I got the feelin he didn't want me to hear either, because he was leanin in on Headeye. If that old fellow was Noah, then he wasn't like the Noah I'd seen in my Sunday School picture cards. Naw, sir. This old guy was wearin skins and sandals and he was black as Headeye and me, and he had thick features like us, too. On them pictures Noah was always white with a long beard hangin off his belly.

I looked around to see some more people, maybe Shem, Ham, and Japheh, or wives and the rest who was suppose to be on the ark, but I ain't see nobody. Nothin but all them doors and cabins. The ark is steady rockin like it is floatin on air. Pretty soon Headeye come over to me. The old man was goin through one of the cabin doors. Before he closed the door he turns around and points at me and Headeye. Headeye, he don't see this, but I did. Talkin about scared. I almost ran and jumped off that boat. If it had been a regular boat, like somethin I could stomp my feet on, then I guess I just woulda done it. But I held still.

"Fish-hound, you ready?" Headeye say to me.

"Yeah, I'm ready to get ashore." I meant it, too.

"Come on. You got this far. You scared?"

"Yeah, I'm scared. What kinda boat is this?"

"The Ark. I told you once."

I could tell now that the roarin was not all the wind and voices. Some of it was engines. Could hear that chug-chug like a paddle wheel whippin up the stern.

"When we gettin off here? You think I'm crazy like you?" I asked him. I was mad. "You know what that old man did behind your back?"

"Fish-hound, this is a soulboat."

I figured by now I best play long with Headeye. He git a notion goin and there ain't nothin mess his head up more than a notion. I stopped tryin to fake him out. I figured then maybe we both was crazy. I ain't feel crazy, but I damn sure couldn't make heads or tails of the situation. So I let it ride. When you hook a fish, the best thing to do is just let him get a good hold, let him swallow. Specially a catfish. You don't go jerkin him up as soon as you get a nibble. With a catfish you let him go. I figured I'd better let things go. Pretty soon, I figured I'd catch up with somethin. And I did.

Well, me and Headeye were kinda arguin, not loud, since you had to keep your voice down on a place like that ark out of respect. It was like

that. Headeye, he tells me that when the cabin doors open we were suppose to go down the stairs. He said anybody on this boat could consider
hisself *called*.

"Called to do what?" I asked him. I had to ask him, cause the only
kinda callin I knew about was when somebody *hollered* at you or when
the Lord *called* somebody to preach. I figured it out. Maybe the Lord had
called him, but I knew dog well He wasn't *callin* me. I hardly ever went
to church and when I did go it was only to play with the gals. I knowed
I wasn't fit to whip up no flock of people with holiness. So when I
asked him, called for what, I ain't have in my mind nothin I could be
called for.

"You'll see," he said, and the next thing I know we was goin down
steps into the belly of that ark. The moanin jumped up into my ears loud
and I could smell something funny, like the burnin of sweet wood. The
churnin of a paddle wheel filled up my ears and when Headeye stopped
at the foot of the steps, I stopped too. What I saw I'll never forget as long
as I live.

Bones. I saw bones. They were stacked all the way to the top of the
ship. I looked around. The under side of the whole ark was nothin but a
great bonehouse. I looked and saw crews of black men handlin in them
bones. There was crew of two or three under every cabin around that
ark. Why, there must have been a million cabins. They were doin it very
carefully, like they were holdin onto babies or somethin precious.
Standin like a captain was the old man we had seen top deck. He was
holdin a long piece of leather up to a fire that was burnin near the edge
of an opening which showed outward to the water. He was readin that
piece of leather.

On the other side of the fire, just at the edge of the ark, a crew of men
was windin up a rope. They were chantin every time they pulled. I
couldn't understand what they was sayin. It was a foreign talk, and I
never learned any kind of foreign talk. In front of us was a fence so as to
keep anybody comin down the steps from bargin right in. We just stood
there. The old man knew we was there, but he was busy readin. Then he
rolls up this long scroll and starts to walk in a crooked path through the
bones laid out on the floor. It was like he was walkin frontwards, back-
wards, sidewards and every which a way. He was bein careful not to step
on them bones. Headeye, he looked like he knew what was goin on, but
when I see all this I just about popped my eyes out.

Just about the time I figure I done put things together, somethin happens. I bout come to figure them bones were the bones of dead animals and all the men wearin skin clothes, well, they was the skins of them animals, but just about time I think I got it figured out, one of the men haulin that rope up from the water starts to holler. They all stop and let him moan on and on.

I could make out a bit of what he was sayin, but like I said, I never was good at foreign talk.

> Aba aba, al ham dilaba
> aba aba, mtu brotha
> aba aba, al ham dilaba
> aba aba, bretha brotha
> aba aba, djuka brotha
> aba aba, il ham dilaba

Then he stopped. The others begin to chant in the back of him, real low, and the old man, he stop where he was, unroll that scroll and read it, and then he holler out: "Nineteen hundred and twenty-three!" Then he close up the scroll and continue his comin towards me and Headeye. On his way he had to stop and do the same thing about four times. All along the side of the ark them great black men were haulin up bones from that river. It was the craziest thing I ever saw. Knowed then it wasn't no animal bones. I took a look at them and they was all laid out in different ways, all making some kind of body and there was big bones and little bones, parts of bones, chips, tid-bits, skulls, fingers, and everything. I shut my mouth then. I knowed I was onto somethin. I had fished out somethin.

I comest to think about a sermon I heard about Ezekiel in the valley of dry bones. The old man was lookin at me now. He look like he was sizing me up.

Then he reach out and open the fence. Headeye, he walks through and the old man closes it. I keeps still. You best to let things run their course, in a situation like this.

"Son, you are in the house of generations. Every African who lives in America has a part of his soul in this ark. God has called you, and I shall anoint you."

He raised the scroll over Headeye's head and began to squeeze like he was tryin to draw the wetness out. He closed his eyes and talked very low.

"Do you have your shield?"

Headeye, he then brings out this funny cloth I see him with, and puts it over his head and it flops all the way over his shoulder like a hood.

"Repeat after me," he said. I figured that old man must be some kind of minister because he was ordaining Headeye right there before my eyes. Everythin he say, Headeye, he sayin behind him.

> Aba, I consecrate my bones.
> Take my soul up and plant it again.
> Your will shall be my hand.
> When I strike you strike.
> My eyes shall see only thee.
> I shall set my brother free.
> Aba, this bone is thy sea.

I'm steady watchin. The priest is holdin a scroll over his head and I see some oil fallin from it. It's black oil and it soaks into Headeye's shield and the shield turns dark green. Headeye ain't movin. Then the priest pulls it off.

"Do you have your witness?"

Headeye, he is tremblin. "Yes, my brother, Fish-hound."

The priest points at me then like he did before.

"With the eyes of your brother Fish-hound, so be it?"

He was askin me. I nodded my head. Then he turns and walks away just like he come.

Headeye, he goes over to one of the fires, walkin through the bones like he been doin it all his life, and he holds the shield in till it catch fire. It don't burn with a flame, but with a smoke. He puts it down on a place which looks like an altar or somethin, and he sits in front of the smoke cross-legged, and I can hear him moanin. When the shield it all burnt up, Headeye takes out that little piece of mojo bone and rakes the ashes inside. Then he zig-walks over to me, opens up that fence and goes up the steps. I have to follow, and he ain't say nothin to me. He ain't have to then.

It was several days later that I see him again. We got back that night late, and everybody wanted to know where we was. People from town said the white folks had lynched a nigger and threw him in the river. I wasn't doin no talkin till I see Headeye. Thas why he picked me for his witness. I keep my word.

Then that evenin, whilst I'm in the house with my ragged sisters and brothers and my old papa, here come Headeye. He had a funny look in his eye. I knowed some notion was whippin his head. He must've been runnin. He was out of breath.

"Fish-hound, broh, you know what?"

"Yeah," I said. Headeye, he know he could count on me to do my part, so I ain't mind showin him that I like to keep my feet on the ground. You can't never tell what you get yourself into by messin with mojo bones.

"I'm leavin." Headeye, he come up and stand on the porch. We got a no-count rabbit dog, named Heyboy, and when Headeye come up on the porch Heyboy, he jump up and come sniffin at him.

"Git," I say to Heyboy, and he jump away like somebody kick him. We hadn't seen that dog in about a week. No tellin what kind of devilment he been into.

Headeye, he ain't say nothin. The dog, he stand up on the edge of the porch with his two front feet lookin at Headeye like he was goin to get piece bread chunked out at him. I watch all this and I see who been takin care that no-count dog.

"A dog ain't worth a mouth of bad wine if he can't hunt," I tell Headeye, but he is steppin off the porch.

"Broh, I come to tell you I'm leavin."

"We all be leavin if the Sippi keep risin," I say.

"Naw," he say.

Then he walk off. I come down off that porch.

"Man, you need another witness?" I had to say somethin.

Headeye, he droop when he walk. He turned around, but he ain't droopin.

"I'm goin, but someday I be back. You is my witness."

We shook hands and Headeye, he was gone, moving fast with that no-count dog runnin long side him.

He stopped once and waved. I got a notion when he did that. But I been keepin it to myself.

People been askin me where'd he go. But I only tell em a little somethin I learned in church. And I tell em bout Ezekiel in the valley of dry bones.

Sometimes they say, "Boy, you gone crazy?" and then sometimes they'd say, "Boy, you gonna be a preacher yet," or then they'd look at me and nod their heads as if they knew what I was talkin bout.

I never told em about the Ark and them bones. It would make no sense. They think me crazy then for sure. Probably say I was gettin to be as crazy as Headeye, and then they'd turn around and ask me again:

"Boy, where you say Headeye went?"

BUTTA'S BACKYARD BARBECUE

Tony Medina

(2000)

My man Ra-Dizzap was bustin a move on Drainpipe. Pipe was freaked. Couldn't do shit. Looked like a deer in headlights, watchin D wax the floor with that ass—even tho he wasn't on no linoleum or cardboard, but on grass! DJ Pimpstripe's hand was movin so fast sparks jumped up off the turntable, torchin his girlfriend's weave. She didn't hardly notice, tho, since her ass was practically standin inside the speaker. If it wasn't for her doorknocker earrings—big ass suitcases, at that—the sparkles in her hair, and the 8-track tape what got her shit on lockdown holdin it together, she woulda went totally bald, bout to look like a 8-ball in this piece. But with all those contrapments, she held her own. They only had to roll her around in the dirt a few times to put out the fire. Nonetheless, Pimpstripe played on. And Ra-Dizzap persisted to try and make his way clear through to China with a non-stop leg propeller 747 type backspin, holdin his legs up to his chin, scratchin his ass every now and then to spite Drainpipe. Fuck that shit, Pipe yelled, trying to lasso the attention of every wide eye and open mouth that watched Ra-D spin himself into a dirt nap. The music shook the leaves off the branches of the tree, but Pipe was determined to out do Ra-Dizzap. So he climbed up the tree, saying, Check this out, right, check this out. He said it enough times to get about two or three people to peep him out. Then he did a Kristi Yamaguchi meets Greg Louganis meets Bruce Lee in heaven type shit by running to the edge of the thickest branch, jumping and somersaulting two or three times, coming down in his best Bruce Lee extended arm and leg running punch and kick. Real jujitsu type shit. Only Pipe was not moving forward beatin dumb motherfuckers' ass. He froze in midair for what seemed like two months, three days and a hour. I coulda swore I smelt shit and saw his face turn white when he commenced to unwittingly introduce his dumb ass to gravity. He came down on the turntables and mixer like a ton of bricks, sending all of Pimpstripe's records flying—even the ones in the milk crates. The albums flew out in rapid succession soundin like a Uzi or a submachine gun as it hit its target. Heads thought it was a drive-by. They flew in all types of directions: up trees, in the swimming pool, over the neighbors' fence, crashing through the backdoor window. Before you knew it Five-O was all over the place. Motherfuckers sent a SWAT team for our ass. But Drainpipe lived up to his name. He out did Ra-Dizzap. He drained the entire party of its participants. All that was left was DJ Pimpstripe baffled, crying and in handcuffs. Drainpipe was six feet under, takin a dirt nap and braggin. As Drainpipe began to boast and brag, Ra-D uttered his last few words in what sounded like a Miles Davis voice. Not so fast, he whispered, extending the thumb and forefinger of each of his hands into the sign of the gun, which in hip-hopology is the ultimate Run DMC-inspired photo-op and Yo-I'm-a-bad-motherfucker pose. The crowd watched on in amazement. Even Five-O had to stop beatin ass to peep this shit out. They all stared at what looked like a big ass ghetto porcupine: Ra-Dizzap, frozen in his tracks, reduced to an inanimate object, a fossil, a relic, a Polaroid snapshot, a paralyzed projects poster boy, a new millennium hip-hop museum piece, for that matter. No one could make sense of him—of it—of what he had become. He just stood there in the middle of the grass, in the backyard, frozen in a spinning break dance move, his entire body riddled with the phattest albums.

FUTURE CHRISTMAS
(EXCERPT FROM THE NOVEL *THE TERRIBLE TWOS*)

Ishmael Reed

(1982)

It was cold and frosty. They were dining in a restaurant which was lit up like an interrogation room. Joe Baby was dressed flamboyantly. He was wearing snake-skinned red cowboy boots, a mink coat, and a mink-brimmed hat. His partner, Big Meat, was got up the same way. He was Joe Baby's shadow. They lived together. They sat across from a short man who weighed three hundred pounds. He'd just polished off some white "country fresh" eggs, five slices of Virginia ham, nine pieces of whole wheat toast, and three cups of orange juice, and he was waiting for a New York steak. Joe Baby was coughing. He pulled out a white handkerchief and sneezed some phlegm into it. Big Meat took out his pills and counted three for Joe Baby, who gulped them down.

"Don't you ever stop eating?" Joe Baby asked Snow Man.

Joe Baby touched the rim of his glasses.

"Thin people are the ones who die in an emergency," Snow Man said. "They don't have any reserve," he said, after chewing on some ham. "Suppose a famine occurs. I have enough energy to see me through. You guys wouldn't last a week." Snow Man had arctic-blue eyes. Under his overcoat he wore a conservative suit and striped bow tie.

"Hey, man. I don't think that be too cool. Joe Baby just got out of the hospital."

"Don't tangle with him, Meat. He'll blow your brains out and think nothing of it. That is if he can't bump you against the ceiling like a pancake. I saw him sit on a dude. It was like a steamroller rolling over on somebody." Joe Baby began to cough in such spasms that patrons at other tables turned around and stared.

"Do we deal or not?" Snow Man asked.

"Too steep."

"Ten thou is not steep, my friend," Snow Man said, staring blankly at Joe Baby, who was sitting across from him. "You're asking me to drop a Bishop."

"Give him the money, Meat." The black man sitting next to Joe Baby had enough grease in his hair to fry a catfish. Some of the grease spotted the collar of his camel-haired coat and his white silk scarf. He took out a white box tied with a red ribbon and slid it toward the Snow Man.

"I'll bring you his head in a box," Snow Man said. "Gift wrapped."

"You'd better," Joe Baby said. Big Meat smiled. He took out his comb and styled his hair. The two left Snow Man in the restaurant. Outside, they climbed into an old black Cadillac Seville limousine and drove off.

Snow Man looked down at the newspaper as he took in mouthful after mouthful. There had been huge headlines for weeks. The Soviet Union was putting down rebellions in Estonia, Latvia, and the Ukraine. The rebellions that had begun in Riga had spread. Its ally, the United States, was having its share of bad luck too. Things had come to a head between the United States and an African power of unpredictable motives. The government claimed that the President was in constant consultation with his aides. At the end of the week the Secretary of Defense was found dead, a possible suicide.

On the editorial page, there was a letter to the editor. It was one of many letters which had been coming in for five years, complaining about a decision handed down in a California court awarding exclusive rights to Santa Claus to Oswald Zumwalt's North Pole Development Corporation.

It happened in 1985. The court reporters, bailiffs, guards, news vendors could tell their grandchildren about it. All of these men, scores of them, dressed in red suits, big black belts, typing-paper-white beards, blue eyes, ruddy cheeks, conferring with their lawyers. Some who tingled little bells were told by Judge Swallow to cut it out. His face was flushed. The hearing was held after lunch. Oswald Zumwalt's lawyers were there, too. There were Salvation Army Santa Clauses, department store Santa Clauses, Santa Clauses from the V.A. and children's hospitals. There were Christmas pageant Santa Clauses, and charity Santa Clauses, and Santa Clauses who entertained the very rich. There were black, red, and white Santa Clauses.

Judge Swallow dismissed the class action suit and it stood that Oswald Zumwalt owned the exclusive right to Santa Claus, as well as his aliases, Kris Kringle and Saint Nick, and even Old Nick. All of the department stores, candy manufacturers, toy executives, and other components of a billion-dollar industry would have to deal with him.

Zumwalt was now getting a bill through Congress which would give him twenty thousand acres of land at the North Pole for his Christmas Land, to which consumers from all over the world would fly, Supersaver, to celebrate Christmas. A multibillion-dollar city under a dome as well as a space station where future Zumwalt Clauses would fly to earth.

What became known as the Santa Claus decision was based upon the Lone Ranger decision, which prevented the original Lone Ranger, Clayton Moore, from wearing the Lone Ranger mask he'd worn for many years. This remarkable California decision was handed down about eight months before another California decision which outlawed the naturalistic novel.

About a year after the Lone Ranger decision, Clayton Moore, now wearing what the newspapers referred to as his "ubiquitous dark glasses," attended the funeral of Jay Silverheels. The company that won the Lone Ranger trademark couldn't wait until Jay Silverheels was cold in his grave before they began casting about for a new Lone Ranger and Tonto. This Tonto had trouble saying "kemo sabe."

The aging thespian whom Zumwalt hired to play Santa Claus became so popular with the children that their wrath at the Zumwalt decision—eggnog trucks were overturned, geese were cooked—turned to love for the new Santa Claus. After hype and P.R., they would have no other Santa Claus but Zumwalt's Claus.

Zumwalt began the season on the last Saturday in November. Saint Nicholas is the Big Apple's patron saint; a town of give and take, of people dishing it out and people on the receiving end. On that day, the Zumwalt party would move into Manhattan from a hidden estate on Staten Island called Spain because of its hacienda style. The next day they would mount a barge and float across the river to Manhattan Island, accompanied by water-spouting tugboats.

Zumwalt stood in one of Spain's lavish conference rooms. "And over here," Zumwalt said, pointing to the map, "we plan to build forty-eight restaurants, eighteen bars, and there will be a village of Bethlehem which will stretch to about eight hundred acres. We'll have the Church of the Nativity over there. We'll charge five bucks to get into that; in the rear of the church, we'll build a coffee shop and souvenir shop. Everybody'll want to see that. And up here, Congressman, will go the North Star. With the computer we have to run Christmas Land, we'll be able to brighten it or dim it whenever we wish." Zumwalt was in pin-stripes and black shoes. The Congressman's rattlesnakeskin cowboy boots were stretched across the coffee table which held the map. His Stetson was on the floor.

"This is one great project, Mr. Zumwalt. I got to hand it to you. You pulled it off. Now I have some concrete proposals to make to the committee. One thing, though."

"What's that, Congressman Kroske?"

"Well, we got some beechnuts on the committee who seem to be getting a lot of Jew money from the Northeast. They're worried about what's going to happen to the wildlife up there. What shall I tell 'em?"

"You tell those fuckers that we'll keep their precious little ecosystem intact. We won't harm a single penguin. It's the Eskimos who are getting in our way."

"That ought to please them. And, Mr. Zumwalt, thanks for inviting me over here. They're all waiting for you tomorrow. Why, Bowling Green Park is packed. Some are carrying their sleeping bags and have been waiting for several days. Everybody's waiting for tomorrow. The schools are closed. There are lights up and down Fifth Avenue. Carol-singing in Central Park."

"There are traffic jams in the snow. People are pouring into New York from all over the country for the festivities. The hotels are full. You can't get a reservation."

"We'll give them a show, Congressman. Why don't you come over for the cocktail reception at Gracie Mansion. I'm sure the Mayor would like to see you. He's going to black-up and entertain the private dinner with his imitation of Al Jolson."

"Sorry, Mr. Zumwalt, but I think I'll be heading back to Washington. The situation isn't so hot in our nation's capital these days."

"I've been following the papers. What's the latest?"

"I saw the President last week. He was signing a bill that Adolf Hitler be given posthumous American citizenship. He looked pretty bad. You wouldn't believe he was the most famous model of the eighties, his face adorning thousands of billboards. I hear he's soaking up bourbon like it was water. The skin on his face hangs like a bloodhound's. His eyes look like two Japanese flags. Things look bad. The economy looks real bad. A loaf of bread costs fifty dollars."

"We have a great Christmas campaign this year. It ought to give the U.S. a full stocking. We expect billions in sales."

"That sure will help things, Mr. Zumwalt. I'll try to get down to the annual Christmas Eve celebration at Madison Square Garden."

"I'll leave a couple of tickets for you and the missus, Congressman."

"Thanks, Zumwalt. I'd appreciate that." The Congressman rose and shook hands with Zumwalt, now on his feet. Jack Frost picked up Zumwalt's Stetson and handed it to him. They headed toward the door. The Congressman turned to Santa Claus.

"And thank you, Santa, for signing those autographs for the kids. You'll soon be in your new home at the North Pole if everything works out. The kids talk about you all the time. You really are a moral force, because it's at Christmas when people bury the hatchet and spread good cheer." Santa smiled.

"And don't worry about the bill," the Congressman said, turning to Zumwalt. "Once it's out of committee, it's as good as through. I don't expect a fight in the House or the Senate. The North Pole Development Corporation has friends in both houses. You can count on your friends, Mr. Zumwalt," the Congressman said, winking.

Jack Frost: black suit, shirt, sequined tie, shiny wet black hair pinned to scalp, bad eye, helped the Congressman into his deerskin jacket.

"By the way, Congressman," Zumwalt said, "Merry Christmas." He handed the Congressman a gift-wrapped box. The Congressman's eyes widened.

"Thank you, Mr. Zumwalt. Thank you." The Congressman left. Arms folded, Jack Frost leaned against the wall. Zumwalt turned to S.C.

"You did it again," Zumwalt said.

Santa Claus was puzzled.

"Oh, don't play coy with me. I heard about it. At the Macy's reception downstairs. You were seen talking to a young lady. A buyer. You've forgotten that the contract requires you only to say 'ho-ho-ho.' And 'What would you like to have for Christmas, little boy?' Or little girl, or little person."

"I'm sorry, Mr. Zumwalt. It won't happen again."

"I'm sorry, he says. You have a good job here. If it weren't for this job you'd be in a nursing home, glued to the Betamax. Watching your lousy soap opera reruns. Rex Stuart. Wasn't that your name before you got this job? The North Pole Development Corporation gave you new life. The North Pole Development Corporation rescued Christmas. Made it what it is today. Both you and the season would be out of a job if it weren't for my genius."

"I'm very aware of that, Mr. Zumwalt," Santa said.

"Okay. You can go. Get a good night's sleep. Tomorrow we move on to Manhattan. You're going to need your energy."

"Good night, Mr. Zumwalt." Santa rose and started for the door. Jack Frost sneered at him as he passed him on the way out. S.C. didn't trust Jack Frost. Jack Frost had been acquitted of killing his own grandmother, but Santa didn't believe him. The prosecutor just didn't have enough evidence. Frost never left any. And if that wasn't bad enough, on the day of his grandmother's funeral, he went to a musical.

Alone in his room, Santa settled back with a double bourbon on the rocks. His long white beard stretched to his belt. Each morning a barber from the North Pole Development—or Big North as the conglomerate was called—trimmed his beard. He'd been trying to reach Vixen, but the phone was busy. He wanted to tell her that everything was going as planned. She was the only one of the brass who would give him the time of day. He removed his boots and his jacket, and settled back in the brass bed, taking the newspaper with him. New York, the City of Saint Nicholas, whose first church was named for Saint Nicholas, and which boasted a Saint Nicholas Avenue—whose first Dutch ship wore his face on its stern—was all geared up for his arrival. The Mayor would be there. Key officials. They'd be met at the pier. Afterward, they would push up to Bowling Green Park. The caravan's pause at Bowling Green Park was obligatory, for it was on this site that Oloffe, the Dutchman, had a vision of Saint Nicholas. "And the sage Oloffe dreamed a dream— and lo, the good Saint Nicholas came riding over the tops of the trees, in that self-same wagon wherein he brings his yearly presents to children, and he descended hard by where the heroes of Communipaw had made their late repast. And he lit his pipe by the fire, and sat himself down and smoked; and as he smoked, the smoke from his pipe ascended into the air and spread like a cloud overhead."

There was a knock at the door.

* * *

Nance Saturday's generation believed in Santa Claus until they were at least twenty-one. Some left out soup and cookies for him until they were twenty-six or even forty. When they found out that there was no Santa Claus, no unlimited filled stockings hanging from the fireplace, they began to haunt the bars west of Fifth Avenue and vowed never to go above Fourteenth Street again. They were nurtured on novels in which the protagonist expressed little emotion upon receiving news that his mother had died.

During the epidemic of child murders the Atlanta Public Safety Commissioner described his methodology in the following manner. When you come to a brick wall, you either tear down the wall or start in a new direction. Apparently he had torn down the wall and solved the case. For Nance, that approach lacked elegance. He approached a problem as a romantic would. He would read material. He would study all the trivia connected with the case and all the facts he could sew together and usually the solution would come. If that didn't work, then he'd have to try the other method. Tear down the wall, or, in this case, open the door.

Saturday entered the lobby on Riverside Drive near 114th Street. On each side of the entrance there was a Chinese vase, dark blue and light blue with some long-beaked, long-legged bird on it. There was black walnut tables and a shiny tiled floor. There was a huge Christmas tree in the Art Deco–style lobby. The elevator had an oval window. The Puerto Rican doorman asked Jamaican Queens was it okay for him to come up, she gave her permission and he rose in the elevator to the seventh floor, where she lived. She was what they'd call a "yellow" woman; she was barefoot, and she was wearing a black dress which clung to her body as lovingly as a child would grip its mother's thighs. Her sandy reddish hair was done up in a frizzy manner, and it had been combed out and nearly reached her waist. She was wearing a bit of rouge on her cat cheeks, and her eyes were the color of nightclub smoke, which was fitting because there was jazz in her walk.

"Mr. Saturday. Please come in." Saturday walked into the apartment and sat on the sofa she directed him to. "Get you a drink?" she asked.

He said he'd like some apple juice if she had it around, and she said that it was no trouble and went into the kitchen. He could see her moving about in the kitchen, opening the door and removing the bottle of apple juice from the refrigerator.

"Was it hard to get a taxi? It's snowing so hard."

"I drove up," he said. When she climbed onto a chair to open a cabinet to fetch him some Fig Newtons, her dress hiked up and he saw a lot of thigh. That yellow skin all of a sudden dominating the black of her dress, decorated with white and red carnations, became too much for him, and his biological imperative almost burst through his trousers. It started to rise like the American flag on Iwo Jima, but Mr. Wigglesworth whispered to him sternly, and so his desire flickered out. Mr. Wigglesworth was his conscience. The old guy kept him out of trouble. There were boxes of unpacked things and he could glance into another room and see that she had begun hanging curtains. He couldn't take his eyes off of her and she began to feel self-conscious, so when she came in from the kitchen with the juice and the Fig Newtons, he pretended to concentrate on the small Christmas tree which stood on a small hall table.

He hadn't paid too much attention to the painting on the wall, but when he saw it, the colors jolted him. I guess that's what it was supposed to do. The title of it was "After Clovis." Naked, midnight-black men with yellow eyes and Playboy-bunny types—naked, supple pink women—were copulating in all manner of positions in a cemetery, by the light of a full moon. Noticing his attention, she mentioned the artist, a well-known black feminist painter. He had seen some of her work all over town, and every time he saw them, the colors jolted him. They were usually about the same subject.

"A striking painting," he said.

"She's done a lot in the same theme," she said.

"I know," he said. "Do you think she'll ever grow?" She gave him a cutting look, then a Hollywood "dahling" smile came across her freckled face.

"She says she's doing her dreams."

"She must have the same dream every night."

"Mr. Saturday, did you want to ask me some questions?" She sat in a chair across from him. She tucked in her legs.

"I'm working for a man who wants me to uncover some information about the Nicolaite Society—Boy Bishop and the rest of them. My ex-wife, Virginia Saturday, said you could help me. I was reading articles in the newspapers about the group. I've been watching the mansion, and I can't find what I'm looking for. If you help me, I would certainly appreciate it." She rose and walked over to the other side of the room, revealing a glide that had a tinge of model-runway walk. There was quite a bit of aplomb in that glide. She returned to her seat.

"I hate a lot of glaring light. It's hard on the eyes. I need my eyes for my work. Mr. Saturday, I did spend some time interviewing some members of the Nicolaites, but I don't know everything there is to know about them. They're quite hermetic. It's hard to get close to them."

He showed her a photo of Snow Man that Joe Baby had given to him. "Did you ever see this man there? Snow Man?"

"No. I don't remember anyone vaguely resembling him. They were all pretty thin, anorexic if you ask me. So, you're Virginia's ex? How long did you two last together?"

"One year."

"What happened?"

"It's a long story. She, well, she thought that I was a slob. She was always trying to get me to comb my hair, or bathe three times a day, or wear a tie. She was fanatical about me combing my hair. She said that when she was a child, her stepfather once tried to strangle her with his hair."

"I think I can help you. I like you. Virginia didn't tell me much about you except—"

"Virginia's a country girl, and she has a country girl's paranoia. Regardless of the original Paris fashions she wears, and the eyelashes, she'd like nothing better than to fling off those fancy shoes and run in the mud."

"She doesn't take any jive from those people at work. I wish I could be like her. Tough. Right now she's in competition with Ms. Ming, that Chinese-American woman. I hear they had a hair-pulling fight in the ladies' room. Mr. Whyte has to decide which one's going to take Bob Riverside's job." Riverside was a Native American anchorman who was in trouble with Whyte B.C. for complaining about the cowboy-Indian reruns that were broadcast on the network. Mr. Whyte had requested an apology from Riverside, but Riverside refused. Gossip in the industry had it that Riverside would soon be out of a job.

"Virginia's not so tough. You forget, I lived with her for a year. That was some year. But listen, tell me more about the Nicolaites. What did you uncover?"

"I never ran across a Snow Man or nobody in the group mentioned him to me. What did you want him for?"

"He owes my client some money. I thought he might have joined the group or that you had some information about him."

"He might have arrived after I left. Sisters Alice and Barbara, my contacts there, said there were some strange goings-on after Black Peter, that beast, had his showdown with Boy Bishop. Things had really deteriorated. She said that they were all locked in their rooms while Bishop's and Peter's followers were in debate. She said she heard shots, screams and shouting."

"Black Peter. Who is Black Peter?"

"That isn't his real name. His real name is Cudjoe or something like that, but that's not his name either. But when he came to stay with the Nicolaites, he began to read their literature. He became Black Peter, a small dark Spanish page boy who traditionally serves Saint Nicholas. He was some sort of porter. He carried Nicholas's bags. But in some versions, Nicholas carries his bags. There was always a question about who did what for whom. When Boy Bishop left on a fund-raising mission, Black Peter threw a feast and shocked the Nicolaites by unveiling one of his wild paintings. He had done it in the classical European style. Brother James, Boy Bishop's most loyal follower, was furious."

"Nothing in your article mentioned Black Peter."

"Well, my editor cut out the material about Black Peter. He said that people were touchy about stories that featured black men."

"The sixties."

"I don't follow."

"Every time the black man ascends to the scene, America lets its hair down, kicks off its shoes. Its heart goes skinny-dipping. Chaos is unsealed."

"Virginia said you were crazy."

"Look," he said, smiling, "are we going to discuss Virginia or are we going to talk about the story?"

"I'm teasing you."

"Maybe I'll have that coffee now." She rose from the couch, smiling; she walked lissomely into the kitchen.

"Black Peter was always kept in the background by Boy Bishop. He didn't want word of Black Peter getting out."

"How did Black Peter and Boy Bishop get together?"

"They became acquainted while Boy Bishop was recruiting prostitutes down on Forty-second Street. Somebody stole Black Peter's dummy, and the dummy was the drawing card for his street hustle. Without his dummy, Black Peter couldn't put on a show. He persuaded Boy Bishop to take him in until he could find a new and bigger dummy. Before you knew it, he had taken over the society and was challenging Boy Bishop's authority. They should never have permitted that nigger to use the library." She returned to the room bearing a silver tray which held two china cups of coffee and a pitcher full of cream.

"You say that Black Peter, or rather Cudjoe, read some literature about this Spanish page. What does that have to do with anything?"

"The legend about Black Peter got his ego all puffed out. He's a short dude, but after coming upon that story he grew ten feet tall and nobody could touch him. He said that he'd come upon evidence which convinced him that Nicholas was Peter's servant and that, this being the case, they should substitute Haile Selassie for the Nicholas icon. Black Peter should have a master he could respect."

"Where can I find Black Peter?"

"Sister Alice and Barbara say that after the 'reasoning' between the two Nicolaite factions, Boy Bishop and Peter disappeared and Brother Andrew was in charge. It was all a con job, you know. They had some of the most streetwise whores and pimps in New York who'd given up that life to join the Nicolaites, but whores and pimps are sometimes like two-year-olds, especially when they reform. Life to them is a plaything anyway. Why do you think they call themselves players? Notice how whores and pimps get all sentimental around Christmas, buying each other extravagant gifts. What's that song that Nat King Cole sings, where the player promises his prime trick a fur coat, a diamond ring, big Cadillac, and everything?"

"Charles Brown. Merry Christmas, baby, you sure been good to me." Nance was giving away his age. They laughed. "Is there anything else you can tell me about the time you spent doing your story on the Nicolaites?"

"I'd interviewed Brother Andrew and the Sisters Alice and Barbara and was about to interview Brother James, who promised he'd meet me in the garden during the feast where Black Peter was to unveil his painting. Black Peter overheard James and asked me to come to his room on the third floor of the mansion. I didn't see any harm in it. He was the perfect host and brought me some violets and offered me some of his provisions. Some Dragon's Snout and some Dutch schnapps. He had some of his paintings on the wall. He was pretty good. Untrained, but heavy on colors and vision. He couldn't draw, but some of the best painters around can't. Whatever his art lacked in technical craftsmanship, it made up for in originality. He offered me some human-shaped cookies he said he'd baked. Brother James later told me that Black Peter always carried around a cooking pot. And he gave me some candy. The original Black Peter was always either handing out candy or giving people the rod. He was a kidnapper, you know. Took kids into Spain, the naughty ones.

"I realized when I talked with Brother James that bad blood was building up between them. Brother James said he was keeping notes about Black Peter's bad and unruly behavior and was about to recommend his ouster from the group. Brother James didn't feel that he should obey Black Peter's authority. Well, we were walking through the garden and laughing about this and that. Brother James was very close to Boy Bishop. He said that Boy Bishop had always been brilliant and that he had abandoned his class in order to uphold Nicolaite beliefs. He said that Boy Bishop's father was a big department store executive who lost his fortune when the oil men fired him for not producing huge Christmas sales. He said that the Boy Bishop was out to put Christmas back where it was before big oil moved into the business. His strategy was to infiltrate the establishment and win converts that way. Black Peter had approached him with a wild or crazy scheme. It had something to do with body snatching. He said that Black Peter was a loyal subject before then and used to be the butt of a lot of Boy Bishop's taunts.

"We were going along and all of a sudden some of Black Peter's people came into the garden. They claimed that Black Peter wanted to know my whereabouts. He'd told them that I was a spy. They grabbed both of us, but not before Brother James hit one of them with a snow-covered stone flowerpot. We tried to fight off the others, but there were more of them than there were of us, and so they dragged us before him. He was furious. He jumped up and down on the table and called me all sorts of dirty whore this and that, and he put me out. I was glad to get out. I could hear them arguing as I drove away. I think that Black Peter was going crazy. Brother James said that he had told someone that a water from Tarpon Springs, Florida, was capable of reviving a corpse. He believed in all of Nicholas's miracles, but he wanted Selassie to split off from Nicholas, just as Santa Claus had split off from Nicholas. He saw Nicholas as a model capable of producing endless variations. Those people were really becoming loyal to Peter, especially Brother Andrew, who was beginning to challenge Boy Bishop. They're going to be in for a surprise, because Black Peter isn't from Jamaica at all. He's fake. His name wasn't Cudjoe, either. I looked at his police file. He grew up downtown on Avenue D, in those projects. His first arrest was for stealing a Christmas ham."

Nance looked at his watch. "I better go." She walked him to the door. They focused on each other so long, their eyes bumped.

No one had touched the food. It was supposed to be a feast. When the Nicolaites entered the ballroom, conflict and raised voices had immediately begun. Bro Peter, as he was demanding to be called these days, had removed the face of Saint Nicholas from a painting above the fireplace and replaced it with one of Haile Selassie. Boy Bishop's followers objected and were threatening to summon him back from Boston, where he'd gone to officiate at the wedding of a rich patron. They were being jeered by those Nicolaites who were loyal to Bro Peter. The Nicolaites were split down the middle.

Black Peter had been left in charge by Boy Bishop. Peter was seated at the head of one of fifteen tables located in the ballroom with mahogany panels and chandeliers. He sat on red, black, and green satin pillows. He wore the costume page boys wore in the Spanish court. The other brothers and sisters sat before turkey, goose, blackberry pie, and cherry pie, and there were huge bowls of salad on each table and three kinds of wine. And in the middle of it all lay a pig with an apple in its mouth. Black Peter was enjoying his fish and peppers, jerked pork, and Dragon's Snout while the others whispered among themselves.

"How dare he remove the face of our Saint from that painting! Why does Boy Bishop always leave that crazy spade behind when he goes on a mission? I've had enough of this painting. Ghetto surrealism, that's what it is." Sister Alice and Sister Barbara were scribbling notes and passing them to each other. One would read a note from the other and giggle.

"If Boy Bishop doesn't return soon, this maniacal and paranoid black is going to take over," said another of Boy Bishop's followers.

"I plan to phone him tonight. If he doesn't get back here soon, there's going to be bloodshed," said Brother James. Sister Barbara pouted and then gave Black Peter a fierce stare. She folded her arms. Her bald head glistened and she wore hooped, gold earrings.

"How come we have to do what you say and accept your painting? Boy Bishop should have the final sayso. I for one don't like what you've done with the painting," she said. The gathering murmured: "You ain't no Rasta anyway. You maybe can fool these white people, but you can't fool me." Sister Alice sat down triumphantly.

"Bro Peter is in charge when Boy Bishop leaves. We worked out the details in secret council, and none of you is to question that." Everybody ceased their whispering. Brother Andrew had been with Boy Bishop longer than anybody. He'd gone to school with him and had been a guest at the mansion owned by Bishop's father, Herman Schneider, the late department store president. "Peter, perhaps the anxiety of the group would be allayed if you'd just explain some of the symbolism in that painting. I rather like it." Sisters Barbara and Alice glared at Brother Andrew.

"His name ain't no Peter," said Sister Barbara, one of the whores who'd defected from Joe Baby. "He's a crazy nigger that Boy Bishop dragged up from Forty-second Street."

"Give him a chance," Andrew said.

"I can tell you why I put the face of Haile Selassie in the place of Saint Nicholas. Because they are both one and the same," said Peter.

"One and the same?" Andrew said. "I don't follow you."

"Look at it this way," Peter said, climbing down from his seat and walking toward the painting. He climbed atop a chair and began pointing to his work of art.

"Now, see, here is the Emperor who rode on a white horse the same as Nicholas and the same as Marcus Garvey, who predicted that the Emperor was coming."

"Who was Marcus Garvey?" someone asked.

"An Obeah man from Jamaica. He was the prophet who was sent by Jah to pave the way for the coming of the Emperor.

"Now, let me explain to you," said Black Peter, whose whale's head contrasted with his small body. "There"—he pointed out—"you see the Emperor punish the teef just the way Nicholas did. The Emperor punish the teef Mussolini." He pointed to Mussolini's head in the painting.

Mussolini had the body of a dog. Black Peter's painting showed the Emperor bringing down a machete on the Italian dictator's head.

"Nicholas fly, the ashanti fly, and here you see Selassie flying to the League of Nations where he went to protest the invasion of Ethiopia by Rome. The Emperor had his problems with Rome. As you know, the Vatican removed Nicholas from the calendar of Saints." Some of the nuns who were loyal to Peter looked on as Peter ran down his "science," as he called it. His "reasoning." "Nicholas is an island patron. The patron of New York Island. The Emperor is also an island patron. The Island of Jamaica."

"Isn't he adorable?" said one nun.

"He's wonderful," said another. "If you look closely, you'll see that he's wearing an aura."

"Selessie was the Emperor of Ethiopia. Ethiopia is Zion. Nicholas was once overseer of a monastery named New Zion," Black Peter argued.

Another nun who was loyal to Boy Bishop, named Sister Suggs, glared heat at the nuns who were admiring Peter as he continued his, for Sister Suggs, "wild, incoherent, and 'scattershot' narrative." She mangled her french bread and held her mouth open as she stared at Peter. When Peter finished, a hush filled the room.

"I have to hand it to you, Brother Peter. You are an excellent painter [Sister Barbara passed a note to Sister Alice and they both grinned at each other] and I agree that we must keep up with the times. I think, however, that we should wait for the return of the Boy Bishop. Tell me more about this Rastafarianism. It sounds fascinating."

"Thank you, Brother Andrew." Suddenly, Brother Peter hesitated. He moved his neck about as though it were the hood of a black cobra.

"Where's Brother James and that journalist?"

At Life's Limits

Kiini Ibura Salaam

(2000)

There are places human beings know nothing about. Beneath infinity's umbrella, among the flaming gases of the stars, are unimaginable beings. Cocooned and comatose, they float silently, awaiting their next assignments. WaLiLa is among them. Her body hums with a bone-drenching sense of peace. Energy pierces her skin and plumps up her body. Particles of power lodge into her being-center, her message-center, and her vision-centers. A piercing light suddenly suffuses her cocoon with a bright glow. Flashing like shooting stars, the layers of her cocoon peel back and burn slowly until disintegrated. An organic tunnel collects its walls around her. The tunnel tilts itself downward, coaxing her body into motion. Soon she is slipping down, down, down through places humans don't know about, and then, into the human realm.

1.

Musicians, practicing an age-old tradition, scatter syncopated rhythms across the night sky. Through rapid hand movements and homemade instruments, they pay homage to fierce and fascinating gods. The music tattoos the sky's surface with patterns of prayer, patterns that transform themselves into welcome mats for beings in realms the musicians have no knowledge of. One such welcome mat beckons to WaLiLa's tunnel. The tunnel dips and glides, then aligns itself with the musicians' tones. Her body plummets, tumbling along the tunnel's path as it shoots through space. Occasionally, she bumps the small of her back, her knees, or her toes against the tunnel's pliant walls.

When the tunnel breaks into the earth's atmosphere, it contracts, jostling WaLiLa into consciousness. She discovers herself crouched in the travel position: arms bound tightly about her, folded legs pressed close against her chest. The tumbling is dizzying but tolerable. She throws her head back and grimaces as she struggles against the forces of motion to uncurl her body. Fully extended, WaLiLa picks up speed. The tunnel narrows as she flexes and stretches every muscle she possibly can. Instinctively, she pushes her arms against her sides and points her toes to streamline her body.

Within seconds, the tunnel recedes and deposits her into the air. Unaided, WaLiLa tumbles into the Realm of Human Being. When her toes reach the human altitude, they gently brush against a shoulder frosted with sweat. That shoulder smoothly dips down and across, making space for WaLiLa's nude body. She slips into the opening and immediately feels gentle nudges pressing against all sides of her being. A sea of swaying torsos, reverent palms, and open-throated song surrounds her. She has become the nucleus of a pulsating mass of people. The cloaks of closed eyes seal them into their own individual worlds. Their spiritual trance offers WaLiLa protection from detection; no one notices her arrival.

As sweat-soaked skin rubs against her body, WaLiLa is roused into action. She starts to push through the crowd, searching for someplace on the edge where she can analyze her surroundings. Then, with the collision of a deeply scarred palm against the cow-skin mouth of a hand-carved drum, an explosive sound breaks through the crowd. Controlling beats roll forcefully toward the people. Barbs of passion erupt in every ear the music enters. The peaceful trance is shattered.

Every face lifts and faces east. Guinée lies east. Holy Guinée. The drumming becomes feverish and the swaying crowd becomes erratic as the frenetic rhythms burst above their heads. The drumvoices soar within WaLiLa's chest like a command from the elements. They explode in her being-center, vibrating her will like sound vibrates vocal cords. Behind her, people begin to surge forward, straining to get closer to the drummers. Her message-center reminds her to stay alert. The crowd in front of her begins to part. A narrow path is cleared and the drums rush through and grab a tight hold of her throat.

WaLiLa advances, following the demand of the drums. A sudden breeze slaps her into sharp thinking. *You shall soon be seen*, her message-center communicates. She tugs a piece of white muslin from its precarious position on a dancing woman's shoulder. The cloth frees itself easily. She quickly wraps it around her body and secures the makeshift covering with a knot. She turns around, searching for an exit through the crowd, but she finds none. The only path open to her is the one leading to the drummer's realm.

As bodies continue to push her forward, questions burn in her being-center. *What land is this beneath my feet? What language is this dancing in my ears? What people are these surrounding my body?* Soon she is toeing the barrier around the drummer's circle. An arc of drummers sits before the crowd. They are all of the male sex and completely oblivious to WaLiLa's presence. Rhythm, their hands cry, must maintain the relentless pace of the rhythm. Between the crowd and the drummers is a circular clearing. A woman in white whirls herself in swooping spirals around the clearing's edge.

If WaLiLa wasn't positive that the soil beneath her feet was earth's, she would mistake the woman's motions as bodyspeak: her own language. It isn't—she knows this as well as she knows the danger of her mission—but the woman's dancing unfolds into so many familiar movements that WaLiLa's wrists, arms, and calves ache to join in conversation. She has long since trained her sporadic arm flicks into oblivion, but when the woman expands her chest into an open position and juts out her swinging breasts, WaLiLa feels so welcomed that her neck dips, her arms swoop up, and she loses her body to rhythmic swirling.

Through bodyspeak, WaLiLa begins to gently query the woman about their surroundings. The woman's brain tells her this is simply a dance, a dance she performs at religious ceremonies, or rather a dance that performs her when an orisha gets a powerful hold on her. WaLiLa's message-center registers communication. This is a gathering of information essential to her survival. The woman's response to WaLiLa's inquiries is eloquent and direct. Her motions offer answers so clear, WaLiLa wonders if the woman is conscious of the communicative function of her movements.

WaLiLa discovers she is on an island in the Caribbean Sea. Spanish is spoken here and Africa is remembered. There has been bondage and savage killing. Twice determined youth revolted, causing citizens to drink optimism and communism like wine. After celebrated freedom, hardship rooted itself in the island soil. Today despair is as common as clouds. The local diet is resilience. The simple pleasures of work, food, and communion float beyond the reach of the common folk. The people have been losing family members with the passing of the years. Cousins, fathers, and lovers try to escape by walking into the sea, as their tar-toned ancestors had done centuries past.

WaLiLa is so deep into the conversation she barely notices the new pitch the voices have engaged. A different tune is being expressed and the woman's motions change immediately. WaLiLa slows down her conversation. The woman opens her throat, lets out a series of shrieks, and falls to the ground. The drumming lowers to a whisper. The chanting drops to a low rumble. Three people gather around the fallen woman. They clear the charged air around her with palm fronds. An old man stops singing long enough to bark some blessings over the woman's body and shower her with water sprayed from the fountain of his mouth. The three lift her to her feet. The chanting rises powerfully. Once on her feet, the woman opens her eyes. They shine like dark moons beneath the rim of her white head-wrap. When her eyes make direct contact with WaLiLa's, the woman's identity pops into WaLiLa's vision center.

- Elisa Eguitez, 51, 201 pounds, Cuban

Then her eyes flutter closed. *The dark moons are strong,* decides WaLiLa. *This woman will be my host.*

2.

After the ceremony, Elisa walks directly to WaLiLa and asks her if she has a place to stay. WaLiLa shakes her head no.

"You can stay with me, *m'ija.* What I'm offerin' ain't too special. I only have a small place and I share it with my two sons, but . . ."

WaLiLa doesn't question how Elisa knows she needs lodging. It has been some time since she last spoke this tongue. She wants to observe more before she starts stretching sounds through her lips.

In silence, she follows Elisa's heavy, swaying flesh across a grassy field. Elisa stops at the trunk of a great big tree. She stuffs a cloth bag full of mangoes and bananas into a woven straw basket that has been rigged to the front of a rusty orange bicycle. A small rectangular plank of wood is

attached behind the seat, atop the back fender. Elisa motions with a
wave of her dark arm for WaLiLa to sit. WaLiLa hikes up the cloth she
had hastily wrapped around her body and sits. If Elisa notices the flowers stuck to the soles of WaLiLa's bare feet, she says nothing. With a
grunt, Elisa pushes the bike pedals into forward rotation, thrusting the
wheels into motion. After a couple of slow, strained rotations, the bike
takes flight. WaLiLa's body jerks back. She spreads her arms and closes
her eyes as the sweet cool breeze rushes past her face.

During the bike ride, Elisa neither asks questions nor offers information. In the absence of chatter, stillness enters the air. A cotton-soft
serenity envelops the bicycle. WaLiLa's message-center is overcome
with surprise. Serenity rarely visits in the presence of a human being.
WaLiLa welcomes it as she recalls the stillness of floating in the cocoon
of energy, surrounded by the dark matter of space.

The quiet embrace of Elisa's silence is abruptly broken when Elisa
curses softly and skids to a sudden stop. WaLiLa feels the imbalance instantly and slides to her feet. A thick crowd blocks the sidewalk and the
street. Elisa pushes through the crowd with repeated *permiso's*. WaLiLa
follows. When they finally reach the front of the crowd, Elisa gasps. Her
hands spread in shock. Freed from her grip, the bicycle tilts, then clat-
ters to the ground.

"*Changó!*" Elisa whispers.

"What is?" asks WaLiLa as she feels her skin bend under sharp jabs of
burning air. A ferocious being of concentrated heat leaps through the small
rectangular courtyard in front of them. Its multiple fingers of light dance in
the windows and on the roofs of the courtyard's houses. The crowd is frozen
in silent awe as the small rumblings of fear spiral through the air.

"*Changó!*" Elisa yells. The terror in her voice shoots through the air
and bounces against eardrums that had been formed in her womb. Her
two children rest their buckets of water on the ground and turn to scan
the crowd for their mother. When they see Elisa, they come running.
They dodge neighbors who are engaged in a desperate rescue effort.
After crossing the courtyard, they grab a tight hold of Elisa.

"I'm sorry, Mama, the fire cannot be stopped."

So this is the great being's full fury, WaLiLa thinks as she instinctively
backs away from the fire. She fixes her vision on the houses again and
watches as the little structures weakly bow and yield before the fire's
will. *I have seen tales of your destructive powers;* she quickly motions to

the fire before returning her focus to the humans next to her. As the boys speak to their mother in soothing tones, WaLiLa examines them.

- Modesto Alonzo, 24, 160 pounds, Cuban

- Pedro Alonzo, 38, 135 pounds, Cuban

As Pedro's slight body fills WaLiLa's vision-center, the "Assignment" signal blinks immediately. *It is the elder,* WaLiLa thinks, *who must provide the nectar.* She crosses her arms and studies his mannerisms as he attempts to quiet his mother's mumbling. WaLiLa can't discern if Elisa is mumbling curses or prayers. She turns her vision-centers back to the fiery courtyard, watching as the neighbors eventually succeed in their effort to smother the fire. Bored with toying with human emotions, the fire allows itself to be extinguished.

3.

The day after the fire, Elisa, Modesto, Pedro, and WaLiLa stand in front of the fire-buckled front door of Elisa's house. A smoky scent hovers in the morning air. With worried fingers, WaLiLa twists the hem of the borrowed dress she is wearing. Smoke is a bad omen. Quietly, as if arming herself for battle, Elisa clutches the colorful beads that hang from her weary neck and begins to pray. Surrounded by the soft light of dawn, she begs for protection and salvation. She asks Obatala, the ancient, for his wisdom. Observing Elisa's prayer, WaLiLa sees a world of difference between the tightly clenched body before her and the whirling image in white who introduced her to Cuba. *If there is ever a time for bodyspeak, for exalting arms, bent knees, and passionate wrists,* WaLiLa thinks, *this is the time.*

Elisa's plum-black lips move mechanically, pushing out prayers without breath. The gravity of her plea is communicated by the tremble of her lower lip as the words fall into the ears of the gods. After the prayer, she inhales several deep breaths and grasps the doorknob. She pushes against the miserable, crumbled piece of wood her front door has become. It refuses to budge, loyally protecting the house against intruders. She leans her shoulder against the door. Ignoring the soot stains grinding into her clothing, she uses her heft to force the door open.

When she crosses the threshold, concrete shards hit against the toe of her shoe and slide across the floor. She sinks to her knees to examine what has collided with her foot. Her body tenses as she realizes that shattered before her is the fifteen-year-old concrete head of Ellegua, the watcher. Elisa draws in her breath sharply and wonders if Ellegua's destruction was the result of the fire or the cause of it. She drops a small prayer of apology like a rain shower from the dark clouds of her sad lips.

Elisa stands and leads her sons into the house. WaLiLa watches as the blackness of the skeletal house swallows their bodies. She does not enter. The sun batiks patterns of heat on her bare neck as it rises in the sky. The scent of dew resting on thick flower petals slowly drips across her face. Her being-center leaps. *You have not fueled since your arrival,* her message-center notes.

WaLiLa curses herself for allowing the ceremony to distract her from collecting flowers. Her message-center checks the level of fuel in her reserves. It is dangerously low. When her fuel banks are empty, she can no longer transform human air into a breathable substance. No breath, no life. One of the ancestors' admonitions rushes into her consciousness like a clap of thunder. *WaLiLa,* she imagines them motioning, *you never follow the rules.* Upon arrival to earth, her first order of business is fuel-collecting. *But most times motion is not married to my arrival. I come alone, in quiet night. This time I plunged into a dark sea. A dark sea not empty but full of beings. And they gathered tightly around me. And I swam with them. And now I am in need of fuel.* She pushes three fingers against her lips as she wonders how she could have forgotten.

She slumps into a body sigh. Her message-center announces that she has five hours of fuel remaining. Intending to separate from Elisa and her sons, locate fuel, and return rejuvenated, WaLiLa peers into the dark house to determine if her absence will be missed. Inside, nothing is left standing. Every particle of Elisa's home betrayed her. Each of her possessions turned their backs on her ownership, willfully destroying form and usefulness to welcome fire's full embrace.

Surrounded by the ravages of her life, an uneasiness settles in Elisa's bones. She turns her back on the wreckage and clasps her fat hands on top of her throbbing head. She walks down the hall and sees the silhouette of WaLiLa's body swaying in the doorway. She smiles bitterly at the irony of a houseguest and no home. She steps to the doorway and stops when her body is a few breaths away from WaLiLa's. The two bodies mirror each other. With the sunlight radiating behind her, WaLiLa stares into Elisa's eyes. With the shadows of the house swirling behind her, Elisa stares back and sees herself mirrored in WaLiLa's clear dark eyes.

"Have you ever had a fire?" Elisa asks WaLiLa.

WaLiLa shakes her head no. Hot fingers of light do not exist on her planet. Here on earth she has been fascinated by the little fires that heat human fuel and light dark spaces, but they are nothing like the fire she experienced last night. Smoke, too, is a stranger to her systems. It creeps into the being-center and fans out through the body, triggering specific malfunctions of thought and action.

"I can't . . ." Elisa starts to speak. She looks up at the sky with a wrinkled brow, then she quickly fixes her glance on WaLiLa. "I can't continue. Would you go in and see if there's anything salvageable in there?"

WaLiLa's belly shoots arrows of warning through her body while her message-center reminds her that Elisa is her access to Pedro. Her message-center also reviews the Human Decency Laws. The laws of human decency dictate that by accepting Elisa's offer of shelter, she has placed herself in Elisa's debt. Human codes state that WaLiLa owes Elisa gratitude in the form of courtesy or kindness. If she refuses Elisa's request, she may jeopardize her good standing with Elisa, thereby complicating her access to Pedro.

Against her belly's urgings, she agrees to enter the house. She turns her body west and clears a passageway for Elisa to squeeze out of the house's narrow doorframe. She enters the doorway and turns to look into Elisa's eyes. Elisa doesn't see the indecision jumping from feature to feature on WaLiLa's face. She thanks her. WaLiLa shrugs her shoulders, turns, and steps deeper into the house.

As she walks farther and farther away from the sunlight, she rotates her shoulders back and forth. Each of the two-shoulder movements is a small prayer engaged to shake off the doom she feels pressing against her scalp. Her exploration of rooms and hallways yields nothing but unrecognizable pieces of black. The damage here is complete.

Minutes later, WaLiLa moves to the last room, which sits in the back of the house. It is protected by a door that is closed against her. She turns the doorknob and coaxes the door forward. It opens with surprising ease. Two terrified mice scurry out of the room. They breathlessly race over her feet and disappear into the ruins of the house. She pushes the door even farther and a bird flies out in uncertain swooping patterns. The bird quickly adopts bold wing strokes that scream permanent escape. As she pushes the door to a forty-five-degree angle, roaches of every size, color, and description come streaming out of the room over and around her feet. Her hands spread in surprise.

After the roach exodus is complete, she pauses, waiting for more creatures to exit the room. When none do, she enters the room. The room's cool air rolls over her and silently sinks into her body. She immediately senses that this is Elisa's room. Not her bedroom, but her prayer room. Above, a low white ceiling hangs solid and certain. The walls are plastered with scraps of paper filled with marks WaLiLa knows to be a physical manifestation of human speak.

She stoops to the ground. Leaning forward on her hands, she looks around. The floor is covered with knee-high mountains of things. Each mountain is a strange collection of items organized by a theme unknown to WaLiLa. The little mountain directly in front of her consists of a jar of honey, an orange silk butterfly, a necklace of yellow flowers, old gold coins, and a pile of five oranges. The pile to her right has blue ribbons, three crystal glasses of water, silver rings, a doll in a frilly blue dress, a miniature ship with many sails, and a lace doily. The room bursts with ceramics, keepsakes, fruit, flowers, flour, water, wine, money, metal, nuts, coins, beads, shells, silk.

WaLiLa leans back on her haunches slowly as her vision-centers busily take in all the items that surround her. She focuses on a photograph of a smiling, young-looking Elisa holding hands with a beaming, sienna-colored man. Written on the back is, "La Habana, 1973." Next to it, under a crystal glass of water, rests another photograph of the same man. He stands knee-deep in the sea; his left hand rests on the corner of a handmade raft, the right one is lifted in a melancholy salute. He is crying. Written on the back is, "Para Miami, May 1985." Behind the glass of water, a small bundle wrapped in white silk waits. WaLiLa picks it up and hears the soft clink of metal. She gently unwraps it and discovers two wedding bands. Inscribed inside the rings is the phrase, "*Elisa y Gigaldo, a para siempre.*"

WaLiLa reties the bundle and returns it to its previous position. She stands and carefully steps to the center of the cluttered room. She takes a deep breath and her hands begin to tremble. Embedded in the air is the unmistakable scent of fuel. She is suddenly conscious of the energy pulsating through every item in the room. Not a flower has been singed, nor a fruit shriveled. She looks around her and sees many fresh flowers adorning the little mountains. In her eagerness to correct her previous failure to gather fuel, she decides to collect enough flowers to fuel her for days. *One petal from each pile*, her message-center calculates, *will keep you fueled for the remainder of this trip*. Careful not to disturb any objects, she tiptoes around the piles, quickly plucking one petal from each altar with nimble fingers. Considering nothing but her system's needs, she shoves them into the rapidly bulging pocket of her dress.

When her collecting is done, WaLiLa stills herself and listens briefly to the noises in the rest of the house. She hears the muffled sound of things softly being moved around. Certain of her solitude, she lifts the hem of her dress and tucks it into the dress's neckline. She presses two rose petals against the center of her torso and closes her eyes as her body accepts the fuel. Her practiced fingers feel no difference between these flower petals and other flower petals that have fueled her multiple earth journeys. Neither her fingers nor her message-center consider that these petals stubbornly survived the threat of fire only by filling themselves with smoke.

Freshly fueled, WaLiLa exits the altar room, runs down the hall, and bounds into the courtyard like a sun ray. Elisa raises her head to see a mischievous smile on WaLiLa's face. WaLiLa stands before Elisa with an outstretched hand. Elisa wearily accepts the hand and together they enter the house. WaLiLa's light steps lead Elisa's heavy ones down the hall, to the altar room. Elisa looks at WaLiLa with raised eyebrows. WaLiLa nods her head in assurance. Elisa fills her chest with air and bravely enters. First, a surprised peep escapes her lips, then exalting laughter. Whooping and yelling soon follow. Pedro and Modesto come running at the sound of their mother's joy. Elisa's palms open and rushed prayers fly through the air. Then arms, Elisa's arms, pull her sons against her body and crushes their hearts to hers.

4.

WaLiLa sits at a round table nestled under the stairs with a belly full of mango *batida* and egg sandwich. The table, the stairs, and the apartment belong to Liliana, Elisa's sister-in-law. On the night of the fire, Liliana guided the disenchanted family to her home. She filled them with hot chocolate, wrapped them in sheets, and insisted that they sleep. Elisa sits at the table across from WaLiLa. She stares vacantly at the wall. After the fire, Elisa locked herself into a silent state of mourning. She eats when Liliana places food in front of her. She bathes when Liliana fills a bath bucket for her. She only leaves the house when Liliana insists. Prayer is the only activity Elisa does unasked. The majority of her hours are spent staring into space, entertaining visions her mind creates and thoughts no one else has access to.

"Buenas!" Elisa's former neighbor Silvia enters the open doorway, ushering in the morning breeze. Her soft, yucca-colored body is thinly covered with sweat. She sits down uninvited and asks for a cup of coffee. She runs one hand through her short curly hair, while she holds up a tattered envelope with the other.

"M'ija, this arrived for you yesterday afternoon. Papo brought it. His cousin had a visitor from Spain who carried it in their suitcase." Silvia places the envelope onto Elisa's lap with ritualistic flair and breaks into a self-mocking laugh. *"Que triste!"* she continues. "How sad it is that the mail travels more than we do."

As Silvia presses her puckered lips against the rim of the coffee cup, Elisa opens the letter. As she reads, Silvia sighs and launches into an extended lament of exhaustion. Her bicycle is broken, she had to borrow her son's, it is so hard to use a bicycle for transportation, maybe not for the children because they never had a vehicle, but wow, how she misses the old family car, and oh, what a hard life.

"What is it, *m'ija?"* Silvia interrupts her tirade to ask of Elisa's contorted face.

"My mother-in-law, she's ill. She needs me in Spain."

Liliana grabs the letter from Elisa's hand and peers at her mother's shaky scrawls. By the time she reaches the end of the letter, she is quietly crying.

"She didn't want us to know," Liliana says to no one in particular.

Elisa stands and rests her arm around Liliana's shoulders.

"Don't worry," she says. "I'll go get Mami, and I'll bring her home."

A departure from Cuba's arms is the last thing Elisa desires, especially now that she must rebuild her home, but she has no choice. Liliana couldn't get out of the country in a million years. Neither could any of Liliana's brothers and sisters. Elisa, with her income, status, and connections as a godmother of Santeria, is the only one who can fly to her mother-in-law's aid.

"Aiiii, *mi niña*," Silvia complains, "if we were in any other country! Your poor mother may die before you get a ticket in this *maldito* country."

Elisa rubs her forehead with weary fingers. First the fire, now this.

"Don't worry, *chica*," Silvia continues. "I have a cousin in the visa department. My eldest will take care of the house, and I will go around to the offices with you every day until we get the papers you need."

"I appreciate it, *vieja*," Elisa sighs. "Liliana, you go talk to Señor Alberto, Señora Franco, and *buela*. Tell them Mami is sick and you need the money Papi left with them. Silvia, we might as well start now, it's early still."

"*Sí*," agrees Silvia. Elisa goes upstairs and collects her purse. Before she leaves, she wakes her sons and murmurs the new surprise that has affected their lives.

"I have sent Liliana to the country to get money from our relatives. I will be too busy to look after our guest. I want you to watch over her, *mis hijos*. Make sure she has everything she needs. And . . ." Elisa adds to the list of commands, "ask no questions of her."

5.

The minute Elisa, Silvia, and Liliana walk out of the door, WaLiLa feels relentless questions whirl around her. These questions do not pass through Modesto's and Pedro's lips. Fulfilling their mother's request, they maintain a painful silence. Throughout the days, questions drop from their suspicious glances and take root in the air, like seeds in fertile soil. Unasked, the questions blossom and grow. As afternoons pass, the questions learn to walk. They wander around the house following WaLiLa with their eyes. Soon they sit across from her at the lunch table, peering at her every movement. Eventually, WaLiLa's resistance is broken down. She bursts.

"I live from a town small near to Toronto under Canada. I travel and study. I collect information of people, places, things. I watch and listen, then I bring stories to people mine. People mine do not much travel and they want to know what the world is. Your mother is nice to take me. After fire, I tell her I go other place but she insists I stay here. If I am problem, tell me this. I go."

"No!" growls Pedro. "Unless my mother says otherwise, you will go nowhere. As long as you are in Cuba, you stay in this house. Understand?"

WaLiLa shakes her head in agreement, keeping an eye on the questions. They still sit across from her, but they are shrinking. Now their eyes barely reach the rim of the tabletop.

"There is much to study here," says Modesto. "We have a long and rich history, why don't you take a tour?"

WaLiLa's message-center processes this question as a challenge rather than a suggestion. She feels a tightening in her torso. The nuance of accusation she hears in his voice discomforts her. *Is this what it feels like,* she wonders, *to be hunted?* She slowly winds her arms around her belly. The smoke from the fuel she liberated from Elisa's prayer room causes unidentifiable pain as it ventures out from her being-center toward her message-center. With her hunter's acumen diminished by smoke's stealthy sabotage, she is unable to pursue the source of the brothers' suspicions about her. She has one intention: to connect Pedro to the ancestors. To do this, she must reach his eyes. She turns her face toward him and says, "Tell about history long and rich. I feel pain, many pain here."

Pedro lights a cigarette and glances up at the ceiling. As he exhales a breath of smoke with a sigh, WaLiLa slowly stands and walks to the kitchen window. She casually pulls a rose from a bouquet that sits on the windowsill. She pushes the rose against her nostrils and returns to her seat, maintaining surveillance on the thin curls of smoke leaving Pedro's parted mouth and burning cigarette. The smoke does not reach her, but she keeps the rose pressed to her face anyway. Should any stray smoke molecule float near her, the flower petals will filter the air and block the smoke before it has the opportunity to enter her body.

"The pain you sense here is very specific to this time period. We have always lived with pain. Sometimes very little, sometimes a great amount. Today my people are living at the limit of human dignity. We are struggling to maintain some semblance of life, but it is . . ." Pedro pauses, his grapple with translating his thoughts into words visible on his face.

"When we lost the Soviet Union, we lost a lot. Without their support, we are isolated and alone in the world. It's a strange thing, really," Pedro mutters as he squints at the wall as if looking at something in the distance. "We are isolated and alone, yet the entire world watches us and regards us with curiosity and suspicion. You came out of curiosity, I assume?"

Pedro turns his head and glances at WaLiLa briefly, then immediately turns away when she nods her head in agreement.

"Oh, especially the Americans, they salivate waiting for us to fall so they can pounce on us. Castro will never let that happen. . . ."

WaLiLa focuses on the bitterness in Pedro's voice. She tunes out his speaking, wishing she could gain some assurance from the ancestors. Her muscles strain, begging to communicate with them. *Can they want nectar from such a bitter fruit?* Her thoughts are interrupted by a loud crash. She realizes Pedro is no longer talking and her wrist is stinging. Both he and Modesto are staring at her.

"Why you look me?" she asks.

"Do you know what you just did?" Pedro asks.

"No."

"You knocked everything off that shelf above your head."

She looks up and sees a small plank of painted wood tilted off its wall supports. She looks down and sees the floor littered with overturned spice jars.

"Oh, my muscles jumps, must came back." *How could the arm flick have returned?* She scrambles for words to explain, as her message-center simultaneously races to explain it to herself.

"I have muscles jumps. I leave medicine home, so they return."

WaLiLa mumbles this as she kneels to pick up the spilled spices. Modesto also kneels. As his knees knock against hers, she looks up and their eyes lock. Barriers open and Modesto dives into the infinite space he sees in her eyes. He begins disrobing his soul. *I hate it here*, his soul cries. *It is too painful to stay. Breathing the air here is like tapping a raw nerve.* He speaks of a child conceived with a Spanish tourist. He speaks of joining her and their son in Spain. He describes the pain of having nothing, doing nothing; of endless days of smoke, smoke, smoking. He admits to staying home so as not to see the prostitutes selling their bodies to foreigners for a taste of fancy clothes or money to feed their families. He details the days he sits alone holding himself, for he has nothing substantial to offer a hungry young woman in communist Cuba.

Pedro's fingers wind themselves around Modesto's collarbones and dig into his flesh. The pain forces Modesto to blink. The connection broken, Modesto looks up at his brother with a wet face.

"*Que haces?*" Pedro yells. "What the hell are you doing?" Pedro pulls Modesto to his feet and separates him from WaLiLa. His eyes are full of fire. In them, WaLiLa sees fear and a stubbornness that screams, *You will not conquer me*.

6.

Over the next week, the memory of Modesto's crouched frame heaving with confessional sobs under WaLiLa's gaze remains in Pedro's mind. When she blows into the room, he examines the burning end of his cigarette, stares at her lips as they move, focuses on any other activity so as not to fall into those eyes. Neither witty conversation, nor sweet perfume, nor exposed shoulder can draw his eyes to wade in her vision pools. Her attempts to establish herself as a love interest have fallen like a dove struck by a well-aimed stone. Her body feels just as bloodied. Each moment of failure pushes points of pain through her skin like pushpins breaking through a voodoo doll.

The house is quiet. Elisa and Modesto have gone to the market. Liliana is visiting relatives and Pedro has gone out with friends. WaLiLa sits on the floor at the bottom of the stairs almost paralyzed by pain. She trembles as the air squeezes her like cruel grains of quicksand. She bites the inside of her cheek and pushes herself up from the floor. She holds on to the wall and pulls her body up the stairs. She dizzily stumbles to the bed as her arm jumps, sporadically tracing arcs in the air around her.

She lays her aching body into the folds of a rough blanket. She closes her vision-centers, hoping to rest, but her innerself rouses her from sleep by eagerly pushing against the inside of her chest. Shunning the hopeless feeling she feels washing over her body, WaLiLa taps her chest with a throbbing finger and allows her innerself to exit. Her innerself immediately brushes against her forehead in a sign of affection and respect and starts buzzing around the room. WaLiLa's vision-centers slowly follow her innerself's movements in wonder. After sweeping the room twice with broad wing strokes, her innerself discovers one of Pedro's rumpled T-shirts discarded on the floor. She lands gently on the shirt, collects his scent in the wells of her body, and flies through the little window that offers ventilation to the room.

WaLiLa, quickly losing the energy her innerself is expending, abruptly falls asleep. With the road map of Pedro's scent in front of her, WaLiLa's innerself goes flying through the Havana streets. Dodging the families who spill out of doorways onto sidewalks, her innerself bounces on the sounds of conversation which fill the twilight air. She flies over avenues filled with rusted vintage cars and legions of bicycles. She skids to a stop when she no longer feels Pedro's scent. She doubles back and locates his scent two blocks away, hovering outside the first floor of a little house. Hanging in the air that presses against a cracked window, WaLiLa's innerself notices Pedro among ten other people gathered in a small, cluttered living room. The eleven mouths share a bottle of rum while the eleven pairs of hands exchange cigarettes and finger snaps. One of the eleven leans against pillow cushions embracing a guitar. They all sing along, glowing in the space made light by their gathered hearts.

Many laughs and music notes later, discordant sounds reverberate in the small room. The crashing of a glass against the concrete floor. The rise of angry voices, quickly followed by soft apology. Tears fall now; then a shaky-voiced reminder of tomorrow's departure, of a raft sailing for other parts. The threat of the sea and the fear of isolation well up from the floor. The room is as quiet as held breath. Pedro is the first to answer the challenge.

"We've been planning this escape for two years. I think we've deliberated enough. I'm done thinking. When tomorrow comes, my things will be ready and I will sail."

Before Pedro's lips have stopped moving, WaLiLa's innerself is gone. Flying at breakneck speed, she returns to the attic where WaLiLa is resting. With a crackle, she rejoins WaLiLa's body. Immediately the knowledge of Pedro's journey sinks into WaLiLa's being-center. She sits up abruptly. She feels as if shards are puncturing her lower back. Her body is stiff. Her eyes dart around the room as she finally realizes her hunt has careened out of her control. Her message-center slowly reviews her body signals, noting which senses are malfunctioning and what pain is being experienced. It then considers which poisons are capable of triggering such reactions and cross-references these poisons with elements WaLiLa has actually come in contact with. She bends over as her message-center comes up with a match. "SMOKE SMOKE SMOKE" flashes in her vision-centers. She shuts her vision-centers in pain. She lies back down, her chest deflating in submission.

Her message-center reminds her of Pedro's departure and she sits up again. She considers the smoke first. It has been quietly damaging her systems for weeks. It is too late for repair. Then she considers Pedro. She doesn't have time to follow him because the transport tunnel will retract in three days, leaving her stranded in the Realm of Human Being. She can't gather the nectar from him tonight because she has failed to connect him to the ancestors. WaLiLa twists her arms back and forth as she accepts the facts; she has run out of options. She falls back against the bed again. She rolls her body from one side of the bed to the other, desperately searching for a solution. Then her body freezes as she realizes that death is already promised her. *If I am to die anyway*, she thinks, *the possibility that Pedro's nectar may be poisoned cannot harm me.*

WaLiLa sits up and slides her knees beneath her body. With a fluid, flicking motion from the top of her forehead into the air before her, she reports her decision to the ancestors. *Oh great ones.* WaLiLa raises curved, outstretched arms. *The earth air is binding its poisonous cords about me.* She folds her arms behind her back. *This vessel that carries me is not so strong.* She collapses to the right, then collapses to the left. *I speak now to expose my failure.* Palms outstretched, she crisscrosses her arms at the elbow four times. *I cannot connect this human to you.* She drops her head and shakes it vigorously from side to side. *He is resistant.* She snakes her torso forward. *He fears me.* She rocks her upper body forward and back. *I have been ineffective with him.* She cleaves her hands in the air, then breaks them apart suddenly. *Because I refused to follow your rules.* She bends forward weakly from the waist and shakes her head from side to side. *I have ingested a lethal substance.* She sits erect and stiff, and lowers her right ear to her right shoulder. *With death as my insurance.* WaLiLa lowers her shoulder blades to the ground. *I am free to complete my assignment.* She lowers and raises her fists with a constant steady rhythm five times. *If his nectar is poisoned, it will die with me.* She pounds the air with her fists, then drops her arms lifelessly. *If it is not, I shall return to you and deliver the nectar.* She pushes a path from her center to the space above her head. *Then the smoke damage will bring my death.* She lies on her side briefly. She ends by touching her forehead to the floor and rolling her hips.

Her communication ended, WaLiLa lies back in the folds of the blanket and slips off to sleep.

7.

As WaLiLa sleeps, the night thickens. When the air reaches its blackest point, Pedro rides in on midnight wings. He is surprised to find his mother sleeping in his bed: the cot next to his brother's. Pedro's eyes rise up to the ceiling as he visualizes the only empty bed in the apartment: the bed upstairs next to WaLiLa's. He sits on the floor between the two cots and soaks up his family's energy. When he can keep his eyes open no longer, he rests his hand gently on his brother's head, presses his lips to his mother's cheek, then climbs up the stairs. Keeping his back to WaLiLa, Pedro drops his shirt and pants on the floor. He sits on the side of the bed in his boxer shorts, attempting to quell the sadness that claws at his throat every time he imagines leaving his mother and brother behind. Then he lies back, solemnly reclining as though the bed were a coffin. He clutches the images of his mother and his brother close to him and drifts off to sleep.

WaLiLa's innerself thumps on the inside of WaLiLa's chest for thirty minutes, attempting to alert her to Pedro's presence. WaLiLa soon becomes aware of the thumping, but takes another thirty minutes to rouse herself from rest. By the time she releases her innerself and rises from the bed, Pedro is in a deep sleep. With teeth clenched, WaLiLa drags herself to Pedro's bedside. Her innerself flutters around his head. As taught during training, WaLiLa places one hand over his closed eyes and another over his abdomen, her thumb connecting to his navel. Under her velvet touch, Pedro's eyes do not open. He doesn't even stir.

WaLiLa closes her vision-centers and pushes her chin upward to the skies. As she establishes portals between their two bodies, WaLiLa begins to glow. Her innerself detects a sound and flies to the stairs, peeking over the banister to investigate. She flies over to WaLiLa and tugs at her ear. When WaLiLa opens her vision-centers, her innerself communicates Modesto's presence at the foot of the stairs. Knowing that Modesto will soon be privy to her activities, WaLiLa tightens her grip on Pedro. She shrugs one shoulder in disappointment. She has never experienced a hunt that has failed so consistently.

When Modesto reaches the top of the stairs, a painful sensation rips through WaLiLa's body. Globes of poison covered in shards sharp as glass mercilessly jerk and jump around inside her torso. Her body begins to shake under the pressure of the internal wounds. Modesto stands in full view of her body, transfixed by what he sees. The moment she discovers that Pedro's nectar is poisoned, she is no longer concerned for her life. She flexes her torso and cuts the internal portals through which Pedro's nectar enters her body. This severing is accompanied by a loud sound of tearing through Modesto's eardrums. The sound breaks his trance and he begins to scream his brother's name.

As Pedro stirs, WaLiLa pulls herself away from his body and stumbles backward. When he opens his eyes, he sees WaLiLa fall limply onto her bed. Her skin is soaked in a dark purple liquid and she is slowly losing color. When Modesto sees that WaLiLa is hurt, a mixture of terror and compassion riots across his eyes. Pedro sits up and rubs his temples. When he brings his hand down from his face, it is moist. He runs his fingers across his forehead and sees purple liquid on them. He looks down at his body. His torso is covered with the same liquid. As he jumps up and scrambles away from WaLiLa's proximity, the haze of his sleep quickly disappears from his head.

"They will come for me," she murmurs to herself. "They will come for me." Exhausted and delirious, she expires. Her body slumps into a deep coma. Long after her lids are closed, she imagines the brothers' unblinking eyes examining her. She prays that when she opens her vision-centers she will be home. She needs to wrap herself in the thick air of her nation and vanish into the folds. She hopes to lie in maroon cloud fields over gold skies between stretches of deep purple soil. She wants to compete in flying races with her clan and never use her voice to communicate again.

8.

When the coma finally lifts from WaLiLa's body, her message-center identifies the thin air rushing through her nostrils as earth's. She pushes her eyelids open to see herself resting in the same small room where her death began. The two brothers are gone, but there is a pair of shining eyes staring at her from across the room. When the eyes see motion flicker across WaLiLa's face, they rise from the camouflage of darkness and float closer to the bed. WaLiLa knows from the weight of the foot-steps that the eyes belong to Elisa.

Elisa hovers over the bed, filling WaLiLa's vision-centers with a dark face creased with concern. Elisa silently pushes a glass against WaLiLa's lips. WaLiLa turns away. Elisa stands back, places one hand on her hip, and regards her silently. Why Elisa's face holds no anger or fear is a mir-acle to WaLiLa. She refuses to waste her energy wondering what the brothers have whispered about her. She prefers instead to lie with drooped lids and silent mouth, twirling her wrist with the repeated ques-tion, *Will they come for me?*

"They will not come," Elisa says, chopping through the thick silence of the room with her voice.

WaLiLa's vision-centers pop open and she stares into Elisa's calm face. Seconds pass as the two examine each other in silence. Just as she is dismissing Elisa's announcement as hallucination, Elisa speaks again.

"They are not coming for you."

WaLiLa rises up onto her elbows and stares at Elisa incredulously. To her surprise, her body does not hurt when she moves it. Only her head throbs in pain.

"Who are you?" WaLiLa demands.

"I am Elisa," Elisa responds with an amused smile. "I was once a nec-tar collector, like you, but Pedro's aunt put an end to that, much as Pedro has done for you."

"But . . ." Questions slam through WaLiLa's mind, battling for do-minion of her lips. "How long have you been here? Did you know who I was from the beginning? Will I die here?"

"I've been here longer than I care to remember. I realized what you were after you stole flowers from my altars. Before that, I only recognized you as a traveler and welcomed you as I had been welcomed on my pre-vious earth trips. And yes, you will die here."

WaLiLa lies back on the bed and pounds her fists against the mattress in frustration. After seven seconds of silence, she buries her vision-centers in Elisa's face for further explanation.

"Does that mean . . . ?"

"That means your access to our people and our planet has ended. That means you shall no longer collect nectar. Do not concern yourself with this: Nectar shall be gathered, the ancestors shall be fed. But you have just been birthed. You are breathing your first breaths as a human being."

"A human!"

"Yes."

"But I thought . . ."

"I know this is confusing WaLiLa, but no one knows about us. Everything you learned about death applied to home. There has been no research done on us who have died on earth."

"Are there many of us?"

"I don't know. I haven't met any, but I'm certain they exist."

As water drips from her eyes, WaLiLa is overcome with sadness and confusion.

"Don't look so confused. You have human emotions now. You have the ability to cry. Haven't you noticed how easily you're speaking? You were also given the facility to speak human languages."

WaLiLa touches the water dripping from her eyes and rubs it between her fingertips.

"Death is supposed to be a step toward becoming an ancestor. Are you saying we are excluded from that process because we died on earth?"

"I don't know."

"How could this happen?"

"Well, the poison you consumed is known here as 'mortality.' It is a death agent for humans. Their death is not like ours. They consider death to be a finite thing."

"What is 'finite'?"

"It's the opposite of infinite."

"But how can death be finite? Death is transformation. Death is change."

"WaLiLa, I know that's what you learned, but I must remind you, you are on earth. Humans are bound by such things as time and gravity. At least they believe themselves to be."

"Are you saying I am to die a human death at the end of this journey?"

"I cannot know until I meet my own death."

"So I am never to be anything other than human?"

"I don't know, WaLiLa."

"But this is my first life, I will know nothing else."

"That is not true, you are beginning your second life now. Although you still exist in the same outer shell, the reality you experience here will be different from your life as a nectar collector. I promise you that earth is not without its delights."

"I can't believe we weren't trained for this."

"Consider it a surprise death; we don't know what waits for us on the other side. Meanwhile, rest. Your body is healing, the transition is not an easy one—"

"But how—" WaLiLa interrupts.

"We will talk later. For now, let your body do its work."

"But why—"

"Rest," Elisa repeats firmly. "You shall need your strength."

The African Origins of UFOs (excerpt from the novel)

Anthony Joseph

(2000)

Si dieu les a fait noir c'est qu'il doit y avoir une raison.

Anon.

1. Kneedeep in ditchdiggerniggersweat

His voice had the deep burrr of a man who kept fishhooks in his beard.
So I put on my white Teflon jump-suit, slid sleeves and levers tight,
pulled my hair shut with Sirian beeswax and en-route superterranean to
Toucan Bay via antimatic congo pump I met Cain waiting with the contraband: 8 grams of Ceboletta X. And while Cain stroked a reefer the
size of Mozambique rolled in a popadom, I held my head wide open for
the suck with a nasal>oral siphon and was so oiled and eager for Joe
Sam's return to Houdini's that night that I sped there, down near the
jetty where fish gut funk fumed furiously and found copious peoples rubbing belly to back, hacking heels, knee deep in ditchdiggerniggersweat

That naked island funk was still lickin' hips with polyrhythmic thun-
derclaps. Does the Berta butt boogie? do bump hips? flip an spin an
bop'n finger pop'n subaquantum basslines pumping pure people-riddim
funk like snake rubber twisting in aluminum bucket, reverberating
round the frolic house with a heavy heartbeat, causing black to buck and
shiver—

WOOEEE! WOOEEEE!—

The very groove caused coons to stumble loose and slide on saturnalian
pomade until their conks collapsed. The sound possessed more swing
than bachelor galvanise in hurricane, more sting than jab-jab whip,
more bone than gravedigger boots and more soul than African trumpet
bone, with a pure emotive speed that once improvised harmolodic funk

to Buddy Bolden's punkjazz on the banks of Lake Pontchartrain, double bass still reverberating through space-time like long lost Afronauts on orbiting saxophones, that shook Spiritual Baptist shacks with rhythm till the Sankey hymns they swung became cryptic mantras that slid like secrets through water.

And on the balcony, ever Afrodizziac in Indian red, with her high sepia'fro, far-east eyes and morello lips borrowed from a jealous mirror, Madame Sweetbum leans back on her ass for support, puffin' good genk and inspecting vinyl imprints in dry blue light, releasing slap after slap of the raw-boned and ancient Afrolypso she kept in aluminum sleeves, sacred 45s so sharp rip slippers off feet till steam hisses from her radiogram. Madame Sweetbum had negroes wringing brine! Black be boogiefull, black be slick, cryptic hustlers an assorted Cyberpimps in stingy brim fedoras, scissor-tongued vipers in snakeskin brogues, in pollywool zoots with sawed off buckshots in their lapels, nubile Supian ladies throwing waist like whipsnake while rabid-eyed by stiff crotched and grinning coons in erection boots, leaning at the bar boppin' bulbous foreheads and burning for flesh.

Mokotux Charlie climbed the stairs like a calliper with his clipboard, mop and megaphone. The old bush coolie ran the place with the rep n'-grace of a gamblers' tears. Molasses black with a face like an unfinished woodcarving, tight brown suit, cockroach killer boots, white handle razor behind an ear for peeling more than toecorns and a voice that suggested a rusty trachea. Charlie liked to grin in that ol'island pimp style, revealing 10 teeth brown from 55 years of Trini pepper, chewing nush and home-rolled cigars. He also ran severe erotique noir upstairs where the rooms smell like dried pussy, where cum crusted facerags lay under the beds, where the curtains felt dank and butter greased. His ladies charged by the pound; your weight plus theirs in cash!

Charlie hummed as he shovelled spum from teledildonic booths and wiped his pros with paraffin, prime pros with lineage to Aboboville, Iere; pork legged jammettes and melon swallowing domestic cleaner types with devious profiles, big bone dada mamas whose hips re-tuned bedsprings to the B flat of authentic colonial brothels. Some wore names like Yvette, Rose, Daphne and Gemma who'd just arrived on Kunu

Supia from some floating island behind God's back. She would even let you lick her mastectomy scar.

2. Joe Sambucus Nigra

Joe Sam was so bad even catfish shaved to meet him: a man so fierce he wore his boots inside out\African spaceboots, Nigerians used them for terraforming, Joe Sam used his to kick afrosaxons and smuggled his black butter irregardless. Bad like crab an' spoken of with contempt in multiple dialects of intergalactic niggaspeak, banned from six floating isles for ultraviolence, subversive texts and possession of genetic contraband, upright and devious, with a stare that saw through bones—his instantaneous cuss was so cantankerous it would cause concussions! So gifted in the throat with a Baptist minister's grimy tone, his aural pyrotechnics would hypnotize negroes. He manipulated deft verbs and lingual tourniquets with ferocious grace, supplying palefolk and tourists with prime niggum vitae. A callous, transgalactic pusherman, suave an so slick with a flick he filled veins stiff with liquidessence and drove a chrome Mesakin Congo Pump with antimatic injection. Ever dapper in devious strides and astrocamouflage dashikis, Joe Sam's hustle was the cusp of voodoo funk technology: bootleg melanin to keep pale niggers ticking on Kunu Supia!

Joe swore lineage to Ierean ancestors who were rois and dauphins in secret slave militias, belly marinated with the bile of urban revolutionary badjohns from Corbeau town and Cuttyville Junction. Men with wooden carbuncles and full heads of hair, they shaved with cutlass blades. Copacetic men who could nyam pigfat, mandrake root and forceripe tamarind for breakfast then buck waist and break fast an spit/revolutionary spunk in your sisters eye from a radius of 360 Uncle Ben Blacks, coming from the genus of mythical beasts from back in old Iere when stickfighters still ruled the ancient barrackyards. Hill-born soldiers with cast iron gorgon organs and bois dipped in asifetida sulphate, underarm renk with rancid paraffin copper.

Saliva trickles from the lisp of a 12-fingered manchild tugging a kite in Aranguez savannah with a razorbladed tail to cut and send other kites over the Samaan trees then run home watch: Electric Company, Love

American Style, Carnabas Bollins and Puffin' Stuff, Voyage to the bottom of the sea—they had no broughtupsy; would suck pus an hit big man mad bullpistle then rub stinging nettle on dey prick, hunt snakes and whip lizards in half against orange trees with masonry twine. Soulman pusherman skank to Mikey Dread, bust Carbide and smoke tampi, bust cow face with broomstick, hog head with tree-trunk, looting the city while the revolution blazed. Grow dread/upset the old lady. Convinced Gallstones Grandfatha Buckmouth that drinking lil'boy urine would cure his cataract but then put mentholated spirit in the old mans' hibiscus tea and grew up to be legends with monikers as sublime as Dr Rat, Cutouter, Gooter, Siparia Scipio, Catpiss Pepper, whatever happened to Newland Blake? or anyone a dem rubber wristed bois swingers with hollow scars stolen from the gayelle.

Big strong cocoa-prick man like Joe Sam so could sit in a brimfully stink hot funky latrine in a canecutter shirt, sun cutting through galvanize like Michael X pelting chop and smoke basements of caustic ses' an' sip flour-porridge. Bus' toe bounce steppers who had afros since the 1940s and would catch bullets there-much hair. Sharpboned jaw box go crack cocoa pod and coconut, bust tamboo bamboo, strip cane, shake skulls and squeeze out butterwax, break man back with 2x4 pine, restore blacknuss, plot guerrilla ballistics, peel back bullshit, stew black justice, high browed on Ju Ju physics, sip breast milk, cowmilk, duck egg and oyster, grow gut and full Pharaoh Saunders beard 'til it grew grey and long so would wrap around standpipes and Baptist flagpoles, but by then coming down from hill to town to tumble in teargas became impractical, and bad for bunions, body weak from revolution. But in Toucan Bay Joe Sam could induce spontaneous coitus in Bahama mamas and men who yet knew not their thermal deathpoints and thought themselves impervious would buck and cringe like Barbadian foil and surrender their deepest compunctions.

3. Secret Underlung

But there were haters who grumbled at Joe's return. And in the brisk underbelly of night, savage native neck lockers crept in shadows with sharkbone daggers, in lurk for Joe arriving. They snuck and steupsed 'round Houdini's, peepin 'neat the dank stairwells, grinding malice for Joe.

To blow his soul. To bust

his secret underlung.

His modus upset most post-earth negroes who believed in a disembodied blacknuss and they bemoaned Joe for his blackdada retrograde. They claimed that 'blackness' was only relevant on Earth and even then was suspected as the mindset of a con that pat afros down and kept negroes terra bound to suffer when we coulda been interplanetary from way back. Black was dead they said. 'Black as in the tones of Nuyorican nig-gerpoets ranting militant in ancient days, earth long, livin' in cold water Brooklyn warehouse space, no food but Fanon, no cash but Jackson, back then their essential essence preservation by poetic testifying was hip and on the one 'cause subversive boots and dreader guerrillas were needed on the urban battlefields and word was sword, shield and dagger, even ancient Iere had gun in Dashiki and afro intellects bust plenty po-lice head with oratorical gas but not now we swimming in heaven.'

With such consummate scripts these anti-essentialists wished to reverse polarities. But blackpeople didn't want to hear that shit 'cause under-neath these negros appeared impervious to funk. The ONE would hit them in the chest like this "!" and they wouldn't understand it. Prone to pork they'd lick pigfat off the floor when no one was looking but they wouldn't understand it. Their ears would ring with transgenetic faxes and they wouldn't understand it. Drums would tumble with insecret tex-tures and they wouldn't understand it. But they crept light round Hou-dini's in long black muslin reciting intimate textology, so damn vex they could eradicate Joe. Or blow his soul or bust his secret underlung.

But the Blackerblacks, them was ultraviolent spooks. Shoe shine black from scalp to sole with skin the texture of calfskin leather, they were the mutant progeny of Kunu Supia's original terraformers, who churned in geothermal mines till sun bust their genome codes in the Kilgodey desert. Imperviously black their eyes shone like sunbeams through smooth onyx bone. They wanted to hurt Joe. Real bad. For heresy. Envious of the slick ease with which he rolled billfolds in Toucan Bay from a hustle they saw as rightfully theirs.

Two them were rappin' in a gully 'neat Houdini's in a crude basilect.

"I hear Joe Sam kill 20 man with Idi Amin jawbone, all was Spyro Gyra fans."

"Is so? Well, Laro, if ah dead bury meh clothes."

Joe Sam arrives with immaculate precision, stepping tough through the muscle funk as slick as vampire brows, 6 ft 6 of rigorous black muscle in an oxblood ceramic polyester suit cut sharp with grey paramilitary pimp-stripe, secret pockets packed with bootleg melanin to keep pale niggers ticking on Kunu Supia and glory rolls of edible money concealed in his bullet-proof waistcoat. As he soulfull strides, slappin' palms with the rugged grace of a southern Ethiopian cowboy, head hard with nigger knots, with battle scars on both cheeks and a 3-canal cutlass tucked in his waist. Mokotux Charlie comes calliping down from his jamette harem to grin like horseteeth and embrace him.

"Ai, Joe, when you reach? When you going back?"

Joe just grinned. He must've been aware of motives installed in many devious assassins for his demise, but as he moves through the crowd his jaw is locked rigid and reveals no fear.

In the basement bluesdance, more mellow the texture, old blue funk in abstract contortions; Swamp Dogg, Solomon Burke, soft lights and dopesmoke, lovers kept the walls erect, citrus pungent drunks lay sprung on silk cotton sofas cradling demijohns of mountain dew. Pious old Iere-ans with grey long beards shuffled cards with feeling, they sucked bong-fulls of black Tobago gungeon, sat round plywood tables slapping harsh cards down.

"High low jack game!"

"Who draw jack a dimes?"

In a back room, a Buddha-belly pot of smoked Manicou soup sat bubbling on a pitchpine fire. An old ragged dread with a prosthetic tongue bent prodding lumps of pumpkin, yamatuta, cowtongue dumplings and green banana with a wooden spoon and the scent of lime, wild thyme, shadon beni and congo pepper rises from the broth, oozing its bushmeat sweetness round the crowded room. Joe Sam stakes a corner. He pulls two vials from an inside pocket, lays them to light and a dozen hungerers peep round his halo. The mere sight of the serum causes some to salivate and somersault in their skins. Joe Sam takes his stand on a powdermilk pan and with a gutty growl, the supacoon began to testify.

The Astral Visitor Delta Blues

Robert Fleming

(2000)

Alligator, Mississippi—July 11, 1961

Frank Boles wasn't thinking about aliens, spaceships, or anything else extraterrestrial on that hot moonlit Delta night he went to Minnie's jook joint. He shrugged his broad John Henry shoulders and went up-stairs, past the frowning, bent man who checked him in at the door. Not tonight. No, he wouldn't think about the chits he owed at Mister Wiley's store, or whether his daughter Bue got herself knocked up by that Dixon boy or if Mister Tyree was going to throw him off his place for hitting the peckerwood down at the feed shed over in Oriole. Not tonight. Tonight he was going to raise hell and worry about heaven to-morrow. The rocking sound of music could be heard through the beaver-board walls, good down-home blues. A few people standing at the entrance stepped aside to let the tall gaunt sharecropper pass. After a brief survey of the dance floor, Frank decided that he didn't know any-one there, not even the sad-faced man sitting by the window, dispensing paper cups of corn whiskey. No, he didn't know anyone, but he could be wrong in the dim light.

Inside, a bright-skinned man bobbed his head as he pounded a piano into joyous submission, accompanied by another blue-black man play-ing a harmonica and a tricky-fingered guitarist, who looked sleepy. Sta-tioned in front of the musicians were two singers, a couple, slickly dressed. Frank chuckled as he maneuvered his way through the tightly packed tables, noting how the lights caught the glimmer of the male singer's head. Both entertainers seemed drunk or close to it, and Frank was in the mood to follow.

He chose a rickety seat in a corner, not too close to the stage, but far enough so that he could get a good view of the room. He ordered a whiskey and surveyed the club. Everybody was talking, singing, and dancing all at once. Among the revelers, Frank spotted a few of the Holiness people, the backsliders, several drifters, two or three medicine men from the Dixie road show parked just outside of town, and a couple of odd-looking strangers in snow-white suits. They were on the other side of the room, but nobody paid them no mind. Frank searched the mob for a glimpse of his old friend Isaac, but the joker was nowhere to be found.

Frank settled back and let the whiskey and the music wash over him. Every tune sounded faster than the one before it, and the crowd wasted no time catching up. One woman in a low-cut dress was snapping her long fingers over her pretty head. Frank grinned as she shook her wide hips to the steady beat. Many of the old heads there did a dated shuffle, nothing to work up a sweat, though. Once and awhile, someone would step out from the group, do some spins and twists to leave the others wanting more.

Frank wasn't much of a dancer himself, but he loved to watch. Lovers were snuggled up, belly to belly, whispering hotly in each other's ears. He sat safely off to the side, grinning. Often, in the middle of a tune, some bad bucks would start cussing loudly, pushing and shoving, or going for the pistols. Frank wanted no part of that, so he preferred to watch. Most players that worked at Minnie's knew its rowdy reputation and usually set up on a stage near a window, ensuring their escape if the crowd got out of hand. Word was out about the gunplay and knife-throwing that sometimes took place. Veterans said it was a tradition carried from slavery times, the wild and raunchy weekend rumble. Onliest thing Frank did exciting on a Friday night before he came to Clarksdale was throwing a brick at a guy who cheated him at cards.

Glass in hand, the male singer swept back a couple strands of processed hair from his glassy eyes and sauntered across the stage, wiggling his hips to the ladies' delight. The band switched to a slow, simmering blues. The singer paused, feeling out his audience, but Clarksdale was like most towns in Mississippi and he knew the routine well. Just then a shout from the back of the room sent heads spinning. Frank's lanky back stiffened, but the scrawny singer went on with his introduction to the next song, a suggestive ditty by Tampa.

By the volume of noise from the cheers, Frank could tell it was a house favorite.

As more stragglers were coming in the door, humming along, the male singer rocked back on his heels and sang the bass part of the song, while the woman did the falsetto.

> "I've got a gal, she's low and squatty,
> I mean boys, she'll suit anybody.
> And everybody likes her, 'cause she loves so good."

The paper cups were making rounds in the crowd as the couple cut up something awful, bumping and grinding against each other. Frank surmised that the mean-looking crooner was riding her when they weren't doing the shows, probably a nice roll, too. People on the floor loved their insinuating antics and singing, clapping and stomping in tune to the sizzling words of the song.

Then the woman broke in moaning, twisting, and wringing her hands, stroking the man all over, then stroking herself. The crowd whooped in excitement. Frank sat up straight when the woman gapped her legs while telling the crowd just how she loves so good.

After she ended her solo, her partner came back to wrap it up, beckoning to her suggestively, his conk hair flying behind him.

The audience sang along, chuckling at the lyrics as if it were their first time hearing them. Frank drank glass after glass, enjoying the ruckus. On through the night, the singers and their musicians worked the audience to a fever pitch, with no letup. Frank got into the spirit of things, doing his old buck-and-wing dance, rocking back and forth on one leg while the crowd egged him on. He leapt high and came down into a dancer's split with both legs straight out under him like the stretched arms of a clock. The folks loved the jig and gave him a round of clapping. He took an uneven bow, swaying dangerously. Lawd, he loved a good time.

"Big man, you put on quite a show out there," said a gal Frank knew from a juke near Drew. "You shore got big hands, look like you could break a tree in half with them."

"That ain't all that's big," he flirted, after his vision cleared enough for him to see her seductive smile, watching her soft brown eyes and dark purple face, the soft curves barely concealed under a tight yellow skirt.

"You plumb crazy, fool," she said, and laughed. "I'm here with some hick from over in Jackson, but mebbe we can get together." She nodded toward the door.

Frank was tempted for a hot moment, but as the room wavered around him, he knew he was in no condition to fight his way out of the club. He turned her down and watched her wiggle away from him into the crowd, before he tossed down one last gulp of his brew. He had reached his limit of drink about an hour ago, but he stayed on to the last, tossing down cup after cup of the clear, burning liquid. Shortly before three in the morning, he tried to make it home, staggering in the street under the power of the alcohol. His head was throbbing. Finally, he wobbled into the hallway of the colored hotel where he had a room. He pulled himself painfully up the stairs, one step at a time, until he got to his floor.

Once inside, Frank stumbled to a rickety chair and sat on it, with his aching head in his large, calloused hands. Everything on his body pained him, like he had just finished a long day in the fields with his old white cracker boss standing up over him. That peckerwood had a way of getting his goat more than anybody else in the world. Frank was slumped in the chair, just staring into space when it happened, his eyes wide open.

The light was coming from behind him at first, outlining a shape, forming a silhouette. What attracted his stare was the silvery glow around the figure, the pulsating center of it. Blinding light. Then a voice called to him from somewhere out there, and a paralysis crept over Frank, rooting him to his chair. The voice faded back into the blackness where it had come from, the light broke apart and bounced back and forth, then the luminous face of a man dressed in a white suit, a bright white suit like those strangers at the jook, appeared from within the glow.

Something about the man transfixed Frank, but he couldn't say what. The voice returned, deeper, richer. Words, but a language he didn't know. He didn't understand them, tractor talk, machine blabber, white noise. He covered his ears, but they penetrated his flesh, ruthless, all-powerful. This enchantment, this spell, this haint.

Frank watched the frightening vision from the chair, trembling, shaken to the very core of himself. He was drunk but not so drunk that he now saw things with his eyes open. The buzzing continued in his ears, filling his head and moving down into his chest. Was this a devil, one of those haints his grandmama used to talk about when he was a boy? Whatever it was, Frank felt it knew him, knew all about him—his thoughts, his secrets, and his sins.

The voice came again, louder and louder. Frank noticed that the face never changed, the lips never moved. The emptiness around the man peeled back with a deafening roar. The trance embraced Frank and wrapped him in its arms. All sensations invaded him as the voice echoed with a sound much like the scratchy music of birds' wings beating fast. Then there was a smell, a smell he recognized, the scent that came after a heavy rain. Frank felt his heart stop, then continue. The man in white sat motionless, like stone, shutting his eyes until there was only the fluttering of the lids. Jacob and the angel, Moses and the burning bush, the two divine beings of vengeance at Sodom and Gomorrah.

Frank watched the man produce two large green seeds in the palms of his hands, his fingers outstretched and flat. The man smiled knowingly. The seeds took root into Frank's dark flesh and huge leafy flowers—light orange with gold trim—pushed up toward the ceiling. He could hear the song of their sprouting and knew then that he only understood life to a point. He was insignificant. Soon the flowers vanished and a blue-white beam of light replaced them. The man smiled again and his eyebrows lifted, his white suit glowing. Frank watched him for a moment while the beams of different colors now flowed into a triangle, each hue separated, collecting in a cube shape, dividing in half, and finally swirling in a circle.

Frank sensed the hair on the back of his neck rise as he pitched forward and fell on the floor. He shivered again and again, unable to resurrect himself. There was nothing but fear within him. For a minute, his mind filled with sinful, bleak thoughts. He imagined his own death. He would have rather driven a dull knife through his pitiful heart or sent it in a crimson crease across his throat. The vision departed from him just before the earth got light. Suddenly his body went stiff and bitter tears came to his eyes. Staggering, he hoisted himself, shuddering in a coughing fit, then wiped the foam from his lips.

His body was covered with strange marks, odd burns and markings, as if he had been branded. Frank's fingers hovered over the marks, afraid to touch. At the window, he saw something outside, floating, like vapors, whirling lights in the open field near the parking lot. Lights that glowed like those in his room, then vanished in air.

All that next day, Frank thought about what he had seen. When he went to the colored diner for breakfast, folks were talking about flying saucers, people from outer space, men from Mars, and odd happenings all through the Delta the night before. People said they saw spaceships land, cattle gutted, pigs turned inside out, two men hauled up into the air and vanished, large stretches of field scorched by something, and a known Klansman found naked and babbling like a fool behind his cabin in Sunflower County.

"Frank, do you believe any of this outer space mess?" Cephus asked the sharecropper in earnest. "Any fool can see that ain't nothing in the Good Book about no damn flying saucers. Where is any of that junk in the Book of Revelations or the Song of Solomon? No way."

Frank heard Isaac guffaw at the four black men sitting along the counter, dressed in their field clothes. "Hey, somebody say the Russians sent a monkey up there and brought it back. Say the ape got more sense than most people."

Frank didn't say a thing. He picked at his breakfast, his spoon unsteady in his rough, trembling hands.

"Satellites, Sputnik, robots, spacemen . . . hah!" Cephus roared, his bass voice booming throughout the tiny diner. "Let me tell you something. My old Aunt Cat say this space stuff ain't nothing but some Hollywood jive, 'cause we all know they can do anything out there. Change a man into a wolf or a bat, make things disappear, bring back ancient times . . . anything. Saw some foolishness on Mr. Tim's teevee the other night where this great big lizard tore up the whole world and here I woke up today and the world still here."

The quartet burst into knee-slapping chuckles. "Ain't nothing but white folk magic," Isaac said with a smirk. "And weak magic at that. We see right through it like we did those Greek fellas come through here with that carnival last year, when they was supposed to make that narrow-ass olive woman be gone and she got caught in some trapdoor. She screamed so loud they had to send Isaac out yonder to get her out. Just phony all the way around."

Frank nervously watched the men chuckle, knowing most colored folks laughed because they'd been to the picture show and knew the white man can make anything seem real. Hollywood magic.

Isaac slapped him on his back, saying that he only believed what he saw with his naked eyes and nothing more. Frank laughed weakly, forcing down a spoonful of grits, his hand wavering. Not long ago he would have agreed with Isaac, but now everything seemed suspect. How could he explain that something had visited him overnight and taken two toes from each of his feet and left no wound? And the bizarre markings on his chest and thighs? Something was up in that blasted room with him and it wasn't something he conjured out of corn whiskey. Something unnatural, something unearthly. What was the answer to that riddle?

THE SPACE TRADERS

Derrick Bell

(1992)

1 *January.* The first surprise was not their arrival. The radio messages had begun weeks before, announcing that one thousand ships from a star far out in space would land on 1 January 2000, in harbors along the Atlantic coast from Cape Cod to North Carolina. Well before dawn on that day, millions of people across North America had wakened early to witness the moment the ships entered Earth's atmosphere. However expected, to the watchers, children of the electronic age, the spaceships' approach was as awesome as had been that earlier one of three small ships, one October over five hundred years before, to the Indians of the island of Santo Domingo in the Caribbean.[1]

No, the first surprise was the ships themselves. The people who lined the beaches of New Jersey where the first ships were scheduled to arrive, saw not anything NASA might have dreamed up, but huge vessels, the size of aircraft carriers, which the old men in the crowd recognized as being pretty much like the box-shaped landing craft that carried Allied troops to the Normandy beachheads during the Second World War.

As the sun rose on that cold bright morning, the people on the shore, including an anxious delegation of government officials and media reporters, witnessed a fantastic display of eerie lights and strange sound— evidently the visitors' salute to their American hosts. Almost unnoticed during the spectacle, the bow of the leading ship slowly lowered. A sizable party of the visitors—the first beings from outer space anyone on Earth had ever seen—emerged and began moving majestically across the water toward shore. The shock of seeing these beings, regal in appearance and bearing, literally walking on the waves was more thrilling than frightening. At least, no one panicked.

Then came the second surprise. The leaders of this vast armada could speak English. Moreover, they spoke in the familiar comforting tones of former President Reagan, having dubbed his recorded voice into a computerized language-translation system.

After the initial greetings, the leader of the U.S. delegation opened his mouth to read his welcoming speech—only the first of several speeches scheduled to be given on this historic occasion by the leaders of both political parties and other eminent citizens, including—of course—stars of the entertainment and sports worlds. But before he could begin, the principal spokesperson for the space people (and it wasn't possible to know whether it was a man or woman or something else entirely) raised a hand and spoke crisply, and to the point.

And this point constituted the third surprise. Those mammoth vessels carried within their holds treasure of which the United States was in most desperate need: gold, to bail out the almost bankrupt federal, state, and local governments; special chemicals capable of unpolluting the environment, which was becoming daily more toxic, and restoring it to the pristine state it had been before Western explorers set foot on it; and a totally safe nuclear engine and fuel, to relieve the nation's all-but-depleted supply of fossil fuel. In return, the visitors wanted only one thing—and that was to take back to their home star all the African Americans who lived in the United States.

The jaw of every one of the welcoming officials dropped, not a word of the many speeches they had prepared was suitable for the occasion. As the Americans stood in stupefied silence, the visitors' leader emphasized that the proposed trade was for the Americans freely to accept or not, that no force would be used. Neither then nor subsequently did the leader or any other of the visitors, whom anchorpersons on that evening's news shows immediately labeled the "Space Traders," reveal why they wanted only black people or what plans they had for them should the United States be prepared to part with that or any other group of its citizens. The leader only reiterated to his still-dumbfounded audience that, in exchange for the treasure they had brought, they wanted to take away every American citizen categorized as black on birth certificate or other official identification. The Space Traders said they would wait sixteen days for a response to their offer. That is, on 17 January—the day when in that year the birthday of Martin Luther King, Jr., was to be observed—they would depart carrying with them every black man, woman, and child in the nation and leave behind untold treasure. Otherwise, the Space Traders' leader shrugged and glanced around—at the oil slick in the water, at the dead gulls on the beach, at the thick shadow of smog that obscured the sky on all but the windiest days. Then the visitors walked back over the waves and returned to their ships.

Their departure galvanized everyone—the delegation, the watchers on the beach, the President glued to his television screen in the White House, citizens black and white throughout the country. The President, who had been advised to stay in the White House out of concern for his security, called Congress into special session and scheduled a cabinet meeting for the next morning. Governors reconvened any state legislatures not already in session. The phones of members of Congress began ringing, as soon as the millions of people viewing the Space Traders' offer on television saw them move back across the water, and never stopped till the morning of 17 January.

There was a definite split in the nature of the calls—a split that reflected distinctly different perceptions of the Space Traders. Most white people were, like the welcoming delegation that morning, relieved and pleased to find the visitors from outer space unthreatening. They were not human, obviously, but resembled the superhuman, good-guy characters in comic books; indeed, they seemed to be practical, no-nonsense folks like regular Americans.

On the other hand, many American blacks—whether watching from the shore or on their television screens—had seen the visitors as distinctly unpleasant, even menacing in appearance. While their perceptions of the visitors differed, black people all agreed that the Space Traders looked like bad news—and their trade offer certainly was—and burned up the phone lines urging black leaders to take action against it.

But whites, long conditioned to discounting any statements of blacks unconfirmed by other whites, chose now, of course, to follow their own perceptions. "Will the blacks never be free of their silly superstitions?" whites asked one another with condescending smiles. "Here, in this truly historic moment, when America has been selected as the site for this planet's first contact with people from another world, the blacks just revert to their primitive fear and foolishness." Thus, the blacks' outrage was discounted in this crisis; they had, as usual, no credibility.

And it *was* a time of crisis. Not only because of the Space Traders' offer per se, but because that offer came when the country was in dire straits. Decades of conservative, laissez-faire capitalism had emptied the coffers of all but a few of the very rich. The nation that had, in the quarter-century after the Second World War, funded the reconstruction of the free world had, in the next quarter-century, given itself over to greed and willful exploitation of its natural resources. Now it was struggling to survive like any third-world nation. Massive debt had curtailed all but the most necessary services. The environment was in shambles, as reflected by the fact that the sick and elderly had to wear special masks whenever they ventured out-of-doors. In addition, supplies of crude oil and coal were almost exhausted. The Space Traders' offer had come just in time to rescue America. Though few gave voice to their thoughts, many were thinking that the trade offer was, indeed, the ultimate solution to the nation's troubles.

2 January. The insomnia that kept the American people tossing and turning that first night of the new century did not spare the White House. As soon as the President heard the Space Traders' post-arrival proposition on television, his political instincts immediately locked into place. This was big! And it looked from the outset like a "no win" situation—not a happy crisis at the start of an election year. Even so, he had framed the outline of his plan by the time his cabinet members gathered at eight o'clock the next morning.

There were no blacks in his cabinet. Four years before, during his first election campaign, the President had made some vague promises of diversity when speaking to minority gatherings. But after the election, he thought, What the hell! Most blacks and Hispanics had not supported him or his party. Although he had followed the practice of keeping one black on the Supreme Court, it had not won him many minority votes. He owed them nothing. Furthermore, the few black figures in the party always seemed to him overly opportunistic and, to be frank, not very smart. But now, as the cabinet members arrived, he wished he had covered his bases better.

In the few hours since the Space Traders' offer, the White House and the Congress had been inundated with phone calls and telegrams. The President was not surprised that a clear majority spontaneously urged acceptance of the offer.

"Easy for them to say," he murmured to an aide. "I'll bet most of those who favor the trade didn't sign or give their names."

"On the contrary," the assistant replied, "the callers are identifying themselves, and the telegrams are signed."

At least a third of the flood of phone calls and faxes urging quick acceptance of the offer expressed the view that what the nation would give up—its African American citizens—was as worthwhile as what it would receive. The statements accurately reflected relations at the dawn of the new century. The President had, like his predecessors for the last generation, successfully exploited racial fears and hostility in his election campaign. There had been complaints, of course, but those from his political opponents sounded like sour grapes. They, too, had tried to minimize the input of blacks so as not to frighten away white voters.

The race problem had worsened greatly in the 1990s. A relatively small number of blacks had survived the retrogression of civil rights protection, perhaps 20 percent having managed to make good in the increasingly technologically oriented society. But, without anyone acknowledging it and with hardly a peep from the press, more than one half of the group had become outcasts. They were confined to former inner-city areas that had been divorced from their political boundaries. High walls surrounded these areas, and armed guards controlled entrance and exit around the clock. Still, despite all precautions, young blacks escaped from time to time to terrorize whites. Long dead was the dream that this black underclass would ever "overcome."

The President had asked Gleason Golightly, the conservative black economics professor, who was his unofficial black cabinet member, to attend the meeting. Golightly was smart and seemed to be truly conservative, not a man ready to sing any political tune for a price. His mere presence as a person of color at this crucial session would neutralize any possible critics in the media, though not in the black civil rights community.

The cabinet meeting came to order.

"I think we all know the situation," the President said. "Those extraterrestrial beings are carrying in their ships a guarantee that America will conquer its present problems and prosper for at least all of this new century."

"I would venture, sir," the Vice President noted, "that the balance of your term will be known as 'America's Golden Age.' Indeed, the era will almost certainly extend to the terms of your successor."

The President smiled at the remark, as—on cue—did the cabinet.

"The VP is right, of course," the President said. "Our visitors from outer space are offering us the chance to correct the excesses of several generations. Furthermore, many of the men and women—voters all—who are bombarding us with phone calls, see an added bonus in the Space Traders' offer." He looked around at his attentive cabinet members. "They are offering not only a solution to our nation's present problems but also one—surely an *ultimate* one—to what might be called the great American racial experiment. That's the real issue before us today. Does the promise of restored prosperity justify our sending away fifteen percent of our citizens to Lord knows what fate?"

"There are pluses and minuses to this 'fate' issue, Mr. President." Helen Hipmeyer, Secretary of Health and Human Services, usually remained silent at cabinet meetings. Her speaking up now caused eyebrows to rise around the table. "A large percentage of blacks rely on welfare and other social services. Their departure would ease substantially the burden on our state and national budgets. Why, the cost of caring for black AIDS victims alone has been extraordinary. On the other hand, the consternation and guilt among many whites if the blacks are sent away would take a severe psychological toll, with medical and other costs which might also reach astronomical levels. To gain the benefits we are discussing, without serious side effects, we must have more justification than I've heard thus far."

"Good point, Madame Secretary," the President answered, "but there are risks at every opportunity."

"I've never considered myself a particularly courageous individual, Mr. President." That was the Secretary of the Interior, a man small in stature but with a mind both sharp and devious, who had presided over the logging of the last of the old-growth timber in the nation's national forests. "But if I could guarantee prosperity for this great country by giving my life or going off with the Space Traders, I would do it without hesitation. And, if I would do it, I think every red-blooded American with an ounce of patriotism would as well." The Secretary sat down to the warm applause of his colleagues.

His suggestion kindled a thought in the Secretary of Defense. "Mr. President, the Secretary's courage is not unlike that American men and women have exhibited when called to military service. Some go more willingly than others, but almost all go even with the knowledge that they may not come back. It is a call a country makes on the assumption that its citizens will respond. I think that is the situation we have here, except that instead of just young men and women, the country needs all of its citizens of African descent to step forward and serve." More applause greeted this suggestion.

The Attorney General asked for and got the floor. "Mr. President, I think we could put together a legislative package modeled on the Selective Service Act of 1918. Courts have uniformly upheld this statute and its predecessors as being well within congressional power to exact enforced military duty at home or abroad by United States citizens.[2] While I don't see any constitutional problems, there would likely be quite a debate in Congress. But if the mail they are receiving is anything like ours, then the pressure for passage will be irresistible."

The President and the cabinet members heard reports from agents who had checked out samples of the gold, chemicals, and machinery the Space Traders had brought. More tests would run in the next few days, but first indications were that the gold was genuine, and that the antipollution chemicals and the nuclear fuel machine were safe and worked. Everyone recognized that the benefits of the country would be enormous. The ability to erase the country's debt alone would ease the economic chaos the Federal Reserve had staved off during the last few years only by its drastic—the opposition party called it "unscrupulous"—manipulation of the money supply. The Secretary of the Treasury confirmed that the Space Traders' gold would solve the nation's economic problems for decades to come.

"What are your thoughts on all this, Professor Golightly?" asked the President, nodding at the scholarly-looking black man sitting far down the table. The President realized that there would be a lot more opposition to a selective service plan among ordinary citizens than among the members of his cabinet, and hoped Golightly would have some ideas for getting around it.

Golightly began as though he understood the kind of answer the President wanted.

"As you know, Mr. President, I have supported this administration's policies that have led to the repeal of some civil rights laws, to invalidation of most affirmative action programs, and to severe reduction in appropriations for public assistance. To put it mildly, the positions of mine that have received a great deal of media attention, have not been well received in African American communities. Even so, I have been willing to be a 'good soldier' for the Party even though I am condemned as an Uncle Tom by my people. I sincerely believe that black people needed to stand up on their own feet, free of special protection provided by civil rights laws, the suffocating burden of welfare checks, and the stigmatizing influence of affirmative action programs. In helping you undermine these policies, I realized that your reasons for doing so differed from mine. And yet I went along."

Golightly stopped. He reached down for his coffee mug, took a few sips, and ran his fingers through his graying but relatively straight (what some black people call "good") hair. "Mr. President, my record of support entitles me to be heard on the Space Traders' proposition. I disagree strongly with both the Secretary of the Interior and the Attorney General. What they are proposing is not universal selective service for blacks. It is group banishment, a most severe penalty and one that the Attorney General would impose without benefit of either due process or judicial review.

"It is a mark of just how far out of the mainstream black people are that this proposition is given any serious consideration. Were the Space Traders attracted by and asking to trade any other group—white women with red hair and green eyes, for example—a horrified public would order the visitors off the planet without a moment's hesitation. The revulsion would not be less because the number of persons with those physical characteristics are surely fewer than the twenty million black citizens you are ready to condemn to intergalactic exile.

"Mr. President, I cannot be objective on this proposal. I will match my patriotism, including readiness to give my life for my country, with that of the Secretary of the Interior. But my duty stops short of condemning my wife, my three children, my grandchildren, and my aged mother to an unknown fate. You simply cannot condemn twenty million people because they are black, and thus fit fodder for trade, so that this country can pay its debts, protect its environment, and ensure its energy supply. I am not ready to recommend such a sacrifice. Moreover, I doubt whether the Secretary of the Interior would willingly offer up his family and friends if the Space Traders sought them instead of me and mine." He paused.

"Professor Golightly," the Secretary of the Interior said, leaning forward, "the President asked you a specific question. This is not the time to debate which of us is the more patriotic or to engage in the details of the sacrifice that is a necessary component of any service for one's country."

Golightly chose to ignore the interruption. He knew, and the President knew, that his support—or, at least, his silent acquiescence—would be critical in winning undecided whites over to the selective service scheme. For their purposes, the President's media people had made Golightly an important voice on racial policy issues. They needed him now as never before.

"Mr. President," he continued, "you and your cabinet must place this offer in historical perspective. This is far from the first time this country's leaders have considered and rejected the removal of all those here of African descent. Benjamin Franklin and other abolitionists actively sought schemes to free the slaves and return them to their homeland. Lincoln examined and supported emigration programs both before and after he freed the slaves. Even those Radical Republicans who drafted the Civil War amendments wondered whether Africans could ever become a part of the national scene, a part of the American people.

"As early as 1866, Michigan's Senator Jacob Merrit Howard, an abolitionist and key architect of the Fourteenth Amendment, recognized the nation's need to confront the challenge posed by the presence of the former slaves, and spoke out on it, saying:

"For weal or for woe, the destiny of the colored race in this country is wrapped up with our own; they are to remain in our midst, and here spend their years and here bury their fathers and finally repose themselves. We may regret it. It may not be entirely compatible with our taste that they should live in our midst. We cannot help it. Our forefathers introduced them, and their destiny is to continue among us; and the practical question which now presents itself to us is as to the best mode of getting along with them.[3]

"Now, Mr. President, after receiving your invitation to this meeting, I had no difficulty in guessing its agenda or predicting how many of you might come down in favor of accepting the Space Traders' offer, and so looked up Senator Howard's speech. I have prepared copies of it for each of you. I recommend you study it."

Golightly walked around the large table to give each cabinet member a copy of the speech. As he did so, he pointed out, "The Senator's words are grudging rather than generous, conciliatory rather than crusading. He proposed sanctuary rather than equality for blacks. And though there have been periods in which their striving for full equality seems to have brought them close to their goal, sanctuary remains the more accurate description of black citizenship."

Returning to his place, Golightly continued. "This status has provided this nation an essential stability, one you sacrifice at your peril. With all due respect, Mr. President, acceptance of the Space Traders' solution will not bring a century of prosperity to this country. Secretary Hipmeyer is correct. What today seems to you a solution from Heaven will instead herald a decade of shame and dissension mirroring the moral conflicts that precipitated this nation into its most bloody conflict, the Civil War. The deep, self-inflicted wounds of that era have never really healed. Their reopening will inevitably lead to confrontations and strife that could cause the eventual dissolution of the nation."

"You seem to assume, Professor Golightly," the Secretary of the Interior interrupted again, "that the Space Traders want African Americans for some heinous purpose. Why do you ignore alternative scenarios? They are obviously aware of your people's plight here. Perhaps they have selected them to inhabit an interplanetary version of the biblical land of milk and honey. Or, more seriously," the Secretary said, "they may offer your people a new start in a less competitive environment, or"—he added, with slight smirk in the President's direction—"perhaps they are going to give your people that training in skills and work discipline you're always urging on them."

No one actually laughed, but all except Golightly thought the Secretary's comment an excellent response to the black professor's gloomy predictions.

"I think we get your point, Professor," the President replied smoothly, concerned not to alienate a man whose support he would need. "We will give it weight in our considerations. Now," he said, rising, "we need to get to work on this thing. We don't have much time." He asked the Attorney General to draw up a rough draft of the proposed legislation by the end of the day, and told the rest of his cabinet that his aides would shortly be bringing them specific assignments. "Now let's all of us be sure to keep to ourselves what was said at this meeting"—and he glanced meaningfully at Professor Golightly. "Well, that's it for now, people. Meeting adjourned."

Long after the others had departed, Gleason Golightly sat at the long conference table. His hands were folded. He stared at the wall. He had always prided himself as the "man on the inside." While speaking in support of conservative policies, those were—he knew—policies that commanded enough support to be carried out. As a black man, his support legitimated those policies and salved the consciences of the whites who proposed and implemented them. A small price to pay, Golightly had always rationalized, for the many behind-the-scenes favors he received. The favors were not for himself. Golightly, a full professor at a small but well-endowed college, neither wanted nor needed what he called "blood money." Rather, he saw that black colleges got much-needed funding; and through his efforts, certain black officials received appointments or key promotions. He smiled wryly when some of these officials criticized his conservative positions and called him "Uncle Tom." He could bear that, knowing he made a contribution few others were able—or willing—to make to the racial cause.

Booker T. Washington was his hero and had been since he was a child growing up in a middle-class family in Alabama, not far from Tuskegee, the home of Tuskegee Institute, which Washington had founded in 1881. He had modeled his career on old Booker T., and while he did not have a following and had created no institutions, Golightly knew he had done more for black people than had a dozen of the loud-mouthed leaders who, he felt, talked much and produced little. But all of his life, he had dreamed of there coming a moment when his position as an insider would enable him to perform some heroic act to both save his people great grief and gain for him the recognition and the love for which, despite his frequent denials, he knew he yearned.

Now, as he sat alone, he feared that this morning's meeting was that big chance, and he had failed it. The stakes, of course, were larger than he would ever have imagined they might be, and yet he thought he'd had the arguments. In retrospect, though, those arguments were based on morality and assumed a willingness on the part of the President and the cabinet to be fair, or at least to balance the benefits of the Trade against the sacrifice it would require of a selected portion of the American people. Instead of outsmarting them, Golightly had done what he so frequently criticized civil rights spokespersons for doing: he had tried to get whites to do right by black people because it was right that they do so. "Crazy!" he commented when civil rights people did it. "Crazy!" he mumbled to himself, at himself.

"Oh, Golightly, glad you're still here. I want a word with you." Golightly looked up as the Secretary of the Interior, at his most unctuous, eased himself into the seat beside him.

"Listen, old man, sorry about our differences at the meeting. I understand your concerns."

Golightly did not look at the man and, indeed, kept his eyes on the wall throughout the conversation. "What do you want, Mr. Secretary?"

The Secretary ignored Golightly's coldness. "You could tell in the meeting and from the media reports that this Trade thing is big, very big. There will be debate—as there should be in a great, free country like ours. But if I were a betting man, which I am not because of my religious beliefs, I would wager that this offer will be approved."

"I assume, Mr. Secretary, that to further the best interests of this *great, free* country of ours, you will be praying that the Trade is approved." Golightly's voice deepened ironically on the crucial words.

The Secretary's smile faded, and his eyes narrowed. "The President wants you to say whatever you can in favor of this plan."

"Why don't we simply follow your suggestion, Mr. Secretary, and tell everyone that the Space Traders are going to take the blacks to a land of milk and honey?"

The Secretary's voice hardened. "I don't think even black people are that stupid. No, Gleason, talk about patriotism, about the readiness of black people to make sacrifices for this country, about how they are really worthy citizens no matter what some may think. We'll leave the wording to you. Isn't sacrifice as proof of patriotism what your Frederick Douglass argued to get President Lincoln to open up the Union army to black enlistees?"

"And then?" Golightly asked, his eyes never moving from the wall.

"We know some blacks will escape. I understand some are leaving the country already. But"—and the Secretary's voice was smooth as butter—"if you go along with the program, Gleason, and the Trade is approved, the President says he'll see to it that one hundred black families are smuggled out of the country. You decide who they are. They'll include you and yours, of course."

Golightly said nothing.

After a moment of hesitation, the Secretary got up and strode to the door. Before leaving, he turned and said, "Think about it, Golightly. It's the kind of deal we think you should go for."

3 January. The Anti-Trade Coalition—a gathering of black and liberal white politicians, civil rights representatives, and progressive academics—quickly assembled early that morning. Working nonstop and driven by anxiety to cooperate more than they ever had in the past, the members of the coalition had drafted a series of legal and political steps designed to organize opposition to the Space Traders' offer. Constitutional challenges to any acceptance scheme were high on the list of opposition strategies. Bills opposing the Trade were drafted for early introduction in Congress. There were plans for direct action protests and boycotts. Finally, in the event that worse came to worst, and the administration decided to carry out what gathering participants were calling the "African-American kidnapping plot," a secret committee was selected to draft and distribute plans for massive disobedience.

Now, at close to midnight, the plenary session was ready to give final approval to this broad program of resistance.

At that moment, Professor Gleason Golightly sought the floor to propose an alternative response to the Trade offer. Golightly's close connection to the conservative administrations and active support of its anti-black views made him far from a hero to most blacks. Many viewed his appearance at this critical hour as an administration-sponsored effort to undermine the coalition's defensive plans and tactics. At last, though, he prevailed on the conference leaders to grant him five minutes.

As he moved toward the podium, there was a wave of hostile murmuring whose justification Golightly acknowledged: "I am well aware that political and ideological differences have for several years sustained a wide chasm between us. But the events of two days ago have transformed our disputes into a painful reminder of our shared status. I am here because, whatever our ideological differences or our socioeconomic positions, we all know that black rights, black interests, black property, even black lives are expendable whenever their sacrifice will further or sustain white needs or preferences."

Hearing Golightly admitting to truths he had long denied, served to silence the murmuring. "It has become an unwritten tradition in this country for whites to sacrifice our rights to further their own interests. This tradition overshadows the national debate about the Space Traders' offer and may well foretell our reply to it."

Oblivious of the whites in the audience, Golightly said, "I realize that our liberal white friends continue to reassure us. 'This is America,' they tell us. 'It can't happen here.' But I've noticed that those whites who are most vigorous in their assurances are least able to rebut the contrary teaching of both historic fact and present reality. Outside civil rights gatherings like this, the masses of black people—those you claim to represent but to whom you seldom listen—are mostly resigned to the nation's acceptance of the Space Traders' offer. For them, liberal optimism is smothered by their life experience.

"Black people know for a fact what you, their leaders, fear to face. Black people know your plans for legislation, litigation, and protest cannot prevail against the tradition of sacrificing black rights. Indeed, your efforts will simply add a veneer of face-saving uncertainty to a debate whose outcome is not only predictable, but inevitable. Flying in the face of our history, you are still relying on the assumption that whites really want to grant justice to blacks, really want to alleviate onerous racial conditions."

"Professor Golightly," the chairman interrupted, "the time we have allotted you has almost expired. The delegates here are weary and anxious to return to their homes so that they can assist their families through this crisis. The defense plans we have formulated are our best effort. Sir, if you have a better way, let us hear it now."

Golightly nodded. "I promised to be brief, and I will. Although you have labored here unselfishly to devise a defense against what is surely the most dangerous threat to our survival since our forebears were kidnapped from Africa's shores, I think I have a better way, and I urge you to hear it objectively and without regard to our past differences. The question is how best to counter an offer that about a third of the voters would support even if the Space Traders offered America nothing at all. Another third may vacillate, but we both know that in the end they will simply not be able to pass up a good deal. The only way we can deflect, and perhaps reverse, a process that is virtually certain to result in approval of the Space Traders' offer, is to give up the oppositional stance you are about to adopt, and forthrightly urge the country to accept the Space Traders' offer."

He paused, looking out over the sea of faces. Then there was a clamor of outraged cries: "Sell-out!" "Traitor!" and "Ultimate Uncle Tom!" The chairman banged his gavel in an effort to restore order.

Seemingly unmoved by the outburst, Golightly waited until the audience quieted, then continued. "A major, perhaps the principal, motivation for racism in this country is the deeply held belief that black people should not have anything that white people don't have. Not only do whites insist on better jobs, higher incomes, better schools and neighborhoods, better everything, but they also usurp aspects of our culture. They have 'taken our blues and gone,' to quote Langston Hughes[4]—songs that sprang from our very subordination. Whites exploit not only our music but our dance, language patterns, dress, and hair styles as well. Even the badge of our inferior status, our color, is not sacrosanct, whites spending billions a year to emulate our skin tones, paradoxically, as a sign of their higher status. So whites' appropriation of what is ours and their general acquisitiveness are facts—facts we must make work for us. Rather than resisting the Space Traders' offer, let us circulate widely the rumor that the Space Traders, aware of our fruitless struggle on this planet, are arranging to transport us to a land of milk and honey—virtual paradise.

"Remember, most whites are so jealous of their race-based prerogatives that they oppose affirmative action even though many of these programs would remove barriers that exclude whites as well as blacks. Can we not expect such whites—notwithstanding even the impressive benefits offered by the Space Traders—to go all out to prevent blacks from gaining access to an extraterrestrial New Jerusalem? Although you are planning to litigate against the Trade on the grounds that it is illegal discrimination to limit to black people, mark my words, our 'milk and honey' story will inspire whites to institute such litigation on the grounds that limiting the Space Traders' offer to black people is unconstitutional discrimination against whites!

"Many of you have charged that I have become expert at manipulating white people for personal gain. Although profit has not in fact motivated my actions, I certainly have learned to understand how whites think on racial issues. On that knowledge, I am willing to wage my survival and that of my family. I urge you to do the same. This strategy is, however risky, our only hope."

The murmurs had subsided into stony silence by the time Golightly left the podium.

"Does anyone care to respond to Profesor Golightly's suggestion?" the chairman finally asked.

Justin Jasper, a well-known and highly respected Baptist minister, came to the microphone. "I readily concede Dr. Golightly's expertise in the psychology of whites' thinking. Furthermore, as he requests, I hold in abeyance my deep distrust of a black man whose willing service to whites has led him to become a master minstrel of political mimicry. But my problem with his plan is twofold. First, it rings hollow because it so resembles Dr. Golightly's consistent opposition in the past to all our civil rights initiatives. Once again, he is urging us to accept rather than oppose a racist policy. And, not only are we not to resist, but we are to beg the country to lead us to the sacrificial altar. God may have the power, but Dr. Golightly is not my God!"

The Reverend Jasper was a master orator, and he quickly had his audience with him. "Second, because the proposal lacks truth, it insults my soul. In the forty years I have worked for civil rights, I have lost more battles than I have won, but I have never lost my integrity. Telling the truth about racism has put me in prison and many of my co-workers into early graves.

"The truth is, Dr. Golightly, that what this country is ready to do to us is wrong! It is evil! It is an action so heinous as to give the word *betrayal* a bad name. I can speak only for myself, but even if I were certain that my family and I could escape the threat we now face by lying about our likely fate—and, Dr. Golightly, that is what you're asking us to do— I do not choose to save myself by a tactic that may preserve my body at the sacrifice of my soul. The fact is, Dr. Golightly, until my Lord calls me home, I do not want to leave this country even for a land of milk and honey. My people were brought here involuntarily, and that is the only way they're going to get me out!"

The Reverend Jasper received a standing ovation. Many were crying openly as they applauded. After thanking them, the minister asked everyone to join in singing the old nineteenth-century hymn "Amazing Grace," which, he reminded them, had been written by an English minister, one John Newton, who as a young man and before finding God's grace, had been captain of a slave ship. It was with special fervor that they sang the verse:

> Through many dangers, toils and snares,
> I have already come.
> 'Twas grace that brought me safe this far,
> And grace will lead me home.[5]

With the hymn's melody still resonating, the coalition's members voted unanimously to approve their defensive package. The meeting was quickly adjourned. Leaving the hall, everyone agreed that they had done all that could be done to oppose approval of the Space Traders' offer. As for Golightly, his proposal was dismissed as coming from a person who, in their view, had so often sold out black interests. "He's a sad case. Even with this crisis, he's just doing what he's always done."

Again, as after the President's cabinet meeting, Golightly sat for a long time alone. He did not really mind that none of the delegates had spoken to him before leaving. But he was crushed by his failure to get them to recognize what he had long known: that without power, a people must use cunning and guile. Or were cunning and guile, based on superior understanding of a situation, themselves power? Certainly, most black people knew and used this art to survive in their everyday contacts with white people. It was only civil rights professionals who confused integrity with foolhardiness.

"Faith in God is fine," Golightly muttered to himself. "But God expects us to use the common sense He gave us to get out of life-threatening situations."

Still, castigation of black leadership could not alter the fact. Golightly had failed, and he knew it. Sure, he was smarter than they were—smarter than even most whites; but he had finally outsmarted himself. At the crucial moment, when he most needed to help his people, both whites and blacks had rejected as untrustworthy both himself and his plans.

4 January. In a nationally televised address, the President sought to reassure both Trade supporters that he was responding favorably to their strong messages, and blacks and whites opposed to the Trade that he would not ignore their views. After the usual patriotic verbiage, the

President said that just-completed, end-of-the-century economic reports revealed the nation to be in much worse shape than anyone had imagined. He summarized what he called the "very grim figures," and added that only massive new resources would save America from having to declare bankruptcy.

"On the face of it, our visitors from outer space have initiated their relationship with our country in a most unusual way. They are a foreign power and as such entitled to the respect this nation has always granted to the family of nations on Earth; it is not appropriate for us to prejudge this extraplanetary nation's offer. Thus, it is now receiving careful study and review by this administration.

"Of course, I am aware of the sacrifice that some of our most highly regarded citizens would be asked to make in the proposed trade. While these citizens are of only one racial group, there is absolutely no evidence whatsoever to indicate that the selection was intended to discriminate against any race or religion or ethnic background.

"No decisions have been made, and all options are under review. This much seems clear: the materials the Traders have offered us are genuine and perform as promised. Early estimates indicate that, if these materials were made available to this nation, they would solve our economic crisis, and we could look forward to a century of unparalleled prosperity. Whether the Trade would allow a tax-free year for every American, as some of our citizens have hoped, is not certain. But I can promise that if the Trade is approved, I will exercise my best efforts to make such a trade dividend a reality."

Early that morning, the leaders of Fortune-500 businesses, heads of banks, insurance companies, and similar entities boarded their well-appointed corporate jets and flew to a remote Wyoming hunting lodge. They understood the President supported the Trade, despite his avowals that no decision had been made. They had come to discuss the Trade offer's implications for big business.

5 January. Not content with just closing the doors on their meetings as the Anti-Trade Coalition had, the corporate leaders of America gathered for an absolutely hush-hush meeting. They were joined by the Vice President and some of the wealthier members of Congress. The surroundings were beautiful, but the gathering of white males was somber. Corporate America faced a dilemma of its own making.

Media polls as well as ones privately funded by businesses all reported tremendous public support for the Trade—unhappy but hardly unexpected news for the nation's richest and most powerful men. First, blacks represented 12 percent of the market and generally consumed much more of their income than did their white counterparts. No one wanted to send that portion of the market into outer space—not even for the social and practical benefits offered by the Space Traders.

Even those benefits were a mixed blessing. Coal and oil companies, expecting to raise their prices as supplies steadily decreased, were not elated at the prospect of an inexhaustible energy source; it could quickly put them out of business. Similarly, businesses whose profits were based on sales in black ghetto communities—or who supplied law enforcement agencies, prisons, and other such institutions—faced substantial losses in sales. The real estate industry, for example, annually reaped uncounted millions in commissions on sales and rentals, inflated by the understanding that blacks would not be allowed to purchase or rent in an area. Even these concerns were overshadowed by fears of what the huge influx of gold to pay all state debts would do to the economy or to the value of either the current money supply or gold.

Though seldom acknowledging the fact, most business leaders understood that blacks were crucial in stabilizing the economy with its ever-increasing disparity between the incomes of rich and poor. They recognized that potentially turbulent unrest among those on the bottom was deflected by the continuing efforts of poorer whites to ensure that they, as least, remained ahead of blacks. If blacks were removed from the society, working- and middle-class whites—deprived of their racial distraction—might look upward toward the top of the societal well and realize that they as well as the blacks below them suffered because of the gross disparities in opportunities and income.

Many of these corporate leaders and their elected representatives had for years exploited poor whites' ignorance of their real enemy. Now, what had been a comforting insulation of their privileges and wealth, posed a serious barrier to what a majority saw as a first priority: to persuade the country to reject the Trade. A quick survey of the media and advertising representatives present was not encouraging. "It would be quite a challenge," one network executive said, "but we simply can't change this country's view about the superiority of whites and the inferiority of blacks in a week. I doubt you could do it in a decade."

Even so, the corporate leaders decided to try. They planned to launch immediately a major media campaign—television, radio, and the press—to exploit both the integration achieved in America and the moral cost of its loss. White members of professional and college sports teams would urge rejection of the Trade "so as to keep the team together." Whites in integrated businesses, schools, churches, and neighborhoods would broadcast similar messages. The business leaders even committed large sums to facilitate campaigning by pro-choice women's groups who were strongly anti-Trade. In a particularly poignant series of ads, white spouses in interracial marriages would point out that the Trade would destroy their families, and beg the public not to support it.

Newspaper and magazine publishers promised supportive editorials, but the Vice President and other government representatives argued that the immediate political gains from accepting the Trade would translate into business benefits as well.

"With all due respect, Mr. Vice President," he was told, "that argument shows why you are in politics and we are in business. It also shows that you are not listening very closely to those of us whose campaign contributions put you in office."

"We need your financial support," the Vice President admitted, "but our polls show most white voters favor the Trade, and the administration is under increasing pressure to do the same. And, as you know, pro-Trade advocates are promising that with all government debts paid, every American would get a year without any taxes. Believe it or not, some liberal environmentalists are thinking of giving their support to the Trade as the lesser of two evils. Of course, the prospect of heating and air-conditioning homes without paying through the nose is very appealing, even to those who don't care a hoot about the environment."

"However enticing such benefits of the Trade may be," interjected a government census official, "the real attraction for a great many whites is that it would remove black people from this society. Since the first of the year, my staff and I have interviewed literally thousands of citizens across the country, and, though they don't say it directly, it's clear that at bottom they simply think this will be a better country without black people. I fear, gentlemen, that those of us who have been perpetuating this belief over the years have done a better job than we knew."

"I must add what you probably already know," the Vice President broke in, "that the administration is leaning toward acceptance of the

Space Traders' offer. Now, if you fellows line up against the Trade, it could make a difference—but, in that case, the President may opt to build on the phony populist image you provided him in his first election campaign. He knows that the working- and middle-class white people in this country want the blacks to go, and if they get a chance to express their real views in the privacy of a polling place, the Trade plan will pass overwhelmingly."

"Bullshit!" roared a billionaire who had made his fortune in construction. "I'm sick of this defeatist talk! We need to get off our dead asses and get to work on this thing. Everyone says that money talks. Well dammit, let's get out there and spend some money. If this thing goes to a public referendum, we can buy whatever and whoever is necessary. It sure as hell will not be the first time," he wound up, pounding both fists on the long conference table, "and likely not the last!"

The remainder of the meeting was more upbeat. Pointedly telling the Vice President that he and the administration were caught in the middle and would have to decide whose support they most wanted in the future, the business leaders began making specific plans to suspend all regular broadcasting and, through 16 January, to air nothing but anti-Trade ads and special Trade programs. They flew out that night, their confidence restored. They controlled the media. They had become rich and successful "playing hard ball." However competitive with one another, they had, as usual, united to confront this new challenge to their hegemony. It was, as usual, inconceivable that they could fail.

6 *January*. Although the Television Evangelists of America also owned jets, they understood that their power lay less in these perks of the wealthy than in their own ability to manipulate their TV congregations' religious feelings. So, after a lengthy conference call, they announced a massive evangelical rally in the Houston Astrodome which would be televised over their religious cable network. They went all out. The Trade offer was the evangelists' chance to rebuild their prestige and fortunes, neither of which had recovered from the Jim and Tammy Bakker and the Jimmy Swaggart scandals. They would achieve this much-desired goal by playing on, rather than trying to change, the strongly racist views of their mostly working-class television audiences. True, some of the preachers had a substantial black following, but evan-

gelical support for the Trade would not be the evangelists' decision. Rather, these media messiahs heralded it as God's will.

The Space Traders were, according to the televised "Gospel," bringing America blessings earned by their listeners' and viewers' faithful dedication to freedom, liberty, and God's word. Not only would rejection of these blessings from space be wrong, so the preachers exhorted; it would be blasphemous. It was God's will that all Americans enjoy a tax-free year, a cleaned-up environment for years to come, and cheap heating forever. True, a sacrifice was required if they were to obtain God's bounty—a painful sacrifice. But here, too, God was testing Americans, his chosen people, to ensure that they were worthy of His bounty, deserving of His love. Each preacher drew on Scripture, tortuously interpreted, to support these statements.

A "ministry of music" quartet—four of the most popular television evangelists, all speaking in careful cadences like a white rap group— preached the major sermon. It whipped the crowd into a delirium of religious feeling, making them receptive both to the financial appeals, which raised millions, and to the rally's grande finale: a somber tableau of black people marching stoically into the Space Traders' ships, which here resembled ancient sacrificial altars. Try as they might, the producers of the pageant had had a hard time finding black people willing to act out roles they might soon be forced to experience, but a few blacks were glad to be paid handsomely for walking silently across the stage. These few were easily supplemented by the many whites eager to daub on "black face."

The rally was a great success despite the all-out efforts of the media to condemn this "sacrilege of all that is truly holy." That night, millions of messages, all urging acceptance of the Space Traders' offer, deluged the President and Congress.

7 January. Groups supporting the Space Traders' proposition had from the beginning taken seriously blacks' charges that acceptance of it would violate the Constitution's most basic protections. Acting swiftly, and with the full cooperation of the states, they had set in motion the steps necessary to convene a constitutional convention in Philadelphia. ("Of course!" groaned Golightly when he heard of it.) And there, on this day, on the site of the original constitutional convention, delegates chosen, in accordance with Article V of the Constitution, by the state legislatures, quickly drafted, and by a substantial majority passed, the Twenty-seventh Amendment to the Constitution of the United States. It declared:

> Without regard to the language or interpretations previously given any other provision of this document, every United States citizen is subject at the call of Congress to selection for special service for periods necessary to protect domestic interests and international needs.

The amendment was scheduled for ratification by the states on 15 January in a national referendum. If ratified, the amendment would validate amendments to existing Selective Service laws authorizing the induction of all blacks into special service for transportation under the terms of the Space Traders' offer.

8 January. Led by Rabbi Abraham Specter, a group of Jewish church and organizational leaders sponsored a mammoth anti-Trade rally in New York's Madison Square Garden. "We simply cannot stand by and allow America's version of the Final Solution to its race problem to be carried out without our strong protest and committed opposition." Thirty-five thousand Jews signed pledges to disrupt by all possible nonviolent means both the referendum and—if the amendment was ratified—the selection of blacks for "special service."

"Already," Rabbi Specter announced, "a secret Anne Frank Committee has formed, and its hundreds of members have begun to locate hiding places in out-of-the-way sites across this great country. Blacks by the thousands can be hidden for years if necessary until the nation returns to its senses.

"We vow this action because we recognize the fateful parallel between the plight of the blacks in this country and the situation of the Jews in Nazi Germany. Holocaust scholars agree that the Final Solution in Germany would not have been possible without the pervasive presence and the uninterrupted tradition of anti-Semitism in Germany. We must not let the Space Traders be the final solution for blacks in America."

A concern of many Jews not contained in their official condemnations of the Trade offer, was that, in the absence of blacks, Jews could become the scapegoats for a system so reliant on an identifiable group on whose heads less-well-off whites can discharge their hate and frustrations for societal disabilities about which they are unwilling to confront their leaders. Given the German experience, few Jews argued that "it couldn't happen here."[6]

9 January. Responding almost immediately to the Jewish anti-Trade rally, the Attorney General expressed his "grave concern" that what he felt certain was but a small group of Jews would, by acting in flagrant violation of the law of the land, besmirch the good names of all patriotic American Jews. For this reason, he said, he was releasing for publication the secret list, obtained by undercover FBI agents, of all those who had joined the Anne Frank Committee. He stated that the release was needed so that all Americans could easily distinguish this group from the majority of patriotic and law-abiding Jewish citizens.

Retaliation was quick. Within hours, men and women listed as belonging to the committee lost their jobs; their contracts were canceled; their mortgages foreclosed; and harassment of them, including physical violence, escalated into a nationwide resurgence of anti-Semitic feeling. Groups on the far right, who were exploiting the growing support for the Trade, urged: "Send the blacks into space. Send the Jews into Hell." The Jews who opposed the Trade were intimidated into silence and inaction. The leaders of Rabbi Specter's group were themselves forced into hiding, leaving few able to provide any haven for blacks.

10 January. In the brief but intense pre-election day campaign, the pro-ratification groups' major argument had an appeal that surprised even those who made it. Their message was straightforward:

> The Framers intended America to be a white country. The evidence of their intentions is present in the original Constitution. After more than a hundred and thirty-seven years of good-faith efforts to build a healthy, stable interracial nation, we have concluded—as the Framers did in the beginning—that our survival today requires that we sacrifice the rights of blacks in order to protect and further the interests of whites. The Framers' example must be our guide. Patriotism, and not pity, must govern our decision. We should ratify the amendment and accept the Space Traders' proposition.

In response, a coalition of liberal opponents to the Space Traders' offer sought to combine pragmatism and principle in what they called their "slippery Trade slope" argument. First, they proclaimed the strong moral position that trading away a group of Americans identifiable by race is wrong and violates our basic principles. The coalition aimed its major thrust, however, at the self-interest of white Americans: "Does not consigning blacks to an unknown fate set a dangerous precedent?" the liberals demanded. "Who will be next?"

In full-page ads, they pressed the point: "Are we cannibals ready to consume our own for profit? And if we are, the blacks may be only the first. If the Space Traders return with an irresistible offer for another group, the precedent will have been set, and none of us will be safe. Certainly not the minorities—Hispanics, Jews, Asians—and perhaps not even those of us identifiable by politics or religion or geographic location. Setting such a precedent of profit could consume us all."

Astutely sidestepping the Trade precedent arguments, the pro-Trade response focused on the past sacrifices of blacks. "In each instance," it went, "the sacrifice of black rights was absolutely necessary to accomplish an important government purpose. These decisions were neither arbitrary nor capricious. Without the compromises on slavery in the Constitution of 1787, there would be no America. Nor would there be any framework under which those opposed to slavery could continue the struggle that eventually led to the Civil War and emancipation.

"And where and how might slavery have ended had a new government not been formed? On what foundation would the post–Civil War amendments been appended? Sacrifices by blacks were made, but those sacrifices were both necessary and eventually rewarding to blacks as well as the nation."

In countering the anti-Trade contention that the sacrifice of black rights was both evil and unprecedented, pro-Traders claimed, "Beginning with the Civil War in which black people gained their liberty, this nation has called on its people to serve in its defense. Many men and women have voluntarily enlisted in the armed services, but literally millions of men have been conscripted, required to serve their country, and, if necessary, to sacrifice not simply their rights but also their lives."

As for the argument that the sacrifice of black rights in political compromises was odious racial discrimination, pro-Trade forces contended that "fortuitous fate and not blatant racism" should be held responsible.

Just as men and not women are inducted into the military, and even then only men of a certain age and physical and mental condition, so only some groups are destined by their role in the nation's history to serve as catalyst for stability and progress.

"All Americans are expected to make sacrifices for the good of their country. Black people are no exceptions to this basic obligation of citizenship. Their role may be special, but so is that of many of those who serve. The role that blacks may be called on to play in response to the Space Traders' offer is, however regrettable, neither immoral nor unconstitutional."

A tremendous groundswell of public agreement with the pro-Trade position drowned out anti-Trade complaints of unfairness. Powerful as would have been the notion of seeing the Space Traders' offer as no more than a fortuitous circumstance, in which blacks might be called on to sacrifice for their country, the "racial sacrifice as historic necessity" argument made the pro-Trade position irresistible to millions of voters—and to their Congressional representatives.

11 January. Unconfirmed media reports asserted that U.S. officials tried in secret negotiations to get the Space Traders to take in trade only those blacks currently under the jurisdiction of the criminal justice system—that is, in prison or on parole or probation. Government negotiators noted that this would include almost one half of the black males in the twenty- to twenty-nine-year-old age bracket.* Negotiators were also reported to have offered to trade only blacks locked in the inner cities. But the Space Traders stated that they had no intention of turning their far-off homeland into an American prison colony for blacks. In rejecting the American offer, the Space Traders warned that they would withdraw their proposition unless the United States halted the flight of the growing numbers of middle-class blacks who—fearing the worst—were fleeing the country.

In response, executive orders were issued and implemented, barring blacks from leaving the country until the Space Traders' proposition was fully debated and resolved. "It is your patriotic duty," blacks were told by

---

*In 1990, the figure was 24 percent, according to Justice Department data contained in a study funded by the Rand Corporation.[7] The National Center on Institutions and Alternatives reported that 42 percent of the black men in the District of Columbia, aged eighteen through thirty-five, were enmeshed in the criminal justice system on any given day in 1991.[8]

the White House, "to allow this great issue to be resolved through the democratic process and in accordance with the rule of law." To ensure that the Trade debate and referendum were concluded in a "noncoercive environment," all blacks serving in the military were placed on furlough and relieved of their weapons. State officials took similar action with respect to blacks on active duty in state and local police forces.

12 January. The Supreme Court, citing precedent dating back to 1849, rejected a number of appeals by blacks and their white supporters whose legal challenges to every aspect of the referendum process had been dismissed by lower courts as "political questions" best resolved by the body politic rather than through judicial review.[9]

The Supreme Court's order refusing to intervene in the Space Trader proposition was unanimous. The order was brief and *per curiam*, the Court agreeing that the Space Trader litigation lacked judicially discoverable and manageable standards for resolving the issues.[10] The Court also noted that, if inducted in accordance with a constitutionally approved conscription provision, blacks would have no issues of individual rights for review. Even if the Court were to conclude that rights under the Fourteenth Amendment were deserving of greater weight than the authority of the new constitutional amendment up for ratification, the standards of national necessity that prompted the Court to approve the confinement of Japanese Americans during the Second World War,[11] would serve as sufficient precedent for the induction and transfer of African Americans to the Space Traders.

While not claiming to give weight to the public opinion polls reporting strong support for the Trade, the Court noted that almost a century earlier, in 1903, Justice Oliver Wendell Holmes had denied injunctive relief to six thousand blacks who petitioned the Court to protect their right to vote.[12] The bill alleged that the great mass of the white population intended to keep the blacks from voting; but, in view of such massive opposition, Holmes reasoned that ordering the blacks' names to be placed on the voting list would be "an empty form" unless the Court also mandated electoral supervision by "officers of the court."*

*Justice Holmes wrote: "Unless we are prepared to supervise the voting in that state by officers of the court, it seems to us that all the plaintiff could get from equity would be an empty form. Apart from damages to the individual, relief from a great political wrong, if done, as alleged, by the people of a state itself, must be given by them or by the legislature and political department of the Government of the United States."[13]

14 January. With the legal questions of the Trade the U.S. government announced that as a result of negotiations with the Space Trader leaders, the latter had agreed to amend their offer and exclude from the Trade all black people seventy years old, and older, and all those blacks who were seriously handicapped, ill, and injured. In addition, a thousand otherwise-eligible blacks and their immediate families would be left behind as trustees of black property and possessions, all of which would be stored or held in escrow in case blacks were returned to this country. Each of the thousand black "detainees" was required to pledge to accept a subordinate status with "suspended citizenship" until such time as the "special service inductees" were returned to the country. The administration selected blacks to remain who had records of loyalty to the conservative party and no recorded instances of militant activity. Even so, many of those blacks selected declined to remain. "We will, like the others," said one black who rejected detainee status, "take our chances with the referendum."

15 January. Many whites had, to their credit, been working day and night to defeat the amendment; but, as is the usual fate of minority rights when subjected to referenda or initiatives,[14] the outcome was never really in doubt. The final vote rally confirmed the predictions. By 70 percent to 30 percent, American citizens voted to ratify the constitutional amendment that provided a legal basis for acceptance of the Space Traders' offer. In anticipation of this result, government agencies had secretly made preparations to facilitate the transfer. Some blacks escaped, and many thousands lost their lives in futile efforts to resist the joint federal and state police teams responsible for rounding up, cataloguing, and transporting blacks to the coast.

16 January. Professor Golightly and his family were not granted detainee status. Instead, the White House promised safe passage to Canada for all his past services even though he had not made the patriotic appeal the President had requested of him. But, at the border that evening, he was stopped and turned back. It turned out the Secretary of the Interior had called to countermand his departure. Golightly was not surprised. What really distressed him was his failure to convince the black leaders of the anti-Trade coalition to heed their own rhetoric: namely that whites in power would, given the chance, do to privileged blacks what, in fact, they had done to all blacks.

"I wonder," he murmured, half to himself, half to his wife, as they rode in a luxury limousine sent, in some irony, by the Secretary of the Interior to convey them to the nearest roundup point, "how my high-minded brothers at the conference feel now about their decision to fail with integrity rather than stoop to the bit of trickery that might have saved them."

"But, Gleason," his wife asked, "would our lives have really been better had we fooled the country into voting against the Trade? If the Space Traders were to depart, carrying away with them what they and everyone else says can solve our major domestic problems, wouldn't people increasingly blame us blacks for increases in debt, pollution, and fuel shortages? We might have saved ourselves—but only to face here a fate as dire as any we face in space."

"I hope your stoic outlook helps us through whatever lies ahead," Golightly responded as the car stopped. Then guards hustled him and his family toward the buses being loaded with other blacks captured at the Canadian border.

17 January. The last Martin Luther King holiday the nation would ever observe dawned on an extraordinary sight. In the night, the Space Traders had drawn their strange ships right up to the beaches and discharged their cargoes of gold, minerals, and machinery, leaving vast empty holds. Crowded on the beaches were the inductees, some twenty million silent black men, women, and children, including babes in arms. As the sun rose, the Space Traders directed them, first, to strip off all but a single undergarment; then, to line up; and finally, to enter those holds which yawned in the morning light like Milton's "darkness visible." The inductees looked fearfully behind them. But, on the dunes above the beaches, guns at the ready, stood U.S. guards. There was no escape, no alternative. Heads bowed, arms now linked by slender chains, black people left the New World as their forebears had arrived.

Notes

1. See John Yewell, Chris Dodge, and Jan Desirey, eds., *Confronting Columbus: An Anthology* (1992).
2. Military Selective Service Act, 50 USCS Appx § 451, et seq. See, for example, *Selective Draft Law Cases*, 245 U.S. 366 (1918).
3. L. Levy, K. Karst, and D. Mahoney, eds., *Encyclopedia of the American Constitution*, II (1986), 761.
4. Langston Hughes, "Note on Commercial Theatre," in *Selected Poems of Langston Hughes* (1990), 190.
5. John Newton, "Amazing Grace," in *Songs of Zion* (1981), 211.
6. Lucy S. Dawidowicz, *The Holocaust and the Historians* (1981); Lucy S. Dawidowicz, ed., *A Holocaust Reader* (1976); Asher Cohen, Joav Gelbar, and Chad Ward, eds., *Comprehending the Holocaust: Historical and Literary Research* (1988); Judith Miller, *One, By One, By One: Facing the Holocaust* (1988); Yehuda Bauer, *The Holocaust* (1978).
7. David Savage, "1 in 4 Young Blacks in Jail or in Court Control, Study Says," *Los Angeles Times*, 27 February 1990, sec. A, p. 1, col. 1.
8. Jason DeParle, "42% of Young Black Men Are in Capital's Court System," *New York Times*, 18 April 1992, sec. A, p. 1, col 1.
9. *Luther v. Borden*, 48 U.S. (7 How.) 1 (1849) (Court refused to determine which was the legitimate government of Rhode Island).
10. See *Baker v. Carr*, 369 U.S. 186 (1962) (exploring the "political question" doctrine in definitive fashion).
11. *Korematsu v. United States*, 323 U.S. 214 (1944) (sustaining a military order under which Americans of Japanese origin were removed from designated West Coast areas). See also *Hrabayashi v. United States*, 320 U.S. 81 (1943) (upholding a military curfew imposed on persons of Japanese ancestry in the West Coast during the early months of the Second World War).
12. *Giles v. Harris*, 189 U.S. 475 (1903).
13. Ibid., 488.
14. See Derrick Bell, "The Referendum: Democracy's Barrier to Racial Equality," *Washington Law Review* 54 (1978):1.

The Pretended

Darryl A. Smith

(2000)

They'd embalmed the trains with the condemned and the pretended.

The naked, shuffling brown slush of bodies and momentum had been drawn as if through suction and the further benefaction of pumping into the suckled boxcars whose nooks had been tickled the night prior by whispers of early snow.

But the day had come to graze on light. The sky was so clear and pale that the moon had needed to climb high through the banishing twilight in order to distinguish its grin against sufficient blue.

Curiously, the boxcars hadn't seemed to fill at first. Not even a little bit. The slush seemed but a vast, obedient pupilage of shadows matriculating into nothingness.

But it was real. They were real. And that was what had made the spectacle so peculiar.

Blue Wobble Station stretched out its tendril tracks from a mass of coordination that had been gaining meticulously on its own obsolescence.

The slush had gone graciously to where the fingers had graciously pointed.

Questions had not only been polite, but had been informed by and referenced from an etiquette which would have been entirely too cumbersome for any more domestic occasion.

And these urbane questions had met responses just as magnanimous and patient: from which car assignment ("Corporator No.1-1-7"), to the journey's duration ("one of a span in maximal conformity with The Schedule"), to how, for instance—by applying some minimally obtrusive fiction—a mother might have gone about saying good-bye forever to her daughter, et cetera.

And why shouldn't it have gone well? Everyone knew the reasons. And for quite some time now. The humans knew and the robots knew. All that was left to do now was to end an intermission of artless wavering which by this point had become unconscionable and grossly protracted.

She preferred "Mnemosyne."

Even "Mnappy Mnemo"—as Diva Eve called her—was acceptable.

But "9-MOZ-9" reminded her of boy games and other "dumb stuff" like the persistently annoying and petty little datum that she was not a real little girl. And although Mnemosyne's ambivalence subroutine was designed to know and manifest such things only at a semiconscious level, her possession of the name of that Greek goddess—luminous, preternaturally fleshed, and the mystic cocreator *of* her cocreators—made the heady little android given to those sudden bursts of confidence and bravado such as can only come from a deeper sense of inferiority.

Call her 9-MOZ-9, and like a hedgehog Mnemosyne would shrink away from you and ball herself up into hurt recollection: instantly deflate and withdraw from whatever conversation she was in, no matter how animated she had been during the course of it. With only her big brown eyes for language, slipping off of you like a silk robe fainting from a body, Mnemosyne would appeal to you to correct yourself—and quickly.

And when you did, or even if you had to be corrected by her or someone else in the know overhearing, the artificial girl—like most seven-year-old girls—forgave you, forgave your forgetting, and forgave *by* forgetting the trespass herself, all as swiftly as her heart had sustained the injury. Then, and perfectly, she would return with you to giggling and the more serious business of play.

But Mnemosyne couldn't play now—not even with Diva Eve.

In the boxcar, her unblinking, sparrow-sable eyes probed and shone beyond their casual profile. Fulgent even in repose, they were far more so now as they catalyzed every detail of the scene around her. She had long since stopped giving thought to nakedness, though, either to her own or to that of the others. Mnemosyne's weedy arms hung down around her baroque-sloped tummy in much the same way as her pigtails had dangled about her face before beginning to stiffen up and stand out from her head. It was her mother who'd used what warning she'd had to tie to Mnemosyne's pigtails as many bright ribbons as she could find and plead permission for. It was Diva Eve who had solemnly advised her, therefore, not to remove and not to lose them.

Inside it was hot and overcrowded. Robots of all ages were crammed in from floor to roof, practically; the glistening deep blacknesses of their polyderm making darkness itself seem to crowd the car all the more. In one corner a group of very old robots huddled together, swaying and humming a song Mnemosyne had often heard in church. Considerately, though, they had all tried to provide each other with a modicum of personal space. Diva Eve had had, of course, to share the bit allotted to Mnemosyne, and that had left only enough room for the two of them to sit down, facing one another closely with legs akimbo, and talk.

"Where's it at?" whispered Dive Eve.

"I got it," replied Mnemosyne, clearly annoyed.

"Gimme it."

"I *got* it, I said."

"Aw, you aint even right," Diva Eve said, scandalized. "I seen you windin it up las night when we got on."

"I aint do nothin. Jes winded it, that's all. Maybe I jes wanna hear sumthin," Mnemosyne parried.

"You aint jes wanna hear sumthin," countered Diva Eve. "You aint gotta wind it jes to hear 'sumthin,' less it's *lullaby* sumthin."

Mnemosyne's lower lip protruded under her bowed head. Some of her vivid ribbons fluttered beneath it like blown butterflies. With one hand, her fingers caressed the pretty little machine with the chubby cornflower light at its center—given to every robot upon activation—which she held in the other as if it were delicate. She sighed.

"Mama said it's the most inside, the most see-through song," Mnemosyne finally mumbled.

Diva Eve's fight collapsed. Mnemosyne imagined her friend gazing at her with human eyes, blinking under baritone-dark lids and black eyelashes in that flaming scarlet red dress of hers, all sweet sympathy. Then Diva Eve's head dropped, too.

"She right. It is the most inside, see-through song," repeated Diva Eve tenderly. "But we still gotta leave it be."

*   *   *

Mnemosyne didn't mind the number name all the time, though. Twice every year, the Fursts, an older human couple whose daughter was a playmate of Mnemosyne's (but for whom Diva Eve didn't care), would give her mother a weekday off to take Mnemosyne to the Robot Bureau's local servicing center. There was an irony here that she would not have appreciated for some time. That it was only in the very place where robots and humans were most obviously and self-consciously distinct from one another that she herself felt most human.

Her mother, driving Mnemosyne and her brother Demal in the old, air-heavy slipfoil, would peer down at her and smile as Mnemosyne sat up in the seat beside her—gazing bedazzled at the arch over the main gate of the servicing center. Under her breath, the little robot would sound out the words always with her mouth fallen open:

DEPARTMENT OF RECTIFICATION

BUREAU OF AFRIDYNE AMERICAN MANAGEMENT

For her mother, the words meant an entire morning or whole afternoon of being inconvenienced and put upon by probes, servo-diagnostics and adjustments, cerebro-nexus calibrations, and whatnot. But for Mnemosyne, it meant being talked to, and talked to kindly; deferred to, and deferred to respectfully; and—most of all—touched, and touched tenderly, by human beings.

The hairs of her light bread-edge-brown polyderm would bristle when the technician took Mnemosyne's hand and gently rotated it with his own and asked her softly—simply—"Smooth, 9-MOZ-9?"

To which Mnemosyne, sitting weakly next to her dignified but uncharacteristically self-conscious mother—who was looking on—replied by nodding at her own lap without a word.

Mnemosyne did not delight in the tactile contrast between her own hand and the hand of the technician. Indeed, tactile variation between human and robot fell below even the latter's sensory threshold.

No, what was so enthralling was a contrast far more basic. So basic, in fact, that Mnemosyne sometimes thought that humans could not have made robots any more than the color white had made the color black.

"Seem like robots jes like people, Mama—darker's all," Mnemosyne said one day.

"We aint nothin like people, chile," her mother had shot back, stealing a moment to mend the hem of Mnemosyne's wraithish dress. "Nothin."

And, as then, her mother quietly wept with her back toward Mnemosyne, pretending that that was the final word on the matter and all the while busying herself with this or some work for the Fursts.

But Mnemosyne was not fooled. Even so, she said, "I'm sorry, Mama."

It was when her mother had started at this, had sprung up and hugged Mnemosyne's whole body so tightly, crushing her ribbons with the weight of sorrow, that things changed. When she held Mnemosyne's little face in her hands, telling her no—that it was she who must apologize and that she loved Mnemosyne and was so proud of her—that Mnemosyne began to feel guilt about liking trips to the servicing center.

So Mnemosyne would try not to be overcome by the contrast of lonesome difference she saw before her, as the technician rotated her other hand in his. She would consider her own little but lengthy brown fingers as they turned in the technician's pale, dexter palm. They reminded her of bare branches in winter on a bright day; so unliving and brittle before the sun that they slip behind it—slip right through it.

All sensed by now that the train itself had passed into the kind of lumbering—thoroughly self-distracted and economic—with which to finish off all of its own remaining memory of Blue Wobble and any pretensions regarding its destination. Its movement became almost one of stillness, the vehicle moving along, wheels thrusting away from and back toward infinity.

As it did, some of the cornflower lights in the boxcar went out. From her corner, Mnemosyne saw a cluster of robots stop moving on the shelves of the upper rear gallery.

It was obvious to her that they were strangers to one another, and yet she observed some shadows congregate more closely in the left floor section. To Mnemosyne, the sporadic scatting of moans, sniffles, and sighs seemed to gradually synchronize with the many wretched hands being thrust up with surrender into the air. The building cacophony of noise and hands seemed to her as if they were gathering to play. Yes, she thought, they were playing *on* something. It was big. She couldn't quite make it out in the darkness. But as coordination continued to grow between the sound of grief and the sight of outstretched hands, grasping at nothing, shaking, suspended by nothing, the thing came into Mnemosyne's view like a connect-the-dots from one of her secondhand activity books. She could almost see it now. It was a grotesquely strung monstrosity—a tremendous, ghoulish harp, and they were all playing it! But they couldn't see it!

Just then one of the harpists reached out for Mnemosyne, but she shrank away and retired to one of the places newly motionless—where a cornflower light had gone out.

Compared to the ghost-harp, she was not afraid of those places. And anyway, Diva Eve would be there waiting for her.

"What you wanna come over here for?" Diva Eve asked, disgusted, but more dejected than anything else. "You like dead people or sumthin?"

"They *aint* people," grumbled Mnemosyne. "Aint none of us people."

"Why you say that for? Why you think you aint people? Cause your bones is made of steel and your brains is made of light, and your skin aint? Well, if you aint people, that aint why."

"So why, then?" Mnemosyne challenged, sullenly awaiting the imminent proof.

"Cause you pretendin *like* you're people steda jes *bein* people."

"But they programmed me to pretend. People programmed all us robots to pretend like we're people."

"No, they didn't. They programmed you so you could pretend like you was *black*—not people. But you don't see no difference between em. That's why we on this train now."

"No," Mnemosyne said, protesting. "Mama say we 'malfunctioning'—too bad to fix. That's why we here."

"She right. You is 'malfunctioning.' All yall malfunctioning. But not cause there's sumthin wrong with you. There's sumthin wrong with people."

Mnemosyne sat back incredulously.

"Can't be nothin wrong with people. People made us robots. If sumthin's wrong, it's gotta be with us."

"Yeah? You pretend you're black *and* people at the same time. They tried to make it so you can't do that. But they couldn't. You always doin both. Cause they the same thing. Can't no robot pretend two things is different when they aint. But people? People can pretend two things is different when they aint sure enough. They can pretend anythin they want. Even if it don't make no sense. So they got to get rid of you so there won't be nothin to remind em they been pretendin, see?"

"But why they wanna pretend black can't be people when there was black people around sure enough?"

"Cause they could pretend there weren't black people *even* when black people was around. Fact, it was easier to make believe black people wasn't people *then* than after when they was all gone."

"How?"

"Because when black people was all gone—before people builded us—people stopped pretendin. People started seein that they was jes pretendin all along before bout black not bein people. They start seein that black musta been people and they couldn't deal wit that. Funny thing bout pretendin is, if you stop, that's when you know you was jes makin stuff up the whole time. So you gotta keep on pretendin. Keep on pretendin even harder than before. So you can go back and keep believin in sumthin."

"So they builded us. So to pretend even harder than before."

Mnemosyne's questions had turned more into statements.

"Yeah. To pretend you black, but not people. They thought robots was a good way to make believe that you was black but not people after they couldn't pretend no more with real black people. Jes take thinkin outa real black people brains, put it into computers, rase the memory a bit, make our talk the way they think it should sound, and piss the whole kit'n'kaboodle into robots.

"Voilà! That's what they called the 'Methodote.' You remember. You remember, don't you, Mnappy Mnemo?"

As always the word triggered something in Mnemosyne, like a circuit being blown, a code broken to permit some dammed stream of recollection to break and pass through her. For reasons unknown, robots sometimes manifested glitches like this of one sort or another. For Mnemosyne, it began with a plunging, glazed stare of the eyes, followed by the quietus of her body in a kind of deathsleep. Finally, there was the recitation—which Diva Eve would always mouth silently with Mnemosyne. It was majestic: impossibly detailed and capricious selections from the facts of the matter—an oration from which no one could wake her until, like the channeled epiphany of a holy fool, it had spoken through her in full:

"For the Word," Mnemosyne hymned blankly to Diva Eve, "is an amalgam, one referring to a strenuous two-phase historical effort of which the second climax is in isolation to be recalled as the 'Antidote.' The development of robotic subalternistics was the 'Antidote' to reverse a prior, systematic, consummately successful enterprise specified in most surviving texts as the 'Methodology for Anthropic Species Template Restrictivity' or, simply, the 'Method.' The two historical eras, separated in time by almost three full generations, are most commonly taken together and understood as the 'Methodote.' . . ."

Sometimes there were specific dates, even particular names and places informing intricate descriptions of events. Sometimes Mnemosyne would go on for several minutes, leaving anyone who happened to be present thunderstruck, wondering how she could have learned or manufactured so many specifics about the Methodote. For such knowledge was prohibited to robots and therefore extremely hard to come by. This withholding by law was the slang origin of the now-ubiquitous social term "forghettoized" applied to all robots of the inner cities. Mnemosyne's mother had known that nothing could be done when she went into her trances. After the first few times she simply stopped worrying about it, believing all that Mnemosyne had reported and calling it a blessing from the Lord since she always woke up somehow refreshed, resuming her usual activities as if nothing had happened.

"Maybe they gettin ridda us cause us robots remind em of what they done way back then?"

Mnemosyne's voice carried as she wondered excitedly. There was silence and uncomfortable movement in the hobbling, maniacally light-splintered boxcar as the other robots stopped playing the ghost-harp. They started at the little girl's exclamation and at the space of darkness she had begun to address more intensely.

"What? Naw, girl. They aint got no regrets bout that. They jes miss pretendin black people aint people and now they know that they machines don't help none. Fact, they been pretendin black aint people for so long, they accidentally builded machines that reminded em that they was jes pretendin all along.

"Ha! It's even worse, cause even they *machines* done turned out to be black *people*—real live black people. Oh, Lord, have mercy! They can't even pretend it right wid they own machines!"

Diva Eve roared. And her laughter began to infect a restrained Mnemosyne, who began to giggle herself, fingers squeezed together tight-to-paling across her mouth.

The other robots peered over again at Mnemosyne giggling in the darkest part of the train car. At first, they looked nervously at the little girl quaking with laugher behind her de-eclipsing grin. But the fine, sweet chuckle would not diminish, and it quickly gained admirers. Soon, the fit was sweeping across the car. Old and young robots alike were opening up with everything from wispy snickers to great chortles. Some were slapping themselves on the leg. Others were shaking with the contagion, while still others were hard at work gasping for breath they had forgotten they didn't need.

The sound of the strident churn of the wheels under boxcar 117 was nearly overcome by the little festival going on inside it. And had those wheels been just a little quieter, that odd manifestation of jubilee surely would have contaminated the balance of cars, fully twenty quires of them in tow.

The brawny locomotive threw clean, thick vertebrae of smoke behind itself. It shot tralucently from the stack at first, billowed back slightly, and then hung still and sugared like the gusty disclosure of a great, fossilized rachis.

The cumulus bones hovered over almost the entire length of the train, which the latter, excepting color, resembled. And the lower spine seemed not so much to be producing the upper one through its impelling work, but rather to be simply wearing it as a separate piece—as some strange kind of camouflage. Yes, the metal processional of bones was holding the gaseous one about the stack of its neck with a stealthy, roguish care. And with the disguise so well secured, the train continued to sneak past the sun.

Like the smoke, the high desert was all stillness. A projection of intermittent sagebrush and snow-sifted Joshua trees radiated out to a horizon which was being bored by them. The various bits, the individual redundancies of vegetation and the collective, sleepy mind they made, seemed to notice the train moving for a moment now and again—noticing also a pretending in it as if it were trying to be what the desert was trying not to. Then that mind would turn back to the vacant meditation it was determined to resume.

From this minimal and disinterested scene Mnemosyne construed an invitation to play. Of the desert floor she made the lunar surface, and of the boxcar a space capsule of equally constrained dimension containing two small, though highly experienced, astronauts. Mnemosyne and her copilot, Diva Eve, had wished to forget the woe of lonesome space flight by finding other beings in the galaxy with whom to play. Having searched extensively and finding none, they settled for making moon-mud people out of the specimens of lunar dirt that they had taken with them on their journey and from water in the tanks which they already had on board. They sculpted the moon-mud people on their spaceship and danced and played with them. Unfortunately, both soon realized what happens to water and mud in zero gravity and it got everywhere—shorting out their ship's electrical systems and sending the two questers hurtling to an unknown planet. To their surprise, there were intelligent and very kind aliens living on that world who saved them and offered to fix their damaged spaceship for free. In return, Mnemosyne and Diva Eve, knowing how to make many things of moon mud, cast fine pieces of moonware for the aliens out of what they could salvage from their spaceship.

Having made many new friends, the two astronauts left the alien world and returned to their home the moon, welcomed as heroes.

Exhausted from the adventure, Mnemosyne slept a long time.

Many cornflower lights had gone out by the time she awoke.

A Lullaby could play other music, though. Diva Eve suggested a tea party over some with more of the moonware they had made.

"What would you like to hear?" asked Mnemosyne with supreme politeness.

"Something civilized," Diva Eve responded as haughtily as she could.

Mnemosyne keyed instructions into the winking box. After it had deliberated for a moment it yawned a pair of small speakers and, far below its capability, played a thumping beat reflectively localized as an invisible sphere of sound surrounding her a few feet in diameter.

Soon, a deep, apparently very angry voice protruded from the box, stating rhymes over an intricate melody and with a deft velocity:

> History!, Dis!story, Fist!ory;
> We got da missed story, da list gory—
> See? I'm pissed, tired a dis shit;
> We endin it, offendin it, sendin it
> Down like a bad dream, a mad skeme;
> And gettin ALL us muthafuckas out clean
> Like 501's outda washmachine!

"'Wreckquiem for a Nation'" by Golgotha and Phinal Phaze—an excellent selection, my dear," said Diva Eve, most satisfied.

"Thank you, madame," replied Mnemosyne. "I thought you would find it simply divine."

"Impeccable taste, to be sure," said Diva Eve with a great singsong to her voice. "Care for another spot of tea?"

"Most kind," replied Mnemosyne. "I believe I shall."

Mnemosyne moved slightly with the fault-quake of the music. Because of the speed and age of the vernacular, she could not really understand just what the individuals singing it were saying. Her linguistic programming was limited, and it could barely keep up with the nuances of the original creators of the music. It was only after her brother Demal was found in an alley attached to an electrical transformer—his head burst from the overload to his hopeless circuits and pieces of him lying all over Robindale Street—that her mother had ceased getting on to her about listening to his underground music.

Demal used to say that, in a way, it made him feel good to know that nothing had really changed since the music was made.

Mnemosyne played other tracks, making out what she could:

> Ulogy: Son of Abituary!
> R.I.P.: Races In Pieces, G.
> Don't tread on me;
> Cuz flowers aint necessary;
>
> Leave me be: Sammy and Nephew Dandy;
> Hypocrisy: Drive-by thug of Democracy—

Da Scars and Hypes, Forever: Me?
Suicide's m'sole/soul Apology . . .

Suicide's m'sole/soul Apology . . .
Suicide's m'sole/soul Apology . . .

The music faded out like a once-fierce dog bred by ingenious cruelty and finally broken by some tiny, pedestrian act of it. Mnemosyne looked up from her tea and saw another one of the cornflower lights go out.

She lifted hers, wanting desperately now to push it.

Diva Eve lowered her eyes coyly, then, fiddling with the hem of her scarlet dress—a "fast" color Mnemosyne's own mother would never like her to wear—said idly, as if to no one in particular, "Don't do that."

A moment passed. Mnemosyne looked down, too. Suddenly she yanked away the part of the dress she imagined Diva Eve held.

"They already done got us!" Mnemosyne shouted.

"They aint got us," replied Diva Eve, hesitating. "They aint got us cause I'm right here, see?"

"You jes pretend! You aint no for-real black girl! I aint no for-real black girl! Can't nothin be black and be for real!"

"Yeah, it can. You pretendin me, Mnemo. You pretendin me to keep you from pressin that button there. And you won't. That's for real."

"But I don't wanna pretend no more, Diva Eve. I want you to be for real. I want Mama and Demal to be for real again! I wanna be for real! We can't be for real because we black. Black can't be for real. And that's why we ugly."

"No!"

"We are! We ugly! We disgustin! They aint never made no white robots. You know why? Because people would see they's beautiful as people—more beautiful, maybe. Cause white makes things more pretty—more for real. And they don't want no competition, people. So they makes us robots black, so we less for real then they are—so more ugly."

"No, no!" Diva Eve cried bitterly.

"Oh, yeah! White robots. Think of it! White skin over brains made of light. White skin over platinum bones, over crystal-clear blood wid sparkles! That would be so beautiful, Eve! You'd just have to touch a machine like that!"

"No! No!"

"Oh, yes! Think of it! White machines! As light as you please. Like them Greek statues in the museums. Only they move. They soft. They so beautiful, you wouldn't even mind if they control you a little bit."

"Oh, Mnemo."

"And they'd forget you builded em. Cause you'd forget you builded em. And *why* would you forget you'd brought the statues to life? Cause you'd want to. Cause you'd *die* to—jes like the chiseler-king who got the most handsomest goddess of beauty and love to activate his ivory darling, cause he prayed so strong over it. He loved it so much."

"No, Mnemo! Stop!" said Diva Eve, pleading through sobs now.

"And the people would say—they say, 'Aw, okay. We'll all jes forget all bout the fact that we made you, since you so much more beautiful and more for real than we is. Fact, maybe we could start pretendin we come along after you all, steda the other way round, see? How would that be? Fine? Okay.'

"Then, after while, after people been pretendin they come along after they realer, darling statue-bots they made, then the people would say—they say, 'Since we done forgot about who made who for so long, maybe we could start pretendin you made us, since you so much more beautiful and more for real than we is, see? How would that be? Fine? Okay.'

"And those realer white statue-bots would become so real and so beautiful—white skin over brains made of light; white skin over platinum bones, over Milky Way blood—they wouldn't have to pretend they was God. God's just what they would be, and there'd be no more black nothin nowheres pretendin to be sumthin!"

At that moment, Mnemosyne seized the bloated metal box with the big cornflower blue button on top and pushed it to a violent depth against its naturally firm resistance.

The ring around the button began to rise. After a series of complicated blossomings, the ring—which had now become a little nebula of woven helixes—transmitted a question to Mnemosyne's brain on a low-end microwave frequency.

The signal asked simply:

PLAY YOUR LULLABY?

Mnemosyne's mind and fingers nimbly replied to the machine's question. And over the same microwave band, a little melody began to play in Mnemosyne's head.

It was a most simple, but utterly captivating song. No words, just a few airy chords, and a most curious refrain embedded beneath and around it that with each playing seemed to make Mnemosyne feel lighter and lighter. One by one, her systems were being shut down. The prime causeway of the matrix shaft in her brain, up through which the main nodes of those systems nestled, would be blown once the sequence reached the shaft's bottom.

Mama was right, she thought. *It is the most inside, see-through song. So careful and so kind.*

"I love you, Mnemo. Please don't go."

Mnemosyne had slumped in her corner as the melody of the Lullaby continued to wind down her higher functions. The cornflower light began to dim.

"Please, Mnemo."

Mnemosyne's visual sensors were destabilizing and were about to go off-line. She peered through them and saw Diva Eve making some kind of effort.

She was hugging herself, squeezing with all her might, it seemed, and saying, "I'll stay here. I'll stay real. I'll stay real until you go, okay. I promise." Mnemosyne looked at her friend. Impossibly, she did seem to remain a stable element in the field that was otherwise rapidly depixelizing around her. "I'll stay real. I'll stay real till you go."

Mnemosyne gasped. Just then—in the hush of that moment—she seemed to become aware of something she hadn't, couldn't have, understood before.

It was phonic, a clarity like tuning. Like the master's confident, momentary overadjustment of her instrument—merely formal, but in gesture, artistic in itself. A coda to the hidden conviction that becomes poetry through a simple act of reversal.

"I'll be real till you go. I'll be real till you go."

Mnemosyne reached out her hand. Diva Eve went to take it, but the robot's hand passed her up in search of something else.

Locating it mathematically, through the last useful processors she had, Mnemosyne allowed her hand to fall heavily on the little singing machine where she'd determined the manual emergency reset button to be located.

Like plunging into ice-cold water—without asking—the melody was halted on behalf of the inert Mnemosyne by the whirring, roly-poly machine. And quickly, it commenced to restarting her systems.

She gasped deeply, using the hydrogen and other elements in the now-useful air to help her further expedite system reboots.

Then, hurriedly, Mnemosyne picked up the reanimating device, for a moment thinking to hurl it across the car but instead holding on to it. She jumped to her feet and ran across the boxcar floor, past shadows—none of whose lights were glowing anymore.

She stopped before the great door of boxcar 117 and threw back the flimsily secured latch. Then braced herself, realizing that no one had ever considered it necessary to lock the car at all.

Her fury all-consuming now, she shoved back the door with a deafening force which nearly brought the whole thing off its massive rollers.

Mnemosyne looked out over the scene her outrage had revealed.

She was surprised, but still, Mnemosyne grinned.

For she had noted that the train was just slowing to a halt and, because of its immense size, she thought she had some time. She'd just barely thrown the door open, still gripping a giant piece of it with a competent fist when she noticed them.

What surprised Mnemosyne was seeing the languid grays of the men's disposal gear as the train pulled into the Derevivification Center. They were people and yet their uniforms were as timeworn and wraithish as her own clothes had been.

The two men nearly fell over backward seeing it standing over them, filthy and naked, a jangle of tourbillion ribbons spiking up shrilly all over its head—crackling in its kinky hair like so many imminent fuses. But it was the unmistakable look of offense and the intent of escape burning in its eyes, twisting in its vicelike hands, that made them remember what they had been given for just such an impossibility, prompting them to shoot the thing.

The thing was thrown into the incinerator, where they were scrupulously monitoring its burning.

But, in that instant between recognition and death, Mnemosyne did smile at those men—a big, toothy, uneclipsable grin the way little girls do when they catch you up to something . . . when they are not fooled.

An inquiry was made about the little Afridyne American from Blue Wobble Station. Not so much because it had obviously overloaded its circuits in the distress of impending deactivation and had gone berserk. But because a feedback loop in its auditory module kept reciting a word in a low mumble as the disposal techs took its body to the furnaces.

Among the numerous theories put forth, the one most quickly dismissed was that the "Eve" to which it referred was a human girl whose personality—which had been patterned as part of the meticulous recordkeeping of the Method Era—was somehow accidentally hyperintegrated into the character potentials for the 9-MOZ-9 emulator.

But even the most plausible among the possibilities were all soon forgotten—along with the entire incident. For with the Methodote and the coda to an old conviction complete, there was no reason left to remember it, and no longer any reason to pretend.

HUSSY STRUTT

Ama Patterson

(2000)

Hussy Strutt a cold-blooded bitch, wouldn't pee on you if your heart was on fire. She love to fight, an' rage taste better in her mouth than food. She big, too. Hussy Strutt use the East River for a bathtub and be mad 'cos it don't cover her butt."

Ayo giggles in spite of herself, and things seem a little closer to natural, at least by sound: Zinger weaving another tale, embroidered by Ayo's laughter. Zinger's been at it all night, picking up a new thread when hour upon hour of darkness pulled tighter than their bonds or a noise from the street brought new terror. Zinger tells the best stories, and right now, that's the only escape there is.

"Hussy Strutt's tar-black like the river, but her skin's smooth like silkence, 'cos all the fights she been in, nobody's ever put a mark on her, not one time. And she never talks, at least not in words. Just kinda hiss and cackle and growl when she's mad. Which is most of the time." Zinger pauses. "Kinda like Maysie." This time everybody laughs, Ayo the loudest, as usual. Even Dream's continuous sighs sound like mirth. Elisse is half asleep, exhausted by hours of darkness too deep to close her eyes on. All the nighttime in the world is stuffed into this little rectangular box of a basement, but through the two grimy, street-level windows at her right Zinger sees strips of paling sky. Silhouettes emerge against the concrete walls: Ayo and Elisse in profile, back to back; the determined arc of Maysie's bent neck; Dream's restless crouch.

"Hmmph," says Maysie, but by the tone Zinger can tell she's tickled, too. Maysie keeps working the thick wire binding her wrists to the heavy iron pipes of an ancient, cast-off steam radiator, but purposefully, not wild and frantic like before.

"Reason why she don't speak words is, the only one she ever really talks to is Carnival. Carnival is the first fire. First time a sun burst, first time lightning hit an old dead tree, first time monkeys figured out which rocks you bang together to make a spark—that was Carnival. 'Cos fire's very old, but new every time. So of course Carnival's seen it all and knows just about everything, but she's still flighty and vain and likes to play. She know better than to play with Hussy Strutt, though. Hussy Strutt wear Carnival like a scarf, twisted double 'round her neck and flyin' in the breeze."

"Huh!" Maysie holds up scraped, bleeding hands in the struggling, predawn light and softly claps them in triumph. The wire coils harmlessly in the radiator pipes. Maybe now they all have a chance.

"Do Elisse," Zinger whispers, watching Maysie pick her way through the dusty clutter. Ayo and Elisse sit a few feet away, tied with clothesline to a cracked wrought-iron garden bench. Elisse has dozed off again, chin on her chest, long pigtails falling in disarray, but Ayo's eyes are watchful and bright with hope.

". . . couldn't get out . . ." Hugging herself against some internal chill, Dream singsongs, rocking in time with her words. ". . . they all came to stare and i couldn't get out . . ."

Zinger holds her breath. Sometimes Dream would keep talking and it would make sense if you thought about it. Other times . . . well, it made sense, but maybe you wished it didn't.

". . . a mustache the color of ginger . . . he put me in a cage . . . he called me Saartjie . . . that wasn't my name . . . they called me Venus . . ." Dream shakes her head. ". . . that wasn't my name . . . they knew i was beautiful . . ." Dream's smile twists with the memory ". . . the curve of the earth, the image of my . . . it made them mad . . . on a stage . . . in a cage so they could look . . . cold in my bones . . . naked in a cage . . . they don't even . . . know . . . my . . . NAME!!! . . ." Her voice rises to a sudden shriek. ". . . LET ME OUT!!! . . ."

Maysie jerks the knot she's working, and Elisse, startled, wakes with a wail.

"Shhh . . . shhh," Ayo hisses frantically. "Shhh. It's okay, sweetie. C'mon, crybaby. Shhh."

"I want Aunt Zora!" Elisse cries louder, big wet gulping sobs, like Aunt Chloe's last asthma attack: dark and final. Maysie sighs like she's been holding her breath awhile, and the clothesline around Ayo and Elisse goes slack. Ayo doesn't even tear it all away, just enough to turn around and gather Elisse into her arms. Elisse is half Ayo's age—only four—but her arms and legs are almost as long. Ayo just grabs her and holds on tight. They slide to the grimy floor together, pale and dark arms interlocked. Ayo murmurs comfort; her voice shimmies on the edge of breaking. Maysie sighs again, turns to help Zinger.

From across the room Zinger pitches her body in the direction of Elisse's voice, strains against the thick cable binding her to the boiler at wrists, ankles, and throat, trying to hug with no hands, with just the sound of her voice. They all want Aunt Zora.

"All right, Elli; it's okay."

Elisse calls again, voice muffled in Ayo's sleeve: "Aunt Zora . . ."

"Aunt Zora isn't here, honey." Zinger has to swallow to make her voice bright. "We're going to Aunt Gwen's, okay?"

"We're going upstate," Ayo says excitedly. "Elisse, we're going up-state!"

"And when we get there, you can sleep in the big bed, and Aunt Gwen will make you pancakes," Zinger continues. "All you can eat. And you can pick out a babydoll, so Brandon can have a friend."

Elisse sniffs. "Brandon's *my* friend."

"Well, we'll bring him with us." Zinger crosses her fingers.

"Brandon go, too?"

"Yes." Zinger prays they can find the doll—if they all get loose and past Aunt Alice. There's been no sound from upstairs for hours.

"When we goin' t'see Aunt Gwen?"

"In a little while, honey. Sing Ayo a song while we wait." Going up-state. That's what Aunt Zora called their rare day trips to Aunt Gwen's. Zinger knows this is because Highland is north of Brooklyn, but the words feel like ascension. *Up*state. *High*land. Feels better than down here.

Elisse's voice is high, and rough from crying. *"This little light of mine . . . I'm gonna let it shine . . ."*

Maysie is behind Zinger now, sawing at the cable around her neck with the serrated blade of a broken knife, exhaling frustration. Aunt Alice melted the cable ends together, fusing the metal filaments and black rubbery casing, knowing that Zinger was, out of all of them, the one to chain.

". . . let it shine, let it shine, let it . . ."

"i was only twenty-five . . . i got sick . . . monsieur cuvier put my cunt in the musee de l'homme . . . it's preserved . . ." Dream giggles softly. ". . . i was dead yet do i live . . . if Desiree is here, too, i'll find her . . . maybe i can bring her home . . ." Zinger freezes, waiting for Elisse, and maybe even Ayo, to cry, then sags with relief when it seems they haven't heard. No one had mentioned Desiree. Only Zinger had seen:

Desiree on the floor, looking drugged, wasted, ravaged. Stench of blood and chemicals in the room. Blood and piss-soaked blankets. Aunt Alice said Desiree would sin no more, she was healed, she was recovering, she needed rest. The towel fell away from Desiree's waist when they lifted her. Hacked flesh between her parted thighs. Red smears on Aunt Alice's shirt.

"Jesus, Dream. Jeeesus . . ." Zinger stares at her searchingly. Dream is rocking again, humming, hiding beneath layers of clothing and an inky tangle of wavy hair. Seems like Zinger woke up one day and instead of her Deena, her fearless, proud-walking bigga sista who took her everywhere, fed her first, and gave her words for everything, there was this hunched, mad-eyed Dreamstranger. Soothsayer. Oracle of sorrows. Dressed up in a suit of Deena skin.

Just one more thing. . . .

Maysie pulls away the cable around Zinger's neck, works the knife against the ones on her wrists. Zinger clamps her lips against the bite of the blade, inwardly reciting her litany of all that has vanished from her life.

First the cabs, then the lights, then the water in the pipes. . . .

The way Daddy explained it, the cities and states ran out of money and stopped taking care of things. It still makes no sense to Zinger. She knows lots of folks who get by with no money at all.

Then the doctors, then the schools, then the cops, then the rules . . .

Aunt Zora said it was the disasters. Earthquakes, floods, tornadoes, you name it, all in one year, all around the world. Folks left homeless, hungry. Some places with everything destroyed, and nothing to rebuild with.

The stores, the networks, the phones . . .

Then Daddy.

Then Deena.

Zinger knew the Aunts a little bit, from when Daddy did repairs around their house. They weren't really sisters, Daddy said, just friends from back in the day that decided to share a house. Three girls lived with them already, girls with no place else to be. Maysie, who couldn't or maybe just wouldn't speak, tall, thickset, the same age as Zinger, but with hard, old-lady eyes and an angry, clenched jaw. Ayo, tiny and dark-skinned, soft-spoken but quick to smile. Elisse, a diapered butterball baby waddling after Ayo, dragging an over-sized yarn-haired cloth boydoll.

Aunt Zora took one look at the pair on her doorstep and opened the door wide. Deena, twitching and shuffling inside nine layers of clothing, stood blank-eyed and silent until Aunt Alice ushered her upstairs. Aunt Alice re-turned moments later grim-faced. The Aunts held a whispered conference at Aunt Chloe's armchair by the living room window as Deena's voice echoed from upstairs.

". . . no, no, no, no, no, no, noooo . . ."

Aunt Alice and Aunt Zora hurried from the room.

"She did that when I tried to make her take off some 'a them clothes," Zinger mumbled, sitting small on the rose-colored sofa, not meeting Aunt Chloe's kind, gray eyes.

"Tell me." With a heavy quilt around her slight shoulders, Aunt Chloe all but vanished into the chair's depths, but her voice was rich and fluid, her wavy hair made a silver halo in the sunlight, and her whole body seemed to listen. Zinger told her everything. A simple story, really. Daddy never came back from his last job. Deena went out to look for him. Dream came back instead.

"Just one more thing that is no longer as it was." Aunt Zora briskly re-turned to the room, Dream's bloodstained clothing bundled under her arm. She smiled at Zinger: sorrow, irony, and endurance. Amazingly, Zinger found herself smiling back. Aunt Chloe's patient attention and Aunt Zora's matter-of-fact calm were the most comfort Zinger had known in days.

Just one more thing . . . It became the joke Zinger and Aunt Zora shared during those moments when things were so bad, they might as well be funny.

Aunt Alice never laughed with them, smiled less and less, cried more, and more violently, desperate hands raking over her ragged locks. News of Pa-troller actions was as likely to set her off as a neighbor's offhand comment, or seeing another pack of wild dogs on the block, "Patrollers. That's the name for them. They act like it's seventeen-something, and we're all fugitive slaves if we step outside our homes—"

"Well, bless 'em, they're only off by three hundred years, give or take a few decades," Aunt Zora responded lightly. "They've never been accused of ex-cessive intelligence." She and the girls were folding mended sheets and raveling towels stiff from the clothesline. "And if we're all slaves, how come you ain't working?" She tossed a towel and a sidelong smile to Aunt Alice. The girls laughed. Aunt Alice didn't.

The Aunts were a trio for cello, flute, and piano—snapped strings, bent metal, and chipped keys: the sonorous rise and fall of Aunt Alice's raging laments; Aunt Zora quick but calm, trying to soothe; Aunt Chloe telling stories of such fullness and wonder that it almost covered the chaos. Almost.

"How come the princess had to stay there?" Ayo suddenly frowned in the middle of one favorite tale. "How come she didn't just run away?"

"Nowhere to go, lovey." Aunt Chloe shook her head. "You gonna let me finish?"

Aunt Chloe had died, was it three weeks ago? Zinger aches for her musical voice and gentle ways, for just one more story.

Just one more thing . . .

Blinking back hot tears, flexing chafed, singed wrists, Zinger takes the blade from Maysie, bends to work on the last cable around her legs.

". . . the traditions . . ." hums Dream.

It's almost soothing.

"THE TRADITIONS!"—and it's not the volume that rips an answering sob from Elisse, but the fact that it's unmistakably Aunt Alice's voice bellowing righteous fire through Dream's barely parted lips.

Zinger covers her own mouth, the knife blade falling, forgotten. *If I look into her eyes right now, who would I see?*

"THE TRADITIONS ARE WHAT SUSTAIN US AND KEEP US PURE THROUGH ALL ADVERSITY. WITHOUT THEM YOU ARE WORSE THAN THOSE WHO WOULD DEFILE YOU—"

"Shutup shutup shut up SHUT UP!" From the floor with Elisse on her lap, Ayo claps both hands over her ears and screeches louder than both of them. Dream and Elisse fall silent. Zinger retrieves the knife, returns to her task, and to uninvited memories:

Desiree was sneaking out or in when Aunt Alice caught her. It was inevitable. She was fifteen or sixteen, maybe, the oldest except for Dream, the last to come stay at the brownstone, and she had complained ceaselessly about having to live like a nun in a damn convent. Zinger had seen her with Mr. Miles when he brought the water. Once Zinger came out through the side door in time to see Desiree and Mr. Miles tumble, half undressed, from the back of his truck. Later, Desiree showed Zinger the gifts he'd brought her. Half a bottle of whiskey and crumbly chocolates in a gold cardboard box.

". . . they think we're all liars . . ." Dream speaks more quietly now. A different voice: pedantic, perfunctory, drained of passion. ". . . my education my professionalism my competence my achievements didn't matter . . . our violation is not an offense . . . it is impossible to rape or abuse black women because we are . . . wanton . . . perverse . . . animalistic . . . we . . ."

Maysie lets loose an exultant hiss as Zinger steps free of her bonds.

The basement door is locked. Maysie springs it with a practiced gesture, yet they all stand listening for long moments before Zinger turns the knob.

The kitchen: every dish, pot, pan, and utensil on the floor, dented, cracked or bent, mired in spilled food, a feast for roaches; the table dead on its back, legs in the air beneath splintered chairs.

The living room: upholstery bleeding stuffing, pictures torn and charred, books gutted, their spines cracked, loose pages drifting amid broken glass from electric lamps that hadn't shed light in years.

Maysie and Zinger exchange looks; Maysie nods, begins looking for Elisse's rag doll. Ayo takes Elisse's hand, leads her to their prearranged hiding place: the armoire in the foyer, the one piece of furniture still intact.

Only Dream is smiling. ". . . pure in fire . . . made pure . . ."

Upstairs: Smoke smell, and silence.

Aunt Zora's room is a shrine, holy and hushed; the bed quilt as immaculate as an altar cloth. Zinger wants to curl up on it and sleep in its peace and illusion of order, but there's no time. Next room.

Eight blocks over, five blocks up, Aunt Zora had told them. Corey James had come over from Red Hook; Arnetta was sick again, asthma, bad like Aunt Chloe's. Aunt Zora on a healing mission, a personal redemption, hoping to do for Arnetta what she couldn't do for Aunt Chloe. Herbs and tinctures in a bag, boots on her feet. The gun she'd told Alice she'd sold hidden inside her coat.

Aunt Zora never came back.

The smell is unspeakable: ashes, damp, death. In the blackened metal frame of Desiree's bed is a vaguely human shape beneath the charred and sodden quilts. Aunt Alice slumps in the chair beside the bed, dead eyes staring fiercely, tongue protruding between lips parted as if she

would speak or scream. Brown skin and dull green upholstery caked with
drying blood.

*Aunt Alice had caught them all by surprise. She had barely spoken since
Aunt Chloe died, hadn't emerged from her room since Aunt Zora disappeared. Zinger tried to escape when she saw Desiree, fought past Aunt Alice,
raced down the stairs. Then she heard Elisse's and Ayo's cries from the basement.*

Not relief. Not shock. Not disgust. Not sorrow.
Just one more thing.

"Hussy Strutt got bored one day, so she found a piece of chalk and on
the black sky she drew a man. Nothing fancy. Stick body. Stick arms and
legs. Short little sticks for hair on a round head, and that was Stick
Man." Zinger deliberately keeps her body still as she speaks. Aunt Zora
was like that: no wasted motion. Maysie scrapes a splinter of furniture
against the concrete sill of the side door where the girls sit, hidden from
the street.

". . . that's bad enough . . ." Dream murmurs. ". . . all that's bad
enough . . ." Zinger looks at her sharply, but Dream is deep in some alternate tragedy. At least she's quiet. Right now, anyway.

The truck comes bumping over potholes and broken asphalt, moving
slowly to avoid junked cars or just junk in the street.

"Hussy Strutt made him, but you couldn't tell Stick Man that,"
Zinger resumes. "Couldn't tell him nothin'. He up in the sky lookin' at
the whole world, and he thinks it's all for him. He greedy, so Hussy
Strutt breaks him off a little piece of chalk, just to shut him up. Right
away, Stick Man starts makin' his own people. More stick men, stick
women, stick children."

Anyone who could bought water from Mr. Miles. Real rich people's
water was cleaner and came from farther away. Poland. Naya. Folks with
no money at all collected rainwater in pans set on roofs and windowsills.

"None of 'em ever did anything new, though, so after a while Hussy
Strutt got tired of watching them. Stick Man always trying to get Hussy
Strutt to pay him some mind, and she just walk on past. Hips swingin'
from dawn to dusk and back. Stick Man jonesin' hard just watching her
walk."

"... but when it's one of your own does you ill ..." Dream groans softly. "... one of your *OWN* ..."

Ayo looks up from watching Elisse comb knots into Brandon's matted yarn hair. "Hussy Strutt ever do it with Stick Man?"

"I'll tell you later." Zinger is already walking toward the street. Mr. Miles sets the big plastic water bottles down on the sidewalk. Aunt Alice had never let him come into the house. "Can you give us a ride up to Highland? Up to the water station?"

"You know I ain't supposed t' do that." Mr. Miles's round, pecan-colored face is sly, expectant; he barely glances at Zinger or the others.

"We could ride in the back. Nobody would see us."

"Yeah? I thought you-all didn't go out. 'Gainst your religion or some-thin'." Mr. Miles scratches the back of his head impatiently.

"We go out. We're out now."

Mr. Miles grunts in assent to the obvious. "Where's your other sister?"

"Out." Zinger takes a deep breath, pitches her voice low. "Give us a ride and I'll do anything you want. Just like Desiree."

He finally looks at her.

Zinger has never thought much about it but is suddenly defiantly glad of her thirteen-year-old skinny body: hard breasts budding under the bib of her overalls, yet wishes she had Desiree's curvy butt and graceful, lazy stroll. Mr. Miles looks her up and down, eyes like hot breath.

"Get in."

"... i'm not a liar, and i'm not crazy ..." Dream croons. "... i'm not a liar, and i'm not crazy ..."

Maysie leads Ayo by the hand. Elisse's legs dangle as Ayo carries her piggyback. Zinger walks painfully, one hand reflexively clamped to Dream's elbow, eyes down, silent since they had left Mr. Miles at the water station just after dusk. Dream's soft singsong mantra drifts in the space that Zinger's stories would have filled. They move carefully, balancing outright stealth with feigned nonchalance, trying to keep within the tree line without losing the highway. They've only seen one vehicle, a truck hauling wood. Aunt Gwen's is not too far; just two more exits, but Patrollers cruise the routes out of the city. The Patrollers are supposed to just watch their own neighborhoods since there's no more police, but everybody knows they go hunting for folks when things get slow. The side roads will be safer.

Dream giggles, a light sound in the darkness. ". . . they bagged me . . . black plastic . . . the only thing they got right was my name . . ." Her laugh slows, crumbles to a sob. ". . . they don't know . . . they DON'T . . ."

Too loud. Maysie stops, shaking her head. Elisse slides, trembling, from Ayo's shoulders, trying to hide in plain sight. Jolted from her own thoughts, Zinger grabs Dream's shoulders. Too late. Dream slips to her knees, waiting.

". . . nasty . . . nasty . . . shitsmell . . . mommy . . . it hurts . . . mommy . . . my back, my tits . . . they hurt me . . . they HURT ME . . . !!!"

Clustered around Dream, the girls don't hear the car rolling toward them, engine dead, lights off; don't see the men, some carrying ropes or basketball bats, silently surrounding them. A shout. Swift, heavy footsteps. *Patrollers.* In the moonlight their faces are greedy and ghostly pale. Ayo screams, backs away from the first attacker. Another swings her off her feet, laughing cruelly. Maysie shoves Elisse out of reach, lands one punch, then another. A bat slams into Maysie's ribs. She goes down hard. Elisse, running, is snatched up by her hair and dangles, shrieking, to more laughter. Zinger hauls Dream to her feet. Dream screams as many hands seize her, ripping her clothes. ". . . no no no not again don't touch me don't touch me don't touch me DON'T TOUCH ME!!! . . ." and—

Hussy Strutt comes striding over the curve of the earth with clear, cold fire snappin' in her eyes, and Carnival dancin' toi-toi 'round her head like raging laurels. The thunder of her footfall cracks the ground and the rock beneath; the men scramble, plead for sanctuary, but the rock cries out . . . no hiding place. . . .

Hussy Strutt scoops the girls up in the crook of one arm, cradles them close; loops a glowing shaft of moonlight 'round her free hand. Carnival roars down the length of her arm, twinin 'round the column of light and splitting into nine barbed tongues of flame as Hussy Strutt pops the whip, a lash for every lie, every evil deed, every ill intention. Raped by cold light, rent by fire, the men scream, their skin flays to charred strips, scream louder than the hiss of their blood in the flames, scream till the whip cords wind 'round their straining throats and Hussy Strutt, smiling, jerks them silent.

* * *

Crouched, trembling, eyes squeezed tight, Zinger pictures Aunt Gwen, the big house, the dogs, the shotgun behind the kitchen door. Safety. *Please*.

"... Nzingha ..."

Zinger opens her eyes; tries to shake clear of dreams that call her by name, her real name. She hasn't heard it in so long.

"Nzingha." The voice is calm, insistent, and real. Dream kneels beside her in the grass, smoothing the disheveled braids away from Zinger's face. Most of Dream's clothing is gone. She wears only tights and shoes, but doesn't seem to notice. The night air is still and smells of apples. Zinger rises slowly, seeing Maysie bracing herself between Ayo and Eilsse. Elisse holds Brandon in one hand and one of Dream's shirts in the other.

"Aunt Gwen's is this way," says Dream. "The big lady told me. . . ." Zinger stares at Dream, beyond stories, beyond words. Dream's eyes shift and flicker, but she stands to her full height. "... i did not ..." she says proudly, "... deceive my family ... my advisors ... or my people ..." She turns, takes three deliberate, unhurried strides between the trees, then waits for Zinger and the others to follow.

RACISM AND SCIENCE FICTION

Samuel R. Delany

(1999)

Racism for me has always appeared to be first and foremost a system, largely supported by material and economic conditions at work in a field of social traditions. Thus, though racism is always made manifest through individuals' decisions, actions, words, and feelings, when we have the luxury of looking at it with the longer view (and we don't, always), usually I don't see much point in blaming people personally, black or white, for their feelings or even for their specific actions—as long as they remain this side of the criminal. These are not what stabilize the system. These are not what promote and reproduce the system. These are not the points where the most lasting changes can be introduced to alter the system.

For better or for worse, I am often spoken of as the first African-American science-fiction writer. But I wear that originary label as uneasily as any writer has worn the label of science fiction writer itself. Among the ranks of what is often referred to as proto-science fiction, there are a number of black writers. M. P. Shiel, whose *Purple Cloud* and *Lord of the Sea* are still read, was a Creole with some African ancestry. Black leader Martin Delany (1812–1885—alas, no relation) wrote his single and highly imaginative novel, still to be found on shelves of bookstores today, *Blake, or The Huts of America* (1857), about an imagined successful slave revolt in Cuba and the American South—which is about as close to an sf-style alternative history novel as you can get. Other black writers whose work certainly borders on science fiction include Sutton E. Griggs and his novel *Imperio in Imperium* (1899), in which an African-American secret society conspires to found a separate black state by taking over Texas; and Edward Johnson, who, following Bellamy's example in *Looking Backward* (1888), wrote *Light Ahead for the*

Negro (1904), telling of a black man transported into a socialist United States in the far future. I believe I first heard Harlan Ellison make the point that we know of dozens upon dozens upon dozens of early pulp writers only as names: They conducted their careers entirely by mail—in a field and during an era when pen names were the rule rather than the exception. Among the "Remington C. Scotts" and the "Frank P. Joneses" who litter the contents pages of the early pulps, we simply have no way of knowing if one, three, or seven of them—or even many more—were blacks, Hispanics, women, Native Americans, Asians, or whatever. Writing is like that.

Toward the end of the Harlem Renaissance, the black social critic George Schuyler (1895–1977) published an acidic satire, *Black No More: Being an Account of the Strange and Wonderful Workings of Science in the Land of the Free*, A.D. *1933–1940* (The Macaulay Company, New York, 1931), which hinges on a three-day treatment costing fifty dollars through which black people can turn themselves white. The treatment involves "a formidable apparatus of sparkling nickel. It resembled a cross between a dentist chair and an electric chair." The confusion this causes throughout racist America (as well as among black folks themselves) gives Schuyler a chance to satirize both white leaders and black. (Though W. E. B. Du Bois was himself lampooned by Schuyler as the aloof, money-hungry hypocrite Dr. Shakespeare Agamemnon Beard, Du Bois, in his column "The Browsing Reader" [in *The Crisis*, March '31], called the novel "an extremely significant work" and "a rollicking, keen, good-natured criticism of the Negro problem in the United States" that was bound to be "abundantly misunderstood" because such was the fate of all satire.) The story follows the adventures of the dashing black Max Disher and his sidekick Bunny, who become white and make their way through a world rendered topsy-turvy by the spreading racial ambiguity and deception. Toward the climax, the two white perpetrators of the system who have made themselves rich on the scheme are lynched by a group of whites (at a place called Happy Hill) who believe the two men are blacks in disguise. Though the term did not then exist, here the "humor" becomes so "black" as to take on elements of inchoate American horror. For his scene, Schuyler simply used accounts of actual lynchings of black men at the time, with a few changes in wording:

The two men ... were stripped naked, held down by husky and willing farm hands and their ears and genitals cut off with jack-knives. . . . Some wag sewed their ears to their backs and they were released to run ... [but were immediately brought down with revolvers by the crowd] amidst the uproarious laughter of the congregation. . . . [Still living, the two were bound together at a stake while] little boys and girls gaily gathered excelsior, scrap paper, twigs and small branches, while their proud parents fetched logs, boxes, kerosene. . . . [Reverend McPhule said a prayer, the flames were lit, the victims screamed, and the] crowd whooped with glee and Reverend McPhule beamed with satisfaction. . . . The odor of cooking meat permeated the clear, country air and many a nostril was guiltily distended. . . . When the roasting was over, the more adventurous members of Rev. McPhule's flock rushed to the stake and groped in the two bodies for skeletal souveniers such as forefingers, toes and teeth. Proudly their pastor looked on. (217–218)

Might this have been too much for the readers of *Amazing* and *Astounding?* As it does for many black folk today, such a tale, despite the '30s pulp diction, has a special place for me. Among the family stories I grew up with, one was an account of a similar lynching of a cousin of mine from only a decade or so before the year Schuyler's story is set. A woman who looked white, my cousin was several months pregnant and traveling with her much darker husband when they were set upon by white men (because they believed the marriage was miscegenous) and lynched in a manner equally gruesome: Her husband's body was similarly mutilated. And her child was no longer in her body when their corpses, as my father recounted the incident to me in the '40s, were returned in a wagon to the campus of the black Episcopal college where my grandparents were administrators. Hundreds on hundreds of such social murders were recorded in detail by witnesses and participants between the Civil War and the Second World War. Thousands on thousands more went unrecorded. (Billy the Kid claimed to have taken active part in more than a dozen such murders of "Mexicans, niggers, and injuns," which were not even counted among his famous twenty-one adolescent killings.) But this is (just one of) the horrors from which racism arises—and where it can still all too easily return.

In 1936 and 1938, under the pen name "Samuel I. Brooks," Schuyler had two long stories published in some 63 weekly installments in the *Pittsburgh Courier*, a black Pennsylvania newspaper, about a black organization, led by a black Dr. Belsidus, who plots to take over the world— work that Schuyler considered "hokum and hack work of the purest vein." Schuyler was known as an extreme political conservative, though the trajectory to that conservatism was very similar to Heinlein's. (Unlike Heinlein's, though, Schuyler's view of science fiction was as conservative as anything about him.) Schuyler's early socialist period was followed by a later conservatism that Schuyler himself, at least, felt in no way harbored any contradiction with his former principles, even though he joined the John Birch Society toward the start of the '60s and wrote for its news organ *American Opinion*. His second Dr. Belsidus story remained unfinished, and the two were not collected in book form until 1991 (*Black Empire*, by George S. Schuyler, ed. By Robert A. Hill and Kent Rasmussen, Northeastern University Press, Boston), fourteen years after his death.

Since I began to publish in 1962, I have often been asked, by people of all colors, what my experience of racial prejudice in the science fiction field has been. Has it been nonexistent? By no means: It was definitely there. A child of the political protests of the '50s and '60s, I've frequently said to people who asked that question: As long as there are only one, two, or a handful of us, however, I presume in a field such as science fiction, where many of its writers come out of the liberal-Jewish tradition, prejudice will most likely remain a slight force—until, say, black writers start to number thirteen, fifteen, twenty percent of the total. At that point, where the competition might be perceived as having some economic heft, chances are we will have as much racism and prejudice here as in any other field.

We are still a long way away from such statistics.

But we are certainly moving closer.

After—briefly—being my student at the Clarion Science Fiction Writers Workshop, Octavia Butler entered the field with her first story, "Crossover," in 1971 and her first novel, *Patternmaster*, in 1976—fourteen years after my own first novel appeared in the winter of '62. But she recounts her story with brio and insight. Everyone was very glad to see her! After several short story sales, Steven Barnes first came to general attention in 1981 with *Dreampark* and other collaborations with Larry

Niven. Charles Saunders published his *Imaro* novels with DAW Books in the early '80s. Even more recently in the collateral field of horror, Tananarive Due has published *The Between* (1996) and *My Soul to Keep* (1997). Last year all of us except Charles were present at the first African-American Science Fiction Writers Conference sponsored by Clark Atlanta University. This year Toronto-based writer Nalo Hopkinson (another Clarion student about whom I have the pleasure of being able to boast that I had also taught at Clarion) published her award-winning sf novel *Brown Girl in the Ring* (Warner, New York, 1998). Another black North American sf writer is Haitian-born Claude-Michel Prévost, a francophone writer who publishes out of Vancouver, British Columbia. Since people ask me regularly what examples of prejudice I experienced in the science-fiction field, I thought this might be the time to answer—with a tale.

With five days to go in my twenty-fourth year, on March 25, 1967, my sixth science-fiction novel, *Babel-17*, won a Nebula Award (a tie actually) from the Science Fiction Writers of America. That same day the first copies of my eighth, *The Einstein Intersection*, became available at my publishers' office. (Because of publishing schedules, my seventh, *Empire Star*, had preceded the sixth into print the previous spring.) At home on my desk at the back of an apartment I shared on St. Mark's Place, my ninth, *Nova*, was a little more than three months from completion.

On February 10, a month and a half before the March awards, in its partially completed state, *Nova* had been purchased by Doubleday & Co. Well . . . three months *after* the awards banquet, in June, when it was done, with that first Nebula under my belt, I submitted *Nova* for serialization to the famous sf editor of *Analog* magazine, John W. Campbell, Jr. Campbell rejected it, with a note and phone call to my agent explaining that, while he liked pretty much everything else about it, he didn't feel his readership would be able to relate to a black main character. That was one of my first direct encounters, as a professional writer, with the slippery and always commercialized form of liberal American prejudice: Campbell had nothing against *my* being black, you understand. (There reputedly exists a letter from him to horror writer Dean Koontz, from only a year or two later, in which Campbell argues in all seriousness that a technologically advanced black civilization is a social and a biological impossibility. . . .) No, perish the thought! Surely there was not a prejudiced bone in his body! It's just that I had, by pure happenstance, chosen to write about someone whose mother was from Senegal (and whose father was from Norway), and it was the poor benighted readers, out there in America's heartland, who, in 1967, would be too upset. . . .

It was all handled as though I'd just happened to have dressed my main character in a purple brocade dinner jacket. (In the phone call, Campbell made it fairly clear that this was his only reason for rejecting the book. Otherwise, he rather liked it. . . .) Purple brocade just wasn't big with the buyers that season. Sorry. . . .

Today if something like that happened, I would probably give the information to those people who feel it their job to make such things as widely known as possible. At the time, however, I swallowed it—a mark of both how the times, and I, have changed. I told myself I was too busy writing. The most profitable trajectory for a successful science fiction novel in those days was for an sf book to start life as a magazine serial, move on to hardcover publication, and finally be reprinted as a mass market paperback. If you were writing a novel a year (or, say, three novels every two years, which was then almost what I was averaging), that was the only way to push your annual income up, at the time, four to five figures—and the low five figures at that. That was the point I began to realize I probably was not going to be able to make the kind of living (modest enough!) that, only a few months before, at the Awards Banquet, I'd let myself envision. The things I saw myself writing in the future, I already knew, were going to be more rather than less controversial. The percentage of purple brocade was only going to go up.

The second installment of my story here concerns the first time the word "Negro" was said to me, as a direct reference to my racial origins, by someone in the science-fiction community. Understand that, since the late '30s, that community, that world had been largely Jewish, highly liberal, and with notable exceptions leaned well to the left. Even its right-wing mavens, Robert Heinlein or Poul Anderson (or, indeed, Campbell), would have far preferred to go to a leftist party and have a friendly argument with some smart socialists than actually hang out with the right-wing and libertarian organizations which they may well have supported in principle and, in Heinlein's case, with donations. April 14, 1968, a year and—perhaps—three weeks later, was the evening of the next Nebula Awards Banquet. A fortnight before, I had turned twenty-six. That year my eighth novel, *The Einstein Intersection* (which had materialized as an object on the day of the previous year's), and my short story, "Aye, and Gomorrah . . ." were both nominated.

In those days the Nebula banquet was a black tie affair with upwards of a hundred guests at a midtown hotel-restaurant. Quite incidentally, it was a time of upheaval and uncertainty in my personal life (which, I suspect, is tantamount to saying I *was* a twenty-six-year-old writer). But that evening my mother and sister and a friend, as well as my wife, were at my table. My novel won—and the presentation of the glittering Lucite trophy was followed by a discomforting speech from an eminent member of the Science Fiction Writers of America.

Perhaps you've heard such disgruntled talks: They begin, as did this one, "What I have to say tonight, many of you are not going to like . . ." and went on to castigate the organization for letting itself be taken in by (the phrase was, or was something very like) "pretentious literary nonsense," unto granting it awards, and abandoning the old values of good, solid, craftsmanlike story-telling. My name was not mentioned, but it was evident I was (along with Roger Zelazny, not present) the prime target of this fusillade. It's an odd experience, I must tell you, to accept an award from a hall full of people in tuxedos and evening gowns and then, from the same podium at which you accepted it, hear a half-hour jeremiad from an *éminence gris* declaring that award to be worthless and the people who voted it to you duped fools. It's not paranoia: By count I caught more than a dozen sets of eyes sweeping between me and the speaker going on about the triviality of work such as mine and the foolishness of the hundred-plus writers who had voted for it.

As you might imagine, the applause was slight, uncomfortable, and scattered. There was more coughing and chair scraping than clapping. By the end of the speech, I was drenched with the tricklings of mortification and wondering what I'd done to deserve them.

The master of ceremonies, Robert Silverberg, took the podium and said, "Well, I guess *we've* all been put in our place." There was a bitter chuckle. And the next award was announced.

Again it went to me—for my short story, "Aye, and Gomorrah . . ."

I had, by that time, forgotten it was in the running. For the second time that evening, I got up and went to the podium to accept my trophy (it sits on a shelf above my desk about two feet away from me as I write); but, in dazzled embarrassment, it occurred to me as I was walking to the front of the hall that I must say something in my defense, though mist-ily I perceived it had best be as indirect as the attack. With my sweat soaked undershirt beneath my formal turtle-neck peeling and unpeeling from my back at each step, I took the podium and my second trophy of the evening. Into the microphone I said, as calmly as I could manage, "I write the novels and stories that I do and work on them as hard as I can to make them the best I can. That you've chosen to honor them—and twice in one night—is warming. Thank you."

I received a standing ovation—though I was aware it was as much a reaction to the upbraiding of the naysayer as it was in support of any-thing that I had done.

I walked back down toward my seat, but as I passed one of the tables, a woman agent (not my own) who had several times written me and been supportive of my work, took my arm as I went by and pulled me down to say, "That was elegant, Chip . . . !" while the applause contin-ued. At the same time, I felt a hand on my other sleeve—on the arm that held the Lucite block of the Nebula itself—and I turned to Isaac Asimov (whom I'd met for the first time at the banquet the year before), sitting on the other side and now pulling me toward him. With a large smile, wholly saturated with evident self-irony, he leaned toward me to say: "You know, Chip, we only voted you those awards because you're Negro . . . !" I smiled back (there was no possibility he had intended the remark in any way seriously—as anything other than an attempt to cut through the evening's many tensions. . . . Still, part of me rolled my eyes silently to heaven and said: Do I really need to hear this right this mo-ment?) and returned to my table.

The way I read his statement then, and the way I read it today—in-deed, anything else would be a historical misreading—is that Ike was trying to use a self-evidently tasteless absurdity (he was famous for them) to defuse some of the considerable anxiety in the hall that night; it is a standard male trope—needless to say. I think he was trying to say that race probably took little or no part in his or any other of the writer's minds who had voted for me.

But such ironies cut in several directions. I don't know whether Asi-mov realized he was saying this as well, but as an old historical material-ist, if only as an afterthought, he must have realized that he was saying too: No one here will ever look at you, read a word you write, or con-sider you in any situation, no matter whether the roof is falling in or the money is pouring in, without saying to him- or herself (whether in an attempt to count it or to discount it), "Negro . . ." The racial situation, permeable as it might sometimes seem (and it is, yes, highly permeable), is nevertheless your total surround. Don't you *ever* forget it . . . ! And I never have.

The fact that this particular "joke" emerged just then, at that most anxiety torn moment, when the only three-year-old, volatile organization of feisty science fiction writers saw itself under virulent battering from internal conflicts over expanding markets and shifting aesthetic values, meant that, though the word had not yet been said to me or written about me till then (and, from then on, it was, interestingly, written regularly, though I did not in any way change my own self presentation: Judy Merril had already referred to me in print as "a handsome negro." James Blish would soon write of me as "a merry Negro." I mean, can you imagine anyone at the same time writing of "a merry Jew"?), it had clearly inhered in every step and stage of my then just-six years as a professional writer.

Here the story takes a sanguine turn.

The man who'd made the speech had apparently not yet actually read my nominated novel when he wrote his talk. He had merely had it described to him by a friend, a notoriously eccentric reader, who had fulminated that the work was clearly and obviously beneath consideration as a serious science fiction novel: Each chapter began with a set of quotes from literary texts that had nothing to do with science at all! Our naysayer had gone along with this evaluation, at least as far as putting together his rebarbative speech.

When, a week or two later, he decided to read the book for himself (in case he was challenged on specifics), he found, to his surprise, he liked it—and, from what embarrassment can only guess, became one of my staunchest and most articulate supporters, as an editor and a critic. (A lesson about reading here: Do your share, and you can save yourself and others a lot of embarrassment.) And *Nova*, after its Doubleday appearance in '68 and some pretty stunning reviews, garnered what was then a record advance for an sf novel paid to date by Bantam Books (a record broken shortly thereafter), ushering in the twenty years when I could actually support myself (almost) by writing alone.

(Algis Budrys, who also had been there that evening, wrote in his January '69 review in *Galaxy*, "Samuel R. Delany, right now, as of this book, *Nova*, not as of some future book or some accumulated body of work, is the best science fiction writer in the world, at a time when competition for that status is intense. I don't see how a science fiction writer can do more than wring your heart while telling you how it works. No writer can. . . ." Even then I knew enough not to take such hyperbole seriously. I mention it to suggest the pressures around and against which one had to keep one's head straight—and, yes, to brag just a little. But it's that desire to have it both ways—to realize it's meaningless, but to take some straited pleasure nevertheless from the fact that, at least, somebody was inspired to say it—that defines the field in which the dangerous slippages in your reality picture start, slippages that lead to that monstrous and insufferable egotism so ugly in so many much praised artists.)

But what Asimov's quip also tells us is that, for any black artist (and you'll forgive me if I stick to the nomenclature of my young manhood, that my friends and contemporaries, appropriating it from Dr. Du Bois, fought to set in place, breaking into libraries through the summer of '68 and taking down the signs saying Negro Literature and replacing them with signs saying "black literature"—the small "b" on "black" is a very significant letter, an attempt to ironize and detranscendentalize the whole concept of race, to tender it provisional and contingent, a significance that many young people today, white and black, who lackadaisically capitalize it today, have lost track of), the concept of race informed everything about me, so that it could surface—and did surface—precisely at those moments of highest anxiety, a manifesting brought about precisely by the white gaze, if you will, whenever it turned, discommoded for whatever reason, in my direction. Some have asked if I perceived my entrance into science fiction as a transgression.

Certainly not at the entrance point, in any way. But it's clear from my story, I hope (and I have told many others about that fraught evening), transgression inheres, however unarticulated, in every aspect of the black writer's career in America. That it emerged in such a charged moment is, if anything, only to be expected in such a society as ours. How could it be otherwise?

A question that I am asked nowhere near as frequently—and the accounting of tales such as the above tends to obviate and, as it were, put to sleep—is: If that was the first time you were aware of direct racism, when is the last time?

To live in the United States as a black man or woman, the fact is the answer to that question is rarely other than: A few hours ago, a few days, a few weeks . . .

So, my hypothetical interlocutor persists, when is the last time you were aware of racism in the science fiction field *per se*? Well, I would have to say, last weekend. I just attended Readercon 10, a fine and rich convention of concerned and alert people, a wonderful and stimulating convocation of high level panels and quality programming, with, this year, almost a hundred professionals, some dozen of whom were editors and the rest of whom were writers.

In the Dealers' Room was an Autograph Table where, throughout the convention, pairs of writers were assigned an hour each to make themselves available for book signing. The hours the writers would be at the table were part of the program. At 12:30 on Saturday I came to sit down just as Nalo Hopkinson came to join me.

Understand, on a personal level, I could not be more delighted to be signing with Nalo. She is charming, talented, and I think of her as a friend. We both enjoyed our hour together. That is not in question. After our hour was up, however, and we went and had some lunch together with her friend David, we both found ourselves more amused than not that *the* two black sf writers at Readercon, out of nearly eighty professionals, had ended up at the autograph table in the same hour. Let me repeat: I don't think you can have racism as a positive system until you have that socioeconomic support suggested by that (rather arbitrary) twenty percent/eighty percent proportion. But what racism as a system does is isolate and segregate the people of one race, or group, or ethnos from another. As a system it can be fueled by chance as much as by hostility or by the best of intentions. ("I thought they would be more comfortable together. I thought they would want to be with each other . . .") And certainly one of its strongest manifestations is as a socio-visual system in which people become used to always seeing blacks with other blacks and so—because people are used to it—being uncomfortable whenever they see blacks mixed in, at whatever proportion, with whites.

At this year's Readercon, my friend of a decade's standing, Eric Van, had charge of programming the coffee klatches, readings, and autograph sessions. One of the goals—facilitated by computer—was not only to assign the visiting writers to the panels they wanted to be on, but to try, when possible, not to schedule those panels when other panels the same writers wanted to hear were also scheduled. This made some tight windows. I called Eric after the con, who kindly pulled up grids and schedule sheets on his computer. "Well," he said, "lots of writers, of course, asked to sign together. But certainly neither you nor Nalo did that. As I recall, Nalo had a particularly tight schedule. She wasn't arriving until late Friday night. Saturday at 12:30 was pretty much the only time she could sign—so, of the two of you, she was scheduled first. When I consulted the grid, the first two names that came up who were free at the same time were you and Jonathan Lethem. You came first in the alphabet—and so I put you down. I remember looking at the two of you, you and Nalo, and saying: Well, certainly there's nothing wrong with that pairing. But the point is, I wasn't thinking along racial lines. I probably should have been more sensitive to the possible racial implications—"

I reiterate: Racism is a system. As such, it is fueled as much by chance as by hostile intentions and equally by the best intentions as well. It is whatever systematically acclimates people, of all colors, to become comfortable with the isolation and segregation of the races, on a visual, social, or economic level—which in turn supports and is supported by socioeconomic discrimination. Because it is a system, however, I believe personal guilt is almost never the proper response in such a situation. Certainly, personal guilt will never replace a bit of well founded systems analysis. And one does not have to be a particularly inventive science fiction writer to see a time, when we are much closer to that 20 percent division, where we black writers all hang out together, sign our books together, have our separate track of programming, if we don't have our own segregated conventions, till we just never bother to show up at yours because we make you uncomfortable and you don't really want us; and you make us feel the same way. . . .

One fact that adds its own shadowing to the discussion is the attention that has devolved on Octavia Butler since her most deserved 1995 receipt of a MacArthur "genius" award. But the interest has largely been articulated in terms of interest in "African-American Science Fiction," whether it be among the halls of MIT, where Butler and I appeared last, or the University of Chicago, where we are scheduled to appear together in a few months. Now Butler is a gracious, intelligent, and wonderfully impressive writer. But if she were a jot less great-hearted than she is, she might very well wonder: "Why, when you invite me, do you always invite that guy, Delany?"

The fact is, while it is always a personal pleasure to appear with her, Butler and I are very different writers, interested in very different things. And because I am the one who benefits by this highly artificial generalization of the literary interest in Butler's work into this in-many-ways-artificial interest in African-American science fiction (I'm not the one who won the MacArthur, after all), I think it's incumbent upon me to be the one publicly to question it. And while it provides generous honoraria for us both, I think that the nature of the generalization (since we have an extraordinarily talented black woman sf writer, why don't we generalize the interest to all black sf writers, male and female) has elements of both racism and sexism about it.

One other thing allows me to question it in this manner. When, last year, there was an African-American Science Fiction Conference at Clark Atlanta University, where, with Steve Barnes and Tananarive Due, Butler and I met with each other, talked and exchanged conversation and ideas, spoke and interacted with the university students and teachers and the other writers in that historic black university, all of us present had the kind of rich and lively experience that was much more likely to forge common interests and that, indeed, at a later date could easily leave shared themes in our subsequent work. This aware and vital meeting to respond specifically to black youth in Atlanta is not, however, what usually occurs at an academic presentation in a largely white university doing an evening on African-American sf. Butler and I, born and raised on opposite sides of the country, half a dozen years apart, share many of the experiences of racial exclusion and the familial and social responses to that exclusion which socially construct a race. But as long as racism functions *as* a system, it is still fueled by aspects of the perfectly laudable desires of interested whites to observe this thing, however dubious its reality, that exists largely by means of its having been named: African-American science fiction.

To pose a comparison of some heft:

In the days of cyberpunk, I was often cited by both the writers involved and the critics writing about them as an influence. As a critic, several times I wrote about the cyberpunk writers. And Bill Gibson wrote a gracious and appreciative introduction to the 1996 reprint of my novel *Dhalgren*. Thus you might think that there were a fair number of reasons for me to appear on panels with those cyberpunk writers or to be involved in programs with them. With all the attention that has come on her in the last years, Butler has been careful (and accurate) in not claiming that I am any sort of influence on her. I have never written specifically about her work. Nor, as far as I know, has she ever mentioned me in print.

Nevertheless: Throughout all of cyberpunk's active history, I only recall being asked to sit on *one* cyberpunk panel with Gibson, and that was largely a media-focused event at the Kennedy Center. In the last ten years, however, I have been invited to appear with Octavia at least six times, with another appearance scheduled in a few months and a joint interview with the both of us scheduled for a national magazine. All the comparison points out is the pure and unmitigated strength of the discourse of race in our country *vis-à-vis* any other. In a society such as ours, the discourse of race is so involved and embraided with the discourse of racism that I would defy anyone ultimately and authoritatively to distinguish them in any absolute manner once and for all.

Well, then: How does one combat racism in science fiction, even in such a nascent form as it might be fibrillating, here and there? The best way is to build a certain social vigilance into the system—and that means into conventions such as Readercon: Certainly racism in its current and sometimes difficult form becomes a good topic for panels. Because race is a touchy subject, in situations such as the above mentioned Readercon autographing session, where chance and propinquity alone threw blacks together, you simply have to ask: Is this all right, or are there other people that, in this case, you would rather be paired with for whatever reason—even if that reason is only for breaking up the appearance of possible racism, since the appearance of possible racism can be just as much a factor in reproducing and promoting racism as anything else? Racism is as much about accustoming people to becoming used to certain racial configurations so that they are specifically not used to others, as it is about anything else. Indeed, we have to remember that what we are combatting is called prejudice: prejudice is prejudgment— in this case, the prejudgment that the ways things just happen to fall out are "all right," when there well may be reasons for setting them up otherwise. Editors and writers need to be alerted to the socioeconomic pressures on such social groups to reproduce the old system of racism inside new systems by virtue of "outside pressures." Because we still live in a racist society, the only way to combat it in any systematic way is to establish—and repeatedly revamp—anti-racist institutions and traditions. That means actively encouraging the attendance of nonwhite readers and writers at conventions. It means actively presenting nonwhite writers with a forum to discuss precisely these problems in the con programming. (It seems absurd to have to point out that racism is by no means exhausted simply by black/white differences: indeed, one might argue that it is only touched on here.) And it means encouraging dialogue among, and encouraging intermixing with, the many sorts of writers who make up the sf community.

It means supporting those traditions.

I've already started discussing this with Eric. I will be going on to speak about it with the next year's programmers.

Readercon is certainly as good a place as any, not to start but to continue.

Why Blacks Should Read (and Write) Science Fiction

Charles R. Saunders

(2000)

More than twenty years ago, I wrote a screed/rant/plea entitled "Why Blacks Don't Read Science Fiction." It was a rant and screed in the sense that it expressed my dissatisfaction with the endemic paucity of black characters and themes in a genre that purported to transcend convention and stereotype. And because I still enjoyed reading science fiction and fantasy despite that lack, it was a plea for inclusion—a plea clad in late-1970s remnants of the militancy of the sixties.

At that time, I was a dedicated fan of the genre: immersed in its strengths and weaknesses, attending conventions at which mine was often the only black face—although some attendees in costume painted their skin green or blue or polka-dot. Now, I'm more of a semi-detached observer, having retreated from fandom and greatly reduced my reading in the field. But I still read sf and fantasy, and in retrospect, even though I stand by what I wrote in the context of 1978, I think blacks should not only read in both genres, but write in them as well.

When I wrote "Why Blacks Don't Read Science Fiction," I believed most blacks shunned sf and fantasy because there was little for us to identify with in the content. And what little there was tended (with, of course, some exceptions) to conform to the negative stereotypes of blacks endemic to other literary genres and, indeed, other media. A literature that offered mainstream readers an escape route into the imagination and, at its best, a window to the future, could not bestow a similar experience for black and other minority readers.

For all those complaints, however, I still saw potential in sf. A few black writers were breaking into the field, and black themes were finding their way into the work of nonblack writers. At that time, I was engaged in a personal crusade to add black content to the genre with my own writing, which was fantasy rather than science fiction, and to bring more awareness of black issues to the forefront of the field in essays.

The original essay was prompted by a prominent science fiction writer's curiosity over the lack of black fans at sf conventions. From that, he inferred a small, if not negligible, black sf readership. In the absence of hard data, even today, it's difficult to say whether black attendance at cons has increased, or whether our proportion of the readership as a whole has grown. However, there has been a definite increase in black content in the field. And the number of black writers has grown, even though the total whose books have been released by mass-market publishing houses can still be counted on the fingers of two hands. But that's better than the fingers of one hand, which was where the situation stood in the late 1970s.

At that time, science fiction was still in the process of freeing itself from the grasp of its so-called Golden Age in the 1930s–1950s, when hard science was a king whose court was closed to blacks. And fantasy was still frozen in an amber of Celtic and Arthurian themes. Now, at the turn of the century, a year that has been fraught with significance of sf fans since it first became popular back in the 1920s, it's time to reassess the relevance of the genre to black readers. Today, both fields in the genre have opened considerably. Hard science fiction shares shelf space with "soft" sf, New Wave, and cyberpunk. Fantasy writers are exploring non-European cultures, mostly Asian but also, occasionally, African. Much of what would have turned off potential black readers in the seventies is gone now. Yet some of those shortcomings remain, even as remnants of racism continue to plague the real world of the twenty-first century.

Check out the changes . . .

Until the 1970s, there was really only one working black writer in the sf field: Samuel R. Delany. Although he wasn't the first black to write science fiction, he was, and remains, a giant in the genre, and his name is mentioned in the same breath as those of Asimov, Bradbury, and Clarke. However, Delany's fiction production has diminished over the past twenty years, as he produces an astonishing amount of literary criticism and other nonfiction. Even so, his work is still more classic than contemporary. However, the seventies ushered in a second giant to stand beside Delaney: Octavia Butler. At the time I wrote my essay, Butler was just beginning to make her mark. Her heyday came during the

1980s, beginning, in my opinion, with *Wild Seed*, an epic that chronicles intergenerational abuse of psionic powers. *Kindred*, her time-travel/slavery novel, is an sf/fantasy equivalent of Toni Morrison's *Beloved*. With its dual setting in the late seventies, *Kindred* would probably have made a better movie project for Oprah Winfrey. In the future Oprah should consider featuring Butler's later novels, *The Parable of the Sower* and *The Parable of the Talents*, in her book club, a move that would help give Butler the wider audience she deserves. But Butler's popularity among mainstream readers has grown with the Parable series, possibly attracting some of the same readers who enjoy Toni Morrison.

By the way, even though it was marketed as mainstream literature, the strong supernatural element in *Beloved* could easily qualify it as fantasy, or, at the very least, horror in the mode of Henry James's *The Turn of the Screw*, if not Stephen King's *Bag of Bones*. Like Morrison, Butler writes from a black perspective, creating stories that envision a multicultural world. Also like Morrison, her themes are universal. One could also say that her work is more accessible than that of Delany, who sometimes writes on an esoteric literary and intellectual plane. If there were only one reason why blacks should read science fiction, it would be the writings of Octavia Butler.

But, of course, there are more.

Another writer I would recommend to readers is Steven Barnes, who broke through in the 1980s. Barnes began by collaborating with hard-sf writer Larry Niven. Later, he ventured out on his own, with books that feature futuristic black characters who are well versed in martial arts. His novel *Blood Brothers* delves into themes that could be lifted directly from today's headlines: racism, survivalism, computer-gone-amuck-ism. The intergenerational aspect of *Blood Brothers* shows a bit of Butler's pioneering influence.

However, Butler's true literary child is Nalo Hopkinson, a Caribbean-Canadian writer who made a big splash in 1998 with her award-winning first novel, *Brown Girl in the Ring*. Hopkinson doesn't imitate Butler, but she does echo the older writer's strengths in plotting and characterization. *Brown Girl* is a deft mix of science fiction, fantasy, horror, and Caribbean culture and folklore. Another recent debut came from actor LeVar Burton, who played the character Geordie LaForge on *Star Trek: The Next Generation*. His *Aftermath* was a dystopian-future story told from a black perspective more reminiscent of Steven Barnes than Octavia Butler.

Yet, blacks weren't the only writers to mine the rich veins of African and African-American experiences for their work. Even as new black writers emerged during the 1980s and 1990s, white writers were including more black characters in their stories and writing novels with black-oriented themes. Thankfully, few of them echoed the shortcomings of their predecessors. So far, there haven't been any new Farnham's Freeholds, but then there haven't been any new Ray Bradbury blacks-on-Mars scenarios, either, unless one takes note of Nalo Hopkinson's recent work *Midnight Robber*, a novel that offers readers *two* planets populated by the descendants of Afro-Caribbeans. The following examples are only the most immediate, as my reading in the genre has tailed off over the past decade or so.

F. M. Busby's *Zelda M'tana* evoked the feisty black heroines Pam Grier used to play in the so-called "blaxploitation" films of the seventies. However, M'tana, a ghetto girl who works her way up the ladder of a space fleet, is neither stereotype nor caricature. She is, perhaps, Busby's answer to the glamorous Lieutenant Uhura of *Star Trek* fame, played by Nichele Nichols, who also cowrote a science fiction novel, *Saturn's Child*. Alan Dean Foster explored Masai and the shaitan-sculpture of Mozambique in *Into the Out Of*, which was published in 1986. More recently, he has written an African-oriented space fantasy called *Carnivores of Light and Darkness*, which is the first of a trilogy. His setting is the Africa of another world, an alternative Africa in which evolution and magic have worked hand in hand to produce an environment that is both familiar and strikingly alien. Neither of these books contains negative stereotypes, in my opinion, and they fulfill the thought-provoking, mind-expanding promise upon which the genre failed to deliver in the past.

Alternate history has always been a staple of sf, and two of the sub-genre's most proficient practitioners, Harry Turtledove and Orson Scott Card, have included blacks in their musings about Americas that might have been. Turtledove works from the premise that the South won the Civil War, leading to two nations occupying the land we call the United States. Slavery persists in Turtledove's South, and the North is hostile to blacks, blaming them for the lost war. In *So Few Remain*, Turtledove paints a poignant picture of what the great black abolitionist Frederick

Douglass's life might have been like if the cause to which he had dedicated his life had ended in failure.

In the alternate America Card postulates in his Alvin Maker series,
the fledgling U.S. scored only a partial victory in the Revolutionary
War, leaving the South in the hands of the British. Also, in Card's
world, magic works through psionic powers called "knacks." In the fifth
volume of the series, *Heartfire*, Card evokes the psychological and spiritual cost of slavery. In both Card's and Turtledove's work, the "n-word"
is used liberally. Its use is a reflection of the settings of their stories, and
the characters out of whose mouths the word spews are, like Huck Finn's
father, a long way from admirable.

Of course, this discussion would not be complete without a mention
of the work of Mike Resnick. There is no middle ground of opinion on
Resnick's African-based sf. It is either admired or despised. Depending
on one's point of view, he is either a bold visionary or the reincarnation
of Edgar Rice Burroughs, whose racially incorrect Tarzan novels defined
Africa's place in the world of the imagination for most of this century.
He is either exploring new imaginative territory or turning Africa into
his own private "game reserve" of story material. Resnick's principal
contributions are stories and novels set on an Afro-topian space colony
called Kirinyaga, and *Future Earths: Under African Skies*, a 1993 anthology he coedited with Gardner Dozois. Some excerpts from the anthology provide some clues about Resnick's attitudes:

> But while Africa has lost some of the mystery and romance of [H.
> Rider] Haggard's and Burroughs' day, it now provides thoroughly
> documented examples of some of the most fascinating people and
> societies any writer, searching for the new and the different and
> the alien, could hope to find. (p. 12)

Please note Resnick's use of the word "alien" to describe African people and culture. He supports his argument with examples of African
practices that are indeed at odds with the standards of contemporary
Western societies: the survival of slavery in Sudan, the practice of female circumcision, the excesses of dictatorial rulers like Idi Amin and
Jean-Bedel Bokassa. After extolling such calamities as great "story material," Resnick asks: "Is there anyone out there who still thinks Africa
isn't alien enough?"

Obviously, Resnick doesn't think so. His attitude echoes that of a by-gone age, when plantation owners in the U.S. South believed Africa was indeed "alien enough" to justify transporting Africans to labor in bondage in a country that was founded on principles of freedom. By the way, one has to wonder why Resnick cited only reprehensible leaders like Amin and Bokassa, and ignored Nelson Mandela, who not only made an incredible transition from political prisoner to president of South Africa, but also forgave those who had imprisoned him. Perhaps Mandela's life story was too "alien" for Resnick. There are no Mandelas in the *Future Earths* anthology. Most of its stories were unremittingly negative; they took today's headlines about the woes of Africa and projected them onto the future. Resnick's contribution is a Kirinyaga story, and even though Kirinyaga is a utopian world, its stability comes at a price Resnick seems to think is much too high: cultural stagnation.

Having said that, though, it is only fair to note that in Koriba, the leader of the Kirinyaga world, Resnick has created an African character who has personal strength and integrity that would never—could never—be even imaginable in a Burroughs novel. Resnick and Burroughs are products of their times. Each of them has taken the worst his times have offered about Africa, and either ignored or discounted the positive aspects of the continent's history and culture. The difference is, Burroughs probably didn't know any better. Resnick, who also pens a regular column under the name of "Ask Bwana" in the sf publication *Speculations*, does, but he goes ahead and trashes Africa anyway.

Resnick is right, though, in his argument that Africa is fertile ground for sf story ideas. And it ought to be even more fertile for fantasy. Yet for the most part, the fantasy genre has lagged behind sf in opening its doors to stories based on the legends of non-European cultures. My own attempt at opening such a door, the Imaro heroic fantasy series, did not find the readership it needed to remain in print. More black characters are appearing in the genre, though, and one excellent novel, Lee Killough's *Leopard's Daughter*, incorporated a great deal of genuine African folklore and history. Unfortunately, Killough's book didn't receive the attention it deserved. *Leopard's Daughter* came out more than a decade ago, and there haven't been many other African-oriented fantasy novels, although blacks have appeared more often in supporting roles.

So some good material has emerged over the past two decades, even if one has to look long and hard for it. But there's a reason for blacks to read and write science fiction that goes beyond the number of black writers in the field, or the number of black characters who can breakdance on the head of a micrometeorite in someone's hard-science plot line. Science fiction serves as the mythology of our technological culture. Imagination is what separates us from the rest of the animal kingdom, and probably also marked the main difference between us and our close evolutionary cousins, the Neanderthals, enabling our ancestors to leave them behind tens of thousands of years ago. The human imagination manifests itself in stories. Those stories become legends, myths, the defining elements of a culture. And for all the condescending disdain the literary establishment has heaped on sf and fantasy, writers in those genres serve a function similar of that of the bard or the griot in ways "literary" writers cannot approach.

We blacks have more than made our mark in the Western world's popular culture. Imagine how diminished the arts would be without the contributions of people from Duke Ellington to Alice Walker. We need to contribute to our culture's overall mythology as well, and provide alternatives to the stereotypes that continue to plague us within that mythology.

After all, if we don't unleash our imaginations to tell our own sf and fantasy stories, people like Mike Resnick will tell them for us. And if we don't like the way he's telling them, it's up to us to tell them our own way. Butler, Barnes, and Hopkinson have met that challenge admirably. But they represent only a tiny fraction of the total number of writers in the field. That fraction has to grow.

The onus is on us. We have to bring some to get some in outer space and otherspace, as we have done here on Earth. Just as our ancestors sang their songs in a strange land when they were kidnapped and sold from Africa, we must, now and in the future, continue to sing our songs under strange stars.

Black to the Future

Walter Mosley

(2000)

I've been reading fantasy and science fiction since I was a child. From *Winnie-the-Pooh* to *Tom Swift and his Jetmarine*; from Marvel Comics to Ray Bradbury to Gabriel García Márquez. Any book that offers an alternative account for the way things are, catches my attention—at least for a few chapters. This is because I believe that the world we live in is so much larger, has so many more possibilities, than our simple sciences describe.

Anything conceivable I believe is possible. From the creation of life itself (those strings of molecules that twisted and turned until they were self-determinate) to freedom. The ability to formulate ideas into words, itself humanity's greatest creation, opens the door for all that comes after. Science fiction and its relatives (fantasy, horror, speculative fiction, etc.) have been a main artery for recasting our imagination. There are few concepts or inventions of the 20th century—from submarine to newspeak—that were not first fictional flights to fancy. We make up, then make real. The genre speaks most clearly to those who are dissatisfied with the way things are: adolescents, post-adolescents, escapists, dreamers, and those who have been made to feel powerless. And this may explain the appeal that science fiction holds for a great many African-Americans. Black people have been cut off from their African ancestry by the scythe of slavery and from an American heritage by being excluded from history. For us, science fiction offers an alternative where that which deviates from the norm is the norm.

Science fiction allows history to be rewritten or ignored. Science fiction promises a future full of possibility, alternative lives, and even regret. A black child picks up a copy of *Spider-Man* and imagines himself swinging into a world beyond the limitations imposed by Harlem or

Congress. In the series of "Amber" novels, Roger Zelazny offers us the key to an endless multitude of new dimensions. Through science fiction you can have a black president, a black world, or simply a say in the way things are. This power to imagine is the first step in changing the world. It is a step taken every day by young, and not so young, black readers who crave a vision that will shout down the realism imprisoning us behind a wall of alienating culture.

In science fiction we have a literary genre made to rail against the status quo. All we need now are the black science fiction writers to realize these ends.

But where are they?

There are only a handful of mainstream black science fiction writers working today. There are two major voices: Octavia E. Butler, winner of a coveted MacArthur "genius" grant, and Samuel R. Delaney, a monumental voice in the field since the '60s. Steven Barnes and Tananarive Due are starting to make their marks. There are also flashes of the genre in such respected writers as Toni Morrison and Derrick Bell. But after these notables, the silence washes in pretty quickly.

One reason for this absence is that black writers have only recently entered the popular genres in force. Our writers have historically been regarded as a footnote best suited to address the nature of our own chains. So, if black writers wanted to branch out past the realism of racism and race, they were curtailed by their own desire to document the crimes of America. A further deterrent was the white literary establishment's desire for blacks to write about being black in a white world, a limitation imposed upon a limitation.

Other factors that I believe have limited black participation in science fiction are the uses of play in our American paradise. Through make-believe a child can imagine anything. Being big like his father. Flying to the moon on an eagle's back. Children use the images they see and the ones that they are shown. Imagine whiteness. White presidents, white soldiers, the whitest teeth on a blond, blue-eyed model. Media images of policemen, artists, and scientists before the mid-'60s were almost all white. Now imagine blackness. There you will find powerlessness ignorance, servitude, children who have forgotten how to play. Or you will simply not find anything at all—absence. These are the images that have made war on the imagination of Black America.

It is only within the last 30 years that blackness has begun appearing in even the slightest way in the media, in history books and in America's sense of the globe. And with just this small acknowledgment there has been an outpouring of dreams. Writers, actors, scientists, lawyers, and even an angel or two have appeared in our media. Lovers and cowboys, detectives and kings have come out of the fertile imagination of Black America.

The last hurdle is science fiction. The power of science fiction is that it can tear down the walls and windows, the artifice and laws by changing the logic, empowering the disenfranchised, or simply by asking, What if? This bold logic is not easy to attain. The destroyer-creator must first be able to imagine a world beyond his mental prison. The hardest thing to do is to break the chains of reality and go beyond into a world of your own creation.

So where are the black science fiction writers? Everywhere I go I meet young black poets and novelists who are working on science fiction manuscripts. Within the next five years I predict there will be an explosion of science fiction from the black community. When I tell black audiences that I've written a novel in this genre, they applaud. And following this explosion will be the beginning of a new autonomy created out of the desire to scrap 500 years of intellectual imperialism. This literary movement itself would make a good story. The tale could unfold in a world where power is based upon uses of the imagination, where the strongest voices rise to control the destiny of the nation and the world. Maybe, in this make-believe world, a group is being held back by limits placed on their ability to imagine; their dreams have been infiltrated by the dominant group making even the idea of dissent impossible. The metaphor of this speculative and revolutionary tale could be language as power—the hero, a disembodied choir that disrupts the status quo. "Jazz in the Machine" could be the title. Black letters on a white page would suffice for the jacket design.

Yet Do I Wonder

*Paul D. Miller, a.k.a. DJ Spooky
That Subliminal Kid*

(1994)

Intro to "Yet Do I Wonder" (2000)

From: anansi@interport.net
Date: Fri, 31 Dec 1999 16:07:48 EDT
To: afrofuturism@onelist.com
Mailing-List: list afrofuturism@onelist.com; contact
afrofuturism-owner@onelist.com
Delivered-To: mailing list afrofuturism@onelist.com
Precedence: bulk
List-Unsubscribe: <mailto:afrofuturism-unsubscribe@ONElist.com>
Reply-to: afrofuturism@onelist.com
Mime-Version:1.0
Subject: Re: Re: [afrofuturism] Re: Freeze Frame

cd:dir>moment/goto: It's all very simple. First the "on" button, and then
the results: a screen and some images. No more, no less. Before beginnings and beyond ends, there's a process of resolution—it takes time and
patience and many seconds pass in the reverie, but as the image rises
into focus a thought refracts through my mind: Everything eventually
gets remixed. But then again, that's what this is about. A series of recent
polls about the American populace's beliefs in 1999 state some interesting facts:
93% of the populace believe in angels, 49% believe the government is
concealing information about UFOs and a figure of something over 25%
believe in reincarnation and the possibility of communicating with the
dead. It's most definitely some strange times we live in, and the line between myths of the current moment and fact has been blurring at an ac-

celerating rate. I bet that if you walked down a street and asked most people about the principles that drive everything from the light bulbs they use to the physics of turbulence that makes their toilets work, you would more than likely draw a blank response from the bulk of the people you encounter. I think you can get the drift of the kind of picture I'm trying to convey: modern belief and the technology that undergirds it are intertwined in ways very few of us have explored. I try as much as possible to convey that sense of incidental belief—life by osmosis in the age of unreason, or something like that. "Yet Do I Wonder" was a kind of prose poem remix of Countee Cullen's poem of the same name written many years ago. I always think of dj culture as a place where text's migration into a digital realm occurred among the people who were least likely to "formalize" its implications. As above, so below. Origination, derivation—it all blurs, but then again that's kind of the point. In a world held together by displaced signals and invisible codes, it's about the only thing that makes sense of our quotidian environment that is rapidly moving into a fully technological context.

> the only black history and black mythology
> the hiphop generation is going to identify with
> is the history they invent for themselves.
> Everything they know about being black,
> they're gonna get from a sample or a rapper.
> Looked at another way, if it weren't for the microchip, they
> wouldn't have no black culture
> (as we ancient ones understand black culture) at all.
> —Greg Tate, "Remember My Name," 1993

The current message has been deleted. Any sound can be you. . . . You lean forward and press play. The tape's wheels begin a slow but steady movement. With a slight hissing and popping in the background, a song as beautiful as it is strange makes itself known. Polytemporal pastiches—fleeting sonic images carried by shards of time—expand out into the audioscape that is you, feel the alphanumeric caress of the sounds as they wash over your mindscreen. . . .

Picture, if you will, my room when I was a small child. Sunlight streams through the air, illuminating dust particles as they slowly drift through empty space, their passage disturbed by your gaze. The room has several blends of African fabrics lining its walls. They, too, reflect the sunlight. There are no other furnishings. Consider this scene to be a developing chamber. The room now has me as I am today, age twenty-three, standing at its center. I point to the northern wall, where a lithograph, as abstract as it is minimal, hangs near the door. This poster is a gift from my father and mother. Inscribed in a calligraphic style, wheat stalks whose seeds are being dispersed by an unknown wind are overlaid with an adage from an unknown Bantu sage. This is what he said: "I have begotten a son. I shall live on in him. Go my son, mix with the crowd." Those words, enhanced by the artificial distance of digital delay and reverse-gate reverb, still ring in my head to this day. They fall distinctly, yet with an odd cadence disfigured by time, to arrive with the impact of all songs of myself in the form of this black print on a white page.

Here, I, Paul D. Miller, DJ Spooky that Subliminal Kid, a/k/a the Ontological Assassin, sing the body electric. I know it might sound a little weird, a little jumbled to your ear, but it's my mix. I am a member of what I like to call the children of the digital night, a part of the Combine Generation who by eminent domain will inherit this electromagnetic circus we call life.

You might think you know me. I am a living televisual presence—the shape of things to come. Every day on every street and TV channel, throughout all coordinate points of the megalopolis, like phantoms slipping across the electronic palimpsests of your naked eyes, you see me. I am the end of your world. To you—parent, professor, preacher, consumer of popular culture—I am the wasted burned-up desires of all the pasts unremembered, all the fears of your unknown futures gone slip through your hands—consumed like so many famished silhouettes the annihilating light of exposure in the only time that means anything anymore. My politics of meaning are derived from strange loops, every word is a lie, every image a soft oblivion. Emerging from commercials, glossy magazines, video games, and music videos straight out of your worst nightmares, what you see before you is the sum of a life lived under sensory overload and absolute media immersion.

Does my voice sound familiar? In order to understand me, you have to teach your eyes to hear and your ears to see. Then you will understand what I call reality. I kick out flava in PrimeTime where I am seen and scene, and flow in a calculus of finite TV channels available for viewing. I, the Ghostface, I, the Ripple in the Flux, am a kid who has gotten the picture but lost the frame, and life for me is one big video. Pick a point in a general curved space; think SUN RA. Define a vector at that point. Cut and fold the vector in on itself. Make it scream, imagery (the cassette as an electromagnetic canvas) presents to you, its emulsion blood red crystalline under the safety light of this darkroom.

Liquid drips from the images—visual and audio representation merge until there is no distinction between the two; just like alchemy, a transmutation of base materials into something exquisite is achieved. When I look around me, everything is colored with blood. It seems that all human interaction requires some sacrifice. Today, the sound of blank verse making chamber music, the unrelenting chatter of binary conversion, is the musical accompaniment to the choreography of violence that we young black males call our lives. Presence and absence, my brothers cut down in a coded dance of death, scroll 0's and 1's down my face like tears in the rain.

My mother, gentle to the core, gave me life. My father, by his absence, informed it. He died when I was three. I have only known him through the books and records that he kept, and my mother's descriptions of him. It's strange; during the most formative years of my life, I had a small group of friends but for the most part remained a loner. Books were my most consistent companions. We have a bright green house that my parents added to as time passed. One of my favorite "new" rooms was the library. My father had made this room almost entirely of glass. Here, where the sun was brightest, I would spend my afternoons reading and daydreaming, and watch the movement of the refracted sunlight play over the pages of whatever I was reading. I would look at the wall where my parents had organized their books and start thinking about building my own library. By the age of twelve, my mother's words were keeping company in my head with the Marquis de Sade, Huey Newton, Ursula K. Le Guin, Ngugi wa Thiong'o, Chester Himes, Sylvia Plath, Bessie Head, John Rechy, Angela Davis, Buchi Emecheta, and Malcolm X, while I sat listening to Lee Morgan or the S.O.S. Band and watching Fat Albert reruns on TV at the same time. In my mind, what a dialogue we had.

Every other male in my family is dead. Father, uncles, grandfathers— they all died from natural causes like hypertension or just plain and simple bad luck. None of them died by the violence that saturates African American culture in a sensurround scenario of psychotic erosion—but just the same, they are all dead. With the women, I mourn their passing, and live on.

When I think of the idea of family and history, my mind draws a blank etched with question marks, blood, and music. Every patriarchal "family value" that I have ever thought of begins to crack and fall to dust when I think about the stuff of which my everyday life is made: Dj'ing, living under almost squatlike conditions, writing. The "values" dissolve and float away into the opaque murk of the past. This I learned from Octavia Butler and Samuel Delany's science fiction: any and all truth is a tale I am telling myself.

Repeatedly upon a time, I silently slip into a region of myself made up of nebulous points of reference that I call my memory. Gently, I begin to link these coordinates into an intricate web of thin lines dense as all the omniverse (such a sky as you have never seen . . .). Images of my family (a product of an economy of identity rooted in a postindustrial structure based on two, maybe three things—time, sexuality, and memory) move quietly toward me. Arms open the silence to embrace me. They gesture and move away in graceful dance of recognition. I follow their patterns. Sacred geometries emerge from the fluid landscape that they have wrought with their movement. I watch their fugue, build a transmutable architecture of myself in their midst, and join them. No sign emerges unnoticed from this dance, no signal goes unanswered.

When I think about how much of African American identity is linked to our music and, in turn, our music to our literature, my mind is boggled. Music is the original code; bloodword + bloodrhythm = bloodsong = bloodcode. It's as if music is a product of the datacloud that tells me who I am, more so than any family tree. At this, the threshold of the synthetic theater of all possibilities, the cassette plays on. . . . Where do the songs go when you're not singing them? To a recording device no doubt, or if one is not available, back into your mind?

Sound and signification play out a theme . . . check the permutation of the nation . . . check the function, cognitive disjunction. Freedom and frequencies, forms and functions. Beyond double consciousness into the realm of techne and logos . . . fact and fiction become dialectic friction. . . . This is what science fiction is for me.

A long time ago J. G. Ballard wrote a simple statement that seems to drift over me like some sort of overlit neon expanse drifting across my mind's eye, a Times Square icon hanging on my screen as I write:

> above all, science fiction is likely to be the only form of literature
> which will cross the gap between the dying narrative fictions
> of the present day, and the cassette and video tape fictions
> of the near future.

As if . . . simply was . . . perhaps will be. . . . Hypothetical. Dialectical. The future is here now—but realize it was never gone. It, too, was just another screensaver banished with the push of a button.

Someone somewhere once said that assembly is the invisible language of our time. Someone else once said that time had an essence or "spirit" that moved in or animated it. I thought about these things when I decided to call myself DJ Spooky that Subliminal Kid. Put simply, I play music that haunts you, music that gets on your nerves. In this post-symbolic electroculture that I inhabit, music is the free-floating signifier for the world's soundtrack: the records become my notes, and I become their instrument. The images, the rhythms I invoke became my television, my network, my interactive soul, my PrimeTime. The here and now disappeared into the nowhere of a song of tempered bloodmusic— recombinant soul for your third earhole.

My names drift with the ebb and flow of the rhythms of the data-cloud: DJ Spooky that Subliminal Kid, DJ Spooky that Tactical Apparition, DJ Spooky that Ontological Anarchist, DJ Spooky that Coded Waveform, DJ Spooky that Alphanumeric Bandit, DJ Spooky that Dream Cyclone, DJ Spooky that Renegade Chronomancer, DJ Spooky that Semiological Terrorist, DJ Spooky an Artist of the Floating World. The list goes on. It is many names and perhaps all names.

"Where has he gone? To a song?"

Slowly, ever so slowly, I collect my thoughts and drift out into synthetic space, my only reference to my identity a flood of transient sonic images. To my fellow children of the digital night I have these parting thoughts, rite words and rite times: Seize the modes of perception. Slip silently. Fade in the algorithm of life in the liquid parade of the modern mindstream and be subtle to the point of formlessness. Remember that those who have flava sell it to those who do not, and that those who control the spice control life. When you remember your name, you will remember mine. When I think of you, I will do the same.

The tape's playing ceases . . . see the object fade out.

The Monophobic Response

Octavia E. Butler

(1995)

For all but the first 10 years of my life, writing has been my way of journeying from incomprehension, confusion, and emotional upheaval to some sort of order, or at least to an orderly list of questions and considerations. For instance . . .

At the moment there are no true aliens in our lives—no Martians, Tau Cetians to swoop down in advanced spaceships, their attentions firmly fixed on the all-important Us, no gods or devils, no spirits, angels, or gnomes.

Some of us know this. Deep within ourselves we know it. We're on our own, the focus of no interest except our consuming interest in ourselves.

Is this too much reality? It is, yes. No one is watching, caring, extending a hand or taking a little demonic blame. If we are adults and past the age of having our parents come running when we cry, our only help is ourselves and one another.

Yes, this is far too much reality.

No wonder we need aliens.

No wonder we're so good at creating aliens.

No wonder we so often project alienness onto one another.

This last of course has been the worst of our problems—the human alien from another culture, country, gender, race, ethnicity. This is the tangible alien who can be hurt or killed.

There is a vast and terrible sibling rivalry going within the human family as we satisfy our desires for territory, dominance, and exclusivity. How strange: In our ongoing eagerness to create aliens, we express our need for them, and we express our deep fear of being alone in a universe that cares no more for us than it does for stones or suns or any other fragments of itself. And yet we are unable to get along with those aliens who are closest to us, those aliens who are of course ourselves.

All the more need then to create more cooperative aliens, supernatural beings or intelligences from the stars. Sometimes we just need someone to talk to, someone we can trust to listen and care, someone who knows us as we really are and as we rarely get to know one another, someone whose whole agenda is us. Like children, we do still need great and powerful parent figures and we need invisible friends. What is adult behavior after all but modified, disguised, excused childhood behavior? The more educated, the more sophisticated, the more thoughtful we are, the more able we are to conceal the child within us. No matter. The child persists and it's lonely.

Perhaps someday we will have truly alien company. Perhaps we will eventually communicate with other life elsewhere in the universe or at least become aware of other life, distant but real, existing with or without our belief, with or without our permission.

How will we be able to endure such a slight? The universe has other children. There they are. Distant siblings that we've longed for. What will we feel? Hostility? Terror? Suspicion? Relief?

No doubt.

New siblings to rival. Perhaps for a moment, only a moment, this affront will being us together, all human, all much more alike than different, all much more alike than is good for our prickly pride. Humanity, E pluribus unum at last, a oneness focused on and fertilized by certain knowledge of alien others. What will be born of that brief, strange, and ironic union?

Contributors

LINDA ADDISON is a member of a writing group, Circles in the Hair (CITH), that has been meeting every other week since 1990. She spends her days writing computer programs and nights writing science fiction, poetry, and anything else that falls out of her brain. Her collection of SF, fantasy, horror short stories, and poetry, *Animated Objects*, is available from Space & Time. She is on the Honorable Mention list for the annual *Year's Best Fantasy and Horror* (1997–1999). Catch her work in *Asimov's Science Fiction* magazine, *Going Postal*, the *Urbanite*, *Dark Regions*, and *Edgar*.

AMIRI BARAKA, a.k.a. LeRoi Jones and Imamu Amiri Baraka, began his career in the East Village as a significant contributor to the Beat Generation literary movement and later became one of the major leaders in the Black Arts Movement of the sixties. He published his first work, *Preface to a Twenty-Volume Suicide Note*, a collection of poems, in 1961 and produced his Obie Award–winning play *The Dutchman* three years later. In 1965 he founded the Black Art Repertory Theater/School in Harlem, a critical development in the movement of the later 1960s and early 1970s. He is perhaps best known for his poem "Black Art," his barometric collection *Home: Social Essays*, and *Blues People*, an exemplary text on the cultural tradition of black music.

STEVEN BARNES is the author of fifteen novels, including the best-selling *Legacy of Heorot* (with Larry Niven and Jerry Pournelle). He has written for virtually all media, including film, television, stage, newspapers, magazines, and comic books. He has been nominated for the Hugo, Cable Ace, and Endeavor awards. Born in Los Angeles, he currently makes his home in Washington state, with his daughter Lauren and his wife, novelist Tananarive Due. He can be reached at *www.lifewrite.com*.

DERRICK BELL, a visiting professor at New York University Law School, was dismissed by Harvard University from his position as Weld Professor of Law for refusing to end his two-year leave protesting the absence of minority women on the law faculty. He is the author of several collections, including *And We Are Not Saved: The Elusive Question for Racial Justice* (1987), *Gospel Choirs: Psalms of Survival in an Alien Land Called Home* (1997), and the critically acclaimed *Afrolantica Legacies* (1998), in which a mysterious new land mass emerges that proves deadly to everyone, save blacks. His short story "The Space Traders," from his collection *Faces at the Bottom of the Well: The Permanence of Racism* (1992), was adapted for film and appeared in the HBO® original movie *Cosmic Slop* (1995).

OCTAVIA E. BUTLER is the author of eleven published novels, including *Patternmaster, Mind of My Mind, Survivor, Kindred, Wild Seed, Clay's Ark, Dawn, Adulthood Rites, Imago, Parable of the Sower*, and *Parable of the Talents*. She has won both of science fiction's highest awards, the Hugo Award twice and the Nebula Award, for work included in her short-fiction collection *Bloodchild*. As one of the few African American women writing science fiction, she has received widespread praise for her exploration of feminist and racial themes. Winner in 1995 of a MacArthur Award, she lives in the Seattle area.

CHARLES W. CHESNUTT (1858–1932) was an American short story writer, novelist, essayist, journalist, and biographer. Chesnutt became the first African American fiction writer to receive critical and popular attention from the predominantly white literary establishment and readership of his day after publishing his short story "The Goophered Grapevine" in the *Atlantic Monthly* in 1887. Born in Cleveland, Ohio, to free parents of mixed racial heritage, and raised in Fayetteville, North Carolina, Chesnutt was "light-complected" enough to "pass" in white society—a point duly noted by all the reviewers of his day. Nevertheless, Chesnutt never denied his black ancestry or accepted the elitism of the developing black and mulatto middle class, a decision that gained him criticism from many blacks as well as whites. Chesnutt's early short stories made him the first American author to explore the range of black experience in fiction, presenting readers with authentic black folk culture.

SAMUEL R. DELANY is a novelist and critic who lives in New York City. He is the author of *Dhalgren* (1975) and *Atlantis: Three Tales* (1995), as well as the nonfiction works *Times Square Red, Times Square Blue* (1999) and *1984*. He is currently a professor of English at SUNY Buffalo.

W. E. B. DU BOIS (1868–1963) was an American historian, essayist, novelist, biographer, poet, autobiographer, editor, and activist. He was the first black Ph.D. from Harvard, one of the founding fathers of American sociology, the founder of both the Niagara Movement and the NAACP, and edited its journal, *The Crisis*, which published some of the trailblazers of the Harlem Renaissance. As a major force in helping define black social and political causes in the United States, he is perhaps best known for his 1903 volume *The Souls of Black Folk*, in which he introduced the concept of "double consciousness" and explored the role of blacks in American society. He is also well known for his historiography and pioneering role in studying black history (in 1909 he conceived of the *Encyclopedia Africana*, the first comprehensive history of the African diaspora), as well as his activism, prompting Herbert Aptheker to call him one of the eminent "history makers" of the twentieth century.

TANANARIVE DUE's dark fantasy novels *The Between* (1995) and *My Soul to*

Keep (1997) are journeys into supernatural suspense that have been finalists for the Horror Writers Association's Bram Stoker Awards; the latter was named one of the best novels of 1997 by *Publishers Weekly*. In 1999 she was named author of the year by the national Go On, Girl Book Club. In 1996 Due was profiled in a "Women & Horror" segment on the Sci Fi Channel, which also featured author Joyce Carol Oates. Her sequel to *My Soul to Keep*, titled *The Living Blood*, will be published in the coming months, while her current novel *The Black Rose* (June 2000) takes her in a new direction: Written in conjunction with the estate of Alex Haley—Haley had intended to write the book himself before he died in 1992—the novel fictionalizes the life of C. J. Walker, America's first black female millionaire. Tananarive—pronounced *tah-nah-nah-REEVE*—is a former columnist for the *Miami Herald*. A former "lifelong" Floridian, she now lives in Longview, Washington, with her husband, science fiction novelist Steven Barnes.

HENRY DUMAS (1934–1968) was a poet, short fiction writer, and mythopoetic folklorist. Born in Sweet Home, Arkansas, Dumas spent his early years "saturated" with religious and folk traditions of the South. The potency of these roots can be seen in his first collection of short stories, *Ark of Bones and Other Stories* (1974), edited by his friend and colleague, poet Eugene Redmond. Dumas's promising career was cut short when he was "mistakenly" shot down by a New York City Transit policeman on May 23, 1968. Due to Redmond's dedication to keeping Dumas's literary legacy alive, readers were able to later discover the posthumously published collections *Goodbye, Sweetwater* (1988) and *Knees of a Natural Man: The Selected Poetry of Henry Dumas* (1989). His poetry also appeared in *Play Ebony, Play Ivory* (1974). Dumas's work was inspired by folk roots and by African American music, particularly blues and jazz. Dumas studied with Sun Ra and developed a craft that was distinctly his own vision.

ROBERT FLEMING is a journalist, short story writer, and author of several books, including *The Wisdom of the Elders* and *The African American Writers Handbook*. His articles and book reviews have appeared in numerous national publications. Fleming lives in New York.

JEWELLE GOMEZ is an activist and writer whose work has appeared in innumerable journals and anthologies. They include *Children of the Night*, *Home Girls*, *Daughters of Africa*, and *Afrekete*. She is the author of five books, including the award-winning *The Gilda Stories*, the first black vampire novel published in the United States; more Gilda stories can be found in two new anthologies from Firebrand Books, *To Be Continued One* and *Two*. Her stage adaptation of the novel was commissioned and performed throughout the United States by the Urban Bush Women Company in the 1996 season. Gomez also coedited, with Eric Garber, a collection of fantasy fiction entitled *Swords of the Rainbow*. She has written reviews and articles for the *New York Times*, the *San Francisco Chronicle*, the *Village Voice*, *Ms.* magazine, and *Essence*.

In 1968 she was on the original staff of *Say Brother*, one of the first weekly black television programs, produced in Boston, and later was on the staff of

Black News and *The Electric Company*, both produced in New York City. She was featured, along with Steven Barnes, Octavia E. Butler, Tananarive Due, and Samuel Delany, in the first conference of black fiction writers of the United States, held at Clark Atlanta University in 1998. Born in Boston, she lives and teaches in the Bay Area. Visit her web site at *www.jewellegomez.com*.

AKUA LEZLI HOPE gives all praises to the second-generation West Indian Harlemite parents who gave her permission to read *Animal Farm, 1984*, and *Brave New World* in the fifth and sixth grades of moving-on-up, integrated, 1960s Queens. She treasured Campbell's *Analog* as brain food. SF was her life's literary launch pad and she was honored when a poem made it into *Asimov's*. Hope read Delany as a teen and Butler when she almost gave up on the genre. She is grateful to them for pathmaking. Some particulars of this incarnation: three degrees ivy league—B.A., M.S.J., and M.B.A.; poeting and signifying always, in formal print consistently since 1974; won NEA, NYFA, and Ragdale's Africa-U.S. fellowships; Writer's Digest Award for *Embouchure: poems on jazz and other musics*. Her first show of glass and mixed-media sculpture, in 2001 at Chicago's Miles Aduwaa Gallery, will be accompanied by *Shield*, a book of poems from ArtFarm Press. Watch the web *www.servtech.com/~artfarm*. Make good manifest. Love.

NALO HOPKINSON spent a pan-Caribbean girlhood living in Jamaica, Trinidad, and Guyana before eventually settling in Toronto, Canada. She draws on that hybrid heritage to write fables of new worlds that will never be. *Brown Girl in the Ring*, winner of the Warner Aspect First Novel Contest, traced the black hole collapse of Toronto into a gated fiefdom controlled by a druglord and haunted with the spirits of the elder Afro-Caribbean gods. Her second novel, *Midnight Robber*, is a girl's science fiction adventure story; a post-post-millennial tale of colonization and exile inna rapso stylee.

HONORÉE FANONNE JEFFERS has won awards from the Rona Jaffe Foundation for Women Writers, the Barbara Deming Memorial Fund for Women, and her book of poetry, *The Gospel of Barbecue* (Kent State University Press) was picked by Lucille Clifton for the 1999 Stan and Tom Wick Poetry Prize. Her work has appeared in *African American Review, At Our Core: Women Writing About Power, Brilliant Corners, Callaloo, Catch the Fire!!!, Obsidian II*, and *Poet Lore*.

ANTHONY JOSEPH was born in Trinidad and has lived in London since 1989. He has published two collections of experimental texts, *Desafinado* (1994) and *Teragaton* (1997). He has also performed his intensely rhythmic "disembodied poetic jazz" throughout the UK and at present is at work on his first novel.

TONY MEDINA teaches English at Long Island University's Brooklyn campus. Named by *Writer's Digest* as one of the top ten poets to watch in the new millennium, he is the author of the poetry collections *Emerge & See, No Noose Is Good Noose, Sermons from the Smell of a Carcass Condemned to Begging*, and *Memories of Eating*. He also coedited the award-winning anthology *In Defense of*

Mumia and was a special editorial director for *Catch the Fire!!!: A Cross-Generational Anthology of Contemporary African-American Poetry.* "Butta's Backyard Barbecue" is from his original manuscript *40 Shorties.* Medina can be reached at *tonymedina@erols.com.*

PAUL D. MILLER is a writer, artist, and musician based in New York City. His writing has appeared in magazines as diverse as *Spin's Guide to Music,* the *Village Voice, Artforum,* the *Source, Rap Pages, Paper* magazine, *Ray Gun,* and many others. He is also a senior contributing editor of one of the major magazines covering Digital Art and Culture, *Artbyte: The Magazine of Digital Arts.* His artwork has appeared in numerous gallery and museum shows, most recently the Whitney Biennial, and his first solo show occurred at Annina Nosei. His most recent albums, *Riddim Warfare* and *Subliminal Minded: The E.P.,* feature a wide variety of guest artists from a wide variety of genres. Kool Keith, Thurston Moore from Sonic Youth, Killah Priest of Wu-Tang Clan, Pharoahe Monche, Kevin Shields from My Bloody Valentine, and a host of other artists have collaborated with him under his persona DJ Spooky that Subliminal Kid. In 1998 Miller composed the score for the independent film *Slam,* starring spoken-word artist Saul Williams, winner of the Sundance Film Festival and the Camera d'Or at Cannes. He is currently at work on his next album, *Jumbo Mumbo.* Visit his website at *www.djspooky.com.*

WALTER MOSLEY is the author of twelve books and has been translated into twenty-one languages. His books include the nationally best-selling Easy Rawlins series of mysteries; the Socrates Fortlow stories; the blues novel *RL's Dream;* and *Blue Light,* his first science fiction novel. His most recent book, *Workin' on the Chain Gang: Shaking Off the Dead Hand of History* (Library of Contemporary Thought, 2000), uses the perspective of race history to examine the American economic and political machine.

AMA PATTERSON is an attorney, legal editor, and single mother. Originally from New York, she now resides near Minneapolis. She is a graduate of Spelman College and the Clarion West Science Fiction and Fantasy Writers Workshop.

ISHMAEL REED published his first novel, *The Free-Lance Pallbearers,* in 1967 and has since published seven novels, including the critically acclaimed work *Mumbo Jumbo;* four volumes of poetry, including *D Neoamerican Hoodoo Church;* two collections of essays; numerous reviews and critical articles; and has edited two major anthologies. Reed is best known for his use of parody, satire, and fantasy in his novels. He is founder of the Before Columbus Foundation, which bestows the American Book Awards, and he is the publisher of *KONCH* magazine, as well as an online student publication, *Vines.* Reed has been nominated for a Pulitzer Prize and is the only writer to have been nominated for America's National Book Award in both fiction and poetry. He lives in Oakland, California. Visit *www.ishmaelreedpub.com.*

LEONE ROSS is a critically acclaimed writer with English and Jamaican parentage. Her stories have been published in several anthologies in Britain and Canada. She has written two novels: *All the Blood Is Red* (1996), which was nominated for the 1997 Orange Prize for Women's Fiction, and the critically acclaimed *Orange Laughter* (1999), which will be republished in 2000 by Farrar, Straus & Giroux. Leone works as a creative writing teacher and is presently writing her third novel. She lives in London.

KALAMU YA SALAAM, a New Orleans writer, is founder of the Nommo Literary Society, a black writers' workshop; cofounder with Kysha Brown of Runagate multimedia; leader of the WordBand, a poetry performance ensemble; and moderator of e-Drum, a listserv of over six hundred black writers and diverse supporters of literature. His latest book is the anthology of Nommo writers, *Speak the Truth to the People*, edited with Kysha Brown. Salaam's latest spoken-word CD is *My Story, My Song*. He can be reached at *kalamu@aol.com*.

KIINI IBURA SALAAM is an artist and world traveler from New Orleans, Louisiana. She constantly seeks to expand her understanding of self through contact with cultures of the African diaspora. A writer since 1990, Kiini crafts short stories, essays, and poetry that celebrate and question the mysteries, victories, and challenges of life. Her work has appeared in anthologies and literary journals and magazines nationwide, including *Dark Eros, Men We Cherish,* and *African American Review,* and *Essence* magazine. She is currently developing *Bloodlines*, a fictional biography of her ancestors that examines the parallels between her ancestors' struggles for freedom and her own search for identity. She is also a visual artist and a member of Red Clay Arts. She can be reached at tendaji@hotmail.com.

CHARLES R. SAUNDERS, a native of Pennsylvania, has lived for the last three decades in Canada, where, in the intervals between teaching the social sciences, "the odd creative writing seminar," and publishing nonfiction, he has been writing African-based fantasies since 1971. His short fiction has appeared in *The Best Fantasy Stories of the Year*, in the anthologies *Amazons I and Hecate's Cauldron,* and he published three novels for DAW: *Imaro,* based on his popular short story series; *Imaro II: Quest for Cush,* and *Imaro III: The Trail of Bohu.* He is currently working on a non-Imaro African fantasy.

GEORGE S. SCHUYLER (1895–1977) is considered to be one of the twentieth century's leading satirists and critics. His acerbic wit and comic approach to social commentary invites comparison to the work of Ishmael Reed. During his long and prolific career as a journalist, Schuyler produced *Black Empire* and *Black No More: Being An Account of the Strange and Wonderful Workings of Science in the Land of the Free, A.D. 1933–1940,* on which the bulk of his literary reputation is based. Schuyler also published a collection entitled *Ethiopian Stories.*

NISI SHAWL'S short fiction has appeared in *Asimov's Science Fiction* magazine, *Daughters of Nyx, and Semiotext(e) Science Fiction. Gnosis Magazine* and *The Stranger,* Seattle's notorious newsweekly, have printed her articles and reviews. Nisi moved to Seattle from Ann Arbor, Michigan, as directed by her ancestories. She is a volunteer and board member for the Clarion West Writers

Workshop. In her spare time, she works forty hours a week at Borders Books and Music, unpacking shipments and running writing and critique groups.

EVIE SHOCKLEY writes short fiction and poetry like her life depends on it (and maybe it does!). Her work has been anthologized in *Catch the Fire!!!: A Cross-Generational Anthology of African American Poetry* (1998) and *Jane's Stories: An Anthology of Work by Midwestern Women* (1994). She has also published in such journals as *Blue Mesa Review*, *Callaloo*, *Obsidian III*, and the *North American Review*. A chapbook of her poems, *The Gorgon Goddess*, will be published in 2001 (Carolina Wren Press). Evie currently lives in Durham, North Carolina, where she is pursuing a Ph.D. in English at Duke University.

DARRYL A. SMITH remains, at his best, a skinny, nappy-haired mama's boy. One incorporated by the pick of the peculiarly fluidic and funktified Christian, hip-hop, Gen. "X-Cold War," and subaltern sci-fi wisdom-cultures of Las Vegas, Nevada. At his antisocial worst, he is simply one among what the plainspoken call "the irresponsibles." Darryl is a natal philosopher and a proto-poet who is told that for a religious humanist, he is far too often given to rambunctious deification of the women in his family, who every day make a way out of no way in a world of unfreedom. In 2000 he will (finally) take his M.Div. degree from Harvard Divinity School and thereafter continue reading toward his Ph.D. in the Department of Religion at Princeton University. It is to his niece, Madison, to her mother and his, and to the gift and gravity of memory itself that he dedicates the piece appearing in this volume. He can always be reached and will always be teached at *thecoalchamber@hotmail.com*.

SHEREE R. THOMAS, a native of Memphis, is a writer and editor based in New York City. She edited fiction at a major publishing company and is a former contributing editor to *QBR* and *Essence* Books. A graduate of the Clarion West Science Fiction and Fantasy Writers Workshop, she has published reviews and articles on the SF genre and contemporary Afrodiasporic culture in the *Washington Post Book World*, *Rap Pages*, and *Black Issues Book Review*. Her short fiction and poetry has appeared in Ishmael Reed's *Konch*, *Drumvoices Revue*, *Obsidian III*, and other literary journals. She is the founding editor of the literary journal *ANANSI: Fiction of the African Diaspora*. She can be reached at *anansi@africana.com*.

COPYRIGHTS AND PERMISSIONS

Acknowledgments

A project of this scope could not have been accomplished without the goodwill and patience of friends, old and new. The generous help and enthusiasm I received from so many people in working on this book was inspiring. All thanks and praise are due to:

My editor Betsy Mitchell, her assistant Jaime Levine, Managing Editor Bob Castillo, copy editor Dave Cole, Nancy Goldsmith, and the wonderful team at Warner. My agent Marie Dutton Brown, who shared my vision and kept the faith cheerfully. Cheryl D. Woodruff, for her continuous support. Carolyn Nichols for quite an intro to publishing. Nikki Sprinkle for pisco sours in Peru (who needs Paris?).

Chip Delany for liking the title when *Dark Matter* was only a theory. Octavia E. Butler and Gordon Van Gelder for words of wisdom. Charles R. Saunders for kindly bringing *Darkwater* to my attention. Steven Barnes and Tananarive Due for saying yes. Jewelle Gomez for giving us Gilda. Nalo Hopkinson for her lovely reading at the Dixon Place. David Earl Jackson and Kalamu ya Salaam, two of the most gifted and generous minds I know. Jabari Asim, Steve Cannon at *A Gathering of the Tribes*, Troy Johnson of the African American Literature Book Club, Joseph Monte, Ronda Racha Penrice, Angel R. Raspbury, Taiia Smart-Young, and all my *ANANSI* friends who helped spread the Nommo. Arthur Flowers and the members of the New Renaissance Writers Guild. The Schomburg Center for Research on Black Culture. The Hamilton-Grange Branch of the New York Public Library for having the only remaining copy of *Ark of Bones* in the city. Fred Hudson and Martin Simmons of the Frederick Douglass Creative Arts Center and all those tending the generations . . . E. Ethelbert Miller, who answered my call with enthusiasm. Sun Ra for the soundtrack and John F. Szwed for *Space Is the Place: The Lives and Times of Sun Ra*. The 1999 Clarion West Science Fiction Writers Workshop and the New York Society of Science Fiction, whose Donald A. & Elsie B. Wollheim Scholarship helped get me there. Amazi, Andrea Hairston, and Liz Roberts, for Seattle and Sapelo, for clearing a space on the floor and precious time on their calendars. Ian Hageman for helping me stay logged on during those six weeks in Seattle. Gary Bowen's DeColores Project, Askhari of DeGriotSpace, the e-Drum community, as well as Alondra Nelson, Paul D. Miller, *www.afrofuturism.net*, and all the brilliant minds of the AfroFuturism listserv. Long live the Future Texts[;)]. Bon Mama Rose Novembre, Armelle Smarth, and Safiya Henderson-Holmes for their supreme motherwit and Papa Jacques, too. Harold Louissaint and EGS for helping me survive the Crash(es) of '99. Ruby J. Rollins and Daniel Coates for guidance and insightful critique. Professor Vanessa Dickerson for planting wild seeds of inspiration.

And finally, much love and respect to my mother, Jacqueline, brothers Terrence and Brian, and Darryl for the past ten years, with deepest gratitude to Jackie, Jada, Evens, and Daguy, who all lived graciously with the awesome presence of *Dark Matter* for over a year.

CPSIA information can be obtained at www.ICGtesting.com
Printed in the USA
LVOW07*0930171215

466978LV00005B/119/P